SAVAGE DECEPTION

The Nickie Savage Series
Book One

***

R.T. Wolfe

Photography by SL Jones Photography

Cover and Book design by eBook Prep www.ebookprep.com

Second Edition, July 2014
ISBN: 978-1-61417-513-1

ePublishing Works!
www.epublishingworks.com

PROLOGUE

Duncan's paintbrush took on a mind of it's own. The lines of his Nickie's face, the curves of her body. Painting her became a drug. She'd fallen asleep; her cautious eyes closed. Her chin resting on her shoulder. With his pre-dawn flight, it was too late to hope sleep might find him.

Time was slipping. A few touch ups were all he needed, but that would have to wait until after some drying time.

So, he washed his brushes, set them to dry and changed into his flying clothes. It was nearing 4 a.m. He debated carrying her to the bed. They'd come so far. She slept in his arms on occasion and hadn't woken with fists swinging in weeks. But he couldn't let her wake on his settee, either.

"Nickie," he whispered.

Groggy, she slithered her arms around his neck.

Cautiously, he lifted. She turned her head into his shoulder, and he swore she inhaled his scent as a small smile lifted the corners of her lips. As he laid her on the bed, her eyes opened.

"There you are." He smiled.

"What time is it?" she asked as she tucked the pillow under her neck.

"Just past four. Get some rest." He kissed her forehead before turning off the light.

It wasn't just the painting, Duncan thought, as he drove toward the airport. There was more pulling him back to his house. More that was incomplete.

His cell rang. It made him smile until he checked the caller ID and saw it wasn't Nickie. It's for the best, he decided. She needed rest.

But why was his brother calling at 4:30 a.m.?

"Andy, who died?" Duncan asked sarcastically.

"That's not funny. What the fuck is going on?"

Duncan pulled his car to the shoulder to talk. "Whoa, little brother. What makes you call at this hour?"

"Where are you, man?" Andy yelled into the phone.

"On my way to the airport. What is it? Is it Mom?"

"No, turn around! I called 9-1-1. It's your house. Rose and I, we heard an explosion. Duncan, we *felt* an explosion."

No. He dropped his phone.

Fear gripped his hands and glued them to the steering wheel. He slammed the car back into gear and spun his tires into a U turn. Nickie. No. No. No. He fumbled with his cell and dialed her number. The ringing was like a gong inches from his ears. He yelled, "No!" as she didn't answer he pounded the steering wheel.

At the sound of gravel, Duncan opened his eyes. He was headed for a guardrail. He swerved, skidded the back end of his car along the metal, then hit the gas again.

Smoke billowed from the trees. It shone in the moonlight long before he reached his long asphalt drive. Nickie. The familiar circling lights from fire engines beat him there. He left a line of rubber from his tires behind him. The flames. Nickie. There were too many flames. They poured out of each window as the firefighters used axes on his doors and roof.

He knew. Somewhere inside he knew it was too late, but the thought was more than he could bear.

He opened the door before he skidded to a complete stop next to Nickie's car. His head was nearing combustion as he ran for his front door.

"Whoa," one of the firemen grabbed Duncan's arm.

Duncan turned, ready for a fight. He used his momentum to land a solid hook to the side of the man's head. He saw it was the chief just as he made contact and could have cared fucking less.

He barely made two more strides before another came at him from the side. This one swung first. A high block sent the dude's arm upward and gave Duncan the in to land three quick jabs with his right followed by a punch so hard that it started from Duncan's hip, went through his shoulder and through his knuckles.

But then more arms were around him. He twisted, head butted and kicked. "There's someone in there! You don't understand!" He sensed people were talking to him, but everything was gray. His only focus was escape and the front door that was now a large, angry hole of flames.

Then, all he saw was pavement. He recognized the voice of the man on his back. Andy. His arms wrenched behind him and the legs that circled his own were a contrast to the pleading voice.

"Duncan, please. It's me, brother. Let them do their job."

Somewhere Duncan knew it was a dream, a memory; yet he couldn't escape the desperate need to save her.

He focused on making the muscles in his slumbering body relax. Andy didn't loosen his grip. The pain from the twist in his arm, the feel of pavement shoved in his face…it was welcomed. "Do something, Andy. They won't let me in. I failed again."

"It's your turn, Duncan." Nickie's alto voice whispered from somewhere around him.

He jerked his head toward the sound of her voice. There. The man. The police captain stood with the fire chief mocking Duncan. They pointed and elbowed each other it the ribs like old friends at Happy Hour.

But behind them. Behind them, Duncan saw the man. Medium height with shiney black hair worn in spikes. The man mouthed the word, 'savage.'

"Who are you?" Duncan yelled to him. His arms and legs were free. He bolted to a sitting position, sucking air and darting his vision around her room. Nickie was there. Here.

"It's your turn," she said again. "You were dreaming."

"Dreaming," he repeated. Not his signature. This time he kept his head still and looked around with only his eyes. They were in Nickie's townhouse. In her bedroom. Her bed. His lungs burned like they'd been singed, but Duncan and Nickie were together and she was safe.

"They can't hurt us anymore, Duncan. Captain Tanner and the fire chief are locked away nice and tight."

It wasn't the captain or the fire chief he was worried about.

CHAPTER 1

Nickie Savage opened her eyes to two cigarette butts, a gum wrapper and a discarded map of Nevada. Cabs weren't any cleaner in Vegas than in upstate New York. With her head between her legs, she reminded herself to breathe.

Duncan's hand rested in the middle of her back. The warmth was more than literal and was a little like walking into a heated home after a cold New York evening. She was grateful, but she wasn't about to tell *him* that.

He called to the front of the cab in his almost-baritone voice. "It's not what it looks like."

What's not what it—oh, shit. She lifted her head and met the driver's cheesy smile in the rearview mirror. Giving him the most intimidating detective's glare she could come up with, she tried to get him to look away and keep his eyes on the road.

She wasn't petty and she wasn't shallow, but besides the driver, Duncan was the easiest target and she needed to yell at someone. Slowly lifting her head, she groaned, "Don't think I don't know why you came along. My captain may approve you as a civilian consultant, but this is federal. I won't make that kind of request to the FBI."

He'd already talked her into flying first class. What if the guys at the station back home found out? Prissy female detective who's too good to ride coach? She'd never live it down. Duncan convinced her it was some sort of compromise to taking his private plane.

He lifted a brow before she could grunt anything else in his direction.

Duncan frigging Reed.

Upstate New York called him the local boy who turned into *The Taste of L.A.* The nickname followed him all the way to, well, L.A. Looking at him, she had to agree. Dark hair, darker eyes, sharp features. Calling the two of them opposites would be an understatement. Yet, somehow they were a couple.

His eyes, steady and lifeless, surveyed her. Most people thought of them as cold and removed. She knew better and didn't know what to do about that.

She opened her mouth, closed it again and decided instead to focus on her appointment at Vegas Metro. Slinging one of her black leather boots on her knee, she dangled a wrist over her shin. She pressed her knuckles against her jaw, turned her chin until she heard a crack, then did the same to the other side.

Her orders were clear. A home in a small town outside of Vegas had been abandoned. In the basement, squatters found two decomposed bodies along with some beds and...cages. It must be bad if squatters reported it.

Reasonable suspicion said the scene related to a mass kidnapping and forced prostitution of girls in their early teens. Since she was the one who traced the group from New York to Nevada, she wanted to know exactly what 'reasonable suspicion' meant. The feds called her in, citing her involvement with a takedown that resulted in the rescue of some of the girls and the arrest of a handful of the johns and perps.

There was much the feds still didn't know.

Covering her mouth with her hand, she dropped her head back down. "I'll be all right," she mumbled from between her knees, trying not to inhale the scent of cigarettes and stale gum. "I don't know my schedule," she said to Duncan. "I might not have time for you."

His hand returned to the center of her back. "I have work. I'm meeting with Johnny Lyons."

She knew why he was here, and it wasn't to meet with Johnny Lyons. Johnny Lyons? Unbelievable. She was sleeping with someone who was going to meet with Emmy Award-winner Johnny Lyons.

Meeting with Lyons may have been part of it, but it was her reaction to the call from the feds that made Duncan tag along. Her heart rate began to rise just thinking about it.

He came to keep an eye on her. To play watchdog. And if she was fair about it, because he cared. It was damned embarrassing. She was a cop, a detective. She didn't want or need him with her on a case...especially a case overseen by the FBI.

"Call me when you're done," he said in her ear. "I shouldn't be long at the Lyons'. I have enough projects to last a few days."

Projects as in painting. He carried his full-sized easel around with him like others did their carry-ons. As the cab driver parked, she sat up and shook her head clear. "I don't know how long they're keeping me."

He got out and walked around, opening her door for her before she had time to gather her briefcase.

"In case you take too long, I sent for my plane," he said and held out a hand.

They stood between two long rows of palm trees

inside the four-story, horseshoe-shaped, mainly glass building that was Vegas Metro. It was easily three times the size of her station in upstate New York.

Briefcase in hand, she balanced on her three-inch heels and turned, giving Duncan her best snarky wink as she left.

The Las Vegas Police Department hadn't changed. Clean, open and modernized. She checked in, took the stairs to the top floor and walked the hallway to the captain's office. Deluxe cabinetry lined the walls, and shag carpet the color of dark red wine covered the floors. She stood at the opened door and knocked.

Two FBI agents stood to the side of his desk. The suits and ties weren't at all practical in this climate. She wasn't about to dress up for anyone and wore her usual snug slacks and boots. The blouse she chose for the day was a sky blue. On her belt hung her badge, gun, phone and cuffs.

Considering his title, the captain was young. About her age. He was a bigger guy, healthy bigger, not heavy bigger. Black hair, black eyes. "Come in," he said to her, then turned to the agents. "This is Detective Savage." Not a return introduction or even a handshake was offered. Typical FBI. The feds liked to come in, take over and won't give anyone else the time of day.

"Detective Savage is the one who came to me several months ago," the captain continued, "with strong circumstantial evidence pointing to a possible mass kidnapping of young teens."

Is that what they said around here when they gave a visiting detective a measly three officers as backup for a takedown that needed at least a dozen? It made her feel somewhat better that the captain had to give up his territory to the feds again. So much was about territory in this business.

"As you know, since this went over state lines, we called in your colleagues—" He spoke to the suits as if she wasn't there. "—as soon as circumstantial turned into sustainable." It was damned condescending. She didn't mind if she was the only one sitting and sunk into the closest guest chair. Slouching comfortably, she lifted her foot and rested her ankle on her knee. The thick heel of her boot had a clump of Vegas dirt on it.

"Detective?" the captain turned to her.

She moved her attention from her dirty boot to him.

The captain must have been done with his part of the briefing. "Thank you, Detective, for coming out on such short notice. Maybe you could brief Special Agents Strong and Lewis on how you ended up here in the first place." He lowered into his high-back leather desk chair.

Was she supposed to stand? Wasn't going to happen. They still hadn't had the decency to tell her their names.

She contemplated which facts were pertinent and decided to share chronologically. "I was assigned to the scene of a murder in the high-rollers section of a casino in upstate New York. Facts led me to discover a child sex trafficking operation. The murdered girl was one of the children. Another of the girls escaped the chaos and was found hiding in a janitor's closet. With her help, I was able to track the rest of the group here. A larger poker tournament was scheduled soon after."

Inadvertently, she paused. How much would they catch onto if she revealed her knowledge of trafficking? She continued but with caution. "Venues like large poker tournaments attract prostitution, so I went undercover and discovered a lead to some younger teens that were sold by the hour. A handful of Vegas officers and I raided the location and arrested six johns, three thugs and rescued four of the girls." She swallowed hard. "Several of the perpetrators got away with the rest of the group."

Uncomfortable silence. More uncomfortable silence.

Finally, the taller one spoke. "Much of your investigation regarding this matter fell on hunches."

She hated hunches. If they only knew how much she hated hunches, they wouldn't say that. Maybe they would. Hunches led to cases that were thrown out in court. Facts. She was all about the facts. But she couldn't possibly share how she obtained some of the facts regarding the missing girls, or how she tracked them across half the country. How would she explain that her boyfriend had a talent for seeing details others missed?

He continued. "You seem to have instincts on the subject."

Her spine tightened. It took all of her focus to keep it from straightening, as it wanted to at that moment. Letting her lids drop to half-closed, she kept eye contact. He hadn't asked a question.

"Good work, Detective." And next came the patronizing. "I'm Special Agent Strong and this is Special Agent Lewis. As you know, an abandoned home has been discovered containing a scene in the basement we feel may be connected to the previous case you orchestrated. We apologize if we haven't been forthcoming with the latest updates regarding the outcomes of that case and appreciate the help you provided the days following the takedown."

They'd used her, then she never heard from them again. Now, they were sorry? Only because they needed her.

Strong must have sensed her attitude because he elaborated. "One of the johns was sentenced. Six months in county. The others were first timers. The perpetrators haven't had their day in court yet. Two of them are working with us on a deal and providing valuable information. The girls are home with their families." And then as a seemed afterthought, he added, "...Thanks to you."

Her suspicions were on overdrive, and suspicions ranked right up there with hunches. They had their place. Proceed with caution.

He picked up a file from the captain's desk and handed it to her. "This will get you caught up as we drive out to the location."

It was thin; it couldn't be a fraction of the full case file.

Johnny Lyons' multimillion-dollar vacation home was set far from the highway. Duncan maneuvered the Mustang convertible rental up the long, winding drive. There were a number of entrances, but the main one was obvious. Brick framed the massive glass double doors. The white stucco that was common in this area covered the outside walls. The sky framed the structure in a brilliant blue, the odd grasses of the arid climate serving as a base. He could have stopped the car where he was, pulled a fresh canvas from his portfolio and painted the house as he sat in the drive.

The mature landscaping told him it wasn't new construction. Johnny and his new bride didn't exactly fit the domestic profile of a couple who would have a home built.

Mrs. Lyons came out before he parked. She was watching for him? She wore a shiny gold bathing suit beneath a head-to-toe sheer housecoat with three-inch ice pick heels. It made him think of how Nickie could maneuver in shoes like this as if she wore sneakers. Women.

"Duncan! You're here," Bebe squealed. She and Johnny had been beautiful and cooperative subjects for his work. They paid him to paint a three-by-five-foot portrait of their wedding picture. If he remembered correctly, they'd hung it in the great room of their L.A. home.

He leaned over and offered a kiss on each of her cheeks. She smelled of something strongly floral.

Taking his hand, she led him around the side of the grounds. "It's good to see you, dear. We get so many compliments on our wedding portrait and, of course, we always share your contact information." She worked around the flagstone stepping bricks like a pro. "An original Duncan Reed portrait in our home. You're getting quite a reputation."

It was true. He was fortunate. It seemed he was a fad and understood it would likely wear off as fads tended to do. He ducked under some low-hanging vines covering an arbor that led to the pool area. He'd smelled the chlorine long before they reached the entry. The area was huge, winding around in the shape of a confused hourglass.

Johnny reclined on a lounge chair with a drink in his hand. It was morning. He didn't get up but offered warm greetings. "Ah, Duncan. Good to see you, friend. What can I have the help get you to drink?"

Duncan waved his hand dismissively yet politely, then offered to shake.

"I hope you didn't come all the way out here for us. Bebe said you were in the neighborhood."

"She's correct," Duncan answered, and sat on the edge of the closest chair, resting his forearms on his thighs.

Bebe sat in the chair between Johnny and him, close

enough to Duncan that he could smell her hairspray.

"How is marriage?" he asked, and reminded himself small talk was a necessary part of his job. Today, he didn't mind. Johnny and his new bride were actually some of the nicer people he'd worked with.

It seemed marriage suited them. They gazed at each other and smiled. "Well," Johnny started, "we don't see much of each other. We're both in the middle of projects, but we did get the next few days off." He reached out and slid his hand around her ankle.

Duncan assumed they wanted more work and waited patiently for them to get to it.

Bebe winked at Johnny before turning to fully face Duncan. "I ran into Coral. Coral Francesca. You remember Coral, don't you, Duncan?"

Uh-oh. He nodded cautiously.

"She showed me a photo on her Smartphone of the portrait you painted of her with the snake. It's amazing. I want one." She placed her hands over her mouth and lifted her shoulders like she'd just told a saucy secret.

He hadn't expected this. Certainly not from these two. Why hadn't he expected this? But it was his reaction that was the most startling. Pain. He felt a sense of pain and betrayal. He'd painted nudes before. Time and time again. Yet, he was speechless.

The two of them glanced between each other like they were picking out sexy lingerie.

"I don't paint nudes anymore." It surprised him how easily that came out.

Their faces fell as both sets of eyes slowly turned to him. Bebe's eyes were actually glassing over.

"What are you talking about, Duncan?" Johnny seemed more disappointed than his wife.

He thought of Nickie posing in his barely-blue open shirt with her legs draped over the edge of his settee.

"I...we...don't expect anything from you, if that's what's stopping you."

His eyes refocused on Bebe's. He knew what she meant and could hardly believe his ears. "Do you think painting a nude means sex with the artist?"

"No. No, of course not," she whined. "We just don't understand. We know you...do that with your subjects."

A few, yes, but what was happening? He stood. "I'm sorry. You're good people and a lovely couple. I'll get together contact information for some excellent recommendations."

Johnny wrung his hands. Bebe pulled her knees together. He'd embarrassed them. He wasn't sure what he was thinking or why. And how he hadn't seen this coming.

"I'm sorry," he repeated, and showed himself out.

CHAPTER 2

———◆ ◆ ◆ ◆———

Nickie's heart beat loud enough that she hoped the special agents couldn't hear it. The abandoned house appeared normal enough on the outside. They always did. Small Tudor ranch, painted a soft yellow. Traveling thorns and tufts of grass covered the expansive yard. A long, weedy gravel drive led to an unattached single car garage.

They bounced over the uneven drive as a single bead of sweat dripped down her back. Keep it together, Savage. This was business. They'd asked the captain if he'd like to stay back. It was rhetorical, of course. No captain or anyone else on any police force would 'like' to stay back while higher-ups investigated a case on their turf. Territory.

Running her hands over the pockets of her slacks, she made sure she had her small, digital camera and mini-notepad. They exited the car, and she took a short detour to look in the garage. It seemed like a normal garage. Two plastic garbage cans, a shelf with motor oil. No car.

She rested her hand on her .45ACP as she turned. Strong and Lewis stood watching her like they couldn't believe she would veer from them. Ignoring their stares, she strolled in their direction in her favorite black boots.

Nothing was familiar. That fact alone lifted much of her tension. The rest she was able to stuff away, focusing on what needed focus. Single door in the front, four windows. Same in the back. The feds pulled away the crime scene tape, took out a single key with no chain and unlocked a box that resembled the kind realtors used.

They stepped in ahead of her. The first room off the back door was the kitchen. It was sparse, and nearly each of the drawers and cabinet doors were open. "Did you find these like that? Or did your guys do this?"

They stopped and turned, looking where she gestured. There was a pause as Strong and Lewis glanced at each other. Were they going to do that every time she asked a question?

"The cabinet doors were like that. We don't know if it was the squatters or the owners."

She read the file on the drive out. The owner's information turned out to be falsified. Identity theft.

The guys watched her too closely. Something wasn't right. She scanned the place, taking pictures as she went. Two bedrooms, one bath. Living room that doubled as a dining room, and a kitchen barely large enough to walk through.

When she'd been told there was a basement, she assumed the house was in a better neighborhood. Most homes in Nevada had a crawl space only.

The door to the basement was heavy and lined vertically with locks. She stepped forward and smelled death. It was faint. She wasn't sure if it was from memory or the real thing. The stairs leading down were wooden and unpainted. They creaked miserably under the weight of the three of them. The walls were filthy with hundreds of dirty handprints. Nowhere in the file was there mention of fingerprinting. Surely they hadn't gotten around to sharing that information yet, she thought sarcastically.

Strong spoke as they descended. "The bodies and evidence have been removed."

What? She hit the bottom of the stairs and spun on them. "What did you say?"

More damned frigging silence.

"We took pictures of everything. Copies are in the file we gave you."

"The fraction of the file you gave me. With the small black-and-white pictures copied on printing paper?" She contained her temper. Barely. "Why bring me out here? Why not email the pictures to me and ask me your questions in a conference call? Oh right, because you haven't asked me any questions. And enough with the creepy silence."

Predictably, they glanced at each other like an old married couple before answering her. "It took a considerable amount of time before a connection was made between this house and the operation you orchestrated on the strip. We didn't learn of your involvement until after we cleared the area. We're hoping you might give us some insight."

She turned and stepped into the basement. It was more of a cellar. Her eyes widened and burned at the sight, tears begging to spill onto her cheeks. Six twin mattresses lined one side like a military barracks. On the other was a toilet out in the open. A shower spigot hung over a drain near the toilet. Two sets of chains were nailed to the brick walls dangled next to two large cages.

Reinforced dog cages. They weren't for dogs. They would be for the girls they left behind when they went out to work a job. Before she could stop it, her hand covered her mouth. Quickly, she moved her fingers over the top of her hair, hoping that was all Strong and Lewis noticed.

Like a bride walking down the aisle, she inched along the row of mattresses. Stains littered the bare material. It appeared some were urine and some the telltale signs of blood, brown and dirty. Deep, square holes had been removed in each, she assumed for forensics. She wasn't ready to turn her head to the other side of the room again. At the end of the row of mattresses was a door. It wouldn't be a bathroom. She knew what would be in there.

Stepping in, she took hold of the knob to keep herself steady. There was a single bed. A double. The handcuffs from the pictures in the skinny file had been removed from each corner. This was what they would call a training room. The girls would have been beaten into submission here, mostly on their backs. Never the faces. They needed their faces to appear innocent and free of marks. Anyone with too many scars was...disposed of in this room. Too many scars, too old or too much trouble. Or too broken.

They wouldn't dispose of anyone off-site. Why throw away an opportunity to scare the hell out of a fourteen-year-old girl? She didn't share these facts with the feds.

She jumped at the hand on her shoulder.

"Detective?"

Shaking her head clear, she took a deep breath and turned. "What was the approximate age of the corpses?" she barked. "Gender? That was left out of the file. The list of items included a bracelet. A man's bracelet. Where was that found? The photo was obviously from down here, but I don't see any chalk, paint or evidence markers."

This time, she ignored the creepy silence and the glances to each other, and instead snapped pictures in between taking notes.

For the first time since they met, Lewis spoke. "The bracelet was found at the bottom of the stairs. Pathology is still nailing down the estimated times and causes of death. We know they had been down here for approximately five months, which is how we made the connection with your operation. It was brilliant, by the way." He held up a hand before she had a chance to respond. "Vegas Metro gave you three officers when you should have had a full SWAT team along with a number of black and whites behind you. We're impressed with how many you took in. The captain is still...paying for his indiscretion."

It was hard to startle her, but she was just that, startled from his praise. Instead of flattered, his comments made her that much more suspicious.

"Coroner estimated the age at thirteen for the body chained to the wall located here." He pointed to the set of chains closest to the toilet. "And nineteen for the one found on the second mattress from the stairs. Cause of death yet unknown for the first, a single gunshot to the head for the second. Evidence suggests the perpetrators left in a hurry. That wasn't in the file."

He said it like he was doing her a favor, like he was giving her classified information. She was angry. Angrier than she had been in a long time. Pulling a band from her pocket, she did something she rarely did, and tied her hair in a quick tail.

Systematically, she took pictures and wrote down dimensions as she spoke. They flew her all the way out here for more than they were telling her, and she wasn't in the mood to play games.

"It looks like they bring the girls out in groups of about nine," she started without facing the men.

"Between one and three would have been kept back, depending on a number of factors. Were they overdosed? Did they have raw wounds?" The girls slept two to a bed, she thought. That's twelve. She wrote that down. Plus the chains and cages. That could be up to sixteen. Were their numbers growing? She'd hoped her takedown in Vegas did some damage.

Lewis spoke again. "You don't think they brought the johns here?"

She stopped, lowered her camera and turned to stare at him. "Here?" Overtly, she turned in a circle, arms spread. "This group of girls was first found in the deluxe section of the Seneca Casino in upstate New York. And I mean deluxe section as in ten grand buy-ins, with antes starting at a hundred bucks a pop." She had Duncan to thank for that information. Duncan. The thought of him helped clear her mind. He did that to her. For a short second, she let herself close her eyes and think of riding horses together in the woods.

Opening her eyes, she continued. "These people don't provide street corner hookers. These are young girls. They want them innocent, stolen and scared." Her voice rose with each sentence. Shaking her head, she ran a hand over the top of her tied hair once more. "Politicians, the rich. I'm sure you read that our previous Northridge, New York, police captain and fire chief were involved."

And she stopped, distracted. The captain and the fire chief. Duncan knew they were involved. It never occurred to her before. How? She'd been so distracted with the girls, with following their trail across state lines, with the shock of the involvement of her own police captain that she'd never considered how Duncan knew.

"Detective?"

Her eyes jerked to the special agents. Shaking her

head twice, she continued. "The girls were found wearing expensive lingerie. Each were showered and found in tidy rooms with satin sheets." She would question Duncan about his knowledge soon. Taking a cleansing breath, she took out her notebook. "They did not, therefore, bring johns here," she said as a final answer to the question and not as an opinion.

If they left with the girls in a hurry, it would have been right after the takedown in the Vegas casino. She wrote the estimated date they would have packed up. She would search for suspicious purchases of homes with basements in a sixty-mile radius since then.

"Cigarette rolling papers were found in the back room, there." Strong glared at Lewis when he spoke. Interesting. "Again, they could have been from the squatters."

She took some last pictures and spoke mostly to herself. "Well, they will have regrouped by now."

"This is our hotel."

Those were the only four words Nickie had spoken since Duncan picked her up at Vegas Metro. He knew what she meant and made the reservation here for that reason. He was able to get the same suite.

The enormous lobby smelled artificially floral with ceramic floors and pillars scattered throughout the area. Bellhops in dress pants, shirts and vests rushed to help guests as the employees in three-piece suits behind reception assisted with check-in and check-out. Even the janitorial help wore black pants and shoes and white, button-down shirts. These facts mattered to Nickie about as much now as they did the last time they'd stayed here. Not at all.

He expected her to be shaken after the day she had. He didn't expect her to be shak*ing*. The slight tremble in her hands was constant. They'd sat folded in her lap as she rode next to him in his rental. She had worked throughout the day and into the dark...as dark as it gets in a town covered in lights like a town in Alaska was covered in snow.

As they headed for the elevator, he realized they were retiring to their room as the rest of the town began their evenings.

He heard them before the elevator arrived. Loud, drunk and male. The doors slid open to a small group of young men. Each reeked of marijuana. One gave Nickie a double take.

"The cop stripper!" he slurred. "I got your card in here somewhere." He patted his pockets. Duncan heard glass clanking inside his loose jacket as he did so.

Nickie wore what she usually did. Button-down blouse, this one sky blue, and black slacks...both tighter than most wear. Nickie was never afraid to use her sexuality when it suited her. Her black boots had thick three-inch heels. Her gun was secured on her belt, along with her badge and cuffs. Duncan saw it all through a haze of red.

The one patting his pockets took out some cash. The others whistled as they pulled out more bills.

Duncan stepped in front of her and noticed as security headed their way.

"Come on, dude. Share!" he said to Duncan.

He wasn't sure whose arm it was, but a hand flew out, fingers splayed and reaching for her breast. Before the hand reached her, Nickie had pushed Duncan aside, twisted the boy's hand and had it wrenched behind his back. Between her teeth, she growled, "That's assaulting a police officer, you stupid piece of shit."

"Hey!" A hand landed on her shoulder. Duncan took it, bending it back until he heard a crack. The man bellowed as his friends stepped in to help.

Fists flew and heads bobbed. They were drunk and young. That excuse wasn't going to help them here. Duncan ducked easily, taking two down with solid hooks as he heard soft heels running toward them.

"Freeze!"

Duncan glanced over his shoulder. His eyes grew large as he noticed the security guard pulling his gun. Everyone put their hands in the air, everyone except Nickie, that is. She pulled her badge from her belt and held it up. "Detective Savage, your captain knows I'm—"

"I know who you are." He didn't appear pleased. "Are you hurt, Detective?"

Nothing like a gun to sober up a group of young men.

"I'm fine."

"Would you like to press charges?" he added.

She raised a brow at the sight of the one holding his strained arm, two others sporting swollen eyes. Straightening her blouse, she smiled and shook her head. Stepping to the one who started the mess, she placed herself inches from his nose. "Stay out of trouble tonight. I know where you're staying."

At the look on the security officer's face, Duncan didn't think they would be staying here.

He and Nickie rode alone in the elevator to the sky loft suite. He didn't ask if she was okay or offer any conversation. He knew from experience she would want independence and confidence at that moment. What he did notice was that her hands had stopped shaking. His Nickie was one complicated mess of a woman. And he was in love with her. Flexing his hand, he surveyed his bloodied knuckles. Damn.

As he opened the suite door, he placed his hand on her lower back, gesturing for her to enter first. They'd packed in haste, but neither would go anywhere overnight without their crutches. His crutch was his painting supplies. Hers was her cello. They'd spent many nights over the past several months painting and playing. Her cello was the one thing that could drown out the lifetime of images, sounds and smells that clouded his mind...ones that weren't conducive to coherent thought, let alone painting. Images from his childhood. Ones from his stint in the Middle East.

Her eyes moved first to the small studio he set up near the windows. He'd been working on a Christmas gift for his aunt and uncle. At the rate he was going, he might be able to give it to them a month early. He'd taken her cello out of the case and stood it next to his easel.

Finally. A tiny smile beckoned the corners of her mouth. "Before I discovered your secret, I thought you were as crooked as the night is dark. Aren't you glad I don't believe in hunches? It's a wonder we ended up together here the first time, let alone again tonight."

He moved his hand from her lower back to around her waist.

She turned to face him now and stared into his eyes. The steel gray color warmed as he watched.

He traced a thumb along the spot under her high cheekbone. Her eyes were wet, but he knew she wouldn't let the tears escape. The only time she cried was in her sleep.

At his touch, her lids dropped. She turned her face into the palm of his hand. "I didn't remember the house they took me to."

Had she thought she might? Apparently.

The bell on the elevator rang as they stood in the doorway. He turned his head. She didn't. Right on time.

"I ordered food. I imagine the captain and FBI ordered pizza delivery and that you didn't eat a bite."

She smiled, stepped into the room and tossed her jacket on the couch.

CHAPTER 3

———— ● ◆ ● ◆———

Nickie worked in her incredibly small office at her splintered desk. Crumpled papers lay scattered around the wastebasket. Empty soda bottles were left on top of file cabinets. It was good to be home.

She finished her official report on the Vegas case days ago. Now, she worked on the unofficial ones. She downloaded the pictures she'd taken and sorted through her notes.

The bracelet. She had no memory of it, just a burning sense of familiarity. Select, copy, new page, paste and print. She would keep a picture of the thing in front of her until it came to her.

Oh crap.

She stood and quickly removed the discarded shirt and stack of files she'd piled on her printer in time for the picture to emerge. Cutting it to size, she placed a piece of ringed tape on the back and stuck it to her desk lamp.

Her intercom light blinked. "Savage," she answered into the ancient system.

"Meet me in my office, Nick." It was her captain's voice. "Bring your coat."

She saved her private files to the cloud, tossed her reading glasses on her desk and shut down her computer. After adjusting her gun belt, she draped her brown leather jacket over her arm and headed out her door. The smell of burnt coffee and stale, empty donut boxes told her senses it was nearing lunchtime.

The common area was deserted other than a few rookies on the phone, pecking at keyboards. Rows of dented metal desks grouped in twos clustered in the center as she passed the office of another Northridge detective. Eddy Lynx lifted his brows, likely due to the direction she was headed. Without him. Shrugging, she turned the corner and stood at her boss's door. The engraved metal plate read Captain Dave Nolan.

Images of her previous captain came to mind. Scumbag piece of shit. She'd respected him. And she was a damned good judge of character, especially male character. How could she have been so wrong? Her burning question now was, how she could have missed that Duncan suspected him before she did? After her day at Vegas Metro, the sky loft suite didn't seem like the right time to drill him about it. Soon, though.

The blinds to the captain's office were up, and the door was open. Always a good sign. She knocked anyway.

"Sir?"

He hated that title and turned his eyes to her. Forcing back a smile, she sunk into one of his padded guest chairs and tucked a leg beneath her.

"A shooting victim showed up in the ER. He's not talking. I want you to see if you can use your powers of persuasion."

She nodded and checked her pocket for her keys.

"How are things with Lynx?"

Eddy. Metaphorical heavy sigh. The man with the occasional lame excuse so he could get close to her. Periodic jabs toward her regarding Duncan. One roll in the hay and she had to be the grown-up about it. "*Things*, sir?"

The heavy sigh from her captain was not metaphorical. "Don't call me that, and you know what I mean."

She let her smile out this time. Dave Nolan treated her with a comfortable mixture of boss, partner and friend with a touch of father figure. The latter was important for a girl in her shoes. "It's all good. I'm a big girl. You don't have to keep waiting to call him in before you have a chance to ask me that."

It was the captain's turn to shrug, and at six-foot-four, pushing two-fifty, it was an awkward sight. He pressed a button on the interdepartmental intercom system. "Lynx. Get in here."

She had gotten the polite invitation, she mused.

Duncan drove his new Audi R8 to just outside Northridge. He pulled onto Highway 2 and drove the short trip to the smooth asphalt that climbed and wound to the topmost spot in a forty-acre property. His forty-acre property.

At the end of the road, the asphalt widened into a circle drive. Three pickups, a classic muscle car and one box truck parked irregularly inside the circle. On the side of one of the pickups, he read, "Don's Electrical." The doors in the back of the box truck were open. Inside, he spotted stacks of drywall.

Granite steps led to a porch lined with cylindrical pillars. Cedar siding covered the outside except for the brick he had installed in the front. The windows were framed with tumbled edge bricks, soldiered on the tops and bottoms. Add architectural roofing shingles and the look was complete.

Other than the landscaping, the house seemed finished from the outside. He liked big. Three stories plus a fully finished basement that would house his pool, gym and theater. With room for a possible shooting range. It all counted as big enough for his needs.

His brother's Jeep sat parked at the bottom of the steps that led to the massive oak door. He supposed it made sense for the general contractor to be here, but Duncan assumed Andy had other things to do. He also supposed it made sense Andy could check on the progress of the house any time he wanted since he lived down the hill. And since he was charging Duncan an arm and a leg.

The noise reverberated in his head before he opened the door. He winced at the sounds as he entered. Drills, air compression hoses and a large boom box blaring AC/DC. The sounds of nail guns beckoned him back to his days in the Middle East. A flashback scratched the back of his mind. He fought it, as he'd been taught to do.

Drywallers walked on stilts. The ease at which they maneuvered the two-story scaffolding was uncomfortable to watch. Climbing the stairs, he responded to single nods of greeting. A man holding a clipboard turned down the music. Duncan had *homeowner* written all over him.

He found himself on the third floor, the only spot he truly cared about. It had to be perfect. The lighting, the space for his supplies, the placement of the substantial cherry wood desk his uncle made for him.

"Boss." His brother came out of the master bath and greeted him.

"You'd better call me 'boss' for what I'm paying you." They gave each other a one-armed hug and smack on the back. "It looks good."

"What are you doing here?"

"I live here. Or will again soon. When will she be ready?" Duncan asked.

Andy shook his head. "You're just like all of my customers. Impatient and have no clue how much goes into making a quality home."

"Lighten up, little brother. As long as I've found you here, I need to ask about some other work we have to do."

Andy squinted at him analytically. He turned his head away slightly, keeping his eyes on Duncan. Shaking his head, he answered, "I can clear my schedule for a few hours. A *few* hours."

"It's more than a brother could ask for," Duncan responded. He pulled favors from Andy sparingly. Andy knew it. And Duncan could always count on his brother.

"You come out for dinner. Tonight. That's the deal. Rose has been after me for weeks, and Abigail gets feisty when you're gone for too long."

Duncan checked his watch. He nodded. "I'll see if I can scrounge up a sexy blonde cop to join me."

Eddy Lynx was a good detective and easy on the eyes if Nickie had to say. But she would never get used to his nonstop conversation. He liked to think aloud. She felt like a heel that it made her squirm.

At least she was the one driving. The ride to the small hospital at the far west side of town seemed much longer than it was. She could smell his cologne. It was a pleasant smell, but it was that musky something that was made to attract females. She wasn't a deer. It was strong enough she would have cracked her window if it weren't just before Thanksgiving in upstate New York.

"Shot in the shoulder. Close range. Preliminary findings from the ER state the wound wasn't fresh. Not a kill shot. Unless the dude had terrible aim."

The captain had already said all of this.

"Married. Two kids in grade school. Pretty young to have two kids in grade school."

Her phone buzzed in her pocket. Relief. Caller ID said it was the captain.

"Savage."

"Are you at the hospital yet?"

"We're en route."

"There's been another shooting. Another shoulder entry. Exited the back this time. A woman. Parking lot of her gym. I'm texting you the name and MO."

"I'll keep in touch." She almost hung up.

"Nick?"

"I'm still here."

"They found the shell. The gun is likely a Smith and Wesson M&P .45 ACP. You got your gun on you?"

She wasn't sure why—she knew her gun was clasped in her holster—but she put the phone between her ear and her shoulder anyway, placing her hand on the butt. "I've got my gun." She disconnected.

"Was that Pretty Boy? Did you forget to tell him where you're going?"

Ignoring the jab, she handed her phone to him.

"Read the incoming text, Lynx. Take notes."

Andy made Duncan drive all the way to the Binghamton internet café. Always the cautious one. They had a system. Had it since they were in high school and first hacked into the Northridge Public School database. They'd deleted their unexcused absences. They justified the breach because they hadn't changed any grades. The twisted minds of teenage boys.

The café was ancient with tall, circular metal tables scattered irregularly. Two matching metal bar stools covered in cheap vinyl were fastened to either side of each table. It smelled of coffee, fruit smoothies and cleaning fluids, and it seemed as if they kept it at a frigid sixty-eight degrees.

Duncan had the memory and the creativity. He remembered passwords and patterns and was able to decode secure sites. Andy was the builder. He was responsible for constructing the safe path of execution so no entrails were left behind. Traceless. After they were in, they had only to wait for someone to log in and key in an ID and password.

The Northridge Police Department system was becoming a regular stop for them. Today, they perused the Vegas files with the FBI on the next burner. That would be a...challenge. They'd hacked into government departments before, foreign and domestic. It was never easy, and he wouldn't want it to be. This way was much more fun.

Again, only under the muse of scruples. It was like an oxymoron.

Duncan had two main objectives. The first was the Asian man whose face popped up into Nickie's past and present. In his dreams. He was there the night of the sting in Vegas months ago. The man had said her name. Duncan couldn't hear over the screams and commotion, but he didn't need to know how to read lips to understand what he said. How did he know her name? That question he needed answered.

Duncan scanned the sketch he'd drawn of the man through the Vegas system. He hoped to get a bite. A name. Anything.

Nothing.

All he had was the memory of a face, some

unconfirmed sightings and a hunch. He wouldn't approach Nickie with this information and bring the nightmares of her past back because of a hunch.

Objective number two was the Vegas reports. They found files on the abandoned house in Vegas Metro's, Nickie's and the FBI's databases. The files included pictures of a basement that resembled a concentration camp. A bracelet. A sparse home. Cigarette rolling papers. He zoomed in on the bracelet and the rolling papers. The bracelet was a man's, showy. The rolling papers deluxe, Bistro Club.

Nickie's reports were like everything she did. Thorough, simple and to the point. Facts only. She never needed flashy but had no trouble using flashy if it suited her. She was smart, resilient and a survivor.

He found something. The feds had left a separate file attached to the Vegas case. Apart from Nickie's. Andy saw it as he did. Together, they read page after page. The feds had searched Nickie's past. Not only the details about her cop life. They searched her childhood. They searched her missing year.

Through a red haze, he copied everything onto a flash drive.

In his peripheral vision, Andy moved in to get a better look. His eyes grew large as he turned his head toward Duncan, then back to the screen.

One of the files had been deleted.

Nickie entered emergency room fourteen with Eddy close behind. Chris Hendrix lay in his hospital bed with a damned lot of bandages for a shoulder gunshot wound.

"Detectives Savage and Lynx, Mr. Hendrix." She held out her badge. "We'd like to have a few words with you."

The room would be small for a single, and yet an

empty bed stood waiting for a roommate. There were no flowers, no cards. The TV wasn't on.

His eyes said he would have shrugged if it wouldn't hurt like hell.

"We're here to help find who did this to you."

"Don't need your help."

"Funny coming from the guy in the hospital bed. What happened?"

He glanced down and to the right. "I fell on a doorknob."

She nodded at his sarcasm. "So, that's how this is gonna be. You okay with being shot at?"

His voice rose this time. "It was an accident."

"Was your wife's shooting an accident?"

Eyes as round as saucers turned in slow motion toward her. That was more like it.

"Lucy? Is she okay?"

"Nice name. Your wife. She was shot in the shoulder. Such a coincidence for a falling-on-a-doorknob accident."

"Is she okay?" He was getting louder but didn't lift from the bed.

"She's conscious. Went clear through, which might be better than what you've got going on there." She gestured to the bandages. "You look like you're wrapped up for football in forty-below wind chill in the dead of winter."

"I let it fester. Should have come in earlier. It happens."

"I have to disagree with you there, Hendrix. Getting shot doesn't just happen."

"When can I see her?"

"I've been told she's en route. I'll put in a good word for you to have that happen if you help us out."

She watched as Hendrix's chest rose and fell deeply.

"I…can't. We can take care of this."

"How? How are you going to take care of this?"

"I don't know," he yelled, then winced.

"You happen to have two of Northridge, New York's finest right here in your hospital room. Use us. We're good."

Arrogant, he shook his head three times slowly.

She tucked her hand inside her jacket and pulled out her phone. Pointing it toward his face, she took his picture. "In that case, we'll try the misses." She ignored Hendrix's protests as she left the room.

"I think I'll stick around in case Mr. Stay-Out-Of-My-Business decides to go on a search and find for his woman."

Eddy was like that. He never was much into macho shit and didn't need to be the center of attention.

"Good idea," she agreed. "I'll be close."

She found Mrs. Hendrix as the nurses prepped her for surgery.

"You can't come in here," one of them said.

Nickie held up her badge. "I'll be just a minute. She's not the only one with a hole in the shoulder."

Not without a roll of the eyes, the nurse conceded. "She's next in line for the OR and she's loopy."

"Mrs. Hendrix." Nickie leaned over and spoke loudly. "I'm Detective Savage. Are you aware your husband is here, also with a gunshot wound to his shoulder?"

The drugs may have made her loopy, but they didn't take away the fear. The woman stared at Nickie and nodded.

"He's explaining what happened to my partner as we speak." Not. "Please tell us your side so we make sure not to miss anything."

"Chris is talking?" she slurred, and gazed around the

room. "Can I see him?"

"No, ma'am. You need the doctor right now. He's coming any minute. I want to help you, Mrs. Hendrix. How old are your children?" Cruel tactic, but it needed to be used.

"My babies? They're six and eight." She started to sit up. "What time is it? They get out of school soon."

The nurse was there fast, gently pushing her back to horizontal.

"We've got time before school gets out. Do you have family that can care for them?"

She closed her eyes. Not sure if she was falling into a drug-induced sleep, Nickie bumped her good side.

"Yes. My mom. She can meet them at the bus stop. My phone." She tried to sit up again. This time Nickie did the honors.

"Listen, miss. I need to know who did this to you and I need to know now. I can call your mother for you or I can call Family Services. I'm sure they'd be interested to know the only two parents your *babies* have are both in the hospital with holes in their shoulders."

Instant tears started rolling down her cheeks.

The nurse started to protest, but Nickie held up a finger.

"Chris is talking?"

"As we stand here."

"Slippery Jimbo was going to help us. We needed some money."

"Slippery Jimbo? James Spalding?"

"Yes, yes, that's him." Her head fell back against the pillow. "We were late. Chris had a deal. We had the mon—"

Nickie knew she could poke her all she wanted, but Mrs. Hendrix was fast asleep. She pulled out her phone and took another picture. Slippery Jimbo. Nickie was going to enjoy hunting him down. She glanced at her watch. Too early for that. About ten hours too early for that.

CHAPTER 4

"It's too dark to go for a ride, girl. Don't be angry with me." Abigail turned her head away from Duncan as he brushed her bare back. He lifted her hooves, checking her shoes as his brother's wife taught him to do.

Andy and Rose kept their barn in impressive shape. The stalls were clean, and the barn had designated spots for saddles, blankets, halters, and pitchforks. A ladder in the corner of the barn led to the loft where bales of hay lay waiting to be tossed to the trough below.

Every horse on the Reed Ranch, as Duncan liked to call it, was well-fed and exercised daily. Abigail, however, was known to hold grudges when Duncan didn't show for several days in a row. When he lived mostly out of L.A., he might miss riding her for weeks and on a few occasions, months. He cringed at the memory of how long it took her to forgive him.

The golden brown in her mane was nearly the color of Nickie's hair.

Nickie.

She consumed his thoughts. At first, he convinced

himself it was the novelty of involvement with someone so completely different from his usual type. It would wear off, and he would get on with life as usual.

It was all quite the opposite.

His agent limited the number of portraits of Nickie in his next showing to six. More would be too many of the same subject, he told Duncan. Duncan never had to force himself to paint, or in this case keep from painting what he wanted in his life.

He agreed to let his agent decide which portraits to use, sent jpegs of each and washed his hands of the decision. His agent gave Duncan his usual jesting about moving from L.A. to the middle of upstate New York without an opera or an acceptable Broadway stage within a two-hour drive. Flying in and out of L.A. was a worthwhile inconvenience. Which was why he bought the plane.

However, this latest art show was conveniently booked in Rochester. His agent said Duncan had a number of Canadians interested in his landscapes. Other than his show in Manhattan, it was the only time he would be able to drive to it instead of fly. And since it was close enough to almost ensure Nickie could make it, they'd decided to showcase her.

He ran his palm down Abigail's single white leg and lifted it, checking her shoe. She snorted but didn't pull away. It would be nice to take a peek at the matching white spots between her eyes if she would quit pouting and face him.

"I'll be back this weekend. I promise."

"You shouldn't make promises to a woman you can't keep." The alto voice was sultry and confident. Unrefined, yet warm. It was a voice he heard in his sleep.

Abigail turned at the sound of it. Figures.

"Hey, girl. I brought you a present." Carrots. That's cheating.

Nickie walked to his horse and rubbed foreheads as Abigail ate her treat. A tan, short leather jacket hung over a loose coral eyelet cover that draped over a matching camisole. Light brown jeans hugged Nickie's shape from low on her hips and into a pair of beige boots with thicker, four-inch heels.

Her phone hung clipped to her hip. He would have thought it ruined the image, but this was his detective. He liked her the way she was. Smart, messy and complicated. The slight scent of sophisticated lavender completed his image, and he understood how much he was exactly where he wanted to be.

Stepping to the two of them, he lowered his lips to Nickie's ear. "Do I get a present?"

She rubbed the spots high on Abigail's snout as she turned her steel gray eyes to his. They were cautious. Not the expression he expected.

Keeping a hand on Abigail, she leaned back against the side of the stall and crossed one ankle over the other. Yes, she knew how to use her sexuality.

He placed his hands up in surrender. "I give. Trail ride this weekend. It's Thanksgiving. We'll have time. Now, your turn."

Slowly, her chest expanded before she let out a long breath. "How did you know my former captain and the fire chief were involved in the kidnapping of the girls?"

He could take a hint. He kept his distance and stood with his legs out, the hand with the brush resting on Abigail's back. "I had a hunch."

She lifted her brows.

"I had a hunch," he repeated, "and kept an eye on them."

Her arms slithered together and crossed. She wasn't

smiling.

"I watched their emails. I felt like it was someone in the department who was involved. Too much was happening from the inside. So, I kept an eye on them."

"You didn't tell me."

Uh-oh. He forced his gaze to remain steady. "You don't believe in hunches."

"I never said that."

This time he did look around and up.

"I said I don't like them," she amended. "Not that I don't believe in them. They cause misunderstandings, useless errors and get cases thrown out in court. You kept this from me."

He had. Why was that? He always told himself it was because of her hatred for hunches. "I hurt you."

"Yes. You did."

"I'm sorry, then."

"Don't let it happen again." Pushing away from the wall, she closed the distance between them, grabbing the front of his shirt and stopping inches from his face.

Her eyes dropped to his lips before she pressed hers to his. It was more of a threat than a kiss, deep and seductive. It was effective.

He wrapped his hands beneath the swell of her backside and dove in. He'd spent years of his life with stick figures carrying globe breasts. That was a distant memory. Nickie was real on more levels than he could count.

Anxious arms wrapped around his shoulders and pulled him against her. She was warm and firm and woman. Sliding his hands to the backs of her thighs, he lifted, wrapping her muscled legs around him.

Their lips and tongues didn't miss a beat.

Her thighs tightened around him. Her boots crossed

behind him. Heat pressed against heat.

And Abigail butted her nose between them, nearly toppling them to the floor.

They sucked air. Nickie leaned over, resting the palms of her hands on her thighs as if she'd sprinted a half-mile.

Ignoring his horse, she lifted her head and carried that damned sexy, seductive smile toward him.

He pointed a finger at her. "Stop."

She didn't.

"Wait. Nickie, I have something to tell you."

Grabbing one of his belt loops, she pulled and said, "So do I."

"It's about the FBI."

That worked. She took a deep breath as she ran her hand over the top of her hair, the long, sexy hair that draped around her shoulders.

He shook his head clear of the image of the curtain it created when they were..."In light of our recent conversation, I think I'd better tell you this now." He reached down and picked up Abigail's discarded brush. "You won't like how I retrieved the information I need to tell you."

Her chest stopped moving. It was a short pause, but he noticed.

"I searched some of the Vegas reports." Don't do it again, he reminded himself. "I searched *all* of the Vegas reports."

"Searched?"

He ignored her rhetorical question. "There is some information they're keeping from you."

She paced now. "They're keeping loads of information from me. Duncan, you can't just do that. It's not legal. I'm a cop."

"I'm not," he interrupted, and put the brush away.

"Come." He clasped their hands together and led her near the entrance where no noises or horse snouts could interrupt them. Taking her shoulders, he placed her against the wall, then held out his hands, palms facing outward in a silent request for her to stay there.

Her brows lifted high, but she didn't move.

"There is information they're keeping from you that pertains to you."

Her brows sunk and she crossed her arms, waiting. It was her suspicious look. That was a good thing.

"Information that pertains to you on a personal level."

That did it. She pushed away from the wall, opened her mouth, but then must have thought twice about it, because she leaned back and waited for him to finish. It was difficult to focus as she lifted a boot and propped it behind her on the wall of the barn. So damned seductive. At that moment, he couldn't look at her and think coherently at the same time. He leaned over and took her boot, placing it back on the ground. There. That was better.

As a result, he did something else that never happened. He paced.

"They know about your missing year."

He opened his eyes and sunk deep into the steel gray. Her eyes weren't red. Weren't glossy. Her lids were half open as she looked back at him. "I figured."

Pulling his head back, he tried to comprehend. "You figured?"

"They were suspicious. Careful. One of them felt sorry for me and shared more than his partner wanted him to. I'm a smart woman. I'm sure if you're the FBI, it isn't that hard to dig up my past. I don't give a flying fuck one way or the other. Who are they going to tell?" She took her knuckles and pressed them along the side of her jaw until it cracked, then did the same on the other side. "Let's get inside."

"Wait."

"No. Rose said she had something she wanted to show me, and I don't feel like talking anymore."

She kicked off the wall and turned to the door.

"There's more," he said, and watched as her feet stopped two beats before the rest of her.

Turning slowly, she glared at him through eyes of stone. Her defense.

"In the FBI report, it reads there was a file they couldn't find. They called it a ghost file. They could see where it had been, but nothing was there." He sighed, trying to think of a way to explain. "It's like noticing that a fireplace mantel has a perfect rectangle free of dust. You know something was there and now it's not, but you don't know what was there."

"Did you…search for the missing file?"

"No." He considered. "Not yet."

"Don't."

"You can't—I won't—"

"Just don't."

He contemplated and decided now wasn't the time to cross that bridge. "There's one more thing."

"Shit, Duncan. What else?"

"Andy was with me when I ran across the FBI reports. He saw, Nickie. He knows."

It was hard to watch the expression on her face. It was one of shame.

"I can't—I'm leaving. Make something up for me."

Grabbing her by the shoulders, he dipped his head so their eyes were in direct contact. "It's nothing compared to…but you know what Andy and I have been through. And Rose too. We get keeping secrets, Nickie, and we get…we get it. Andy is a good man."

"Duncan?" It was Rose. Nickie's eyes widened.

"I see Nickie's car," Rose yelled. "I'm trying to stomp loudly on my way in. Don't want to interrupt anyth—Oh, there you are." Rose threw her arms around Nickie, glanced at him, then back to Nickie who was still frozen. Rose tucked her arm in the crook of Nickie's and pulled her along. "We made a plate of fresh fruit and the biggest apple chicken salad you've ever seen. You have no excuse not to eat."

CHAPTER 5

Nickie wasn't sure exactly what was happening. She didn't have girlfriends. Didn't have friends really. And as of yet, no one, other than her parents, knew about her missing years. Her foster mom didn't even know, and she was the closest thing to family Nickie had. And then Duncan found out, and Strong and Lewis. Now, Andy and Rose?

A fog settled around her as Rose pulled her along, talking about their new baby. Nickie's ears were ringing loudly and she honestly didn't comprehend much of it. Her legs moved on autopilot toward the ranch home.

Andy was in the kitchen. Nickie felt someone pull the jacket from her shoulders, but all she could focus on was her hands. She willed them not to shake. She knew she was staring at Andy. Knew her eyes were as big as gray moons. Except he didn't stare back. He stood at the kitchen sink, explaining how long the baby had been asleep as he cut broccoli.

"Hey, Nickie. We heard your car," he said and wiped his hands as if nothing had changed. Like he wasn't standing in a room with a woman who did what she did to survive. He walked over, greeting her with a kiss on the cheek before opening a cupboard that held plates and cups.

He gestured to Rose, and she took his place cutting vegetables at the kitchen sink. It was like an unspoken dance between two people who worked as one. "Rose was determined to run out to the barn and catch the two of you fooling around. I told her Duncan was too much of a geek."

Without changing expression, Duncan gave Andy a swift elbow to the ribs. Like friends. Like brothers.

Andy had learned her secret. Her disgusting secret. They knew what she was, what she did. Yet here they stood as if Nickie was a normal person having dinner in their lovely home. Duncan and Andy jeered like they were high school boys.

Tears tried to well in her eyes. She wouldn't let them.

"I changed my name." It just came out. It was like a confession, and for some reason made her shoulders lighter.

At that, everyone stopped. "My birth name is Nicole Monticello." She wanted to keep going. It was incredible. Turning to Andy and Rose now, she stepped toward him as Duncan's hand slithered around her waist and rested at the lower part of her back. "I was taken from my home when I was fourteen. I fought. I fought for eighteen months as they made me...*work*."

Rose dropped the bowl she had in the sink. Andy hadn't told her.

"I'm so sorry, Rose. Andy inadvertently discovered this with Duncan, and I feel...I *want* to explain." It was like sunlight struggling to find a break in the clouds.

"They called me Savage. I was the only one I know

of who ever escaped. My parents didn't want me after they found out what I'd done. In fact, they never publically acknowledged what happened to me. To the world, I was a rich, spoiled teenage runaway." The hand at her back flexed. She closed her eyes as she finished. "I moved around foster homes until I was eighteen years old, when I changed my name in honor of the girls I left behind."

Andy's expression was unreadable. Rose turned to face her with red eyes.

As she wiped her eyes, Rose tossed the towel from her shoulder into the sink. Nickie watched, not sure what to expect. What had come over her? This was their home. They had made her dinner, and she—

"Well, aren't we a group of misfits," Rose said and walked to Nickie. "Duncan and Andy grew up without parents and gave their aunt and uncle years full of shit as they sorted through that. I was held at knifepoint by my extortionist biological father." Rose threw her arms around her neck and whispered in her ear, "You're in good company," before pushing Duncan in the center of his chest and ordering him to set the table.

"You have more work tonight?" Duncan protested as he sandwiched Nickie against her car. She wasn't sure she'd ever heard him groan before. Cold metal pressed along her backside, heated steel against the front of her. It was clear he wasn't happy to be sleeping alone that night. His warm breath tickled her neck as he worked to persuade her to stay.

It was…convincing.

Magic hands traveled over her hips and inside her jacket. The cold car quickly became a welcome method of regulating her temperature. The air in a town the size of Northridge was never polluted, but out here, the trees and open fields made it surreal.

Her head fell back as his lips trailed a line along her jaw and down her collarbone. She opened her eyes to millions of stars against a backdrop of ink black.

"You could come back later," he purred.

"Mmm. Tempting. We both have work in the morning."

He pulled back and ran his thumb across her lips. "The responsible one."

The irony. "I need to catch up with an informant. A wannabe informant," she corrected, "who's maybe an informant. He's only out at this hour." That wasn't all of it. She was revitalized and ached for a fresh lead in the Hendrix case.

It was the strangest sensation. She had friends. She'd spent an evening with people who knew who she was—who she really was—and still wanted to spend time with her. She was in love and had friends. Two things she'd never expected or thought she wanted.

"Slippery Jimbo?" he asked.

Tilting her head, she looked into his chocolate eyes. "You remember him?" she asked, momentarily forgetting who she was speaking to. "Actually, I can't believe I asked that." Digging in her pocket, she found her keys.

"I'm coming with you." He took the keys. "We can take my car."

She stuck her hand in his pocket and took them out again. "Lynx is on this case with me. He's waiting for my call."

A cool breeze rushed between them as he pulled away. "Lynx is not only waiting for your call, he's sitting by his front door with his keys in one hand and his cell in the other."

Refusing to give him the satisfaction of rolling her eyes, she opened her door. "Lynx is harmless. I can handle him."

If Duncan was nothing else, he was a gentleman and took the door handle, waiting patiently for her to disappear fully in the car. "Dream about me," he said before leaning in to kiss her, then shutting her door.

Duncan's request wasn't random, she realized, as she maneuvered down the long, winding drive. He was concerned for her in more ways than one. He was the first man she'd spent the night with—an entire night—in years. The memories of her past didn't taunt her by day. But she had little control of her dreams.

You never get over something like that. Duncan's words reverberated in her mind as her car climbed onto the highway. Look who's talking, she thought. She'd caught him more than once using swimming as a way to drown out the lifetime of sounds and sights that permeated his mind.

He had a photographic memory, eidetic he taught her was the technical term. It was much of what brought them together in the first place. She was suspicious of him, she remembered, as she cruised along Highway 2. He recalled details like he was reading them from a textbook. She thought he had rehearsed them. Had something to hide. Then, his sight became invaluable. He was able to memorize scenes, see details others missed. He was the one who noticed the telling scars on the first dead girl discovered only twenty miles south of Northridge at the Seneca Casino.

At first, she thought his memories were a gift. But crystal clear memories of learning your parents died in a plane crash at the age of four were not a gift. Neither was remembering witnessing the beloved aunt who raised him like a son as she was blindsided with a baseball bat. The time when he was eight years old and was used as bait in the attempted murder of said aunt. Memories of his time in the desert. An overwhelming sense of sadness encompassed her each time she thought of it.

Her dreams were something altogether different. They were embarrassing and sometimes dangerous. She'd woken to find Duncan holding his chin from one of her mindless uppercuts. Never once had he shown a desire for her to leave his bed. He loved her. Duncan Reed loved her.

Shaking her head, she remembered Eddy. "Damn," she said as she pulled over to call him.

Duncan tried to put the finishing touches on his Christmas gift for his aunt and uncle. In his mind, they'd earned it. They put up with him for years, never once showing frustration with his exaggeratedly rebellious and dangerous teenage years. He owed them his life. Literally.

His morning of virtual meetings had gone smoothly. The lighting in his studio was ideal at this time of day.

But his head wasn't in his work, and he was reluctant to paint when his head wasn't in it. Where were Nickie and her cello? Nothing worked better to clear his mind. Oh, right. She was with her ex. That was a petty thought, he knew. He trusted her. But Eddy was a different story. She was right, though. She could handle him.

He still wanted to break something.

Instead, he opted to move to his computer. He was anxious for his house to be finished. The place he'd been renting was becoming tiresome. He plopped his shoes on the furnished ancient desk and set his laptop on his thighs.

The price of silver was nearing a year-low. He put in an order to balance his portfolio and sold some bonds. A few of the plots of land he'd been keeping an eye on had dropped in price, but not to the amount he had in mind.

His appointment with the governor's personal assistant wasn't until Tuesday. Nothing much he could do about him until after that date. The man had been present at the press conference announcing Nickie's return home at the age of fifteen. His name was on her transfer papers when she moved to the Northridge Police Department as Captain Nolan's assistant. Coincidence? Not likely. Was Duncan going out of his mind? Was he suspicious of anything that had to do with this woman? Definitely, and he wondered if this was what happened when people were in love.

In the corner of his desktop was a sketch, one he had drawn himself. The man was about forty-five, short black hair, black eyes, round face, Asian descent.

He was the man who said Nickie's name at the operation in Vegas five months ago.

Duncan had a few unconfirmed bites as to the whereabouts of the man, but what he really needed was a name. Was the guy a casino customer who had skipped the evacuation and heard others using her name in the confusion? Or was he one of the johns that got away and heard her name called from the other officers? Or was it what Duncan feared? Did he work for the scum they were searching for?

It was becoming an obsession. He could admit it. He walked to his small, makeshift studio, took out his darkest pencils and chalks and drew him again. He didn't need the physical drawing. He had the picture in his head. It was a photograph in his memory. But it pleased him to hold the concrete drawing in his hand. He would make this one with more shading and crisper lines. He wouldn't include the casino surroundings as he did in his previous sketches.

Before he began, he wrote the word SAVAGE in all caps and in quotations before beginning. It was the single word Duncan had read from the man's smiling lips before he disappeared at the end of the hallway in the casino.

Time was nonexistent when he sketched. It didn't erase the lifetime of sounds, smells and images that permeated his senses. Not like Nickie's cello could. She once called his eidetic memory a gift. It was more of curse for him. He used the side of his thumb to blend the shading as he thought of the methods he used to cope with his curse. His post-war therapist would be proud.

As he scanned and printed the new image, he thought of the look on Nickie's face when he told her Andy had found out about her missing year. It was nearly more than he could take. And when she spilled her guts to Andy and Rose. His head shook from side to side just thinking about it.

Hunches. He had hunches about the Asian man. He would get something more concrete, then if something came of it, he would go to her.

In addition to the Vegas system, he'd already hacked the National Crime Information Center database and ran the man's sketch. Nothing.

He changed to his email. His agent left him three messages, all with the subject line: ART SHOW. His agent picked fifteen pieces for his upcoming show and reserved a highly willing museum as the locale. *Local Artist Takes the Northeast.* He reminded Duncan of the recent, sweeping Canadian interest. It was his agent's thing, not Duncan's, and he trusted him.

He realized Nickie could be called into work and miss it. He hoped not since six of the portraits were of her. He needed her there but accepted the downfalls of dating a cop.

* * *

Slippery Jimbo was easy to spot. He sported his usual light-brown, calf-length trench coat. His receding hairline was covered by bangs he let fall over his forehead. Usually, he hung around the more greasy bars of Northridge, although living where she had lived in her life, the term greasy had a watered-down meaning. Yet, here he was, in the midst of a group of smokers hanging around outside Get Lucky's bar. They stood in a dusting of snow, shoulders hunched, bouncing on the balls of their feet to keep warm.

The bar's windows were void of neon signs or posters. In fact, if she paid close enough attention, they didn't seem to be windows at all. Each was covered with black shades drawn completely down. Cigarette butts littered the walk and the ground in front of the only front door. A single wooden sign read 'Get Lucky's' and hung over the single entrance door.

Nickie knew she should wait for Eddy, but instead pulled her oversized town car to the curb. No one ever spotted her as a cop. She didn't dress like one, didn't act like one and didn't drive a car that screamed 'unmarked.' But, Jimbo knew her car. His eyes spotted her, but he pretended not to notice. At least he didn't run away this time. She couldn't decide if that was a good thing or not.

She definitely knew how to swagger in her boots like she wasn't a cop. Bumping Jimbo's shoulder on the way to the nasty door, she noticed he didn't flinch, convincing her he took the hint. Glancing behind her on the way in, she noticed Eddy as he parked his car. It did scream 'unmarked.' He parked far enough away that she hoped no one noticed.

Diet Coke in hand, she waited at the end of the bar.

She wasn't going to wait long and planned to kick Jimbo's ass if he didn't hurry it up. Lucky for him, he beat Eddy in the door.

Eddy followed him down the long, narrow hall leading to the bar area, flanking Jimbo as they neared.

"Hey, what's going on?" Jimbo gestured to the way Eddy crowded him. "I'm an upstanding citizen of the town of Northridge now. Aren't I, Detective? I got me a woman. Wanna see a picture?" He waved down the bartender, ordering a draft as he took out a photo.

She had little patience for a man who she had arrested nearly a half-dozen times only to have his lawyer get him off on technicalities. Holding down the hand with the picture, she dug in the inside pocket of her jacket and pulled out her phone. She brought up the picture of Chris Hendrix, then laid her phone on the bar. "I've got my own picture, Jimbo." Leaning back, she took another drink and waited.

The bartender brought Jimbo's draft and held out his hand. Jimbo looked to Nickie, then leaned over and whispered, "Aren't you gonna pay? I'm on duty here, as an official police informant."

"I'm not paying for your beer," she said. "You tell me the story behind this man, and I might have something for you."

Jimbo paid the bartender and rubbed his hands together as if he was getting ready to open a present. "That's Hendrix, Chris Hendrix. His wife's a babe."

"She's a babe with a hole in her shoulder."

He seemed honestly concerned. His head moved from her to Eddy and back again. "You're shittin' me."

Nickie slid the photo of Chris Hendrix over and revealed the one of his wife. Turning her phone to Jimbo, she plopped a hip on the bar stool and watched his reaction.

Definitely concerned. "Rex Baxter," he said. "Owns

a boxing gym in the basement of Hardware By Joe."
He turned his head and took a long swig of his beer.

Eddy spoke up from the other side of Jimbo. "I
know Rex. He's a mid-level loan shark."

She met eyes with Eddy and jerked her head once in
a silent agreement. She handed Jimbo some cash. He
scoffed at it. "That's it? I could get my ass kicked for
talking to you."

"Consider it an entry- payment. Take your woman
out for dinner."

She heard him mumble in his beer as they headed
for the door. "Where do I take her? To the local gas
station?"

At the feel of a hand on the center of her back, she
stopped, craned her head at it, then turned her eyes to
Eddy.

He didn't take the hint. Or he did. "We're
undercover." His smile was from ear to ear.

Nudging him soundly with her elbow did the trick.
He pulled his arm from her and tucked it close to him.

"You think Baxter will be in his *gym* this late?" she
asked.

Eddy shrugged as he rubbed his side. "Could be. I'll
drive."

They opened the door of the bar to cold air and the
smell of cigarettes. She loved this town.

"What do you think about the sorrowful Slippery
Jimbo?" he asked as they walked to his standard-issue
four door. "I can't believe you're using him as an
informant," he added before she could answer.

"Possible informant," she corrected.

"How many times have you tried to lock him up?"

"More times than I can count. I can't stand the sight
of him. He's ruined my record."

"No one can ruin your record. You've got the best

conviction rate of all of us. By far."

"If we count only Slippery Jimbo, I don't. How do you think he got the nickname Slippery Jimbo and my general and complete loathing?"

"That was you? I'll be damned. I thought it was on his birth certificate."

Nickie stared out the window as they drove the short distance to Hardware By Joe. She didn't even know it existed.

She glanced over. Eddy wasn't so hard to deal with. She just nodded her head and grunted in agreement every once in a while as he rambled on. It appeased him. She hoped he didn't ask her any questions, because she had no idea what he was talking about. She was still thinking about dinner that evening at Andy's home. And about riding Duncan's horse this coming weekend. And about missing sex with him that night. Baxter had better be here.

The store was dark, of course. They walked around to the back in silence. In the absence of streetlights or building lights or even moonlight, she took her gun off safety.

CHAPTER 6

Nickie felt Eddy's arm pressed against hers but didn't elbow him in the ribs this time. Rarely did she feel fear, but it would be nice to be able to see a damned thing. Resting her hand on her gun, she resisted the urge to pull her coat tightly around her waist.

Supposedly, there was a lower-level entry. "If he's down there, how do people see to get in and out?"

A car turned down the alley with its brights on. "Ah. That could be it." She and Eddy stepped into the closest doorway a few stores down.

The car parked. The occupant turned on his cell phone flashlight and jingled a set of keys.

Eddy leaned close to Nickie. "That's Rex Baxter. I can tell."

She turned and found his face inches from hers. She smelled mint and his musky men's cologne. "How do you know?"

She saw his white teeth in the dark as he answered. "He's a giant. I hope there aren't going to be any more giants in there."

Pushing him away with her arm, she followed the

light, careful not to make noise with her boots. Before she stepped fully into the alley, she noticed another person was in the back of the car. The windows were tinted, but the inside light was on. Female, blonde. Sticking her arm out, Nickie stopped Eddy. "Do you see that?"

"I do. This isn't smart. We're going in blind here. Let's wait and come back in the day."

He was probably right, but it didn't take away the disappointment. She was still on her high from her evening and ready for a tussle. "Chicken."

The man who was possibly Rex Baxter didn't stay long. They drove away but not before Nickie had a chance to get their license plate number, make and model of the car.

Duncan pulled into the parking lot of his office building. He got out of his car and considered the first time he brought Nickie here. She'd had no faith in him. Understandable. She assumed their relationship was a fling and he would soon return to L.A., since it was where he did the majority of his work.

This was the tallest building in downtown Northridge, as tall as the police station and still only four stories high. He popped his trunk, retrieved his briefcase, then beeped the lock. Straightening his tie, he unlocked the back door of the building and headed for the elevator. Other than the janitorial employees, he was generally the first one in the building. As if on cue, the elevator rang and old man Jimmy came around the corner, pushing his cart over the ceramic squares.

"Good morning, Mr. Reed. Fine morning we're having now, isn't it?" Jimmy asked as he shuffled.

"That it is, Jimmy, and please call me Duncan."

"Will do, Mr. Reed."

It was the same conversation they had each morning. Things like this made him sure about his decision to move back here. That and a feisty blonde cop.

The doors opened on the fourth floor. It was here, in front of his office door where he first told Nickie he was in love with her. He unlocked the glass door as he realized this office was as much of a symbol of his commitment to their relationship as an engagement ring might be to others. She'd always been commitment shy, and he suspected it had a deeper meaning than either of them realized.

He had an hour before his assistant arrived and two before his first appointment. It was good to sit at a decent desk with appropriate equipment. He turned on his printer and maneuvered around it as he remembered he left his latest sketch of the Asian man in the one at the rental house.

Shrugging, he booted up his computer and made another copy. He flipped through his records books. When had he obtained so much property? The economy was finally turning around. He had spent the last several months buying up land that was too cheap to pass up.

He had a soft spot for sellers who were forced to unload their properties for ridiculous amounts. There were too many predators watching for that precise scenario. In an effort to ease the minds and the pocketbooks of landowners, Duncan ended up with pages and pages of details regarding the land he now owned. He was making a profit and made sure to pay a fair price to the former owners. It was how he obtained the forty acres, where his brother was rebuilding his home. Most people didn't need to rebuild a home after an arsonist burnt it to the ground. Most people weren't dating Nickie Savage.

He browsed the latest price per acre for each plot he'd purchased, decided if it was time to resell and took notes regarding each.

And, as he generally did, he became sidetracked searching images of the assistant to the governor. For a government official, the man spent a lot of time at sports venues and populous events. New York's Madison Square Garden made sense to Duncan, but Mardi Gras, the Daytona 500 and the Kentucky Derby? Ah, to have such a schedule.

Nickie would have liked to have gotten to Rex Baxter's gym earlier, but she had court. At least Eddy didn't argue when she insisted on driving this time. They parked in the front, ignoring the fact that they knew about the back entrance.

Hardware By Joe didn't look like it sold a lot of hardware. Dust covered the sparsely stocked shelves. Her suspicion lights blinked in her head. "I'm going to talk to the owner. You wanna walk around?"

Eddy shrugged and took the long way around, moseying like a shopper.

An elderly woman with a visible wad of chew in her lip came out from the back. "What do you want?"

The woman might as well have called her a cop. Nickie had on her three-inch heeled brown leather boots, a pair of matching snug slacks and a white button-down blouse. Her hair fell over her shoulders in the large waves she preferred. Her gun and badge were tucked away under her hip-length brown leather jacket. How did the old hag peg her so quickly?

She guessed she definitely wasn't dressed as someone looking to find a gym, so she went with it and pulled her coat aside to display her badge. "I'm trying to find the entrance to the gym. Is Rex around today?"

"Humph." The woman pointed to the back. Eddy was already making his way there. Nickie followed.

"I'm sure a phone call downstairs announced our arrival," she said to him as they descended the steep stairwell. "This is like a cellar."

"Guys like this shit. It makes us feel manly. Me Tarzan—"

"If you finish that sentence I'm going to kick your ass."

Boxers must not work first shift, because there were plenty there. Eddy gave her a nudge when Baxter was in sight. Yep, he was watching for them. Holy cow, he must be six-foot-five and pushing three hundred.

She walked up to him with Eddy on her heels. Chicken shit. As she got closer, she moved her jacket enough for him to see her badge, but without making a scene. "Detectives Savage and Lynx. We have a few questions for you. Is there a place we can talk?"

He gave her a slow once-over. So, it was going to be like that, was it?

Baxter led her and Eddy to an office, then shut the door behind them. It was a big space with framed posters advertising past fights. The guest chairs were up against a sidewall. A door in the back could be a bathroom or a hallway, maybe another exit.

Baxter walked around his desk, then slouched into his office chair, folding his hands in front of him. "What brings you to my gym?" he asked with a pronounced Jersey accent. His shaved head would have made his tanned face stand out even without the rows of star tattoos behind his ears.

Eddy spoke first. "Do you know anything about a Mr. and Mrs. Chris Hendrix?" Okay. Right to the point, then.

Baxter scratched his head. "Can't say that I remember the names, but loads of people use the gym.

Are they in some kind of trouble?"

She squinted. He was so full of crap she could smell it. Digging out her phone, she loaded the hospital picture of Mr. Hendrix and stepped forward, holding it out to him. He opened his eyes as if sudden recognition just graced him. "Hospital bed? Poor dude. His face rings a bell."

"Listen, Baxter the boxer." That got his attention. "I just thought that up. I bet you get that all the time. It's hilarious."

"No one says that," he growled.

She nearly choked. "I doubt that, Baxter, but you do have a great gym here." She nudged Eddy with her forearm. "We could come by every day, couldn't we? Or even at night. Say, around 11:45 p.m. through the back door?"

She watched as his face fell. The plates they ran from the late-night car belonged to the mayor. It must be more of a secret than she thought. No more arrogance or annoyance. Just old school pissed off.

"I dunno anything about Hendrix. It's the truth. Take it or leave it."

Her face was stone cold. "You're going to have to do better than that."

"He has a bookie, probably more than one." Baxter stood and pretended to straighten the papers on his desk. "And I dunno the name, so don't ask." He took the handful of papers beneath his fingers and crunched them into a ball.

"Still not good enough." She turned to Eddy. "Whose car was that, partner?"

Eddy didn't appear to be so sure about this, but he took her lead anyway. "I think it was the mayor's wife's, Savage."

It was likely most people cowered when Baxter turned the colors of red he was right then. She wasn't most people. She smiled and pulled her hair over her shoulder.

"Try Seventh and Olive Street," he grunted. "Asshole owes me money anyway."

"Name?"

"Dunno. He owns the pawnshop. Can't miss him."

"Don't go too far, Baxter," Nickie said.

She let herself out, but not without hearing him mumble, "Bitch," under his breath.

"Like I haven't heard *that* one before," she said before shutting his office door.

The bookie turned out to be an out-of-town bookie, or so the employee of the pawnshop said. Nickie called in his name and business address to the station. They would get his home address and any other phone numbers, plus search his name in NCIC.

The misses was all sewn up and out of the hospital. Mr. Hendrix wasn't so lucky. He was dealing with infection. That's what happens when you get shot in the arm and wait two days to see a doctor.

The Hendrix's place was in a better area than her townhouse. Fenced in yard around four apartments. The group of apartments stood out from the rest of the neighborhood. Although the building was maintained, there were no bushes, no trees, and the walks weren't shoveled. Last summer's toys littered the front of each apartment.

The blinds were drawn. She parked in front.

"You called me partner," Eddy said. "I liked it."

She turned, brows low, to find him smiling wide. "We're not partners. I was playing the moment. He could have used a little Eddy Lynx sarcasm, by the way. What's your deal?"

"He's Rex Baxter. I've seen him fight."

"Chicken shit," she called him for the second time.

She got out before he had the chance to come around and open her door. This wasn't a date. He opened the gate of the metal fence. She rolled her eyes as he gestured for her to go first.

Through the door, they heard children and a loud television. At the sound of the bell, both quieted.

Mrs. Hendrix opened the door. The room was dark, but from the door, Nickie could see two twin mattresses strewn on the living room floor and a large man sitting in a recliner around a cloud of smoke in the corner. The TV had been muted, and the kids were nowhere to be found.

When the misses recognized who was at the door, she darted her eyes up and down the yard and street.

"Good to see you out of the hospital, Mrs. Hendrix. We have a few questions. May we come in?"

Mrs. Hendrix glanced over her shoulder, then stepped outside, shutting the door behind her. She hugged her bad arm in the chill.

"He's not here."

"Who? Chris? Yeah, we know that," Nickie said. "Sorry to hear that."

"I got nothing to tell you."

Seems to be a reoccurring theme these days. "Slippery Jimbo turned out to be helpful. We're getting closer to finding the person or persons who did this to you and your husband."

She lowered her brows and took a deep breath. "I don't know any Jimbo. You questioned me when I was drugged. I don't even remember you bein' in the room."

"You remember we questioned you, but you don't remember we were in the room?"

"Listen. Jimbo's a pal. He has his shit together and tries to help us. He's got nothing to do with this."

"It's nice of you to have his back. Now, what about your husband's bookie?"

Her face fell. "I got kids, Detective. Do you have kids?"

The mere thought made her cringe. She loved Gil's kids, but ones of her own? "No, but I know you're in trouble and it's not going away."

"It is going away. I'm taking care of it."

"How much?" Nickie asked.

Mrs. Hendrix's focus dropped to the sidewalk. "I've got a plan."

"Does your bookie know you have this plan? I heard he was out of town."

There it was. Surprise mixed with a dose of confusion. So, the bookie wasn't out of town. Big shock, she thought sarcastically.

"Chris'll be out of the hospital in time for Thanksgiving. We have a family. Please leave us alone."

Without turning her back to Nickie, Mrs. Hendrix turned the knob on the door. Nickie laid a gloved hand on her arm. With the other, she slid into her inside coat pocket and pulled out a business card. "Call me. I can help you."

Mrs. Hendrix curled the corners of her mouth and nodded, sticking the card in the back pocket of her faded jeans.

CHAPTER 7

Duncan was used to a bigger family. He and his brother were two and four when his uncle inherited them. After Nathan married Brie, they had kids of their own. Between the seven of them and Brie's seemingly endless line of siblings, nieces and nephews, he was used to changing diapers, all-out squirt gun wars, and could handle preteen female hormones along with his twin cousins who could cause enough trouble to challenge General Lee.

They had already celebrated Thanksgiving with a day at his aunt and uncle's home. "Are you sure you're up for this?" Nickie asked as they reached the front door of a small ranch house. Cars lined the drive and road nearly halfway down the block. The walks and drive were shoveled to perfection, and a dusting of snow topped simple evergreen bushes.

"I can take anything, and I'm not at all worn out." He looked down his nose at her. "And you'd better not wear yourself out, either. I slept alone last night." The idea took the blood from his head and sent it flying south.

A visit to Nickie's former foster home made

Duncan's family seem sparse. He considered this more
of a scene from Black Friday. Organized mass chaos.

The anticipation in her eyes made it worth it. She
worked diligently to disregard her wealthy
upbringing. The boots, the hoop jewelry, the long
loose hair. Even the language she often spewed but
avoided in front the woman who gave Nickie her first
true family. All of it was her rebellion to the debutant
society she grew up in. The society that rejected her
when it learned what she had to do to survive during
her time in captivity. Here, she was more woman than
cop, more daughter than woman. It was a sensation he
couldn't quite find words to describe.

"Mista Weed! Mista Weed! Daddy, Nickie and
Mista Weed are here!" Gilberto and Teresa had two
sets of twins. This set was the one old enough to
charge him.

Gloria had added on to the kitchen, making the
square ranch home more of a T shape. There was a
room for watching whatever sport was in season,
another for video games, although Gloria called it the
family room, and an area for the double-leaf extended
table. It held twelve chairs comfortably.

The furniture was worn but well kept, the carpet
threadbare yet free of crumbs or dirt. Photographs
hung on the wall in frames that didn't match. None
were store-bought, and all contained an array of
generations of family. He shook his head and smiled
at how Nickie was the only white person in the
frames.

"Lela. Neva." Nickie squatted down to the young
girls, each of who was wrapped around one of
Duncan's legs. "Where's your mama and papa? I need
to talk to them, and Mr. Reed needs to eat some of
Grandma's appetizers."

As the girls ran off, dodging bodies, she lifted to a

standing position. Leaning his lips to her ear, he whispered, "You are ravishing."

Her shoulders shivered once. "Says the cover model for last May's *People to Watch in L.A.*"

"But right now I need to slaughter a few hundred zombies," he continued.

"Ah, so that was just one of those compliments given so you can escape without protest," she said, leaning around him to peer into the room packed with teenagers intensely focused on their video games.

"Nickie Savage, I hear you out there." The smooth, liquid tone coming from the kitchen was in direct contrast to the words. "Get in here and help with dinner."

Games were played, dinner feasted on and remember-when stories told. Nickie never spoke of these people as her family, but it didn't take a genius to see she belonged here. She didn't have any girlfriends he could think of. Gilberto was one of her best friends, but Duncan thought of him as more of a brother to her.

He found her sitting at the kitchen table, drying silverware as Gloria packed leftovers in plastic containers for her children, Nickie included. Gloria was a stunning woman. Considering her age, lines had escaped her face, and only a few strands of gray twined through the silky brown to give away her age.

A washrag came at him from the sink area. He grabbed it before it hit him in the face, giving him a quick, crystal clear screenshot of a moment in the Middle East when he had a less desirable object thrown at him. As he'd done with the grenade, he chucked the rag to the only spot in the room free of people. The incessant talking stopped.

Nickie must have assessed the scene accurately. He couldn't quite gather himself to offer a quick explanation.

"Nice reflexes, Reed," she said and lobbed him another washcloth. "Now, go wipe off the tables. No one eats for free. You know that."

***

Nickie helped pass out desserts at the dining table, kitchen table and card tables that were set up wherever there was a spot. Many ate their choice of pie or cheesecake with a plate on their lap. She checked her phone. No messages. Always a good thing.

Her foster family was endlessly impressed with Duncan's ability to remember every name, nickname and detail about each person. If they only knew he remembered those details after his very first time here. He and Great-Grandmama played an older version of Halo, balancing their desserts on their legs.

Duncan had both apple pie and a slice of traditional cheesecake. He didn't know how much it pleased Gloria that he took both.

They fit, she and Duncan. She wasn't exactly sure what to think about that, and she certainly didn't understand how it was possible. He loved her. She was a cop with a sordid past. He was the *Taste of L.A.* She shook her head, trying to take hold of the idea. The long, lanky muscles of his arms and back flexed as he worked to beat Great-Grandmama, who cussed like a sailor. Duncan didn't give her an inch.

Little Nala hung onto the back of his neck as they played. "Cwap! Shit!" she copied her great-great-grandmama.

"Now, you've done it," Duncan said. "You'll have your mom and dad to answer to. I've been a perfect gentleman. There! You're running out of ammo, old woman!"

"Old woman!" little Neva repeated.

Amid protests and more less-than-child-worthy language, Nickie walked over and stood in front of the television. Crossing her arms, she stared at Duncan. "It's after ten. What great-grandmothers stay up past ten? It's past their bedtimes too." She gestured to the twins, winked at Duncan seductively, and reveled in the way he stood and fumbled his controllers.

"It seems we're leaving." Leaning down, he kissed Great-Grandmama's cheek. "I forfeit this time only."

She was older than the hills, free of most lines, as was Gloria, but with a full head of long, sleek gray hair. "Good night, Duncan. Be good to our girl."

Nickie's eyes filled at the comment. Great-Grandmama smiled, and the invisible lines erupted around her eyes and the sides of her mouth. The house thinned from the loads of people. The ones who were still there lounged in front of the television with the buttons of their pants undone.

Together, she and Duncan stopped in to say their good-byes to Gloria. Duncan lifted a heavy stack of plates into the cupboard for her.

Nickie wrapped her arms around Gloria's substantial frame. "Thank you. For everything."

Gloria's eyes were nearly the color of Duncan's. A dark brown so glossy they were almost black. They shone at her as Gloria took hold of her face.

"Thank you, my child."

Gloria turned to Duncan and gave him a small push. "You've done enough around here tonight. Take care of our Nickie." As she had done with her, Gloria wrapped her arms around him in a bear hug before taking his face in her hands the color of caramel. "You have many secrets, Duncan Reed. They have lasted many years. I hope you have someone to share them with."

It took Nickie aback. Her eyes darted from Duncan

to Gloria. No one elaborated, and he seemed as surprised as she was.

Duncan refused to ride in Nickie's piece of crap unmarked. He found it difficult to believe the police force allowed cars like it. Big, gas guzzling and old. Then, he considered that it might be why they chose the car. She was a terrible driver.

"I thought we were going to your place," she commented when he drove past the turn to his rental. She never missed a thing. Damn smart woman.

He shifted and reached over, linking fingers with her. "We are."

Her head turned to face him. "You mean—"

Shaking his head, he shrugged. "Not exactly. But you'll see."

Just outside of town, he turned up a long, winding asphalt drive that led to his home. His real home. A lone trailer had been left for the holiday weekend, and a thin sheet of snow covered the mud. He took her bag from his trunk. She packed for overnight like he would for a week. It made him grin.

They walked, glove in glove, up the flagstone steps. She craned her neck as she looked over the siding and pillars. "You do like big," she commented.

It was true. He unlocked the front door and opened to visqueen, five-gallon buckets of paint and stacks of trim.

She stopped a foot inside the door. "There is a bathroom, right?"

He turned to face her and snaked his arms around her sides. "Do you trust me?"

Her eyes thinned. "Maybe."

Leaning in, he let his lips touch hers once, twice, before sinking into the place that was his detective. Her lips were cool from the weather, her tongue warm and inviting. Her arms wrapped around him, making his mind clear, then fog. He was home.

"Come," he said before they got carried away. Rarely did they make it to a bed. Taking her hand, he led her up the first set of stairs.

She studied his house like a first-time guest. Much of the painting was done, some of the hardwood floors installed.

When they took the set of stairs to the third floor, he complained, "I should have installed an elevator."

"People shouldn't use elevators."

It made him consider where he could install one. As they reached the top of the landing, she stopped. "What have you done?"

The top floor was finished to his specifications...with a few additions. "I had them rush the third floor along."

He considered it more of an enormous studio apartment rather than a master bedroom. On one side was the wrap-around cherry wood desk his uncle made for him. On and surrounding it were his desktop computers, towers, scanners, printer and fax machine. Under the skylight windows was his painting studio, complete with the short wooden stool he preferred, three easels and the chestnut settee he couldn't help but replace.

She turned in a circle, gazing next at the four-corner oversized canopy bed.

"It's amazing. Who lives in a place like this? Did you think of all of this or did Andy help you?" She turned to him. "It's perfect. Thank you for sharing it with me."

Striding to him, her arms snaked up his chest before she released the top button of his shirt. He took hold of her wrists before his eyes crossed. "There's more."

He led her to the bathroom he had made twice the

size he would have if not for her. The woman took more time in a bathroom than any Hollywood actress he'd ever dated.

She held out her arms and turned in another circle. Two vanities, adjustable lighting, separate shower and hot tub, an island for drawers with a bar stool tucked beneath near a magnified lighted mirror, and outlets for a hair dryer and irons. He didn't tell her about the heated towel bars and floors.

She covered her mouth with her hand. "Let's hurry up and have sex so we can shower. No, let's shower then have sex."

He was determined to break in the bed and turned her around, pushing her out the door. It was then she spotted the second desk.

"Why do you need two desks?"

"I don't."

Her feet stopped, causing him to nearly trip over her. She spun, her face not at all seductive or impressed with the area any longer. "I'm not living with you."

He wasn't planning to ask…yet. It had been difficult enough to get her to keep the key to his first house. The way she said it stung nonetheless. It was one more attempt on her part to keep their relationship from moving forward.

"I hurt you," she corrected. "I hurt you on such a perfect day. I'm sorry."

"It's a desk. I bought a stand for your cello too. It's not a ball or a chain, and isn't this something the man is supposed to concern himself with?" He smiled and watched as she blinked rapidly.

"I'm going to ignore the chauvinist comment, because right now, I want you so badly I can't think straight." She grabbed hold of his shirt and took him to the floor with her. Her strong legs wrapped around him as he pulled her sweater over her head. Beneath, silk the color of powder blue barely held her in. It made his toes curl.

She yanked his shirt from his pants and fumbled with the buttons. Seductive lips sent him from zero to sixty in seconds. They gave up on the buttons and, together, pulled it over his head, exposing the tattoo of Black Creek across his left pectoral. Zippers were released and clothes tossed as they rolled on the soft, new carpet, twining limbs and lips.

He couldn't get enough; he always needed more.

"I love you. I love us," she gasped. Her fingertips traveled down his torso. He nearly choked when she found him.

Nickie's back arched as impatient anticipation flooded her. His strong fingers traced the curve of flesh that refused to stay tucked in the blue silk she chose purposely for their night together. She loved the way he could multitask and quickened her pace around him.

Savoring the way his eyes turned opaque, Nickie didn't let go and maneuvered herself until she straddled him. His eyes, his face, the sensation of primal need. His hands. His glorious, magical hands took hold of her through the blue silk. The fingers of one traveled and dipped below the matching bottoms.

Her head flew back, and he reached behind her, both holding her up and releasing her from the silk. She fell into his hands, and he took hold as he flipped her around until he hovered over her. His eyes moved from one of hers to the other as his hand trailed a line down her neck, over her stomach in a line to her center.

It was more than any human would be able to take. She was completely in love, and it scared her as much as it thrilled her. She'd never held such need, such intensity as she did when she was with him. Barely keeping her eyes on his, she went over with a cry that seemed distant. He didn't let go, didn't stop, and only slowed his pace long enough for her to climb upward again.

Desperate for purchase, her nails dug into his shoulders. She wrapped her legs around his back pulling stronger, deeper. "I need you," she breathed. "It has to be now. Tell me it can be now."

He didn't answer her words, but lowered over her until they were sinking together in light and darkness. Joined. The artist and the cop, as if this were meant to be from the day they met. They raced like their lives depended on the last inch closer.

She heard the air escape his lungs and knew it was time. Time for them. Here. Tightening around him, she choked on a gasp as they went over the last peak together. A sheen of sweat lay between them as they moved together in the final push.

The weight of him collapsed over her, with nothing moving other than their hearts and lungs. It took longer than usual for their breathing to return to a semi-normal rate.

"We didn't make it to the bed," he breathed into her hair.

She smiled, knowing what that meant to him. Lifting her heavy limbs, she wrapped her legs around him, linking the backs of her feet together and clasping her fingers behind his neck. She clung to him like an infant chimpanzee. He lifted, carrying her to his new bed. Still twined, they squirmed until they crawled beneath the covers. It was an early evening for them, and she looked forward to a solid night of sleep next to her friend and lover.

CHAPTER 8

Nickie sat on one of the two stools at the wet bar Duncan installed next to his painting studio. Her hair was wet, and she wore her detective gear; black pants, black boots and a button-down blouse, with her gun in her holster and badge secured on her belt. He wore a three-piece designer suit, not a chocolate-brown hair out of place. Even the obvious difference in their appearance couldn't kill her mood that morning.

He'd stocked the mini-fridge with orange juice and a fruit salad. She ate with him as the sun rose through the windows. A bag of whole grain bagels and cherry-filled donuts sat between them. Metaphorically, she was the donut and he was the bagel. Except, he knew her too well and set a donut on his plate only. Damned Monticello fat genes.

They ate in silence, not needing useless small talk to fill some kind of awkward space. Absently, he ran his thumb over the back of her hand as he read some documents that had more numbers than words.

He lifted his head and turned an ear toward the door. She hadn't heard anything, and she was the cop. But Duncan seemed to have a constant awareness of the sights and sounds around him.

"Andy's here." He straightened his papers and slipped them in his briefcase. "And Lynx." He reached in his pocket and took out a silver circle that held the single key to his new house. He held it toward her, letting her make the next move.

She smiled at him as she stuck out her hand. It was a short, silent conversation only they would understand.

Now, she heard them. Eddy was early. Figures. They were due to check out the home address of the bookie Rex Baxter hit them onto. She glanced at her watch. Not at this hour, though.

"I'm coming up, brother," Andy called from below. "You two had better be dressed."

Between Andy and Rose, she was beginning to suspect everyone thought all she and Duncan did was fool around. As usual, Duncan was a man of few words. He crossed the room and opened the door for them.

Swallowing her last gulp of juice, she stood and adjusted the gear on her belt. Andy came through first and made a beeline for the food. Eddy stood, legs apart, inside the doorframe.

She checked out the room. No clothes on the floor, and Duncan had made the bed. Relief.

"Help yourself to a donut, Lynx," Duncan said as he buttoned his suit jacket.

Andy spoke with his mouth full. "Trimmers are coming this morning. Time and a half due to the holiday weekend. You know this is illegal, right?"

Unlike Andy, Eddy took the long way to the food, browsing through the expansive room like a visitor in a museum.

"Hmm?" Duncan asked as he lifted his briefcase.

"Staying here. It's nowhere near ready for

inspection."

Duncan turned his eyes to her with an expression no one else would be able to detect. It read sultry sarcasm. "You should call the cops."

Andy washed down the donut with some OJ. "Very funny. I'm glad you're here, legally or illegally. I have a few things to run by you."

Duncan stepped to her and ducked his lips near her ear. "I'm pretending to whisper something profound so I can nibble on your earlobe before I deal with Andy's 'few things.'"

And he did. It took great restraint not to shiver from the sensation or smile at his rare attempt at humor.

"Eat on the go, Lynx," she blurted. "We're crowding the work crew." As if on cue, the sounds of a diesel engine rumbled outside. Eddy stuck a donut between his teeth, mumbling his thanks to Duncan as he fooled with some papers in the inside pocket of his leather jacket.

"I told you I trust your judgment," Duncan said as Andy drilled him about faucet hardware, tile design and which second-floor guest rooms should have a gas fireplace.

Andy shook his head in frustration. He pulled a pencil from behind his ear. The gesture reminded Duncan of their uncle.

"When is your next gig?" This was his brother's affectionate term for 'creating a painting for a client.'

"I leave for L.A. in ten days. I have an appointment with the assistant to the governor Tuesday." Duncan washed the few breakfast dishes and put the rest away in the small cupboard above the wet bar sink.

Andy wrote something in the notebook he'd taken from his back pocket. "Wait a minute, the assistant to the governor? Of New York?"

Duncan nodded again, this time more prominently and with a lift of his brows.

"He's the dude we hacked not too long ago," Andy said like it hit him at that moment. "I have a feeling this isn't a coincidence."

"True enough. I'd like to make my own assessment of him and his property."

"You are one ballsy bastard."

Duncan lifted a corner of his mouth.

They headed for the crew that unpacked on the first floor. Duncan locked the door to his master bedroom. The area was done, and he didn't believe in tempting anyone who could use some state-of-the-art equipment.

"Speaking of," Andy added, "you need someone to go with you on Tuesday? I could have my secretary move some things around for me. You shouldn't go alone."

"I'll keep you on speed dial. Other than that, it's a regular appointment with a potential client. I've done it a hundred times." They rounded onto the final flight of stairs, stepping over visqueen and around paint cans.

"A regular appointment with someone you think might be involved in your girlfriend's past. Have you told her? Is that what Lynx was getting out of your printer?"

Duncan's feet stopped, and he grabbed the unpainted railing in the middle of the stairs. "Excuse me?"

"Ahha. Not many times I catch something you don't. Points for me."

How had Duncan missed that? What was in there? Lynx was Nickie's friend, her partner. Sort of. It was possible he needed a piece of his paper to use as a notepad. Duncan oftentimes did that.

"I don't have anything to tell her yet. There is no

need to upset her or put unfounded ideas in her head."

"It's your neck."

The crew needed the stairs, so he and Andy made haste and got out of the way. They nodded greetings as they passed.

Thanks to the desk guys at the station, Nickie had a face, a name, two addresses and two phone numbers. What she didn't have was a suspect. The bookie was MIA. Something didn't add up.

So, she decided to wait. She hadn't done a stakeout in a whole six days, she thought sarcastically. Eddy was the tricky part. She didn't have the patience or the professionalism to handle his talking for potentially hours while sitting in a stagnant car. She considered taking a beat officer. Or wearing headphones? Alone?

The thought made her realize that during the last handful of calls, Eddy had refrained from his rapid chatter. He must be taking the hint. Go you, Eddy.

Luckily, they agreed to split up. She was parked in front of the bookie's home and he in front of the bookie's business. If either one saw anything, they would call the other. It was a small city. Couldn't take more than ten minutes for one to get to the other.

She thought about her transfer here. Northridge was big enough to have a hospital, a place to shop, great restaurants, and a movie theater. But it was small enough that her captain was a stepdad to Duncan's sister-in-law. She was glad she didn't have to say that aloud ten times fast. And she was glad she was here. She'd learned a lot, good and bad.

She and Eddy hadn't mentioned the day's plan to Captain Nolan. Better to ask forgiveness rather than permission in this situation.

While she waited, she used her tablet and did a deeper search for both Rex Baxter the boxer and

Hendrix's bookie. She took down names of their employees and did a search on them individually, creating a spreadsheet that included photos of each.

The house she watched was a single-family with evergreen bushes that fought the winter weather and offered a glimpse of the season yet to come. The car got cold, but she didn't want to turn it on and attract attention with gas fumes creating steam from her tailpipe. She blew into her hands so her fingers would move over the screen of her tablet.

It looked like Rex Baxter was a naughty boy. Two stints in county and a mistrial that should have taken him to the big house for five to seven. The bookie was more careful. Questioned on suspicion of money laundering, but no arrest.

A black SUV pulled into the curb space between the bookie's house and the next-door neighbor's. Nickie got out her digital and cursed that it didn't take better pictures from this distance.

It was a man. A man who was not Hendrix's bookie or Rex Baxter. He appeared as if he might work out at Baxter's gym. In his hand, he carried…two bags of fast food? Feed the kids while he does the wife. Gross. She was taking the best pictures she could when her cell rang.

"Savage."

She heard a woman sucking air and sobbing on the other end.

"This is Detective Savage," she repeated.

"My kids. Detective, my kids."

"Calm down, miss. How did you get this number?"

"You gave it to me. He's…he's targeting my kids. I don't know what to do." It was Mrs. Hendrix. She should be glad Nickie wasn't the type to say, 'I told you so.'

"Where are you? Where are your children?"

"They're in school. I checked. I'm home. Oh! Do you think I should leave? They sent me pictures." She was barely audible through her sobbing. "They took pictures of my kids."

One thing Nickie learned from her years on the force is the fact that damned near every mother loved their children. They may love their drugs more, want their abusive husband more, but they all loved their children.

Her own mother served as an exception to that rule.

"Lock the doors. I'm on the way. Can you do that?"

"Uh, huh. I keep them locked all the time now."

"Are you alone?"

"Yes, ma'am."

Settled in his office, Duncan booted his equipment. 'It's your neck,' resounded in his head. His view out the top story window displayed downtown Northridge. It was like something off a postcard. Business owners took care of their stores and office buildings. Some tall, some short, they all carried fresh paint and maintained brick or clean siding. The top of each was dusted with picture-perfect white. He tucked the memory away for a future painting and turned his attention to his desk computer.

He had exactly two hours to fit in a virtual meeting with an out-of-town realtor, a face-to-face with his agent and a conference call with his next L.A. client. The last two pieces for his art show were nearly completed, but if he didn't get in some hours on them, they wouldn't be ready on time.

His growing list aside, what he really wanted to do was spend time on an image search for the assistant to the governor. He checked email, the price of silver and a few of his real estate investments. Finally, he gave up, plopped his shoes on his desk and set his tablet on his legs.

He found mostly the same images of the governor's personal assistant he'd found previously. Few were taken in New York State. Yet, the press loved this guy. Thurmond Moody. He had twice the number of pictures taken at sporting and gambling events than he did at charities or political venues.

He dressed well, Duncan would give him that. There was the photo of him at Mardi Gras with strings and strings of beads dripping around his neck. One of him at the Kentucky Derby surrounded by obnoxiously bodacious women in their enormous racing hats. He had to scroll to page seven to find the one he'd been searching for, the one of him at the press conference discussing *the* Maryland Monticellos' daughter, who had come home after eighteen months on the run.

In the picture, Nickie's parents clung to each other near a podium. Moody wasn't in the foreground, wasn't announcing, so why was he there? And why was he the assistant to a number of consecutive governors regardless of political party? And, most of all, what the hell was he doing at a Maryland press conference?

Finally, there was the photo, years later, of Moody announcing Nickie's transfer to Northridge PD. Coincidence? Duncan wasn't like Nickie. He counted on hunches. It wasn't that Nickie didn't believe in them, he knew, but she was a cop. She could only use what would hold up in court. He was most definitely not a cop. And for him, there were never coincidences.

He stood as he saw it, thumping his feet on the ground as he did. Setting his tablet on his desk, he leaned in to get a better look, then zoomed in on Moody's wrist. There it was. How? What? How? The bracelet. Thurmond Moody, the personal assistant to the governor of New York State, wore the same bracelet found in an abandoned home in Henderson, Nevada.

A dozen possibilities and connections ran through the red fog that quickly became his vision. Pressure filled his skull, and firecrackers seemed like they were exploding inches from his ears. He saw dust and blood, army fatigues and gaping wounds.

No. He wouldn't let himself go back there today.

He grabbed hold of his desk until his knuckles turned white. He shook his head three times hard, then woke up his desk computer. Quickly, he re-searched the image, zoomed to the center and printed. He went back and printed the images of the sick prick at the announcement of Nickie's transfer and of the day he stood in the back at her teenage coming home press conference.

Standing with both hands on the side of his desk, he locked his elbows and dipped his head low. This was circumstantial. She wouldn't like it. He wanted to scream, to punch something. Instead, he sat down and decided to research jewelry stores to see how common this bracelet was.

Nickie knew Eddy would be pissed she hadn't call him for backup, but he was needed where he was. Instead, she called dispatch for the closest beat officer. The dude was already there when she arrived. She recognized him as the one who assisted her with some evidence in a bridge underpass search. Officer Parker. He was built like a brick and, if she could describe him, acted like a brick; stiff and formal.

"Ma'am," he addressed her as he approached.

Shutting the car door, she walked to him. "Do I look like a ma'am to you, Officer?"

Clearly baffled, he opened his mouth, closed it again, and then stuttered, "Uh…"

"It's Detective or it's Savage." She didn't care if it was petty.

Mrs. Hendrix ran out of her house, waving a white, business-sized envelope in her good arm. Black makeup dripped in straight lines down her cheeks.

Nickie took a pair of plastic gloves from a compartment on her belt and slipped them on. "Let me help you." The pictures were, indeed, of her kids. Each of them. Playing in front her house, in the yard at the school. "We can send an officer over to pick them up from school. Do you have a safe place to stay? Preferably an out-of-town friend or relative?"

She nodded and wiped her nose on the sleeve of her shirt.

"Let's get you inside and get you a coat. It would be better if you went with the officer to the school. The kids will feel safer rather than going with a stranger."

As they sat in the lounge at the station, Nickie handed Mrs. Hendrix a bottle of water and a bag of pretzels.

"Thank you, Detective. I owe you." Her eyes were bloodshot, half from crying and half from whatever she was taking. Nickie hoped it was only a prescribed dose of pain meds.

"All you owe me is a name. You keep saying, 'they.'"

"The hospital says if Chris's numbers stay steady through the night, he gets out tomorrow."

Nickie hated this part of her job, but it had to be done. "You're waiting for his instructions? His advice put your children in danger. Both of you have been shot."

The sobbing started again. Nickie had little

tolerance for hysterics. It never did a damn thing except cloud judgment. She got the woman a tissue, counted to ten in her head, then continued.

Taking out her photo of Rex Baxter, her husband's bookie and a handful of other photos, Nickie asked, "Do you recognize any of these men?"

Mrs. Hendrix's eyes turned to Nickie, then back to the photos. "None of these men shot us, Detective Savage."

Nickie was losing her patience. "Are any of the men who worked for any of these men responsible for the shootings of you or your husband?" Without opening it, she placed the white envelope containing the pictures of Mrs. Hendrix's children in front of her.

Tears dripped on the table. "They'll kill us. We owe so much money, and now with the hospital bill..."

"We can help you."

"Chris says you can't."

"Chris isn't the one saving your kids' butts. You did that. You did that by letting us help you."

Nickie reached behind her for a pad of paper and a pen, and then pushed them in front of Mrs. Hendrix. "I need a name, an address and a phone number. For your children, Mrs. Hendrix."

"I didn't recognize the man who shot me. Chris says it was the same guy. You won't tell him I told, will you?"

"Of course not," Nickie lied.

"And I don't have a name, but I know what he looks like."

"We have people for that, Mrs. Hendrix. Come with me."

George Henery was a pushover, the poster child for OCD and an excellent sketch artist. Nickie left Mrs. Hendrix with him and decided it was time to call Eddy. She pulled out her cell as she made the corner to her office. And nearly ran into him. A waft of new leather and the cologne he liked to wear breezed over her.

"You ditched me," he said flatly.

"Not really," she lied again. "You were needed where you were. I had this under control. Did you find out anything?"

He turned from her and headed into his office. "Just that the bookie thinks his wife is having an affair." He was saving face as he spoke with his back to her. Male posturing got tiresome, but Nickie followed anyway.

"Mrs. Hendrix is working with Henery on a rendering of the man who shot her. Says the same dude got her husband."

She followed into his office and flicked on the lights. Her eyes drew like a magnet to a paper on his desk. It was a regular-sized piece of paper, 8 ½-by-11, but to her it was as big as a billboard. Her feet gave out beneath her as she grabbed the sides of the doorjamb to keep from falling to the floor.

"I need to show you something," he said.

The air felt like it had been knocked out of her lungs. Her head bobbed, but her eyes couldn't leave the paper. It was a drawing, a rendering. And it was of the man who held her captive for eighteen months of her childhood.

CHAPTER 9

Nickie noticed as Eddy turned to finish his sentence, but she was concentrating on keeping herself conscious. She bent over and Eddy grabbed a garbage can, placed it in front of her face. Smart man, because she emptied the contents from her stomach then and there.

Sucking air, she asked, "Where did you get that?"

"Where did I get wha—? Oh, that." He set the soiled wastebasket down, held her under her arm and reached to grab a box of tissues. Guiding her to the floor, he reached over his desk and retrieved the paper. "That's what I wanted to talk to you about. I found it in Pretty Boy's printer this morning at his place. Since it had your name written across the top, I figured it had to be for you."

She knew he was lying. He'd taken it. Somehow she knew she should be glad, but right then, her heart was breaking in so many pieces she didn't have room to comprehend anything.

Duncan took the elevator to the top floor of the police station. His head spun with millions of possibilities. How was the personal assistant to the governor of New York involved with the kidnapping and forced prostitution of young girls in Nevada? How far did this reach, and what was his interest in Nickie?

The elevator doors opened as he unbuttoned his coat and extracted the photos from his inside pocket. If Moody was involved and knew of Nickie's past, why didn't he take her or keep an eye on her or...maybe he was.

He and Nickie would find out soon enough. This would classify as a viable hunch, even in her cut and dry mind. Her office was dark. He should have called first. He wasn't thinking straight. Kicking himself, he almost turned around before he spotted her. She was on the floor near the doorway of another office, sitting on her heels. Her hair draped in long, flowing waves down to the center of her back.

And over her hair were the arms of her ex.

Duncan's first instinct was blind jealousy. But he trusted her. Next, he realized she was trembling, and his feet charged into a run. She turned at the sound of his footsteps. Her eyes spoke to him. No tears. Never any tears. But they were red and screamed anger and betrayal.

She slid one of her arms from around Lynx. In it was a paper. It was the man of Asian descent Duncan had obsessed over for months.

"How long?" Her voice was raspy and nearly inaudible.

Time turned into slow motion. Pieces fell together in his head. She knew this man. Well enough to cause this reaction.

The paper slipped between her fingers, just as she slipped between his.

He looked down at his hand. He held the prints of

Thurmond Moody. He couldn't remember why.

He could explain. "It was a hunch." It was only a picture. "The Vegas casino." Panic set in. His feet didn't retract, yet the image of her grew smaller and smaller.

"I think you know what you can do with your *hunch*," she said to him as she turned and buried her face in Lynx's shoulder.

"Detective?"

Nickie lifted her head to find Mrs. Hendrix standing in the doorway of Eddy's office. Her knees were flattened with dents from Eddy's berber carpet. In her good arm, the misses stood holding the rendering of the shooter.

"I don't mean to...uh...interrupt, but Mr. Henery told me to give this to you myself because you make him nervous. His words," she added as a disclaimer.

The woman's pathetic stance, slouched and pouty, gave Nickie the will to try her legs. She was working on autopilot and hoped it didn't malfunction. This overwhelming rush of defeat was something she never allowed.

Taking the sketch from Mrs. Hendrix's hand, she said, "Good, good, let's—"

Dipping her head, she brought her eyes closer. She'd seen this man. He was at Baxter's gym stalking around with a clipboard. Turning it to face Eddy, she asked, "Recognize this man?"

He shrugged.

She put her face in her hands and took a deep breath. There was too much in her head to know where to start with sorting it out.

"We were sent on a wild goose chase, Lynx. Mrs. Hendrix, you wait here. We're gonna be a while. I'm going to put someone in charge of you. They can get you anything you need—food, something to drink, cigarettes. Please wait in the lounge for a few until I can wrangle someone up." Mrs. Hendrix nodded nervously as Nickie took Eddy by the arm.

"Come on," she growled. On the way out, she dipped into her office and grabbed a warrant application. Duncan was long gone.

"Are you going to tell me what's going on? I'm talkin' about you and Pretty Boy. What happened back there?"

"I don't wanna talk about it." It was almost the truth. She *couldn't* talk about it, not if she wanted to keep her head on straight. She was broken and overwhelmed and didn't plan on letting it take hold of her. Broken maybe, but she was in control. Had to be. Survival was what she did best. No man was going to break her. And no man was going hide things behind her back.

Eddy took her arm. "Slow down."

She shrugged from his grip.

"Are you going to tell me where we're going? Tell the captain, maybe?" His tone was short and sarcastic.

"We're going to the hospital, then to Judge Foster, then to Baxter's gym. The sketch was of one of his employees. You call and notify Nolan." She took the stairs two at a time.

Nickie drove. Eddy rode with his hands planted firmly, one on the dash and one on the door. And in true form, not quietly. "Whoa, Nick. I'm too young to die."

She barely heard him.

She parked in front of the ER and turned her lights on. There was still enough room for an ambulance to get through. "You coming or not?"

Eddy took a pronounced breath before slinking out.

She ignored him and walked ahead. She stepped in front of the person waiting at the reception counter and slapped her badge on the white Formica. "Chris Hendrix's room number."

The receptionist gawked at her like she had three eyes.

"You wanna come to the station with me for obstruction of justice?"

Rolling her eyes, the woman tapped at her keyboard. "Room 223." She popped her gum.

"Nick, wait." Eddy took her arm.

She glared at his hand like it was a bug, then lifted her focus to his eyes.

He released her and held his hands up, palms out. "Slow down, man. What's the matter with you?"

"Come or stay. Your choice."

She barged into Hendrix's room to find him sitting up with unidentifiable hospital food on a tray in front of him. He pushed it away when he saw her like he'd just lost his appetite.

"Do you know about these?" She set the envelope with the pictures of his kids on his lap.

He didn't open the envelope. "Maybe."

"Listen, asshole. The only way you're going to come out of this alive is if I put this guy away."

"I don't disagree with that, except you're not going to put anyone away." He crossed his good arm over his chest.

"I don't mean only the shooter. I mean Baxter too. You're going to stop this game, man up and take one for your family, you bastard."

"You can do that?"

"I guarantee it," she said as Eddy poked her in the back.

Hendrix took too long considering.

"Ticktock, Hendrix. I need a statement. How do you know Rex Baxter?" She noticed a nurse stick her head in the door. Nickie stuck out her badge, using it as a stop sign.

She was about to conveniently bump his bad arm when Hendrix took a deep breath and finally spoke. "Rex Baxter runs a money laundering and loan shark business. I owe him money I used to pay off some gambling debts. I was late, and he hired one of his dudes—"

"Was it this dude?" She showed him the police artist's sketch. His eyes said it all. "The rest is circumstantial." She walked around Eddy to the door. "I'll keep in touch," she added as they left.

The pool in his house wasn't ready, so Duncan tried laps in the one at the Northridge Y. The water was too warm, and he had to share a lane with a man who was much too slow for the pace Duncan needed.

Relationships.

Impossible.

He kept his head lower in the water than usual, following the line painted on the floor beneath him. Between muffling outside noises, the rushing sound of the water helped dull the inside noises. The ones from his memory that were always there.

He'd come to her with what he had. And what he had was information on Thurmond Moody.

He had nothing on the nameless Asian man.

What he had was crucial, and now it sat on the seat of his Audi. She wouldn't answer her phone. The sensation in his gut was one he'd never experienced. Not when his parents died. Not in the desert. Not even the first time he spotted the scars on Nickie's back. Six thin lines drew away from her right shoulder blade to just below. And three small, round cigarette burns.

All returned to the color of skin with the passage of time.

He drove into the wall at the deep end like he was finishing a race, dipping his body and reaching for the edge. It wasn't a race he was finishing. He needed air. More air. It sucked into his lungs, but it wasn't enough.

The Chinook had taken a hit. Sand stuck to every inch of him, clinging to sweat and blood. His commanding officer yelled orders to check on the rest of the platoon, but all Duncan could see was gaping flesh and blood. Blood covered the wall of their helicopter around a hole the size of a small car.

"They're gone, sir," he said, dropping his head low.

"Who's gone?" a young male voice spoke to him. Duncan blinked and saw his goggles floating in the gutter of the pool. He lifted his head to a lifeguard who squatted next to him. "Who's gone, sir? Are you okay?"

Shaking his head, Duncan darted his eyes from one side of the pool to the other. "The cramps. My cramps are gone," he lied, slipped his goggles on and dove back in, breathing between every stroke.

He would give it another five-hundred yards, then go to his office and email the pictures to Nickie. Email and send them snail mail if he had to. Then, he would wash his hands of the whole mess. He was sure she would recognize the bracelet. She was a smart woman. She could decide what to do next.

CHAPTER 10

The gated community had been left open on this day after the holiday. Nickie pulled in front of Judge Foster's home. She parked with one wheel partially on the curb and slammed the gearshift into park.

"Nick—" Eddy started.

"I need a warrant, and it's the damned day after Thanksgiving. Wait here, if you want."

He didn't budge. She knew she was acting like a bitch. If the shoe fit.

She trudged up the absurdly long walk to the front door and searched for a doorbell. What the hell? Who doesn't have a doorbell? Awkwardly, she lifted the large brass ring and knocked in the center three times. It took so long for anyone to answer that she almost left. It was a butler who opened the door, in full butler getup.

"I'd like to see Judge Foster. Tell him it's Detective Savage, and it's an emergency."

"Of course, Detective."

He didn't offer to let her wait inside and, instead, shut the door, leaving her in the cold. She'd been through worse. But it turned into dead time, which was something she couldn't afford.

He lied to her. Duncan told her he wouldn't keep anything like this from her again, and at the same time, he was sitting on a picture of Jun Zheng?

Jun Zheng. She hadn't let herself think that name in over a decade. Without considering, her head craned to one side as her eyes squeezed shut. It was like being slapped in the face. Again.

The door opened and she straightened. "You may come in. The judge will see you now."

The butler led her to a library where Judge Foster was pouring himself a glass of water from a bottle. "Detective." He sat on the edge of a brown leather couch. "You're at my house," he said flatly. "At dinnertime."

"Yes, sir. I need a warrant, and it can't wait until Monday." Thinking she'd better, she added, "Please." Then, took out the forms.

He picked up the papers, and without reading them, set them down next to him on the couch. "Tell me what's going on."

She didn't have the patience for this. Clenching her fists, she forced herself not to bite the hand that feeds her.

"I have two witnesses who tag a Rex Baxter of running a loan shark and money laundering business. They've both been shot, not fatal, and one of them has IDed a man who works for Baxter as the shooter. The bullets were from a Smith and Wesson M&P .45 ACP. The warrant is for the confiscation of any guns fitting this description, and any computer hard drives and files from Baxter's place of business and home."

A flash of the expression on Duncan's face ran across her mind, her thoughts. It was his confusion when he first saw her in Eddy's arms. Not jealousy or anger, but honest confusion.

"And this couldn't wait until Monday, because…"

"Hmm? Oh. No, sir. The couple has children. Pictures were sent to the mother. Pictures of their children. Someone is threatening them."

"I'm going to assume since you've never been desperate enough to come to my home that you are exactly that, desperate," he said as he reached for the papers and looked them over. "You've got a good track record, Detective. Your cases are solid. You make my job easier. Don't make this a habit." He took a pen from his pocket and signed the warrant.

She should have been flooded with relief, but at that moment, rational emotions were nowhere to be found. "Thank you, sir," she said mechanically. "I won't."

"Do you want me in here, or should I wait in the car again?" Eddy was understandably pissed.

Nickie took a cleansing breath, and turned down the alley behind Hardware by Joe. She pulled close to Baxter's back door and rested her forehead on her steering wheel.

"Oh, shit. I didn't mean it." He ran his hand up her arm, over her shoulder and behind her hair. It was warm. Eddy had always cared about her. That was never the problem. With his other hand, he took hers and linked fingers. She glanced at their joined hands, then up to his eyes. They were the softest blue. She pulled her hand away.

"No. It's my fault," she said. He was sincere, it seemed, as he looked from one of her eyes to the other. She placed her clammy palm on his cheek. "I need some time. I've been through worse."

They exited the car as she took her gun off safety. "I've got a plan."

"I always like the sound of that," he said as he closed his door.

Before shutting hers and locking the car, she tossed her coat on her seat. She wanted her gun and badge on display for this asshole.

Pushing open the back door of the gym, she let it slam against the wall, announcing her entrance. It was effective. All eyes turned. The place had the scent of rusty metal, sweat and the feel of damp concrete.

She scanned the place but didn't see the dude from Mrs. Hendrix's police rendering. She did see Baxter. He wasn't happy to see her.

She knew men and needed to get this one agitated. Just the way she liked them.

"Maybe we should talk in my office, Detective," Baxter said as soon as they were within whispering distance. Step one, check.

Before they left the open area, she stood her ground in front of the thin group of employees and members, each of whom had yet to get their eyes off them. "You first." Gesturing with her arm like she was a chivalrous man allowing the woman to enter before her, she reached for the door before he had a chance. The glare he shot at her was priceless. Step two, check.

For a quick moment, she saw Duncan. It was the time he held the door open to his new office. The one he bought so he could spend more time in Northridge, spend more time with her. The wash of emotion that spilled over her was not welcome.

"Detective?" Baxter barked from inside his office.

Her eyes saw nothing but fog. Confusion. Hurt. Disappointment and a haze.

Eddy shut the door behind them more softly than she would have preferred. Turning on Baxter, she walked up to him, chest out, stopping inches from his face. She paused and smiled. "You sent me on a wild goose chase, Baxter the boxer."

His face turned all sorts of colors, and he spoke through his teeth. "You're gonna want to step back, pretty lady."

She adjusted her hair. "Pretty lady? Why thank you, Rex." She stepped close enough that only a thin line of air lay between them. "I lost my beauty sleep sitting in front of Hendrix's bookie's house."

She pulled out Mrs. Hendrix's police rendering from her back pocket. Shoving it in his face, she crooned, "Where is this man?"

He took a step back to focus on the sketch. She countered and took a step forward. His eyes showed a flash of recognition before they turned stone cold. Step three, check.

"I don't know what you're talking about," he said through smiling teeth.

"Of course you don't, dear." She took a step closer, causing him to step back and hit the wall behind him. She heard his piece clunk against the wood paneling.

It was a dance of wits, and he was easy prey. Taking the warrant from her other pocket, she crooned, "How about this? I've got two witnesses implicating you and your two-bit money laundering and loan shark joke of an operation. One who identifies your employee as the man who took a hit on two citizens. He's been stalking their kids. Left an envelope of candid kiddie pictures for the mama."

"Pictures of kids? What the hell do you take me for?"

He was sincere about the pictures. Interesting.

"The warrant covers every piece of computer equipment and every scrap of paper." She glanced around his back. "And for any gun matching this description. Let's start here..." She slid one hand over her gun as the other reached around him, careful not to touch him.

He didn't disappoint. Two thick hands spun her around and backed her to the wall. "You stupid whore. You have no idea what you're doing." Step four, check.

The expression on his face was perfect as she dug the end of her Smith and Wesson into his belly. "I'll shoot you in the gut and watch you bleed on the floor," she whispered in his face. No need for Eddy to hear that part. Baxter's response was textbook. He knew he lost it, and that he lost it to a woman. Men could be so damned predictable.

"Rex Baxter, you're under arrest for assaulting a police officer, obstruction of justice and lying to an official. You have the right to remain silent..." Keeping the gun pressed to his belly, she slipped around him, letting Eddy do the honors of cuffing him as she finished reading him his rights.

Duncan sat on the stool in his studio, contemplating the landscape his agent insisted he finish for his upcoming show. His most delicate brush was in his hand. The oil paints sat beside him. The lighting was perfect. Natural sunlight with a haze of cloud cover. His hands didn't budge.

He'd emailed the pictures to her. Put the hard copies in snail mail. But there was no sensation of closure.

He turned his eyes to the cello stand that stood empty. As empty as the hole in his heart. 'It's your neck,' his brother had said. What had he done? He'd hurt her is what he had done. Again.

The look on her face. He'd kept the picture from her. As well as the ones he brought to her.

Lynx took the former. Stole it from his home. He would deal with that when the time came.

But this was on Duncan's head, not Lynx's. The expression in her eyes was one of betrayal, but there was more. His sketch meant more to her. Did she know the man? He didn't want to think of the possibilities if that were true.

He dropped his brush and placed his hands on the sides of his head. The phone rang. Tipping his stool, he picked it up from where it sat on the wet bar. It was his aunt. He couldn't face anyone at that moment and set the phone down without answering.

Grabbing his jacket, he headed for the stairs. He stepped over the plastic and around the paint cans, and realized none of it seemed to matter anymore. Losing her was like losing an arm.

The boxes containing a state-of-the-art security system lay in the foyer. The company was due out next week to do the install. He hadn't bought the system for himself.

His feet led him to his car, his car to the airport. He would pay his pilot accordingly for the short notice. Waiting on the runway was a pitiful metaphor to what he was doing—running away.

The flight to L.A. was a business venture, he told himself. He had a string of potential clients he could check on. Convincing himself of the reason for the trip wasn't that difficult. He was panicking.

He had the worst flashback he'd had in months, and he had no one to blame but himself. Taking a deep breath, he gazed out over the runway. His plane was stored to the side behind a row of propeller planes in the small Northridge airport. The air was crisp and seared through his cheeks. The pain was welcome.

When his pilot arrived, he approached Duncan and glanced around the back of him. "No bags, sir?"

Duncan wasn't sure what to say. "I...it's a last-minute trip, as you know. I'll pick up some things when we touch down. Thank you for coming on such short notice." He made himself remember he wasn't the only one alone on a holiday weekend. "I'm surprised you weren't with the kids."

"I saw them yesterday," his pilot answered as they headed for the plane. "They're with their mom for the rest of the weekend. We have clearance to taxi in twenty. You'll wait on the plane, I assume?"

Duncan nodded as they reached his plane.

His pilot reached for the stair release. Duncan took his hand. "Wait."

"Sir?"

"This is wrong." This is what he did. Ran away. He'd done it for thirty-plus years. It was Nickie who made him want to settle in Northridge, but it was Northridge that made him want to stay. His aunt and uncle, his brother, his new nephew.

It was against everything his gut wanted him to do, but he told his pilot to go home.

The man gawked at the large bills in his hand. "I didn't do anything. I can't take this."

"Take it. Yes, you did. It's a holiday, and I'm going home."

Nickie had enough to keep Baxter for at least twenty-four hours. He could sleep on his transgressions in the comfortable cell he shared with a handful of meth addicts and petty thieves. It made her smile for the first time that day.

She sat straddling her cello with her laptop open in front of her. Her fingers did the dance of a spider over the strings on the wooden neck. She'd done everything she could think of; finished reporting on her day, checked her email, ignored the ones from Duncan, checked her voice mail, ignored the ones from Duncan, and now she sat, running her bow along the strings in a slow, sad rendering of Bach's "Sonatina."

The search engine stood empty on the screen.

Waiting. Taunting her. She wasn't in a hurry, she convinced herself. It had been fifteen years.

Closing her eyes, she moved her bow as she led her mind to places that would soothe. The time she took down Captain Tanner for his involvement in over thirty years of using barely teens to get his kicks. Except, Duncan had been there for that. And was the main reason she wasn't sitting at the bottom of Seneca Lake with bricks tied to her ankles.

She led her mind to the ecstatic relief on a college girl's face when Nickie had freed her from the soundproof bunker where the sex offender had trapped her. Except, Duncan was the one who'd found the bunker.

The cello wasn't working. And her cello always worked. It as the single thing she took appreciatively from her upbringing as a Maryland Monticello.

She set it aside and scooted her stool closer to her laptop. Setting her fingers on the keyboard, she made them type out the name 'Jun Zheng.'

CHAPTER 11

Her fingers trembled as she pressed enter. The screen listed 'About 1,280,000 results.' She took a deep breath and chose an image search. It came up with endless pages of photos of men and women, sports enthusiasts and chemical engineers.

Rubbing her hands over her face, she took her machine, curled in her lounge chair and set to work. She wouldn't forget his face. Fifteen years of aging wouldn't change it enough for her to forget.

Time passed as she studied each picture. Memories she'd carefully packed away became real…in color and stereo surround sound. He'd laughed at her. Again and again. He loved it when she fought. To him, it was like poking a caged animal through the bars and watching it react. And she reacted. Every damned time.

What a fool she'd been. She should have been smarter, kept her head down and did as she was told. But she wasn't like that. Not then, not now.

She pushed her laptop from her legs and let it slide to the floor. Enough. Turning her eyes to the clock, she noticed it was 2 a.m. She curled in a ball in the chair and laid her head on the armrest. The last she heard was the beep from her phone signaling another voice message.

As she'd requested, they had Baxter waiting for her in Interrogation One when she arrived at work. It was 7 a.m. Her hair was damp from her morning swim, and she was getting a caffeine headache.

She made sure Baxter saw her through the thin window on the door as she took the long way to Eddy's office. A slow stop at the soda machine, turn on the lights in her office, boot up her desktop, and head to Eddy's office.

He was sitting at his desk when she knocked.

"You never have to knock," he said as he stood.

Right. "Anything from IT?"

"Baxter's office computer was clean. That would have been too easy. Home computer, same. They had an external hard drive, but so far, it's all family stuff on there. They found a computer in a back office with encrypted shit. They're working on it."

"Family stuff?" She plopped down in one of his guest chairs, slouching as she folded her hands over her belt. "Baxter has kids?"

"Two. And a wife to go with 'em."

"I'm going to visit IT before I tackle Baxter. The wait will do him some good."

His brows dropped as he tilted his head. "Did you listen to the message I left you last night?"

Which one? She sat up, back straight. "What message?"

"We found the shooter. A Rob Ramsey. He's in interrogation two."

"What? Where?" She missed that? This was wrong. This mess with Duncan was affecting her job performance. "Where is he?"

"We found him at Baxter's house. No shit. Right there at Baxter's home. If you hadn't gotten Baxter to shove you around, we couldn't have booked him. Then, he would have been able to call and warn Ramsey while we confiscated the computers and files. I don't get the impression Ramsey was there for the wife. He's not talking, by the way. Lawyered up before we got his mug shot and prints."

"Okay. You wanna take Mister Tight Lip? I want Baxter. I've got a plan."

"I love it when that happens." He smiled at her. It sent a refreshing wave of rejuvenation through her.

With a Diet Coke in hand, Nickie strolled into Interrogation One and set a white envelope in the middle of the table. She had the officer on watch contain Baxter with cuffs attached to the table. Not that she was scared of him, because she wasn't. She just wanted him good and pissed.

Turning her chair backward, she slung a leg over the top and sat. "We found your friend Ramsey. You lied to me, Baxter the boxer. Not only do you know Ramsey, but he was cozying up with your wife." She smiled wide as she lied, thrumming her fingers on the table. With a pronounced shrug, she added, "No harm done there, except Ramsey's not so happy with you. Bad news is ballistics found that the bullets shot from the gun registered to you match the ones taken out of Chris Hendrix's shoulder." She shook her head and lifted a corner of her mouth.

Baxter smiled back.

"When we met up with Ramsey—at your house— we may have mentioned the possibility that you could roll on him." She made her voice as sweet as the Maryland Monticello she once was. "I suppose anything's possible," she crooned.

He didn't speak. His arrogance would be his downfall.

"He thinks you might do it," she continued as he sat in silence. "Because it seems as if he might have gotten himself a little collateral." She enunciated each syllable of the last word.

That got him to turn his eyes to her. Momentarily.

"He's looking at two counts of Man 1. You wanna be in on that? You're just the guy who works with him. He did the shooting. I'd rather be an accomplice than the shooter, that's all I'm saying." She pushed the envelope within arm's reach of the cuffs. "I always thought collateral was in the form of a flash drive or a secret safe deposit box filled with incriminating documents." Leaving the envelope for him, she added, "Some guys are dirty mean."

She brought out her best blonde voice. "We have him in interrogation two. I'm going to go check on him. He'll be interested in all the talking you're doing. Oops. Did I get that wrong? I hope I don't get that backward when I speak with him."

She figured he would know she was watching through the two-way mirror, but she didn't care. She went directly from Interrogation One to the room on the other side of the mirror.

Eddy walked in shortly after. "Ramsey's still not talking. Asshole."

Baxter turned his gaze to the mirror, then to the ceiling. Acting like he didn't care about the envelope, he put on that arrogant smile and pulled it open enough to see inside.

It was like watching a favorite movie. The muscles in his face fell. His eyes turned to the mirror like he could see through it. The glare was the first honestly intimidating one she'd gotten from him, and he couldn't even see her. With as much room as he could get with the cuffs secured, he turned the envelope upside down and shook the contents on the table. Scattered were a handful of photos of his two children. At home, at school, at the park. He wasn't too happy about it.

She gave him enough time to decide to roll on Ramsey, but not so much he might think up an alternative plan. After all, she had court at 10 a.m.

Walking in, she repeated her first entrance, turned her chair backward, slung her boot over and sat facing him. She moved the photos to the side and replaced them with a notebook and a pen. He didn't speak at first. Suited her. She had time to let him sit here while she went to court if needed. Using her knuckles, she pushed her jaw until it cracked.

"It was his idea. I told him not to. Hendrix has kids."

Yada, yada, yada. She kept quiet as he made this up.

"He took my gun. I didn't know."

He'll be glad to know you said that, she thought.

She pushed the notebook closer to him. "The DA might very well see it that way." When hell freezes over.

Patiently, she sat as he wrote. When he finished, she took her time reading it over before gathering up the photos and handing them to him. "Give these to your wife for me, will you? I found them on your home computer. I expect she'll appreciate 'em."

As she left the room, she heard the chains from the cuffs strain under a Baxter the boxer-sized tantrum.

Duncan couldn't bring himself to cancel his appointment with the governor's personal assistant. His feelings had ranged from defeat to denial to rage and now simple vengeance. The home was about an hour north of Manhattan Island. The two-hour drive for him was proving to be therapeutic.

New York was stunning country. Rolling mountains. Enormous trees that were strong enough to withstand nor'easters and coastal storms. Long fields and plenty of creeks, lakes and rivers. The scenery brought him to terms with what had happened and gave him enough painting inspiration to last months.

He hoped Nickie had opened his email or at least the envelope with the copies of the pictures he sent her. His curiosity burned as to why the sketch of the man of Asian descent caused the reaction it did. He was sure she would have been online doing her own search regarding the picture. Researching and keeping her meticulous notes on whatever she did or did not find. He refrained from hacking into any of it.

His life had been one long, incredibly tiring string of secrets. His eidetic memory. The events of his childhood. His time in the Middle East. They were decades he spent basically alone, but this was the first time he could remember feeling truly lonely.

He'd experienced love. He'd experienced Nickie Savage. There was no going back.

The bumping of his tires as he crossed the bridge to Thurmond Moody's home woke him to the present. Emotions ran from fury to expectation, so much so that he purposely turned it all off and focused on taking pictures in his mind of the grounds. He'd already searched satellite photos of the property— several acres in the middle of an upscale neighborhood in the medium-sized town of Alabaster.

He approached an expansive wrought iron fence. It opened as soon as he came within ten yards of it. Cautiously, he scanned the area before continuing on the drive.

An enormous berm lined the inside of the fence with an array of evergreen and deciduous trees topping the acres-long hill like jewels in a king's crown. He remembered from the satellite photos, the home, if that's what you could call it, stood to the north, and four warehouses, possibly for storage, were to the south. A building that appeared to be a home for the help stood farther down the south trail.

The grounds contained rolling hills and was heavily forested in trees planted in rows like soldiers. Security cameras littered the drive, affixed to trees, fence posts and lampposts. He took mental note of each as he went. They weren't the latest models but were an excellent brand. He'd used the same in his previous home.

Coming to a fork in the road, he took the south direction. He could claim ignorance later. The first warehouse came to view on his right. The other three soon after. Each was identical—corrugated metal in a creamy green color. Each had two doors big enough for a large truck to clear the opening. He could see from the road a single window on each of the sides that were covered in horizontal blinds with a single visible door near the corner.

He assumed they held the mowers, tractors and equipment needed to maintain property of this magnitude. But four of them? Maybe Moody stored his extra vehicles in one or more. He wanted to pull over to check the doors, but with the cameras watching him, he wasn't sure how he would talk himself out of it.

Playing as if he were still searching for the main house, he kept driving to the last structure he remembered from the satellite image. He was surprised the road didn't turn to gravel, but continued as smooth asphalt all the way to the end. Two dogs came bounding toward him before he reached the house where the road stopped.

The house was a white, two-story Victorian with a fully lit parking lot on the far side. He slowed his car to a stop. The dogs circled, barking with lines of drool dripping from the corners of their mouths. One was a Doberman, one a Rottweiler. Cliché.

The house was dark, the blinds open. He supposed the help would be working at this time of day. He'd expected something a bit more modest for the employees of a man who likely was involved and had been involved for decades in the kidnapping and forced prostitution of young girls.

Right on time.

Between the barking, he heard the tires of a vehicle rolling along the drive as he executed a slow three-point turn. A man about his age exited an SUV wearing black pants, a white shirt, black tie and vest. He tossed the dogs something flimsy and red. Duncan put his car in neutral, pulled the emergency brake and rolled down his window.

"Mr. Reed?" the man questioned.

Duncan held out his hand through the window. The dogs ran to the food. "Yes, that's correct. Forgive me if I don't get out." He gestured to the dogs. "I seem to have taken a wrong turn."

The man didn't introduce himself, and awkwardly accepted Duncan's offer to shake. He'd been trained to fit the status of *the help*. Remain as invisible as possible and don't make eye contact. Such bullshit. "If you would follow me, sir. I can lead you to the manor. Mr. Moody is expecting you."

The Manor? Duncan would have laughed if that was something he did. They returned to their cars. He tried to hide the fact that he already knew how to get there.

CHAPTER 12

———◆•◆•◆———

Nickie sat in the captain's guest chair, only half listening to him. Her back was straight and her ankles crossed under the chair. Her eyes were hazy from spending the last three days searching for something, anything about Jun Zheng.

Not a bite. How did a guy run this show for decades and not have a single piece of information on him anywhere? She'd taped the sketch of him right next to the copy of the bracelet on her monitor. Had he worn it? Is that where she recognized the thing? No, that wasn't it.

To have been so close. To have stood where he did only months before. She'd run Duncan's sketch through NCIC's facial recognition database, although she knew Duncan would have done that already. If he had any idea who Jun Zheng was, had found out anything about the sketch, Duncan would have brought it to her. Somehow, she knew that. Her eyes closed hard. This is why people shouldn't fall in love. It screws with everything.

"Do you want me to put Lynx on this one?"

She opened her eyes and recognized the concern in

Dave's. "No. No, I was just thinking."

"You haven't been yourself lately. You can talk to me."

I can't talk to anyone. "I'm on it, Captain. Give me the address." She held out her hand, waiting for him to pull off one of the many yellow sticky notes from his desk and give it to her.

As she said her good-byes to Dave, she thought of her foster mother. It wasn't that she didn't have anyone to talk to. She was wallowing. Sulking. And it pissed her off more than anything.

She headed to her office to gather her things. Eddy stepped out of his and into her path. She smiled up at his blue eyes.

"You look like hell." His eyes told her it was said in jest, cop to cop.

"Back at you, buddy." She put her hands on her hips. "Is there a reason you're not letting me through?"

"Food."

"Excuse me?"

"Food. It's nearly lunchtime, and I have a feeling you haven't had any."

"I never miss breakfast."

"Yogurt covered in birdseed doesn't count as food."

She held up her telltale sticky note and waved it at him. "I've got a call. Rain check?"

He brushed a strand of hair from her eyes, nodded and answered, "Rain check."

She gathered her coat and checked her gear, giving Zheng one more glance before she left. She would check out the assignment from her captain, stop by to see her foster mother if she had time, then see if she could find some minutes to search a little deeper for Zheng.

After flicking the sketch between the eyes, she

flipped her light switch and left.

Duncan sat in one of the heavy black chairs adorning Moody's four seasons room.

He thought he'd prepared for his reaction to sitting in the same room with him. After all, masking his emotions was Duncan's specialty. But he'd never sat face-to-face with a man involved in kidnappings before. Involved in the kidnappings of preteens. Involved somehow with Nickie. He hoped his face was blank, because it took everything in him not to sprint from his chair and take Moody down where he sat. Images of beating Moody's head against the hardwood floor helped to keep his cover intact.

The room was floor-to-ceiling glass on three sides. It was big, bigger than the entire third floor of Duncan's home. A white couch sat between a matching love seat and chairs, all with white cushions and throw pillows. The floor and end tables were sandalwood beige, white candles centered on each.

The glass looked out over a layered brick patio, which was home to a number of wrought iron tables and chairs. The dogs must not be allowed this far. Everything was covered with an inch of untouched white that made the room seem to melt into the outside. Beyond were pockets of landscaping plots containing dead ornamental grasses that whipped in the breeze. The force of the wind complemented Duncan's needs.

Next to him was his large portfolio case containing examples of his work.

"I have to say, Duncan, I was surprised when you called." Moody sipped his tomato juice. Duncan was sure he smelled vodka. "Reviewing your credentials, it doesn't seem you need to make phone calls."

Slowly, Duncan crossed his legs and tilted his head.

"I'm a New York native, Mr. Moody. I'd like to move my business closer to home. And I have a great admiration for your work." Bile threatened his esophagus.

An honest hint of surprise crossed Moody's face. It was followed by an air of suspicion. "Is that so?"

"Anyone who can cross political lines and remain bi-partisan enough to serve as the personal assistant to a number of governors in this state is someone worthy of admiration."

Obviously, Moody agreed. Sick bastard.

Duncan pulled his portfolio closer to him. Untying the top, he selected a photo and slid it from the case. "This is a piece that will adorn the landscaping portion of my next art show. It is a rendering of the estate of the mayor of Las Vegas." Not knowing what Moody would be interested in, he added, "The mayor in particular had requested images of his grandchildren acting naturally in and around his grounds. The grounds here on your property are spectacular. The multitude of towering evergreens creates quite a sense of power. With the dusting of snow, I see the power turning omnipotent."

What Duncan didn't see was the help. Other than the man who escorted him to the manor, he hadn't seen a single maid, butler or grounds crew.

He pulled out another example. This one was more of a formal pose, including two of Hollywood's latest and greatest as they stood in front of their flaming, wood-burning fireplace. The portraits in Moody's *manor* were contemporary abstracts. Duncan didn't draw abstracts. He didn't have high hopes for landing a contract with him, making this appointment all the more important.

"Let's retire to the den, Duncan. I've ordered some canapés." Moody stood and gestured to Duncan's glass. "Are you sure you wouldn't like something more...substantial?"

Duncan nodded once. "I'm driving, thank you."

Duncan liked big, generally the bigger the better. However, Moody's den was so exaggerated, it swallowed them up. He assumed that was what Moody was hoping for.

A photo of him and the governor sat on a desk made completely of ebony. The desk must be worth tens of thousands. In the photo, Moody wore the bracelet that matched the one found in the abandoned home in Henderson, Nevada.

His mind reacted as it often did, more so in the absence of a certain detective. Without warning. Without permission. The sand stuck to every inch of his body, whipping around in the air as the Chinook spun toward Earth. No.

"What do you think about a portrait of you with the governor?" he asked, sweat lining his back. "Or one of you in front of this manor you've created and embellished. I could draw the three governors you've assisted in hazy outlines behind you." Working Moody's vain side seemed to be taking him in the right direction as the pedophile lifted his brows and nodded.

The same man who'd escorted Duncan to the manor served the food. Moody spent time between drinks casually drilling him for information about his past, his present and his clients. He was fishing, but Duncan had played with fish before. And playing with tipsy fish could be simple.

"I can draw up some preliminary samples. Shall we take a drive so I can get a lay of the land?"

"Fine, fine. I'll call—"

"I'd be pleased to do the honors, Mr. Moody."

Duncan drove them in his Audi R-8 to the enormous

circle drive in front of the house. He had Moody in his car. How easy it would be to choose a spot between surveillance cameras, backhand him in the face, beat him unconscious, and dump him in Seneca Lake.

Moody brought his drink, refreshed by the single escort/chef/butler/maid. In the confined quarters of the vehicle, the alcohol was rank.

"This is an excellent angle," Duncan said as he took a few photographs with his phone. As if he needed pictures.

Shifting, he veered down the drive. "I imagine it's just as lovely in the spring, but the dusting of snow sets off the house and powerful trees as they tower in the crisp sun. Do you have many visitors?" It was the first non-business topic Duncan had dared.

It was hard to disguise reactions when you'd had a few Bloody Marys. Moody wasn't pleased with the semi-personal question and snapped to attention. The overreaction didn't go unnoticed. Duncan changed the subject.

"I leave for L.A. in a few days. Then, the holidays will be here. I'm free the following week."

"The holidays." Moody rested his head on the headrest. "There was a time when I participated in the events at Times Square." He lifted his brow as if it were an annoyance. "I avoid crowds whenever possible these days. Follow the road to the west." He ordered Duncan with his finger.

Pretending to misunderstand, Duncan took a road he hadn't noticed in the satellite images.

"Not this way," Moody slurred.

Duncan slowed, but Moody shook his finger. "Never mind. It won't matter."

Avoided crowds? Like the Indy 500, the X Games and the World Series? The pictures Duncan found of him weren't old.

The missing road turned out to be a back way to the white house. Duncan pulled in front of it. "This is where the help found me. I'm embarrassed to say it's so beautiful I'd thought for a moment it was your home."

"Phssst," Moody growled. "I didn't tell you to stop here."

Duncan didn't ask about the house but didn't make the same mistake when they came to the row of cloudy, green warehouses. "Do you keep your cars here?"

"Cars? No. This is for equipment and quarters for the help."

He had his help stay in metal warehouses? Why was Duncan surprised? "Surely you have a favorite. Mine is a '72 Barracuda. I only take her out in warm weather."

"I'm not into the classics. Mine is a Jaguar c-x75."

"Ah yes," Duncan crooned. "Zero to sixty in under three seconds. To one hundred in six."

"That's the ticket," Moody snapped. "You've sold me. I see me in a tuxedo, standing in front of my Jaguar with The Manor behind me." He used the term *The Manor* like the place could be found in Wikipedia. "Here's my personal number." He scribbled it on the back of a business card.

Pulling up the short drive, Nickie felt better already. The small, square house was the closest thing to a home she'd known. Why hadn't she thought of coming here before now? The drive had been shoveled from edge to edge. It made her roll her eyes before she smiled and wondered who Gloria had do the chore of clearing a drive in upstate New York of a *dusting* of snow.

As usual, the front door was open. The storm door

was covered in steam, or maybe it was frost. She couldn't tell as she rounded her car.

She came from an interview with a college student who had been raped at a school party. It made her feel sorry for herself, something she also didn't allow. The last several days had messed with her head. For a short second, she thought her captain might have been right and should have given the case to Eddy. This was all Duncan's fault. Or at least her fault for letting herself have these feelings for him. For anyone.

Gloria would clear things up for her. Gloria always cleared things up for her. She would help her focus, and then Nickie could get back to work. She didn't mind being alone, but life after Duncan seemed…off.

"Hello!" she called as she walked in the front door.

"Child." Nickie heard Gloria call from the kitchen. "Come back and see me."

She followed Gloria's directions and found her standing at the sink, draining whole grain rice. Covering the dish with a large towel, she set it aside and dried her hands. The house was empty, a rarity. It made the kitchen seem bigger somehow.

"I love surprise visits from my Nickie." Gloria gave her a bear hug and told her to sit. Nickie obeyed as Gloria took two mismatched mugs that hung from hooks beneath a cabinet. She poured herself a cup of coffee before taking a can of Diet Coke from her fridge.

Nickie nearly salivated at the sound of the tab releasing pent up carbonation. It was like a symbol of the entire scene.

"What brings you home?"

Home. It sent a blanket of calm over her. The thick, ancient plastic counters, the mismatched chairs around the small table in the middle of the kitchen. The larger table on the other side of the sink, and the enormous one in the dining room next to them.

"I was in the neighborhood." She smiled wide and poured her soda in her coffee mug.

Gloria did little more than lift her brows, holding the steaming mug with both hands, her long, glossy hair falling over her shoulders.

"I was in the neighborhood, and I decided to break things off with Duncan."

Expertly, the expression on Gloria's face was unreadable.

"He lied to me."

Still no expression.

"Well, he didn't exactly lie to me, but he withheld things from me. Some*thing*. Things that had to do with me personally. He does that—keeps things from people. Or he just doesn't talk about shi—stuff," she corrected.

"I wonder why that is?" Gloria asked.

Gloria didn't know about Duncan's eidetic memory, but she did know about the events of his childhood. "He doesn't want to remember any more than he has to," Nickie continued. Why was she defending him? "He had a gun dug in his temple at the age of eight. Watched his aunt blindsided with a baseball bat. So, he doesn't talk about it. Hides it from everyone, really. He had just kept something from me. A big something. I told him not to do that ever again. So, it's the same as lying, don't you think?"

Gloria smiled at her and brought the mug to her lips.

Nickie stood and walked to the freezer, taking a handful of ice cubes from the tray. "He digs into my business, my personal business, and doesn't tell me. It's the same thing as lying," she convinced herself as she plopped the ice cubes into the mug one at a time for emphasis.

Sitting back down, she crossed her arms, not caring

that it was childish. "He says I don't like hunches, and he didn't want to bring something to me that was a hunch." She ran her forefinger in circles near her ear. "Men. Who could have known how much drama and confusion a relationship could bring. I feel better already."

Gloria patted the top of her hand like Nickie had lost a beloved pet.

"He keeps calling," she added. "Leaving messages, emailing me. He even mailed me a large envelope. I've ignored them all. Cold turkey. It's better this way." As much as she tried to avoid it, a chill formed at the base of her heart. "It's better this way," she repeated. She suddenly felt tired. It wasn't the lack of sleep over the past several days. It wasn't the interview with the college girl. "I can't be with a man I can't count on, one I can't trust." A small tear threatened to fall over her lid. She blinked it away.

Gloria was pretty. Even at her age, her skin was still the smooth color of caramel candy. She had the biggest, rounded, deep brown eyes Nickie had ever seen.

"If you don't mind, I think I'm going to rest in the guest room for a while," she said, and rinsed her mug in the sink.

CHAPTER 13

Other than the small Northridge museum, The Pub was the oldest building in Northridge. The wood floors were splintered. The tables for four were too small for two. And Nickie loved it. People of all ages came for clean, honest music and spirits. They had their share of fights, some prostitution and the occasional drug sale. But for the most part it was a place to sit back and get away.

The stage was small and in the shape of a triangle. She was surprised Gilberto could fit his drum set back there and still have room to play. In front of him sat his wife on a short, swiveling stool. Teresa had a clear soprano voice with a hook so saucy, they were asked back time and time again. Since this wasn't Ireland, people didn't bring their kids to a bar. Gil's brother had the twins—both sets of them—for the evening.

At one of the tables, Gloria sat on one side of Nickie, her grandmama on the other. As usual, Gloria's biological children trickled into the bar every half hour or so. It was what Nickie needed, a comfortable evening with the people who took her in without blinking an eye. Not that anyone would dare to blink anything at Gloria. Nickie caught the few times Teresa glanced over her shoulder, winking at her Gil.

So, why was the gaping hole in her heart still here?

"The art show is tomorrow." Gloria hadn't asked her an actual question, but Nickie knew better than not to answer.

"I'm not going, of course," she responded respectfully.

"He is counting on you."

"No, he isn't." That didn't come out at all respectfully. "What I mean is that of course he isn't expecting me. We haven't spoken in over a week. It's over." The impact of hearing those two little words aloud was worse than any street fight she'd been in. In the midst of loud music and the smoky haze that wafted in from the front door, her eyes instantly burned. Tears threatened, but she was strong. She would survive this like she survived everything else in her life. It was simply a new kind of pain.

"He is counting on you," Gloria repeated.

Nickie expanded her lungs completely before emptying them. He didn't need her. But arguing with Gloria was moot. He said six of the twenty or so portraits were of her. She hadn't remembered him painting more than a few, but with his memory, he really didn't need her to pose.

She was to be the guest of honor, so to speak. What if the art show was the subject of his voice mails? Or his emails? Or the envelope he sent her through the mail?

This was crazy. It had to stop.

"No." It was more of a declaration than it was an answer. "No, this has to stop," she repeated from her thoughts. "I've had secrets kept from me most of my life. I can't be with a man who keeps things from me.

Things that pertain to me."

Gloria placed her soft hand over hers, then leaned close to her ear. "You are not the only one with history, my child. Against your will, you've had secrets kept from you. Against Duncan's will, he's lived his life forced to keep secrets. It's all he knows."

Nickie sat behind the wheel of her 'piece of shit oversized town car' as Duncan called it. Damn if that didn't make her smile. Her police issue Smith and Wesson was locked in her glove box. The piece she bought to use as a spare rested under her seat. Her badge, cuffs and cell sat next to her as she drove the 90 to Rochester.

What the hell was she doing?

In her dented, tainted, rusted, unmarked, she wore the flowing ivory dress Duncan had bought her months ago when they cased the ten grand buy-in poker game in Vegas. Purposely, he chose one with a high back to cover her scars. Sitting alone in her car, the thought of the personal gesture meant more to her than it had that evening in the casino. The shoes were ridiculously tall and ridiculously spiked. Nickie had ankles of steel, but this was, well, ridiculous.

She'd gone home alone from The Pub the night before. Nothing new there. She hadn't had the strength to hear his voice on his voice mails. But she did bring herself to open the envelope he sent her. The one that sat on the tiny table in her tiny foyer for days, burning like a beacon each time she had passed it.

In it were photos of the personal assistant to the governor. One of the photos was a zoomed shot of a bracelet he wore. *The* bracelet. Duncan didn't need to send that one. She would have spotted the bracelet in the full-body shot he'd included.

The bracelet.

She wasn't sure if it was seeing it on his person or if it was the photo of him standing at the back of the press conference announcing her teenage coming home. But it was the bracelet. The bracelet of one of the men who had been involved in the kidnapping of countless young girls.

Her heartbeat rose in direct correlation with the closing distance to the museum. Letting the GPS on her phone tell her where to go, she worked on coherent thought. "What the hell am I doing?" she said aloud this time.

She wasn't about to have any part of valet parking. She knew how to walk. Instead, she parked her car in the lot, facing away from the museum. She sat with both hands on the wheel, ten o'clock and two o'clock. She could go home. No one would know. She could count it as a nice drive through scenic upstate New York.

Wimp. She checked her lipstick and decided against a purse. No gun. No badge. She didn't know exactly what she wanted, but she did owe him this. Standing, she stretched the hours of road from her back and shoulders, then remembered she was in an evening gown. Straightening, she brought back her Maryland Monticello family training and turned for the entrance.

She didn't have a coat to go with the dress. Hadn't needed one in Vegas. Since there was nothing in her closet that would come close to matching an ivory, sequined, tea-length dress, she wore her brown leather jacket that hung below her hips.

As she climbed each of the dozen steps, she forced her mind into survival mode. It was her specialty. Step, step. She wasn't Nicole Monticello anymore. Step. She was Nickie Savage. Step, step. Survivor. Cop.

Thick pillars flanked the entrance and corners of the enormous concrete porch. A host waited at the door like this was a funeral home, opening the massive piece of wood as soon as she neared.

The doorman was dressed in a three-piece tailored suit. He held out his hand and offered, "May I check your coat and bag, miss?" At least he didn't call her, 'ma'am.'

"I didn't carry a bag today, thank you." She slid out of her coat and handed it to him, impressed with the way he didn't blink an eye at the leather. He tried to hand her a ticket. "Oh, I don't have a purse." She turned her eyes down to her dress. "Or pockets, of course."

He bowed his head. "I won't forget you, miss."

She glanced in one of the many planes of mirrors along the entrance walls. Makeup was never a problem. And her hair had stuck. She chose an updo similar to the one she wore for the Vegas undercover stint. A meticulous French twist with a few strategic dripping curls.

She followed the voices to an area off to the right and stopped when she turned the corner. In front of her was a life-sized portrait of herself. In the ivory dress.

As if she wasn't going to stand out as it was. Her feet begged her to turn around and head for the highway.

Survival.

Pulling her shoulders back, she strode into the room. How could she be this nervous to see him? She wasn't a child. She hadn't been a child even when she was a child. Expertly, she flipped on her Monticello charm and strolled in.

The portraits were amazing, of course. Duncan painted like a photograph. That's what everyone said.

She found one from the set he made for the Vegas mayor. It made her smile. Three of the mayor's grandchildren tumbled in endless green with the massive estate behind them. Clumps of organized color dotted the landscape in the form of roses and other flowers she couldn't name.

"You're the one in the portraits." The voice was familiar, and it brought Nickie from the memories of the weeks Duncan had worked on the mayor's paintings.

She turned to find a goddess. A woman that could be Aphrodite. Tall, thin, sun-kissed blonde hair with the most beautiful eyes Nickie had ever seen.

Bebe Lyons. This was the woman Duncan had gone to visit weeks before when they were in Nevada.

Bebe must have assumed Nickie knew who she was because she offered no introductions. "You have *got* to be the reason Duncan won't paint me," she said as she placed an arm around Nickie's shoulder.

Nickie had no idea what Bebe was talking about and politely turned to face her. Smiling quaintly, she responded, "I'm afraid I don't understand, Mrs. Lyons."

Bebe pulled her along like longtime friends browsing a clothing store. "You're that girl."

It wasn't the first time someone had said that to her, although it was usually said as an insult.

"You're the girl in the paintings."

They turned a corner, and it was as if the walls were covered in mirrors. She knew the paintings would be here. But she didn't remember they were this big. It was unnerving.

"I'm sorry Duncan turned down your request. I'm sure he was just busy." Nickie used her most enunciated speech.

"Oh no. It's quite all right. Johnny and I made

terrible fools of ourselves. I'm embarrassed just thinking about it." Bebe pulled her along a little farther until they stood in front of a painting of Coral Francesca, Best Supporting Actress Oscar winner. Ah, yes. Nickie remembered this one. Coral stood naked surrounded by angry colors and sharp lines. She wore nothing but a snake, strategically covering areas of her model-perfect body.

Bebe shook her head. "This is what I asked him for."

So? "Maybe he'll have time in the coming months." Nickie honestly didn't know how to handle this woman or how to read her.

"You don't know, do you? He *won't* do it." Bebe slid her arm in the crook of Nickie's. "I took it personally at first. How self-centered of me. I'm not used to being told no. You can imagine."

Yes, she could. The woman was Bebe Lyons. Super star who married super star. She was one of those people who went by a single name only. Bebe. It was easy for her to take Johnny Lyons's last name, as she'd never used her own.

"Johnny and I got to wondering why. We did some digging and found…you."

It would be repetitive to say she didn't understand. So instead, Nickie smiled.

"Coming here confirmed our suspicions. You see, he told us he wasn't painting nudes anymore. Now I see why. You're completely lovely, Nickie Savage." Bebe kissed her on the cheek, leaving her more than a little stunned.

Not painting nudes anymore? Was that true? She watched as the woman walked and found her star-studded husband.

Duncan knew she wasn't the jealous type. It was his business. Now that she thought of it, she hadn't

noticed a nude on his easel in the months they were
dating. Dated.

She was here.

His reaction to the sight of her was more than
Duncan could have prepared for.

Wearing the gown he bought her months before in
Vegas. Gliding across the marble floor as if she were
made for this. He wasn't sure what Bebe Lyons had to
say to her, but the way the two of them carried on, he
would have thought they were friends.

It seemed like months since he'd seen her, and she
was more beautiful in the flesh than even his eidetic
memory recalled. The way she moved was
disconcerting. The graceful slide of her feet, the
poised movements of her shoulders, her neck tall, her
hands slightly bent. It wasn't real, of course, and he
reveled in the fact that he was the only one in the
room who knew it.

She was here. How would he ever live without her?

Browsing his work as if she were window-shopping,
she stopped and responded to everyone who
recognized her from his portraits. He leaned against a
supporting pillar, covered in white wainscoting. She
spoke to Louie Star, quarterback for the enemy. He
kept his hands off. Smart man. Smoothly, she placed
her fingertips on his forearm as she turned to browse
further.

She stopped when she spotted him. Her expression
softened. Her shoulders relaxed.

And his heart fell out of his chest and landed at her
feet.

They didn't speak or move. The world went on
around them. The tiniest of smiles beckoned the
corners of her mouth. No one would notice. But he
noticed. He knew every inch of Nickie Savage and

didn't have the first idea how to make this right.

Straightening like she might roll right over him, she strode his way, her poise painfully matching that of the dress she wore. As soon as she got within whispering distance, she kept her poise but spoke in the voice of his detective. "You're not doing nudes anymore? What do you take me for? I work side by side with my ex. I trust you. You trust me. Where did this shit come from?"

"There you are," he said as he realized she spoke to him in present tense. It nearly made his knees give. "I don't want to do nudes anymore."

His comment seemed to take her aback. He took the moment to move a step closer to her. Close enough he could smell the slight breath of lavender that seemed to forever flow around her. Smart. Sophisticated. "I'm so sorry." A burn crept into the backs of his eyes. He knew it would be evident to anyone who paid attention. He didn't care. She would know he wasn't referring to his change in painting guidelines.

"I know," she said softly.

He took the sides of her face and brought her to him. Her lips were warm and forgiving. Her beautiful arms twined around his sides, burning a trail all the way to where they landed on his back. He didn't know what happened to change her mind. It didn't matter.

She was here. And she was his.

Her cheek was warm beneath his thumb, the lower of her back soft. Their lips moved together in a conversation meant only for them. Slowly, they heard it. It wasn't the hoots or jeers they may get from friends who might suggest they get a room. It was a refined clapping that soon turned into the kind of applause one hears at a golf tournament.

He pulled away and smiled, moving his focus from one of her gorgeous gray eyes to the other and back again. She blinked rapidly before taking his hand and dipping her head in polite embarrassment. Glancing forward, he spotted Johnny and Bebe Lyons blowing them a kiss as they wrapped their arms around one another.

The clapping dissipated, and the circle of friends and strangers went back to browsing, or eating or drinking his complimentary glasses of celebratory champagne.

All but one pair of guests. A couple who appeared to be in their late fifties or early sixties stood statue still with what Duncan judged as an aura of arrogant condescension. The woman was nearly as big around as she was tall. The man only slightly trimmer. Duncan could spot the best of clothes, and these two didn't hold back. They seemed familiar in a way. His instincts told him he didn't want to know how.

He nearly stepped forward to introduce himself if not for the way Nickie stiffened as she turned. Jerking his head to her, then back to the couple, he knew why they seemed familiar. They looked like Nickie.

CHAPTER 14

———— ◆ ◆ ◆ ————

"Nicole," the man and woman called, walking to Nickie as their eyes traveled down their noses from the top of her head to the bottoms of her feet.

He could sense the contrast between the unrefined detective who wanted to show her teeth and the woman dressed as hostess for an elegant art show. He preferred the former.

"Hello, Edward. Ivanna. What brings you this far north of the border?"

It seemed to be a stab meant for only the three of them.

Their smile was slight and as phony as Coral Francesca posing with the snake.

Edward answered. "We came to see if the rumors were true, darling."

"Rumors?" He could hear the vile in Nickie's voice.

Edward leaned his head from one side to the other, overtly judging Nickie's dress, her hair. "The rumors that our Nicole has finally embraced the upbringing she was provided."

Her lungs expanded beneath Duncan's hand as it rested on her back. After a painstaking silent standoff, she responded confidently, "I'm not playing this game with you, Edward."

Edward smiled. It was evil. It was cruel. And it washed Duncan in sadness.

"At the very least you could introduce us to the infamous Duncan Reed." Edward held out his hand.

Infamous? Duncan waited before accepting, working to take Nickie's lead with this.

"Duncan Reed, Mr. and Mrs. Edward Monticello. Edward and Ivanna, this is Duncan Reed."

Duncan shook once with each of them before sliding his hand into the pocket of his pants.

"See, dear?" Edward turned to his wife, who may have been a mute for all Duncan could tell. "She's dating a man who holds company with our kind of people. Exquisite upbringing."

Our kind of people? Did they honestly mean those in the crowd who were wealthy or famous?

The muscles in Nickie's jaws flexed and released.

Duncan stepped slightly between the trio. "It's nice to meet you, but my agent would like to see us now. Good day."

Her fingers dug into his palm as he took her hand and led her around a square beam the width of a dining table. "We can go," he said as they walked, only loud enough for her to hear.

"Fuck that. They aren't running me out of here."

He understood her need to pull a street-smart Nickie Savage retort. It made him proud. The contrast in her language to the way she glided across the floor, even more so.

"Twenty minutes tops, then," he bargained. "I think you've spoken to everyone in the museum already."

She turned to him, and he watched as her face relaxed one muscle at a time. "You were watching me."

Bringing his lips to her ear, he whispered, "I always watch you."

He kept an eye on the clock. He would give her twenty minutes to save face before he would take her out of here. He'd never seen her so unraveled. Like a pro, she smiled and thanked guests for coming. Several of the pieces that were for sale dangled sold signs drawn in gold letters in the bottom corners. The prices were ridiculous. His agent must be dancing all the way to the bank. Duncan had given away a number of business cards with promises of calls for appointments.

Graciously, Nickie accepted the compliments from his guests. Quite differently than she had from her parents. Her parents. Were they truly here to see if she cleaned up well? He suspected there was more to it.

Exhausted, Nickie dragged herself down the steps of the museum. Her arms and legs were heavy. It seemed like two in the morning, yet the sun was only beginning to set.

Duncan carried much of her weight. If she didn't have her pride, she would crawl into his arms and let him carry her to the car. She dreaded the thought of the drive home without him.

When they turned to the parking lot, she kept walking but he didn't.

"You drove *that*?" He gestured with his chin toward her unmarked. "In *that*?" His glance moved to her dress.

How could he make her smile at a time like this? She'd spent the last week on the biggest emotional roller coaster she'd experienced in her life. More so than the wretched home she grew up in, more so than the time she spent in captivity.

"What else would I drive?"

He exaggerated a headshake, then caught up with her. Pulling the belt of her leather jacket tighter around her waist, he held out his hand. It's what he did when he insisted on driving.

"What about your car?"

"My agent is having one of his people drive it to Northridge for me."

"You're letting a stranger drive your car?"

He shrugged and caught her before she leaned her backside on the metal.

"Don't touch the car with that dress." He pulled her into his warm body. She turned her head and let it fall on his shoulder, both literally and metaphorically. As she did so, he dug in her pocket for her keys. She didn't argue.

There was so much to say, much to talk about. He didn't ask a single question. Instead, he let her lay her head on his lap and sleep as he drove her piece of shit, oversized town car home.

The drive gave Duncan the necessary time to process the events of his evening. His Nickie slept on his lap. Her beautiful face contorted in grimaces as she dreamed. He knew better than to wake her when she was like this. They could crash.

What made her change her mind and come to him? Pity? Duty? Was it that he would...No, that he could never paint another naked woman because of how he felt about her? Was that why she let him take her in his arms, why she was sleeping on his lap at that moment?

Or was it the pictures of Thurmond Moody? Had she seen them?

And her parents. He didn't know where to begin. All he could piece together was the disdain she carried for them and the lack of parental nurture they held for her.

She must have sensed the climb up his drive because she sat up, startled, and sucked air.

He held up his free hand in a sign of surrender.

"Oh." She sighed and slouched in the dress that likely cost more than her car. "I feel like I haven't slept in days. We're in Northridge? This is your house."

"Yes."

"Where are the trailers? The equipment?"

"They're done."

"They're done?"

"Mostly. A few touch-ups. Don't be too impressed. Other than the third floor, the home is empty."

He parked in the garage and turned to see her deep in thought, brows tightly together. It was the most defeated expression he could remember on her beautiful face. He walked around the car and opened her door. Extending a hand, he said, "Come. It's getting late."

Willingly, she held out her hand and leaned on him as they climbed his steps.

When they entered, he picked her up beneath her knees and back, and carried her the two flights of stairs to the top floor. Ignoring the burn in his legs, he kissed her forehead as if she were breakable before she tucked her head into his shoulder.

He kicked open the door to the third floor, and instead of letting him lay her on the bed, she slid down and wrapped her arms around him. Painfully, he pulled her away. "We should talk."

She shook her head. "I don't want to talk."

Normally, a comment like that would send them tumbling to the floor. But not tonight. "We need to talk."

"You're right. I know." Instead of complying, she set her fingers on his lips. Her gaze was sincere and pleading and held for the longest of moments. One at a time, she stepped out of her shoes, then tugged the shirt from his pants.

This would be different. He was determined. He was different. They were different.

He took her forearms and brought the palms of her hands to his mouth. Closing his eyes, he took in her scent before trailing a line with his lips down the tender skin on the inside of her wrist. Replacing his lips with his fingertips, he slid them lightly along her forearms, inside the crook of her elbow and up the sensitive skin of her inner arms. As he crossed her shoulders, her eyes drifted closed.

"Look at me." He hoped it sounded like a request. He needed to see her, to see inside her.

His thumbs made a line over her jaw and around to behind her neck. There he found the top of her zipper, and as painfully slow as he could, let it sink. The zipper didn't catch until well beneath her lower back. The skin exposed was smooth and firm. It melted into his hands as if it were made for him.

She unbuttoned his shirt and teased the flesh beneath his tattoo with her fingertips. He kissed her once, carefully, gently, before dipping his lips across her cheeks. Lazily, he trailed a line under her jaw and down her neck. Tugging on a strap of her dress, he slid it off her shoulder, letting his lips follow the exposed skin one painful inch at a time.

The air cooled the sheen of sweat that had formed on his chest as she pulled his shirt from his shoulders and let it fall where they stood. Like a dance, they released each piece of clothing, exposing themselves to one another as their garments dropped to the floor in a circle around them.

They didn't plunge to the carpet in a frenzied need, and he didn't lift her into his arms. Instead, they walked together, hand in hand, to the enormous bed he bought with no one in mind except his Nickie.

Pulling the covers away, he placed his hand behind her head and led her to a pillow. Her head turned and she crooned, moving in response to his hands. She lifted her knees, and he tucked himself between them. Her eyes were the color of steel, strong and solid. They turned to him with tenderness.

Nickie welcomed his gentle affection. Her insides melted with liquid need. Her eyes willed to roll to the back of her head, but his were unwavering, staring at her, in her. She was exposed in a way that created a net of safety and a melody of want.

Their hands explored as if it were their first time, releasing the last pieces of clothing serving as a barrier between them. His glorious lips danced over her skin in the moonlight that shone through the skylight windows. A small tug with his teeth, then a pull with his lips and she purred in a warmth that shivered through every inch of her.

Her fingers clasped his sides, muscles flexing beneath her touch. His hand traveled, explored and stopped dead center. She fought nature as he moved in circles. A little quiver. It was too soon. He paused.

She gasped and lifted her head. "Don't stop." Her brows dug deeply together.

"Come to me."

She arched and lifted, her legs quaking like a volcanic eruption. Not the kind that explodes, but the kind that pours over the sides of the mountain, long and hot. Rocking into him, his words echoed in her mind and through her body until he brought her down, slow and easy. Her cries were a mixture of the old and the new. Her body wanting both, all. Until she realized all the want was him. She led him to her.

"Not so fa—"

She couldn't stop herself. She led him to her until there was nothing more between them. She heard the choke, the gasp followed by his moan. They were joined, united. Together they moved as one, slow and purposeful. It was the calm before the storm. Still, she wanted both.

Slowly, they arched to each other, gaining rhythm, gaining momentum. His hands grasped chunks of the sheets on either side of her head, his arms trembled.

"I love you." It came out of her as a breath, but it seemed to take his control. They quickened, then quickened some more, working to get the last bit closer, the last moment of need to release. Safety nets were gone. They flew over without restraints. Natural, instinctual. Like the sounds erupting from their lungs. She was nearly spent but couldn't stop, neither of them could. They grasped and moved, clinging and arching until their muscles gave out completely.

Her arms and legs might not be able to move for hours. For the first time in ten days, she smiled, truly smiled. He lay across her like a protective blanket, unwavering and unmoving. Irony.

"I love you too." The words were a whisper, and she kissed his shoulder in response.

Nickie slept like the dead for the first half of the night. Duncan had never remembered her so still. As he feared, it didn't last. The small twitches, the minute whimpers had brought him fully awake long before the sun.

He showered quickly, then watched her carefully as he booted his computers. She lay on her stomach, her long, honey-wheat hair resting over her shoulders and back. With the blankets tucked around her waist, her scars peeked through the blonde waves. He'd seen them dozens of times, but for some reason, this time sent a new vengeance through him with which to find the ones responsible for putting them there.

Wet hair and unshaven, he'd barely pulled on a fresh shirt before it hit.

The tears she would never shed when conscious turned to growls as he walked over and sat beside her.

"Nickie." He was ready for it, but she was lightning quick. His ability to block the twisting left uppercut was mocked by the returning right hook that landed soundly on his left temple.

CHAPTER 15

"Duncan."

He held up his arm, partly as a sign of surrender, partly as a signal he was okay, and partly as protection in case Nickie wasn't fully awake. It was the first time in months she'd woken swinging, and his heart hurt worse than his left temple.

Her face dropped into her hands. "Why do you insist I stay the night?"

Head throbbing, he took her hands and pulled them from her face. "Because I'm in love with you." He let his glance drop. The blanket curled around her hips, her hair not much of a cover. "And for other reasons."

Whipping the blanket to the side, she stormed to the mini-fridge. "How can you joke at a time like this?" She opened the tiny inside door and took out the ice tray.

He leaned back against the headboard and watched as she walked to his fridge, unashamed, making an icepack for his head. It damn well made the slug worth it.

"Here." She held out the ice. "Let me grab a shower."

Accepting the ice, he placed it on the sizable bump forming on his head.

Well aware the phrase, 'grab a shower,' meant at least forty-five minutes, Duncan finished dressing and set to work in his studio.

Nickie had been seeing Duncan for eight months. Or was it nine? Ten? She might not be sure when they officially started seeing each other, but she never remembered him using a hair dryer. And yet there it hung, next to the pink toothbrush that had shown up around month two. Or was that month four?

She hadn't planned on staying the night. His art show. Their reunion. They were perfect and full of love. Only to be predictably ruined by her past, by her issues. She shouldn't have stayed the night. That was apparent from the red circles around each of the knuckles on her right hand. And the thought of Duncan's head. She didn't want to think about it. She simply wasn't made for this kind of relationship.

But he was in love with her, she thought, as she began the slow process of drying her hair. He moved his downtown office here to be with her. It was surreal. How did *The Taste of L.A.* end up involved with a cop who carried her kind of past?

And yet she didn't want to think about the idea of running into her parents without him. She hadn't seen them since she was sixteen. They looked old. He was there for her. Exactly how she needed him. They worked like a team, each knowing when to speak, when not to. He let her stay at his show long enough to keep her pride, yet took her away when she couldn't hold it together any longer.

On the other hand, she would never have seen her parents if not for Duncan. He was the reason they showed up. It was like they were telling her the reason she landed someone of his stature was because of their upbringing. Turning the hair dryer off, she dropped her forehead to the granite counter.

The house key to his place was more of a trick. Make her fall in love with him, then at her weakest most swoon-worthy moment, stick the key in her hand.

She lifted her head to eyes of steel that stared at her in the mirror. She knew she acted unreasonably, possibly childishly, but that was the whole reason she didn't get involved with men and certainly didn't allow herself to fall in love.

She had no makeup, no change of clothes, not even a clean pair of underwear. It was Sunday. If she didn't get a call from her captain it might be okay. Except, she would have to wear that dress back to her place. It made her almost start laughing. Almost, except she knew she had to tell Duncan about Jun Zheng and what it would do to him.

She finished drying her hair and made sure to hang the dryer back on the brass hook he so intentionally placed next to the outlets. Her stomach growled as she readjusted the oversized white bath towel that wrapped around her. First stop, fridge.

The image of him made her feet falter. He sat in his absurdly uncomfortable swivel stool with a thick, black drawing-something in his hand. His hair was tied in a low tail, his eyes thoughtful. He was beautiful.

His head didn't move, but his eyes did. They met hers in a sort of a conversation, much like their lips had the evening before.

"I should have chosen smaller bath towels," he said.

Her lips curled and she decided to skip the fridge. She sauntered to him, sat in his lap and let her lips slide across his. "Good morning," she mumbled.

Breaking from him, she craned her neck. "You're um…awake." She let her eyes drop south.

"I have a beautiful woman in a towel sitting on my lap."

"What are you drawing?" She turned, inadvertently swiveling his stool. Except there weren't paintings of famous people or the landscapes he often preferred. It was a list. A list written horizontally in dark pencil across the top of a huge sketchpad.

It contained the names James Spalding, alias Slippery Jimbo; former Northridge Police Department's Captain William Tanner; his accomplice, incarcerated ex-Fire Chief Brian McKinney; the personal assistant to the governor of New York, Thurmond Moody; and the words, 'Asian Man.'

Her head turned back to him. "We need to talk." They were his words from the night before.

He nodded.

"I think I need to borrow a pair of your work out pants and a T-shirt."

"You can, of course, but you have a drawer."

"I have a what?" It took everything in her to keep her composure. She wasn't suited for a drawer, and she hadn't agreed on a drawer. "What's in it?"

He shrugged and stood, causing her to stand or fall. "The stray pieces of clothing you leave when you stay."

So much for the effort of hanging the hair dryer. It was true. She was a slob. He was the opposite. One more example of how different they were and one more reason to proceed with caution. The taste she'd gotten of what it was like to lose him while they were still casual was hard enough. She didn't want to think about losing him because of a drawer. "What? Where? Which one?"

He moved toward his coffeemaker. "Left side of the bed, top drawer."

"The top drawer?"

He kept walking away from her, but responded flatly, "It's a drawer."

She stormed toward the designated dresser. "It's a toothbrush. It's a key. It's a hair dryer." She didn't know if he heard her grumbling.

"A hair dryer?" he said as he poured.

The clothes were neatly folded and stacked. "Don't try to tell me you didn't put that hair dryer in there for me." Her words echoed in her head. She sounded like a sixth-grader. Less than twelve hours ago, they were twined in passion and a mutual understanding. And there was the sweater she'd been looking for. Her sweater and a large stack of neatly folded underwear.

Thankfully, he ignored her childishness, but she had an inclination he wouldn't do so forever. Cross that bridge when...

She had an entire outfit, mismatched as it was, including a pair of sneakers she remembered trading for her work boots the morning after riding Abigail. Then, riding Duncan. Her head dropped, and she smiled at the thought.

It was too bad she hadn't forgotten some makeup on his floor. Since she wasn't in sixth grade she said, "Thank you."

"That had to hurt."

"And, I'm sorry."

"Ouch."

"That's not funny."

"We have much to discuss. Let's cross that bridge when—"

"What did you say?"

"I said we have other equally important matters to

discuss that are more time sensitive."

That was not what she meant, but the classic Duncan-Reed-formal-grammar made her smile. "Okay." She grabbed a yogurt and a Diet Coke from the fridge, adding them to her mental list right under, 'drawer,' and pulled a bar stool next to his short swivel stool.

She crisscrossed her legs and faced his list of names. "Thurmond Moody. I opened the envelope you sent me."

"I met with him on Tuesday."

"You what?"

"I met with him about some work, some portraits."

"Bullshit."

"Well, I know that and you know that—"

"No, I mean it's bullshit. Think about it, Duncan. You sent me pictures of him at the press conference announcing my return home. And again, when I was sworn in as detective. I remembered his bracelet. I can't remember him wearing it, but that can't be a coincidence."

"Yes, I've thought of the possible connection with him, but you and me?"

She dropped her legs and turned to face him. "We seem to be gaining some public...*something*. I'm no Bebe Lyons, don't get me wro—"

"I don't want a Bebe Lyons."

"I know. It's confusing." She trailed the words. It was a million-dollar puzzle.

"I'm not famous is what I meant. Yet the Lyons knew who I was. Even my parents had gotten wind of us and came all the way from their precious Maryland to slum in upstate New York."

"Your portraits were on nearly every wall." He leaned in and bit her earlobe. "I earned a half-dozen new clients thanks to those portraits. You think he knows I know." A sinister light bulb seemed to appear over his head. "You think he's setting me up as I try to set him up."

"You got it."

"I can use that."

"Oh, no you don't. *We* can use that."

She nodded to the chart paper before he could turn away. "Why Tanner and McKinney?"

"I'm thinking of everyone who was either involved with you on an illegal level or might somehow be. Did you read my email explaining the sketch of the man of Asian descent?"

It had to be done sooner or later. Slowly, she stood and took the black pencil from the chalk tray at the base of the easel. Taking a deep breath, she faced him. "I have something to share with you that isn't going to sit well. Will you promise to keep it where it belongs, in the police investigation?"

"No."

She sighed but continued. Reaching for the end of his list, she drew a single line across the words, 'Asian man,' and above wrote the name, 'Jun Zheng.'

"You know who he is?"

She nodded.

"That's why he—?"

"Said my name at the casino in Vegas, yes. He must have recognized me."

"But then…that means…fuck. Fuck." He rose to his feet, hit the easel hard enough to send it to across the room in pieces. "He was one of them. Is one of them, and I've been sitting on this for how long?"

"In your email you mentioned Slippery Jimbo had spotted him in town."

Duncan stopped at his wet bar, braced himself, elbows locked, and shook his head back and forth.

She'd seen him lose his temper, and it wasn't something she thought this shiny new room could withstand.

"Yes, and I think he might have been the driver in Tanner and McKinney's get-away truck."

She wrapped her hands around his sides. His head hung low between his arms.

Taking in this new information, she sorted through it as she tried to calm the storm. "You didn't know," she crooned.

"I knew something. I kept it from you. I don't even know why."

For the first time since she'd known him, he sounded vulnerable. She could have handled angry, dismissive, passionate, or even protective; these were familiar. "I know why," she said as she stepped to the side of him.

He turned to her, brows together.

She repeated the words Gloria had spoken. "You've been forced to keep secrets your entire life. Big secrets. Ones no child should need to keep."

"And you forgave me. Twice. And for something like this." It wasn't a question.

"We're a pair of something, you and me. I just have no idea what that is yet."

Duncan sat in the love seat he had installed in his plane. The plush carpet and table lamp atmosphere did little to settle him. When did his life turn around to where leaving New York caused nerves? He went over his time estimates for his next few projects, reread the schedule his secretary had made for him and started outlining his next move.

Zheng was a wash. Duncan had dragged Andy to three different, distant Wi-Fi spots, leaving a traceless virtual maze through eight states and three countries as they searched. He used every system, scan and database he had access to. And a few he didn't.

For now, Nickie would track down her Slippery Jimbo, and Duncan would concentrate on Moody. He thought he could pull one over on Duncan. He might have, but not now. Duncan had a plan and decided to include the police department for a change. It seemed necessary that he become accustomed to working with the police. Irony at its finest.

Pulling out his phone, he sat back and placed his feet on the coffee table secured to the floor in front of him. He punched in Nickie's cell and texted,

> *'detective, i'd like to set up a meeting with your captain.'*

He set his laptop on his legs and added a conference call he'd scheduled with a realtor in Louisiana for the following day to his secretary's planner. Opening the master spreadsheet of the properties he owned, his cell vibrated.

Nickie answered,

> *'r u sure ur ready?'*
>
> *'yes. I'll be back sat. afternoon. late.'*
>
> *'this isn't his jurisdiction.'*
>
> *'do we have options?'*
>
> *'FBI. i'll have 2 do it on my own.'*

Of course. What had he been thinking? Sliding his phone into the inside pocket of his jacket, he stared blankly at the sea of numbers in front him.

Any doubt he had about Moody's involvement with the kidnappings was erased. There may be more than one man who owned a bracelet like the one found in the abandoned house in Nevada. It was little more than circumstantial evidence to say the photos of

Moody wearing one that matched led him to the scene of the crime. But when Nickie remembered it, that was good enough for Duncan. Circumstantial still, for Nickie's set of cop rules and guidelines, but he wasn't a cop. Moody was involved. Involved enough to have been in Nevada. Involved enough to have been in that out-of-the-way house of horrors. Involved enough to have something to do with Nickie.

Moody told him he kept away from crowds, that he wouldn't be around Time's Square for his own state's traditional dropping of the ball. There was more to it. Duncan was sure of it. He couldn't find a single photo of Moody at any of the Times Square New Year's Eve celebrations.

Picture after picture showed Moody in the center of Mardi Gras, poker tournaments and NBA finals. Nickie explained to him that the men took the girls around the country to anywhere large numbers of wealthy men gathered.

The white house. The white house on Moody's property was used for this. It had to be. There was a parking lot. Why else would he have a parking lot? Why was such a decorated place dug deep into his property?

New Year's Eve.

CHAPTER 16

The nonstop week at the station should have made time fly. Instead, it was the longest week Nickie could remember in a while. She sat in her car in the parking lot next to the small Northridge runway. Duncan's plane was due on time, but she kept checking her watch anyway. Get a grip, Savage.

An investigation into several stolen objects that turned up in the local pawnshop, a couple of teenagers missing from a winter hike in the mountains who ended up missing on purpose, follow up on the rape victim who was only now softening to the idea of coming forward. It was all part of the job. And Nickie was a woman. She could multitask. Regardless, the itch in the back of her head grew as time went on.

She was anxious to see him, anxious about their meeting with the feds and anxious at how she allowed herself to be anxious. Hers was the only car in the lot. It wasn't meant for regular customers. Only a handful of planes landed and took off in the time she waited. He'd taken trips before. Dozens of them, some longer than this one. But she wanted him, needed him and wasn't sure that was a smart thing to let herself do at this point in her life.

Each plane that came into view made her sit up. They all looked the same, dammit. As soon as she was sure it was him, she bolted from her car like a high school girl. It was crazy. They still had to do the taxi thing and the shutdown thing. It took a while to lower the stairs. And yet, there she stood, behind the fence, freezing in the wind.

The pilot came down the stairs with him. They were making some kind of arrangements. Duncan always treated the people who worked for him with respect and attention. As soon as they shook hands, he turned, scanning the inside observation area first. Yeah, she *should* be in there. When his eyes turned to search the outdoor waiting spot, he found her. In one of the rare Duncan Reed moments, he smiled, teeth and all. It was brilliant. Tiny lines radiated from his eyes, the sharp features that framed his face softened. Her knees nearly betrayed her.

He motioned toward the end of the gate. As if she had all the time in the world, she strolled to the spot where he directed, forcing her feet to walk at a normal speed. Meeting up with her, he took her arm and dipped her into a dramatic kiss. The surprise should have made her stiffen, but she trusted him to keep her from falling. It was a damn good metaphor.

"I missed you, Detective."

A few jeers came from the grounds crew and the boy who carried his luggage.

He pulled her upright, and she ran her fingers through the top of his hair. "I thought about you once or twice."

For a moment, he turned his head, judging her sincerity. Then, he tossed her over his iron shoulder, bouncing her like that as he headed for her car. A few yards from it, he stopped abruptly. "I really hate that car," he said.

As he slid her to the ground, she said, "Be nice to her. She's sensitive."

"She is not sensitive." Nickie wasn't sure if he was talking about the car or her.

Duncan reached around, opened the driver's side door and popped the trunk. The boy who carried his luggage tossed them in.

"The feds agreed to first thing Monday morning unless something else comes up," she said as he tipped the boy.

Duncan slid into the passenger side, and she followed into the driver's side, surprised he was up for her driving, which was perfectly safe. Before she could start the ignition, he leaned over and gave her another quick kiss. She grabbed hold of the back of his head. She'd waited for days for his lips to be on hers, his hair in her grasp. He wasn't getting off that easy. His hair was soft and just long enough to lace her fingers through and grab hold. Sensations in her body played like an orchestra with the melody waving from head to toe and the harmony centered directly in her heart.

They spent the evening dining at Nickie's favorite hole-in-the-wall bar and grill, followed by a round of toe-curling sex at his place. Her eyes drifted closed as she sat with her cello between her legs. She'd played a solid hour as Duncan painted. Wagner's Lohengrin, Chopin's "No. 3 in E Minor." The reddening calluses on her fingertips were well worth it. She could live this way for the rest of her life.

The thought brought her back to reality like a roller coaster screeching to a halt. Her bow stopped. Her fingers stopped.

He turned his eyes to her, then squinted.

She was literally choking on her thoughts and waved her hand as a signal it was nothing. Alluding to the pretense that she was done playing anyhow, she set her instrument on the stand he'd bought for her. She reminded herself to add it to her mental list, right under house key and drawer, when her eyes stuck to his chart paper. The one with the list of men he decided were involved in the kidnapping and prostitution ring.

"We can't find anything on Zheng." She said it like they hadn't already known it.

His arms quit moving at the sound of Zheng's name. He didn't answer, but she hadn't asked a question. Only his eyes moved to her, and this time they stayed there.

"You found Moody in the background of pictures— the press conference announcing my return from being a rebellious teenage runaway, the one regarding my transfer to Northridge. He was tagged in those, of course, because he's been the frigging personal assistant to how many governors?"

He stood and came to join her, also letting his eyes roam the list of names.

"We know the former captain of police and fire chief were involved. We could search for images of them—"

"And search for Zheng in the background. You are a genius." He grabbed her hand, linking their fingers together and squeezing hard enough to make her eyes water. But he didn't notice. His eyes were glued to the names on the paper, written appropriately in the darkest of black.

Nickie sat in her office, polishing reports that were due as she waited for the feds. She and Duncan had spent hours Saturday night searching hundreds of images for Jun Zheng. Sunday was much of the same, moving the number of images searched into the thousands.

The three pictures of him they found had been shrunk and taped to the edges of her computer monitor. They were getting closer, and she was going to take down the rat bastard.

Before she had time to savor the gleeful image of doing so, the ancient intercom system on her desk buzzed. "Savage," she answered.

"Special Agents Strong and Lewis here to see you, Detective."

"Send them up." She rose and closed the blinds to her office. Looking around, she noticed there wasn't a single clear place to sit or set a briefcase. Quickly, she stacked papers, files and books in a corner next to her printer, and threw away papers from the floor that had missed the trash.

Then, she eyed the shots she and Duncan had found of Zheng. She took the pictures and tucked them into her bottom desk drawer. She wasn't ready to share Jun Zheng with the feds.

Strong and Lewis stood outside her open door. Lewis knocked. They didn't come in. It made her want to roll her eyes and cringe at the thought of everyone in the common area staring at them.

"Come in, guys. Shut the door behind you."

They seemed out of place in her dismal office and rickety chairs.

"Any news?" She wondered if they would offer any information.

Lewis glanced at Strong. Lewis was the one who shared with her more than she had the impression he should have.

"We flew out here to hear what you think you've uncovered."

So damned condescending. "I suggested a conference call," she retorted.

There was a long silence, which would have been awkward if it didn't feel so good.

Lewis blinked first. "We have a lead that says they're taking some girls to Madison Square Garden. We've got a man on the inside posing as a customer."

"Is this the 'important information' you mentioned that the thugs I arrested in Vegas gave you in their plea bargain?" From the looks on their faces, they must have assumed she forgot about that. Not a chance.

"Yes," Lewis answered flatly.

"I want in," she said just as flatly.

They glanced at each other before Strong jumped in. "What do you have?"

She supposed it was her turn. That was fair. She couldn't resist, however, baiting them. "An acquaintance of mine recently had a meeting with Theodore Mundy, personal assistant to the governor of New York."

"Thurmond Moody," Strong corrected.

She mispronounced Moody's name on purpose. And since she didn't think even FBI special agents had memorized the names of the personal assistants to every governor in the nation, Moody must already have red flags surrounding him.

"Right. Moody. So, this guy has a meeting with an acquaintance of mine about some work—legit work— a portrait Moody wants painted of him in front of his Jag."

"Is this acquaintance Duncan Reed?" Strong smirked. Male posturing was so annoying. She supposed they didn't know that she knew they'd been digging into her personal life.

"Sure, it's him. Duncan likes to do simple

background checks on potential clients. I noticed a photo he'd printed of Moody." It was mostly true.

She opened the bottom drawer of her desk and took out the print. She turned it to face them, but they didn't seem to catch the bracelet that hung below the sleeve of his shirt. Reaching back into the drawer, she pulled out the close up of the bracelet and held the pictures for them side by side.

They had how many cases? She didn't know. Maybe a few. Maybe dozens. So, she gave them an imaginary thumbs up that they recognized the bracelet.

"It's circumstantial," Lewis said, although it was definitely with reluctance.

"I'm not finished." She took a sip of soda from her large Styrofoam cup. "Duncan mentioned that Moody made a point to tell him he doesn't like to attend big ticket venues anymore, specifically mentioned Times Square on New Year's Eve. As he is the personal assistant to the governor of New York, that made me curious. I did some searching. I found him cheezing for the camera at dozens of big-ticket venues, and not always political big-ticket venues. Super Bowl parties, bigger poker tournaments, the Kentucky Derby, NBA Finals. You get where I'm going with this? All places known for hosting prostitution rings, both adult, child and coed."

Strong opened his mouth, but Nickie held up a hand. "Still not finished. Duncan took a wrong turn when he entered Moody's property." Sort of. "It took him past four warehouse buildings and down farther to a spectacular, two-story white house fully equipped with a lighted parking lot. Moody turned up his nose to Duncan's suggestion this might be the quarters for the help. In fact, Duncan was with Moody for over two hours and only ever saw a single person serving the man. I think Moody uses this house for guests. I think he brings the girls there. His place is close enough to the city. An hour drive from the city for an all-night party in lush accommodations is about right."

They sat still, listening without taking notes. "Thank you for the information. We'll do some digging and see what we come up with." They were going to leave. Dismissive assholes.

"Still not finished." It was good to be on her own turf. "I want men. I am requesting that you wave that wand of yours, talk to the Alabaster, New York, captain in Moody's jurisdiction and get me some squad cars. I want them for between 1 a.m. and 3 a.m. outside the perimeter of Thurmond Moody's property the night of New Year's Eve."

They were meeting at Get Lucky's of all places. Duncan ordered a draft. When in Rome.

The bar was sticky and his seat was cracked. Innards from the chair's stuffing poked his backside. Nickie wanted to catch her Slippery Jimbo.

Duncan's bar stool sat at the far end and gave him a beeline view across the room, down the narrow hall and right to the entrance door. The streetlight shone through each time the door opened.

No one paid attention to them. He sat with his legs straddling hers, his hand tucked around her thigh. Nickie rarely looked like a cop. She didn't walk like a cop. He could spot a cop. Her heels were too high, her pants too snug. Her jacket hugged her female hips right below where it tied around her waist.

She carried herself as more of a warrior, sizing her surroundings. She didn't do it in only sleazebag bars. She did it everywhere. She was a tall, sexy, cop warrior. And she was his.

He ringed one of her belt loops and pulled her into him. He kissed her on the cheek before touching his lips to hers.

"Technically, I'm on duty, Reed," she said pitifully weakly.

He closed his eyes and savored the taste. "Mmm. I'm helping keep your cover. And besides, I haven't seen you naked in—" He glanced at his watch. "—fifteen hours."

She crossed her legs and let her hip fall to the side of her stool. Loosening the top button of her work blouse, she glanced over her shoulder and checked the door again.

"That's not helping," he croaked.

She squinted, then raised a corner of her mouth. "It's not meant to."

She set her elbow on the bar, then lifted it, investigating what was making her arm stick to the Formica.

"If you had James's cell," Duncan reminded her, "we wouldn't have to meet in a place with a sticky bar."

"If you would have told me months ago Jimbo had spotted Zheng, we wouldn't be here at all."

Point taken. "Finish telling me about your meeting with Strong and Lewis."

"They agreed to my request."

"Nicely played, Detective."

"I think we need a plan B. And possibly C."

"Because Moody is likely onto us. Of course. What did you have in mind?"

He kept an eye on the door for James as he listened to her plans B and C and ran his thumb in circles over the back of her hand. And she always told him men couldn't multitask.

She was right, Moody knew. The idea of the portrait with his Jaguar had been forced. That was simple enough to see.

They planned for another hour. He switched to water and let her knees sink between his as they sat. He was warming up to Get Lucky's and all of its illegal smoking and couples who could easily choose one of the rooms in the back to do what they were doing in the booths.

He explained that Moody's security system was identical to the one he owned before he upgraded. He could hack into it enough to pause the system for a few seconds, he was sure of it. She explained details of the visual and audio bugs she hoped to plant on Moody's property as part of their plans B and possibly C.

"Don't look now," he said. She was one of the few people who could hear that phrase and wouldn't look.

"Let me know when he gets closer," she said. "I don't think he'll bolt, but it's happened before."

He dipped his head closer to her, running the end of his nose along her jaw as he watched James saunter in alone. He wore his usual light-brown trench coat, his hair slicked back. An unlit cigarette stuck behind his ear, he scanned the place as he walked and spotted them. His eyes closed. Duncan sensed that behind James's lids, his eyes were likely rolling.

Nickie must have read the recognition in Duncan's eyes because she rotated easily, leaning an elbow against the sticky bar. James's face read something between phony elation and reservation. He gave a heavy sigh before walking toward the two of them.

"Detective, dude. What brings you to this less-than-adequate place of business? Of honest business, I might add."

Nickie snorted. "As if what is going on in those back rooms is legal." She said it as a statement, quiet enough that the bartender didn't hear. "Come. Sit. Let me buy you a drink."

The suggestion seemed to make James lower his brows deeply and slow his step. Gingerly, he placed a hip on the stool two seats from Nickie. She switched to the one next to him. Placing her hand on his shoulder, she must have squeezed hard, because he lifted his shoulders and ducked away from her grip.

"Hey, Savage. What's that for?"

"It's Detective Savage to you, Jimbo. I need you to look at a picture." She slipped her hand inside her jacket and pulled one of the better close-up pictures they'd gotten of Jun Zheng and set it on the counter.

James shook his finger at the photo. "That's the guy. That's the guy I came to you about last winter. The one who was asking around about you. See how valuable I am?"

"Valuable? Do you have a name for me?"

James shook his head.

"Do you have an address? Have you seen him more than once?"

He lifted a shoulder and dipped his head. "No, but—"

"I want the entire conversation, beginning to end."

"It was a long time ago, ya know?"

Nickie placed her hand back on his shoulder. Duncan imagined she must have pinched the spot around the tendon that led from the neck to the collarbone, because James dipped his shoulder and winced again. "Hey, what 'cha gotta do that for?"

"I want to know."

She released him, and he rolled his shoulder as he answered. "He spoke like an American. You know, no Japanese accent."

"Chinese, but go on."

"He had your picture. Wanted to know where you

went and who you used for information. I didn't give you up." James patted himself on his good shoulder.

Duncan closed his eyes tightly.

"Who else did he talk to?" Nickie asked.

"I don't know. I didn't see." He lifted a hand ready to block Nickie's arm if necessary. "For real, detective dude...Detective Savage, dude. I only saw him the one time. I didn't think it was a big deal. I could keep an eye out for you."

Nickie handed him a bill and paid for his beer. "You do that, Jimbo."

She pushed away from the bar and Duncan followed. This was making him crazy. It was late and he was suddenly very tired.

The muscles in Nickie's body tensed, waiting to spring. She sensed she was dreaming, but couldn't convince herself it was a dream. He was coming. He was coming and she was ready.

They'd put her in the red room. They named each for their color like it was the real White House. The white house. They'd put her in a duck yellow, lacey bra with matching *panties*. That was what they liked to call them. They never put makeup on her. They wanted her to look like she was a virgin. They'd taken that from her a long time ago.

This one liked her. They'd brought him to her before. He called her Savage like the rest of them. She'd show them a savage. He came in with his deep voice busting out over something the guard said. Lifting his arm once to the guard, he shut the door and turned his eyes to her. She scrambled to the edge of the bed and curled her legs tightly into her. It was only partly an act.

He huffed a half-laugh and emptied his pockets like her father did when he came home for the day.

"I'd hoped you'd be that way, honey," he said like she was some sort of little girl.

She shook with fear, more from her plan than of him.

CHAPTER 17

⬤ ◆ ◆ ⬤

The man in Nickie's dream tossed his jacket over a chair and pulled at his tie.

"They..." Nickie could hardly get it out. "They record us, you know."

His hands stopped. He didn't turn his head, but moved his eyes from one side of the room to the other.

"There," she said, pointing to the lion's head on the wall.

He continued with his tie, tossed it on a chair, then untucked his shirt.

He didn't believe her. He had to believe her. Please believe her. He was going to ruin everything.

He took his shirt off, his blubber hanging over his pants so far it hid his belt. Taking his jacket from the chair, he walked with it to the far wall.

She took her chance and pulled his tie from the chair to the bed.

He tossed his jacket over the lion's head before he came to her. "There we go, honey. Just you and me."

She put her mind somewhere else. Somewhere safe. Her lip trembled as the weight of him sunk the bed and tilted her toward him.

"Now, where did we leave off last time?"

Bracing, she let him pull her legs until she was horizontal, then reached with her arm as his clammy body pressed against her. She could smell cigars and alcohol as his hands searched and squeezed.

She found it. She found it and she was going to do it. She grasped his tie and started thrashing like a fish. He'd expected it. That was why he chose her. Always be the smartest person in the room, she told herself, as she wrapped the tie around his neck.

A hand lay gently on her shoulder. She sat up and spun. Somewhere she noticed the room had changed, but it didn't matter. She swung like a savage at the figure behind her.

"It's okay." He blocked it like he knew it was coming. "It's me."

She held her arm back, fist tight, chest rising and falling like a rabbit's. "Oh no." She crossed her arms in front of her and made herself sit down at the edge of the bed. "Not again," she breathed. "Are you okay?"

"I'm always okay." He placed his hand back on her shoulder and squeezed before he slid it to the back of her neck and leaned over to kiss the top of her head.

Falling on her pillow, she gave herself a moment to let her breathing slow. He stayed. He always stayed. Knowing. Who does that? Turning her head, he lay next to her with his eyes closed as if nothing happened.

She asked him once why he never questioned her about how she escaped. He told her she would tell him in her own time. If it weren't for the muscles in his jaw that flexed and released, she would assume this was a regular morning for him.

She watched his beautiful face as he slid his hand

down to find hers. "It's almost Christmas Eve," he said with eyes still closed.

"Hmm?"

He lifted one lid and eyed her.

"That's right." She tried to smile. "It's almost Christmas Eve, and we're going to your aunt and uncle's."

He smiled. No teeth, just a warm, safe smile that made her feel exactly that.

Nickie pulled to the curb in front of the home Duncan grew up in. She looked down at her 9-by-13 pan of mini-strombolis and started laughing. It was the same thing she brought the first time she'd come to his aunt and uncle's home.

Today was different, even if her dish-to-pass wasn't. She was free of jitters and feelings of inadequacy. His family was as welcoming and nonjudgmental as Gloria's. She sat in awe of the idea there were two families in existence like them.

And yet, she parked in the street. She may be welcome, but the oil that leaked from her car would drip on Nathan's driveway. Her boots crunched in the few inches of snow that had fallen. They were lucky it wasn't a few feet. It was beautiful. The towering trees stood covered in white guarding their property like soldiers.

Duncan's aunt was a landscape designer. In the winter months, she changed to yard-decorator. There had to be a better word for it. Lining each side of the drive was a row of trees wrapped in hundreds of tiny white lights shining beneath the new snow. The evergreens that stood tall at the corners of their enormous house were wrapped in the same, as well as the thick pillars that stood guard outside the front door.

This must have been where Duncan learned his love of *big*.

Someone had to have seen her and let Nathan and Brie's golden retriever out the front door. He tore down the drive to greet her. In one hand, she held her pan of appetizers, in the other was the gift she brought them. As the dog came bounding toward her, Nickie reminded herself Brie was a whiz at training dogs.

Sure enough, a few feet before he reached her, he put on the brakes and sat. "I'll be damned, Red. You are a good boy." She noted the contrast between his frozen head and his butt and tail that wiggled like a crazy man. "Come on. Let's see who let you out."

They'd told her not to, but she couldn't help it. She knocked and waited. One of Duncan's cousins answered. It was one of the twins. She could never tell them apart, so she smiled and offered generic holiday greetings.

"I'm Jonathon," he said as he helped her wrangle her coat and gifts. He must have known. The place was filled with dark green and deep red decorations wrapped around the stairs and hanging from the doors. Beneath the arching staircase was a portrait of Niagara Falls painted by an eight-year-old Duncan. She thought it was good enough to put in one of his shows.

"You're late." Speak of the devil.

"I texted you."

He kissed her with the stromboli as a barrier between them. "That you did. Come."

She understood why the foyer had been free of people. They were opening gifts. So much for not feeling awkward. Duncan took the pan from her and leaned over to place it on a counter filled with enough food to feed a small army.

When she was growing up, Christmas meant a

mountain of presents with her name on them…all from her parents. Dresses she didn't want to wear, and as she got older, wouldn't wear. Ballet slippers for the classes she didn't want to take, and English riding gear when she would have preferred riding bareback. It was no wonder her parents didn't search for her when she disappeared.

Nathan and Brie sat on a couch. Next to them, propped against the wall was the painting of the creek that flowed behind the house. It was the portrait Duncan had been working on for them. Their three nearly grown biological children sat on the floor. Duncan and Andy, Rose and the baby were there along with their grandparents, who were so old they made her grandmama seem like a teenager.

Brie stood and everyone stopped talking. She was staring at the gift Nickie held in her hand. It wasn't wrapped. How do you wrap a hardwood maple sapling? "Oh," Nickie said, breaking the silence. "I remembered you…lost some trees last summer." At least she remembered to tie a bow around the pot.

"I don't know what to say," Brie said. She walked to Nickie, then wrapped her arms around her in an embracing hug.

Nickie held the tree to the side and used her other hand to pat her on the back.

"It's perfect," Brie said. "So personal. Thank you." The rest of group greeted her and offered wishes of happy holidays.

She wanted to say it was nothing because it was nothing, but instead, she said, "Merry Christmas."

Duncan persuaded Nickie to park in his garage. As silly as it was, it was a step. A storm was headed in, and the term 'storm' had a different meaning in upstate New York. He'd hooked the plow to the end of his

SUV and backed it in the third spot of his double-deep three-car garage.

As they opened the door to the service entry, he pulled her coat from her shoulders. "I have a surprise."

"I've learned to go on alert when you say that."

"You'll like it."

She turned to face him and squinted. "I believe you."

He hung up their coats, dropped her overnight bag at the bottom of the stairs and took her hand. The back of the house stairs were circular and wound up and down. For the first time, he took her down the descending passage.

The basement was finished. Nickie had squashed his hopes for a shooting range, reminding him she was a cop and that it would be illegal. Her feet stopped before him, and he looked around the open space like a tourist. This side wasn't what he wanted to show her. It was more of a man cave. A large screen television sat in front of two recliners, which served as bookends to a double-long leather couch. A large table for cards was positioned on the other end of the room with a lengthy wet bar on the side.

"Nice." He knew she meant it.

"Walk this way." He guided her through the closest door. "This is what I wanted to show you." He opened it and gestured using his best Vanna White impression.

Her eyes lit in such a way he wanted to do it all over again just so he could watch them.

He'd installed a four-lane, twenty-five yard lap pool. It lay next to the glass walkout sliding doors that led to the woods behind his house. Room for a future sauna and guest bathroom were to the side, and on the other was a set of weights, an elliptical and a heavy bag.

"Is the heater working?" she asked as she lifted her shirt off. The blood instantly drained from his head, leaving anything more than basic conversation fruitless. She was naked in seconds. He stood, stunned like an idiot. Why hadn't he had the pool installed first, he wondered, as he stripped.

The snow was coming down outside, covering the ground with a thick blanket of white. His Nickie was in his arms, safe and without reservation. He wanted the snow to come down, trapping them there for days, maybe weeks.

Foreplay in the water was followed by more on the deck of the pool. They made love like it was their first time, or maybe their last. He cursed himself for not installing an elevator as they walked to the third floor, wrapped in towels with their clothing piled in their arms.

They curled in the covers of his bed like mummies, legs twined and her head on his arm, using it as a pillow. They gazed at the ceiling as the skylights piled with white.

"Do you remember your real parents?" she asked.

"My memories of my childhood are much like other children in the sense that the ones of my early years are less clear. I do remember learning to walk, though."

"Yeah," she said with sarcasm dripping from her tone. "That's just like the rest of us humans."

"I remember my parents, yes. The sound of my mother's voice. She sang to me at bedtime. My father played catch with me. We used Velcro mitts and tennis balls."

He rubbed his thumb over her silky shoulder.

"The waiting sucks."

Said in the true form of his detective. He knew

where she was going with the change in subject and didn't have an answer. They'd found some pictures of Zheng, but nothing recent and nothing tagged or hinted at his identity. James 'Slippery Jimbo' Spalding had been of little help. So, they waited. Waited for New Year's Eve when they would hopefully find some answers and 'bust some heads,' as his detective would say.

She leaned over and bit his earlobe, letting her hand travel south.

He turned his head to face her. "After what we just did in the basement, I might need a Gatorade or something."

"Hmm," she crooned, maneuvering over him. "If I know you like I think I know you, that might not be altogether true."

She lifted, bringing heat to heat as he admired her silky skin. Sure enough, his body…woke.

Her smile was breathtaking. She shifted just enough to make his toes curl. "I thought so," she said. She arched her head back and pulled his mouth to her.

Duncan heard the telltale sounds of pots and pans banging on porches and entire boxes of Black Cats igniting. "Happy New Year," he said as Nickie taped the surveillance wires to his chest.

"Why are you smiling?" She sounded honestly irritated.

"It's our first New Year's together."

"I'm not comfortable with this."

"Being alone in a strange room with me?"

"I'm ignoring you," she said as she buttoned his shirt.

He took her hand and finished the buttons himself. "The rush. Don't you feel it?"

She shrugged. "I suppose."

"Must be a guy thing," he said, lifting his brows up and down.

Taking his hand, she turned it supine and placed a small handful of small, circular devices in his palm. He brought them closer and noticed they had a paper backing. Stickers?

"The ones with the red paper are visual only, the green ones audio. See if you can plant some of these suckers. They work outside, but we'd like to get some on the inside."

Before he finished tucking in, she opened the break room door. They were upstairs in the Alabaster police station. Moody's hometown. This police department was far different from the one in Northridge. Everyone except reception seemed to have a personal office. It was absent of the large common area he had come to believe was a staple feature in any police station. It seemed odd without metal desks bunched in twos and scattered throughout. The carpet was new, the walls were painted with a fresh coat of yellow and the coffee in his hand was a dark espresso blend, fresh.

The two special agents she worked with were there, along with four detectives from Moody's hometown police force. No one questioned why they were walking out of a closed room while Duncan fastened his belt. Full-tactical SWAT waited in the basement. Duncan thought it was overkill, considering what they had in mind.

He'd barely had his arms in his suit jacket before she reached in his pocket and grabbed hold of the jammer he'd rigged in the garage of his home. Granted it would have been hard to miss. It was big enough that she had trouble extracting it from his pocket. It was her turn to lift her brows.

"I told you Moody uses the same security system

model I did previously. Andy and I worked this to match the frequency. It should jam it temporarily."

"Should? How temporarily?"

"An average of fifteen seconds from our tests. It jams only to the current state of the system. Cameras stop rotation, the gate freezes closed...or open. In theory."

Nickie rode with the feds. Duncan was alone in his Audi R8. He wanted to drive his SUV, but she insisted he drive the same vehicle he had during his first visit to Moody's. He couldn't argue with the logic. He wanted to be discovered—just not right away.

As he drove, he slipped his Beretta from beneath his seat and tucked it in the back of his pants. Placing the security system jammer on the seat next to him, he checked his pockets for the bugs Nickie had given him.

Her actions had been cool and rehearsed. To others, they would read it as a cop who was smooth and knowledgeable. Not that she wasn't. But he had learned to read it as her automatic pilot mode. She had the ability to shut down her emotions, to close everything out and focus on her goal.

CHAPTER 18

The neighborhoods were quiet and dark. Twice, they passed homes lined with a dozen or so cars, lights and movement inside. Apparently, the pot and pan bangers had either gone home or found a spot to gather for an all-nighter.

The FBI staged their arrival a few blocks from Moody's property. The unmarked cars parked at the end of the cars at the party house three blocks north of Moody's main entrance. The SWAT vehicles waited in a neighborhood park the same distance south.

Duncan's heartbeat quickened as he pulled in behind the SUV Nickie was in. It was just the two vehicles alone in a dark spot at a far edge of Moody's property. She got out and went right to the driver's side of his car. Turning off his ignition, he opened the door and stood.

"Change in plan," she said and untucked his shirt. Reaching in, she pulled the wires from his chest.

Damn. His jaw flexed and released. "What—" One of his eyes closed involuntarily. "—was that for?"

"I'm not comfortable with this." She held up the wires, then stuffed them in her pocket. He cringed at the thought of what the FBI would have to say about it.

Visibly, she took a deep breath. "And I'm going with you."

"That's more than a change of plans."

"The risk of you getting caught wearing the wire is too high. You could be outnumbered, and the target is too far from the road. We wouldn't be able to get to you fast enough. And you're a civilian. I had no trouble convincing Strong and Lewis."

"Do I need to remind you I specialized in covert tactical explosives in the Middle East?"

"No, you don't, because I'm still going with you."

She got in, slid the passenger seat back as far as it would go and placed the homemade jammer on her lap. Sticking her arm out the window, she signaled to the FBI, then rolled it up.

"Okay," he breathed, more out of confusion than nerves.

"Does Moody's system have audio or visual only?"

"Visual only," he answered.

She nodded.

The grounds were dark. He hadn't expected it with the lights Moody had installed, but he supposed it made sense. And Duncan didn't need the lights. Moonlight between the trees was enough for him. He remembered the grounds like a map taped to the inside of his eyelids. The location of each camera and each turn in the road.

He pulled over before they reached the scope of the entrance camera.

"What are you doing?" she barked.

He lifted a brow and took out a bottle of Boones Farm. "Toast?"

"What the hell?"

He twisted the cap, took a long swig, gargled and swallowed. "I would have explained had I known you were coming with me."

Her eyes were wide and her mouth open. It was a most endearing mix of disbelief. But she said nothing more.

When he covered the end of the bottle with his fingers and turned it upside down, she nodded in understanding. He dabbed the wine on his neck, hands and jacket like a woman putting on perfume.

"You smell disgusting."

"Good. Now we wait."

"We what?"

"We wait."

"I thought you had your jammer thing?"

"I do. It's a jammer, not a key."

"Oh boy." Bringing the walkie to her mouth, she notified the rest of the crew. "We're in a holding pattern, gentlemen. Stay tuned." Readjusting her belt, she reclined her seat and slouched.

"This is anticlimactic," he said into their first hour.

"This is what most police work is."

"Nickie," he said as a bright red Ferrari pulled to the gate.

"I see it." She tucked her long legs close to the rest of her and slipped into the space in front of her seat. Impressive. "Are you going to move?" she barked.

"Not yet." He waited for the gate to open, the car to enter and for the gate to begin to close.

"Duncan," she growled.

He thought of the time of night, the men who waited around the neighborhood and truly hoped this was going to work. He waited for the gate to begin to close, leaving enough room for his car to fit before activating the jammer.

It stopped. Fifteen seconds, he reminded himself.

His tires squealed as he pulled away from the curb. He approached the gate and tucked between the metal, scraping the side of his car. "Damn," he said, spinning his tires in deep snow before reaching the road. He really liked this car.

He checked his rearview mirror and watched as the gate stood frozen. "Traceless," he crooned.

"Sometimes you scare me," Nickie said, but she didn't sound scared. She sounded positively jovial.

Trolling painfully slowly down the drive, he worked to swerve and hit the grass every twenty to fifty yards. The trees stood in the calm evening air like a painting. They lined the road as if they were watching, waiting. The drives were plowed clean. Footprints littered the deep snow everywhere, human and animal alike. This was much different from the last time he was here.

He took another swig of the Grey Goose, threw his head back to gargle and reapplied some to his clothing. "My car is damaged and smells."

"And he worries about his car," she said to the air.

He approached the white house, surprised he hadn't been stopped before then. So far so good. Until he got closer.

It was dark.

Other than the streetlight over the parking lot, there were no lights. No cars. No people. No kidnapped girls. No johns.

"You said this would happen," he said to her, but was still disappointed.

"Yep. He knows. It sucks. Plan B."

He pulled his car to the grass near the only corner he remembered the cameras didn't reach. She called in their current position. Purposely, he bumped the house and, leaving the car in neutral, pulled the emergency brake. "You have exactly ten feet in each direction," he whispered. "Here." From his pocket, he removed one of the camera bugs and an audio only bug, then handed them to her.

As she slid out her door, he opened his, staggered into camera view and called out for Moody, loud and drunken. "Moody! Where are you?" He clutched his Grey Goose and purposely tripped on his feet as he pulled a red sticker from the first bug and headed to the closest window. Slapping his palm to the window frame, he stuck the visual recording device to it as he dipped his head and pretended to choke. Then, he tipped the bottle in the air and faked a long drink of nothing.

Over his shoulder, he noticed Nickie. She was already slithering back into his car. Something was wrong. He wanted to go to her, but this might be their only chance.

He pounded on the window, turned in a circle, and fell on a bush, leaving an audio only device at the base. Nickie said they worked outside. He hoped they were water resistant. When he reached the front door, he set his bottle on the concrete step and laid his right hand high on the jamb. He placed a visual device high on the outside framing of the door as he pounded with his left hand. He heard the tires coming but was determined to get one more bug placed before he was stopped.

Stumbling around the side of the house, he pounded on the window that overlooked the parking lot and placed a visual bug in a crease between the wooden siding.

A car door opened and he spun, making sure to trip on his feet, stagger and right himself. The gun pointing at his head would make other men lose their composure. But Duncan had a gun pointed at him more than once in his life, and the rush of adrenaline was more than enough to keep it interesting. After all, he knew Moody was onto him. Moody wouldn't believe Duncan was here by drunken chance and might be privy to the location of the SUVs waiting outside his property. The most Moody could accuse him of was trespassing, and he had a plan for that too.

"Mr. Moody would like you to stay where you are until he gets here, Mr. Reed."

Duncan leaned his back to the side of the house and slid down to the snow. "Whad ja gotta gun for?" He threw back a swig of nothing.

He ached to place one more bug along the house or in the bush that slept in the winter next to his leg. But he knew they were recording his every move and decided to take his winnings and run.

Then came the red Ferrari. Did Moody know or care how cliché that was? Moody came to a controlled stop and stepped out fully dressed in a three-piece suit. "Are you disappointed it's only me here this evening, Mr. Reed?"

Duncan stared at him with lids half closed.

"I can have the police here in five minutes." He pulled off his gloves, one finger at a time. "Maybe less, as it seems they don't have far to go. Did you think you could outsmart me?"

"For wha?" Duncan slurred. "I have an appointment." He took the business card Moody had given him at their previous appointment, held it up and turned it over. On the back, Moody had listed his private phone number and the words 'week after Christmas.'

Moody tore it up in a small tantrum. "At two in the morning? I have cameras, Mr. Reed. Cameras that will prove you broke onto my property in the middle of the night and—"

"And?" It was difficult to continue the show for the

cameras. "I made a copy of yer card," he said, and threw back another drink of nothing. "Never can be too careful. And I didn't break onto yer property. W-w-why w-w-would I do that?" Pushing up along the siding, he inched his way to a standing position.

"How did you get in, Mr. Reed? The gate was not opened for your car or anyone else."

"I followed the red car. Can we get started? I brought my s-s-stuff." He staggered toward his Audi.

"Consider our agreement terminated. You're not welcome on my property again, witnessed by my help, here." Moody sounded completely exasperated. "Make sure he gets out," he heard Moody say as Duncan staggered to his car.

Duncan was reluctant to speak to Nickie. Scared to glance down at where she curled at the foot of the passenger seat. Resisting the urge to spin his tires, he inched the wheels to the asphalt. It didn't matter what Moody thought. As long as he didn't go running his fingers along the windows and doorframes, the evening was a success. And they never had to move to plan C.

The worst thing Moody could prove was that Duncan was driving drunk and had a poor sense of deciphering the back of a business card. Camera footage wouldn't show the lapse in time when Duncan passed through the fence. Let Moody watch that stretch of tape a few hundred times.

As soon as they were out of sight, he spoke to her. He was reluctant, wondering if the cameras might be able to see him talking. So, he tried to speak without moving his lips.

He continued to swerve along the road at a snail's pace. "I planted three visual and one audio, Detective. I want a raise. I want an accommodation and a raise."

She didn't answer. He allowed himself a full look at

her. Her body was shaking as if she had been standing in the cold for hours. Tucked tightly in a fetal position, her arms covered her head. Her hair was three shades darker with the dampness of sweat.

"Nickie. Nickie, what's the matter?"

He heard nothing but whimpers. Screw the cameras. He pulled out his cell to call the special agents. "Shit," he said aloud, realizing he had no number to call, and tucked it back in the pocket of his coat. He hit the road and leaned in to take her walkie from her pocket.

She grabbed his wrist as if she was hanging onto the edge of a cliff. "No."

Her face turned to the side as she spoke. She was white as a sheet with dark makeup smeared around her eyes.

"Nickie. They're waiting for us. A lot of people are waiting for us. What do you want me to do?"

Lifting into the seat, she shook her head and tried to move away the damp hair that stuck to her forehead.

He pulled in front of the SUV that held special agents Strong and Lewis. The exited their vehicle as he did.

"There's something the matter with Detective Savage. I'm taking her to a hospital."

They offered no sympathies and turned to gawk at each other. "Now?" Strong asked as he peered over Duncan's shoulder, checking on her through the front windshield. He winced at the sight of her, pale, sweaty and trembling.

"What the hell happened to her?"

"Look," Duncan said. "I planted three visual and one auditory bug. I'll draw up the exact placements, and you can debrief us tomorrow in Northridge. I'm getting her to a hospital now."

He crawled back into his car and slammed it into gear.

"No hospitals, Duncan, please."

"I know. Let's get you safe and dry."

Nickie knew she was technically in the first bed and breakfast Duncan had found on his GPS. But the white house was too fresh in her dreaming head and deeply seeded in her subconscious memory.

She was a little girl, shaking in the corner of the four-poster brass bed. Her whimpers were only partially artificial.

"I'd hoped you'd be that way, honey."

She told him about the camera. She didn't think he believed her, but he tossed his suit jacket over the lion's head anyway.

The weight of his body pressed on top of her. It made her sick to her stomach, but she focused, focused on the tie. Reaching it with her fingertips, she maneuvered it around his neck. Thrashing, she scrambled behind him and tightened the tie until her arms shook.

The man paused, but only for a moment, before he began shaking his body from side to side and grabbing at her. She wrapped her thighs around him as tightly as she could and pulled the tie like a crazy girl. Like a savage.

Covering her face, she knelt, sucking air as Duncan came into the room dressed and with wet hair.

CHAPTER 19

———◆ ◆ ◆ ◆———

Duncan dropped his towel and reached Nickie in three strides. Relief that he was there washed through her. No words were spoken. He sat in front of her on crumpled sheets and pushed away the strands of hair that were stuck to her brow. She focused on his face. It was the most stable thing she had in her life. Taking her forearms, he pulled them together and lowered them to her lap. She hadn't realized they were shaking, still aching from pulling on the tie in her dream.

Gingerly, he propped his back against the antique headboard and pulled her to his chest. She listened to the sound of his heart through his shirt. It beat faster and faster, a direct contrast to his calm demeanor.

"There is much I don't remember. I was young."

She sighed, letting the draw of his hand over her hair soothe her heart and clear her thoughts.

"But I recognized Moody's voice." She sat up and looked him in the eye. "And the house. I've seen the bracelet. I've seen it when it was on his wrist. I think he was one of the—" She dropped her head back to his chest. "—men who came for me."

His hand stopped on her back, only for a fraction of a second, but she didn't miss it.

"But he wasn't the one that night. I'd never heard his name before, but...the white house is the house I escaped from. I remember the night, the room." The man. "Moody organizes parties in the white house. That's what he calls them. He doesn't always use girls. I've heard them talking about groups of women and some men they bring in. It depends on the clientele."

She wanted to cry but couldn't bring herself to do it. The other half of her realized a sense of clarity. She could breathe. Lifting again, she gazed into the deep chocolate of his eyes, and for the first time that night noticed the specks of tawny brown that came out only when he was the most intense. They were stiffly composed, but she could see through them. Far in the back, there was pain. But he was here for her and she would use him. Crossing her legs, she faced him fully.

"I planned it for months. He kept dogs. I used to hide some of the food they gave us and snuck it to them through the cracks in the basement windows. I kept some in the pockets of the silk housecoat they gave me to wear."

She turned her eyes down. His fists were clenched, knuckles white. A sudden stabbing pain pierced her heart. "I can stop if you want."

A man of few words, he shook his head.

Letting her chest expand, she expelled a long breath. "I...got away." She stared at her hands like they weren't her own, then sniffled defiantly. "I crawled out the window. The dogs were there, but they weren't a problem. They knew I had food. I should have been caught, should have froze. I ran in the cold until I found a wrought iron fence. I climbed a tree and jumped, rolling in the snow, and then ran for I don't know how long. Almost everything was dark. I pounded on some doors, but no one answered. Until, I found a house with two police cars. I could see now they were answering a domestic disturbance call. I cried out at the door, afraid I had been followed. The beat officers almost tackled me to the snow at first. When they saw what I was wearing and recognized my age, they let me stay in the back of their car until another black and white could get there."

Duncan swung his legs over the side of the bed, his chest rising and falling rapidly. He buried his face in his hands. "I had him within my reach. I had his neck within my reach. I could have snapped it with my hands."

Scooting beside him, she took his hands and pulled until he faced her. "I need you. If you end up in jail…"

His eyes turned down to their joined hands, then up to her face. His eyes were murderous. "I'm going to shower, Duncan. Are you going to be okay? Because, I'm okay. Then, we need to debrief with Strong and Lewis. I'll call and see if they'll let us do it at the Northridge station. I'm better, Duncan." She brought his hands to her lips and kissed his knuckles. "I'm going to be okay. You do that to me. I love you."

She watched as his gaze morphed from lethal to helpless. He smiled. It didn't reach his eyes, but he rubbed his thumb along her cheek. "You are my everything."

Nickie wanted her captain present. She wasn't sure why. This had nothing to do with him. Maybe it was so she could be that much more on her own turf. Maybe it was because Dave had been a sort of a father figure since back in the days when he was a detective and she was his assistant.

Regardless, if the feds wanted in her head, they

were going to have to do it on her terms. They went through the empty politeness of inquiries into how she was feeling. Although they were agreeable to the idea of her captain attending her debriefing, they were firm about keeping her and Duncan separate. She didn't put up a fight to the latter, only because she would have made the same decision had it been her pulling the strings.

She'd gone over the events step-by-step, but left out the part about regaining parts of her memory. Pieces from a broken, fifteen-year-old girl didn't seem credible. Instead, she formed her knowledge into the opinions they seemed to value above all else.

"In my opinion, Moody uses the house as a place to host mass prostitution parties. I expect he caters to more than exclusively the men and women who prefer early teens. It's likely he changes venues depending on the demands of his clients."

"We backed you up on this, because of the previous success you've had in…this area."

Duncan's hacking into their files or not, did they really think she wouldn't figure out why they took such interest in her knowledge? Why they came to her of all people for her *expertise*?

"We've spent man hours planning, executing and paperwork on this project. We have basically nothing. What facts do you have to back up your opinion exactly, Detective?" Strong asked, moving nothing but his lips. Now they want facts?

So, that's how this was going to be. "Exquisite house set in the back corner of a forty-acre property. Duncan testified that Moody stated he didn't allow his help to use the place."

"Why isn't it a house for guests?"

"With a parking lot for sixteen cars?"

"This is all good in theory, but we have nothing

concrete," Strong repeated, clearly exasperated. As if she cared.

"Which is why we have the bugs. Now, we wait."

Or, they could wait while she made a visit to an old friend in the U.S. Penitentiary in Terre Haute.

Duncan was in interrogation. The FBI could call it debriefing if that was what looked good on their books, but he knew enough to realize this was nothing less than an interrogation.

It was for Nickie, he reminded himself. He said as little as possible and gave only facts. She would want it that way.

"And why did Detective Savage suspect Mr. Moody's involvement?"

What kind of question was this after the fact? "I'm not comfortable answering for her."

"And you just happened to have a client that is a suspect in the detective's eyes?"

Point for Special Agent Lewis. "I have high-profile clients all over the country, yes."

Lewis pulled out a preliminary blueprint of the white house. "And these are the locations of the bugs you think you planted?"

Think? Playing the game, he turned his eyes to the markers he'd written on the prints himself. His façade of patience was classic. "Yes." They'd had him mark the audio bug with a green marker and the visuals with red. Prints that were side shots showed close ups of the windows and shrubbery. They'd had him mark the exact locations on these also.

He wanted to ask if the bugs were up and running and what they had seen, but he could find that out on his own later.

"What made you think Moody was onto you?"

"I never said that."

Lewis smiled. "Was it you who came up with the cover of drunken artist coming to find his client?"

"Yes."

"Did he seem to fall for it?"

Nope. "I don't know."

It went on like this for an hour and a half. Duncan was ex-Army. He had enough endurance to last a day and a half.

Strong turned his eyes away from Nickie and down to his file before he asked her, "Why did you suspect Moody's involvement?"

Nickie glared at him and scowled. "You should probably check your notes, Strong. And it's a little late for reviewing motive."

He smiled. "It's procedure, Detective. You know that."

She wasn't about to reveal the pictures of Moody at the press conference announcing the return of the Maryland Monticello's runaway daughter. Or the one of him over fifteen years later announcing her transfer to the Northridge police force. "His need to share an aversion to crowds in order to explain his absence from his state's high-profile celebration of the New Year in Time's Square." She leaned back and crossed her ankles in front of her captain's desk. "The large number of photos, many recent, showing him at said crowds that weren't necessary, needed or beneficial to his career.

"He was lying and he was covering," she continued. "When Mr. Reed discovered Moody's lack of grounds employees, the size of the warehouse that housed his supposed grounds employees, and the random exquisite home in the far corner of his property, suspicions were enough for recon, but not enough for a warrant."

"And what should I write regarding how Mr. Reed happened to have a client that is of suspicion to you?"

Pushing her chin to the side, she cracked her neck, then again on the other. "Mr. Reed has prestigious clients all over the nation."

"You suspected Moody was onto you, yet you didn't share this with us."

It wasn't a question.

Strong leaned back and rolled his pencil between both hands. "Why did you suspect Moody was onto you?"

"I didn't." Duncan did. She just agreed is all.

"But you sent Mr. Reed in with bugs. That indicates you thought you wouldn't find what we were looking for on Moody's property and that you wanted to get something out of the operation."

"Sending Mr. Reed in with bugs was smart detective work. I'm sorry if it confuses you."

His face fell. Too damned bad. She was tired of jumping through federal hoops. She had cases on her desk, leads to catch up on and a horse waiting to be ridden.

"Whose idea was it to put on the drunken façade?"

It made her smile, and she reminded herself to stick as closely to the truth as possible. "It was Duncan's idea."

It was time to turn the tables. "I'm going to visit Tanner about it."

He lifted his brows at the mention of her now-incarcerated former captain.

"I want to see what I can get out of him. I need some leverage, just in case he's on the fence, deciding whether or not he feels like sharing with me. What can you give me?"

He took a deep, exaggerated breath. Her lips ached to smile, but she kept a straight face.

* * *

They still had a few hours of daylight. Duncan watched as Nickie rode in front of him through the thinner parts of the well-worn trails his brother and Rose had created from exercising their horses. Nickie rode his Abigail as if she hadn't taken a fifteen-year hiatus from riding. Her long hair bounced behind her as she led the way through ancient trees and miles of white. The lower heels of her brown boots dipped behind her stirrups. He wondered if she wore shoes with flat heels anywhere other than the gym.

Pausing, she directed Abigail onto a spot of virgin snow that led to their favorite resting spot. They hadn't visited the spot since early fall, and it surprised him she would be up for it in the cold. Winding between the trees, she didn't miss a turn and pulled to a stop when they reached the clearing.

The air was cold against his cheeks, but otherwise he was warm in his winter riding gear. The air was crisp and clean. It gave him a sense of cleansing and renewal. He could only hope it did the same for her. Comfortably, she swung her leg over Abigail and set her boots down in the snow. "I brought matches," she gloated.

The comment took him aback. "You want me to make a fire?"

"No." She smiled and tied Abigail on the outside of the large circle of fallen logs. "I'm doing it."

He tied his horse near Abigail and took some treats from his coat pocket for them. "Really," he said as a statement.

"Don't say that like you think I can't. I've been watching you."

In warmer, dryer weather, he thought.

She had discovered parts of her childhood she had repressed for years, repressed for a reason. She was drilled through her lunch hour by the same people who claimed to want to work with her, and she wanted to build a fire in the snow. He was in love with this woman.

He worked on brushing the snow from some of the bigger sitting logs as she cleared the area between the small circle of rocks. Lying back on his preferred, flatter log, he crossed his ankles and enjoyed the show.

She knew to remove the snow and the first few layers of foliage to find the dryer leaves and sticks beneath. Knew to make a tepee shape out of the smaller twigs before adding a layer of thicker ones. And she made a pile to the side of bigger sticks and a few of the logs she'd uncovered from the bottom of the pile of wood left from last fall.

All in her lower-heeled brown boots and snug, brown denim pants that made him want to scrap the whole idea and take her to bed.

Before lighting the first match, she ran her hand over the top of her hair and glanced at him. Swinging his legs to the ground, he sat and let his forearms rest on his thighs.

The leaves smoked, but no flames offered appreciation for her tedious work.

"Can I—?"

"No." She answered before he finished.

The sun would set soon. He would hate it if she did all this work only to turn around and have to leave without a fire. He nearly insisted on helping her before a small flame flickered. She blew too hard, creating another smoke signal to the wildlife in the trees.

One more flame and she blew again, but gently this time. The flame grew, licking the twigs before catching them all on fire. The noises that came from her mouth were nearly more excited than the ones she made when they had sex. It was enough to make any man question his abilities.

Adding the bigger sticks, she walked around the fire like an all-star wrestler who won the heavy weight title. "I made fire! I am the king!" He saw pieces of the little girl she was never allowed to be, a carefree skip in her step she would never let anyone else witness.

The heat began to reach him where he sat. His knees first, then his toes. Heat rose in his pants that had nothing to do with the fire.

Swinging her hips, she approached and straddled him like he was Abigail. She linked her fingers behind his head. "You are one lucky man, Duncan Reed. You have a genius winter fire starter wrapped around your little finger." The kiss was long and confident. Any coherent retort escaped him.

He splayed his gloved hands on her backside and tugged. The heat from the fire was nothing compared to the heat between them. If it were six months from now, he would take her there on the forest floor.

"Wrapped?" he asked without taking his lips from hers. "I could use that."

"Hold that thought." She swung her legs off him and went to add some smaller logs. The flames grew as quickly as his desire.

When she came to him, she sat between his legs, facing the fire instead of him. Tough luck.

Taking his coat, she pushed the sleeve of his left arm, exposing the tattoo on his forearm. He had to assume the fire she just created with her hands made her think of it. The blacks and grays were meant to be as symbolic as the fire that licked up his skin.

"You did that yourself." She shuddered, and he was certain it wasn't from the cold. "I have to admit, it looks like your work, even if the...canvas is a different material."

She took off a glove and ran her fingertip along the veins in his arm as they twined and mixed with the flames. So much of his life had to do with fire. Not happy fire, one worth circling in a dance of conquer, but fire of destruction.

"I'm going to visit Tanner," she said.

CHAPTER 20

Duncan's lungs stopped moving at the change in subject. He knew this, but still couldn't get them to move. The sounds of the forest around them that had helped create their moment disappeared in a breath.

She craned her head to face him, turning her gray eyes from one of his to the other. She was reading his reaction. He had no idea what she saw.

"I can go alone," she said.

"I know you can." It came out as a bark and was too late to retract.

"But you're coming with me anyway."

He tried to soften his voice this time. "I am."

"They won't let you in."

"Where is *in*, exactly?"

"The United States Penitentiary in Terre Haute, Indiana. Don't you have work or meetings?"

"I'm the boss." He took her bare fingers to his lips and kissed them. "And isn't Indiana State in Terre Haute?"

Her eyes took a circle before she answered. "Yes. I think it is."

"Nice place to put a top-security prison," he said

sarcastically.

She shrugged. "I wonder what happened to him in prison to earn the transfer. Inmates don't like child molesters." Her smile was from ear to ear.

"I assume you're bringing the picture of Zheng."

"You assume right."

"It might cause a leak that you know about Zheng, that you're looking for him."

"Exactly."

He used to like the way she enjoyed living dangerously. Now, it just made him crazy.

They'd taken Duncan's private plane. Nickie had to admit, it was damned convenient. She enjoyed threatening him with his life if he told anyone about it.

And he couldn't have simply chosen the most fuel-efficient sedan rental or at least a car that was big enough to be considered remotely safe. Instead, they drove to the prison in a silver BMW. Ostentatious was an understatement.

He knew enough to dress down for the occasion. Dressing down for Duncan was a cotton button-down shirt, sleeves rolled to three-quarter length, boots that might be considered work boots, and a pair of dark blue jeans.

Making it only as far as the first waiting room, he found a small table and opened his tablet. She sat next to him for a moment. He lifted his brows at her quizzically.

"You sure you're okay?" she asked.

"This isn't my first time as a visitor in a big house."

She remembered. "I don't know how long I'll be."

He didn't lift his eyes from his tablet this time as he responded. "I have work. Take your time." Most people would think it was rude or dismissive. She knew better. He didn't want her to be pressured or to think of anything except what lay ahead of her.

The prison employees were expecting her, but she still had to wait. She carried no lasting animosity toward her former captain. She was over it. She'd thought Tanner was an upstanding captain. He duped her. End of story. That's how she worked.

There were plenty of nerves, however, surrounding the purpose and possible outcome of her visit, good or bad. She checked her file for the tenth time. The 8 ½-by-11 photos that involved Jun Zheng were tucked neatly inside. In the pictures, he was mostly somber, blending in as an observer in the background. She remembered him differently.

Zheng was as sarcastic as he was sadistic. He didn't get angry. He enjoyed when girls fought, enjoyed when they cried.

"Detective?"

She stood and followed the prison employee escort through a second set of doors. Here, they had her stop in an office and hand over her gun, cuffs and phone, then did an over-the-clothes search. They checked through her file folder before handing it back to her. "Sorry about that, Detective. You're not in Kansas."

She shrugged. "Don't be sorry."

"He's been in isolation much of his time here. It's for his own good."

Yep, she thought. Inmates don't like pedophiles. It made her warm all over.

"We got you a room and a guard."

She was surprised, although she made certain not to show it. "That'll be helpful. Thanks."

The prison guard showed her to the room. She wasn't sure if the sight of her old captain would bring a reaction from her or not. It didn't. It took a lot to get a reaction out of her from anything.

He was thinner, much thinner, but she must have expected this because it didn't faze her either. He looked ten years older. She wondered why he hadn't offered a deal, why he didn't roll over on any of his accomplices but not enough to waste time asking him about it. Subsequently, his trial was fast, his incarceration faster and his transfer to one of the country's highest-security prisons faster yet.

She nodded a greeting to him as she sat.

The room was probably the size of his cell, small, five by nine. Brick walls, painted gray. Duncan wouldn't have much to memorize in here. Tanner sat at a metal table and chair. As she lowered to her seat, she noticed the legs of his were bolted to the floor. Tanner wore some kind of restraints that were a cross between a seat belt and a straightjacket. His hands were cuffed to a dip in the table. Northridge had to get one of these, she decided. The guard stood behind her.

She sat and leaned back in her chair, letting the feet in the front hover above the floor.

"What brings you to my humble home, Nick?"

No greeting. No small talk. Good. She slid the first print from the file folder and turned it to face him. It was an older photo of Tanner in Manhattan. He was a detective at that point. She'd never known he worked in Manhattan. Most cops didn't run background checks on their bosses. The picture was at a routine press conference. Zheng stood in the background like he thought he was Secret Service.

Tanner's eyes went from the photo to her. Was it because of Zheng? She could wait him out if necessary and rocked on the back legs of her chair again.

"Did you fly halfway across the country to ask me about a cut and dry closed case?"

"Just trying to piece together some loose ends." She

placed the next photo in front of him. He didn't look at it. She was losing him. He stared at her long and hard before dropping his glance. This one was of Tanner as he accepted accommodations for 'outstanding detective work' in the dismantling and arrest of over a dozen perps involved in a prostitution ring. She and Duncan had mused they were likely the competition. She didn't mention Zheng in the background for this print either.

He stared at her long and hard. She could practically see the suspicions running through the backs of his eyes. "What is this about, Nick?"

It made her cringe to hear him loosely use the nickname most everyone in the police force used with her.

He didn't stop there. "Are you piecing together cases that happened when you were...in high school?" The pause was slight, but she caught it. He knew. He knew about her past. How long had he known? Bastard.

The final print she slapped down on the table with force. Tanner wasn't in this one. It was one they had found of Thurmond Moody. Thurmond Moody and the captain of the Baltimore, Maryland, Police Department.

Moody had an arm up, clearly deflecting the questions from the mass of reporters gathered around them. Next to the Baltimore police captain stood two officers who were tagged as New York cops. The ones that had found her, fifteen, barefoot and dressed in yellow lingerie, pounding on the door of the residence they were investigating. And next to the officers was a teenage her. She was dressed in white jeans and a light blue winter coat. The final pair in the line was her parents. They stood and appeared as relieved as any parents who found a lost daughter. Nickie clung to the officer nearest to her, not to her parents.

Zheng was in the background dressed as a driver and stood near the back passenger side of a large black car. She'd looked at this photo before and never noticed him. His demented, sick, jovial aurora was absent. This was the only time she could remember seeing Zheng angry. Flustered and angry. It had become her favorite picture of him.

"You have no idea what you're dealing with," Tanner said, sounding suddenly tired.

"Which brings us to why we're here in your *humble home*," she said, using her fingers to make quotation marks in the air.

"It could be worse," he said.

"What are you talking about? Zheng isn't a drug cartel."

He visibly winced at the mention of the name.

She took the chance and kept rolling. "He isn't in a gang with ties inside the prison system. I, on the other hand, can get you isolation. Permanent isolation. Not the kind you earn because you've been used as a boy toy by other inmates due to the nasty little habits you had before you came here."

They sat there like that, at an impasse for what seemed like twenty minutes. It was probably only one or two. Sensing she was losing him, she tried a different tactic. "What about Moody? How high does he go? He's been in this, after all, for at least twenty years." She hoped she was right.

"Moody's a tool. A drunken tool."

She remembered Tanner's use of the term back when he was her boss. He meant it as an ignorant pawn whose only use was routine, mundane operations.

"New Year's Eve is a regular night for early teen prostitution. What others?"

She knew her former captain well enough to know he was considering her offer. She didn't have more to offer him.

"You know anyone who likes boxing?" he asked.

Nickie slept soundly, the rise and fall of her back slow and steady. Her long waves of honey wheat splayed across her back and pillow. The scars peeked between strands like haunting beacons, reminding Duncan of her past.

He knew of four people who were in some way responsible for them. Two of them sat behind bars. Zheng and Moody were the other two, and they consumed his thoughts.

He hadn't prodded her with the dozens of questions that filled his waking moments. Was Zheng the one who put the scars there? Or was he one of the ones? What about Moody? Who was the man she strangled when she escaped the white house?

He'd rigged the computer he used only for such an occasion to his separate feed of the three visual and one audio eavesdropping devices he planted at the white house. At least three times a day, he did a scan for movement or audio. Thus far, the drives around the house hadn't even been plowed. The only footprints around the place were from the dogs.

He worked on preliminary prints for a painted rendering of a movie poster starring actress Jessica Lambodos in the forefront and the rest shadowed in the background. It was more abstract than he was used to, but a good diversified challenge for his talents.

It wasn't like him to turn off the sights and sounds around him, but sure enough, there she stood. He hadn't seen or heard her. Her powder blue panties peeked just below the shirt he assumed she plucked from his nightstand. She must not have dreamed through the night, at least not anything harsh enough to make her wake swinging.

She was flushed, her eyes puffy from sleep. He wanted to pull her down in his lap, the painting be damned.

"It's still dark," she yawned.

"It's winter in New York."

"True. I'm going for a swim. Wanna join me?"

"Then we won't get in any swimming."

"True," she repeated and headed for the stairs.

"Nickie."

"Hmm?" She turned and leaned against the doorjamb.

He knew he should wait for a better time, and yet it came out anyhow. "How did you get moved from Child Protection Services in Maryland to a foster home in New York?"

Her eyes seemed to search the floor for an answer. Then, they darted to him as she reached and gripped the sides of his doorway. She hadn't thought of it. What had he done?

"Savage." Nickie answered her phone as she sat at her desk researching boxing tournaments within an hour radius of Moody's home. The feds said they had a lead around or during the January scheduled fight at Madison Square Garden. She worried they would bring the girls to the site of the match. It's what they most commonly did. But they didn't have bugs at Madison Square Garden or Broadway Boxing. The bugs they had were at the white house.

On the other end of the phone was the mother-in-law of a noncustodial parent who was suspected of taking his son and daughter out of town. The kids had been due back with their mother the night before. The woman thought she knew where the man was hiding.

Nickie listened carefully and took notes meticulously, but her mind was clouded.

They'd already issued an Amber Alert, covered all the bases there. "Thank you, ma'am. We'll check this out right away." She even broke her own rule and addressed the woman as, 'ma'am.'

She wasn't sure how she'd spent the last dozen years without ever questioning the logistics of moving foster homes from one state to another. She'd never really taken time to do any kind of search through historical files regarding the time around her disappearance. It was in the past. She didn't want to relive it. It belonged in the past.

Questioning her impossible foster home transfer from one state to another meant she should have suspicions about Gloria. How could she possibly have a single suspicion toward Gloria? It wasn't right. And it was a hunch. It was a hunch to think Gloria had something to hide, and it was a hunch to decide she didn't. That was why she hated hunches. What kind of judge was she about the sincerity of people? She could read perps. She could judge the antics of men and how they ticked. But this? She ran her hands over her face.

Pushing away from her wooden desk, she grabbed her notes and headed for her captain's office. Eddy lifted his gaze to her as she passed. She nodded toward him once in greeting. He looked back down at his desk. Still not talking to her.

She knocked and waited for Dave to acknowledge her.

He turned his eyes to the door and smiled. At least someone was happy to see her. "What can I do for you, Nick? Come in."

"Got a call on a possible whereabouts of the Amber Alert suspect. It's about a thirty-five minute drive.

You want me to go myself? I have the time. I can call the town captain and see if they have anyone available."

"Go check it out. Take Lynx."

Oh shit. "Are you sure? Should we leave the station without—?"

"I would say the same thing to him. You know the rules. Domestic disturbance. Two go."

"Yes, sir."

"Don't call me sir." He smiled.

It was hard to be mad at him when he was right.

"Come on, Lynx." She leaned her head in his office. "We have a call. Captain's orders."

"I'm driving." He grabbed his coat and keys without facing her. Men and their need to save face.

She stopped in her office and grabbed her tablet, the pictures of the kids, the dad, and the pic of Zheng she seemed to carry with her everywhere she went. Might as well get something done during their thirty-five minute sure-to-be-silent drive.

She found two boxing matches in the month of January; the one at Madison Square Gardens and one at Broadway Boxing. There were some other amateur matches at Friday Night Fights, but the girls she was searching for only did upper class. Literally.

She explained to Eddy where they were going and why. He still didn't talk. Men could be much worse than women when it came to grudges. And what was he mad about anyway? Because she decided to forgive Duncan? Of course, that was why he was angry.

Her phone buzzed on her hip. Checking the caller ID, she saw it was Gil.

CHAPTER 21

———— ♦ ♦ ♦ ————

Her hand didn't seem to want to move as her phone buzzed in her palm. Fear crept beneath her skin. Fear that she didn't have the family she thought she did.

"Nick?" Eddy nudged her.

Her eyes shot to his, then she answered the call. "Savage," she croaked and didn't know how to keep her voice neutral.

"Nickie, it's Gil. Did I catch you at a bad time?"

She looked around, her heart beating like mad. "No. What do you need?" That was too formal.

"The twins are sick. Teresa and I have that gig tonight at The Pub. Can you fill in? Please tell me you can fill in."

Her chest rose and fell. "I…"

"We didn't want to ask you to watch sick babies, but we need you, little sister."

Sister. "Okay." The words stuck in her throat. She cleared it. "Okay," she said louder.

"You are saving my life. And my marriage. Thank you. Be there at eight?"

"Eight," she repeated. "See you." And hung up on him.

"You okay?" Eddy finally spoke. When times were tough, he'd always been there for her. That said something. Pursing her lips together, she tried to grin and nod her head.

Gesturing to the exit, she spoke up. "This is us."

He took the ramp in the direction of a small town about a mile from the highway.

The address was to a trailer in a mobile home park. It didn't seem to be an average mobile home park. Trash was piled in the streets and broken, plastic toys littered nearly every overgrown yard.

"I should've worn my other boots," Eddy said.

He took lead and knocked on the tin door of one of the nicer trailers as she stood back, checking the perimeter. A woman covered in freckles answered with at least four sets of eyes standing behind her.

"Detectives Lynx and Savage, miss. We'd like to have a word with you."

The woman's expression didn't change.

Nickie noticed a man dart from behind one car surrounded by overgrown grasses to another.

"Perp," she said calmly to Eddy as she took off.

Knowing it could be anyone running from the police for any number of reasons, she was regardless itching for a chase. The dude must have heard her boots and took off from behind his rusted cover.

"Freeze! Police! No kids in sight." The last part was for Eddy.

The man was wiry and dirty, but it was their man. And he was quick. Pausing at the edge of the mobile homes, he looked left, then right, and then took off, giving her enough time to take a running dive at him.

The dude couldn't have expected she was going to take air for his sake. She didn't even expect it. Flying through the air, she made it to him. He was small and Hispanic, his black hair curling around his ears like

Gil's. She caught him by his coat, grabbing handfuls of it and letting the rest of her body fall as it may.

They went down like rhinos, sudden and hard. Wrenching his arms behind his back, she dug her knee in his spine and cuffed him. His children weren't foster kids and they weren't from another state, but her adrenaline was racing so hard she could scarcely tell the difference.

"Where are they?" she yelled as she flipped him on his back, taking his gun with her as he went. She stuffed the gun in the back of her belt and dipped close to his face. "You can answer with a jaw intact, mother fucker, or answer me through a broken one."

He glared at her and spit. She pulled back her fist.

"Whoa there, Detective. Let me help you with that." Eddy referred to the man as a *that*, and lifted her to her feet.

"You hear what she said to me?" the man roared.

"I heard her ask where the kids are."

She let Eddy take over and stomped back to the trailer. The front door was shut, and she pounded on it with the side of her fist. Cries erupted from inside, the cries of little children. Did they belong there?

The freckled woman's blank expression hadn't changed when she cracked the door.

"You wanna keep your kids? Aiding and abetting an abduction is not going to do that for you. I suggest you tell me where I can find his." Nickie thumbed a finger over her shoulder to Eddy as he dragged the man toward his unmarked.

The woman opened the door and stepped aside. The little girl and boy from the photos ran to her, each grabbing one of her legs. They trusted the woman with the badge. Who had Nickie trusted to take her across two state lines and into Gloria's home?

* * *

Nickie sat on the small triangle of a stage in the corner of The Pub. Her acoustic sat comfortably on her thigh, the microphone like a finger pointing, directing all eyes to her. The music would tune them out. It was the one thing, the only thing, she appreciated from her parents. They started her onto string instruments at a young age. She gravitated toward the cello. They didn't argue. The cello was deep, tall, possessive. It didn't need to be the center of attention and instead served as backup to the little guy.

All one, big pile of symbols.

Her traverse to the acoustic guitar was one of the dozens of avenues she used as release. It was probably more of a rebellion against her parents' expectations. But it wasn't rebellion she was feeling this night. It was mass confusion.

The bar was the same, comfortable. The crowd was large since it was a Friday night, filled from wall to wall with mostly twenty-five to thirty-somethings. People younger and older dotted tables along the sides. The cool breeze that blew each time the door opened was a relief even with the smell of tobacco that followed.

It was the people she was with who confused her. Gil sat behind her, thrumming his brushes on his cymbals as she strummed her guitar and sang about better days. It wasn't her first time filling in for Gil's wife. She'd filled in for weeks at the end of both of her pregnancies. Tonight shouldn't be a thing, but it was.

Duncan had arrived. His eyes told her what she must look like. He was worried. Her family...Gloria's family didn't often come if Teresa wasn't singing. She never thought anything of it before. Now, she wondered if she should.

She felt like a caged animal, disoriented and trapped. She wanted to run out the door. Gil laid a hand on her shoulder between songs, something he always did. Except this time, it made her stiffen.

"Thank you," she said into the microphone. "We're going to take a short break." She glanced to find Gil with his mouth open, staring at her in pissed off wonder. They weren't due for a break for ten more minutes. Ten-minute break? Twenty-minute break? What was the big deal?

Setting the system to prerecorded, she headed for the bar. "Diet Coke. Lots of ice."

Duncan came behind her and brushed aside the sweaty strands of hair that stuck to her neck. She hadn't realized she was sweating.

"Nickie—"

"Don't. It's one more set. I'll be fine."

"I was going to ask if you drove."

"Oh." She shook her head and her forehead tightened. "Don't think I don't see how you're looking at me. I'm fine."

"You mentioned that."

"Gil picked me up. You can take me home." She looked just in time to see his chin jutted back and his brows lifted high.

"Please," she added as a sarcastic afterthought.

He straightened and looked down at her. She knew she was being a bitch and couldn't find it in her to care. Her four-inch heels put them right about nose to nose. She took her soda and stood in front of him, her chest expanded like a friggin' silverback gorilla. She set down her untouched drink and stormed out the door. Air.

Barreling through the group of smokers, she let her chest heave and sucked in the cold, welcoming the burn. How did she not think of it? She remembered a random woman who picked her up from her last foster home. She remembered struggling to keep her eyes open in the four-door sedan. And then waking, freezing cold, in the woman's car. They were in the driveway of Gloria's square, ranch home.

"Hey, babe. Nice pipes." The male voice was close to her, and she realized it was much too close.

She wanted to kick herself. She never let her guard down to her surroundings and whirled on him. Fist cocked, she stepped forward only to have Duncan step between them.

His back was to her as he addressed Mr. Babe. "We're together," Duncan said calmly enough that it pissed her off more.

"Sorry, man." The guy held up his hands, palms out.

"You don't have to finish the set, Nickie."

"Did you talk to Gil?" She was mortified. "This is my gig. I'm getting paid. And if you say one damned thing about covering my check…"

He had the nerve to hold her arms down at her sides. Blood boiled in her veins.

"Gil came to me at the bar. He cares about you, as do I."

She strained against his arms, but he didn't let go. "But you're not taking a swing at me or anyone else," he added.

She forced her body to relax. He waited an annoyingly long stretch of time before he trusted her enough to let go. Then, she stormed back into the bar and picked up her guitar. The owner generally liked them to slow down the last set before closing time, bar closing time that is. But her fingers wouldn't have it tonight. She didn't glance back at Gil and knew he would follow her lead. They played about jungles, the city and not backing down. The crowd shook the floor with their last chance at foreplay before leaving for the night.

The pain and worry in Gil's face was more than she could handle. She'd been an idiot. It didn't matter that she had been fifteen. She should have known better. No one moves foster homes to a new state. It was one more thing she had shoved into her subconscious, like her memories of the white house. And look at all the good that did her.

"I'll get the cleanup, Nickie. Go home."

Gil's words stung. They always did that together. "Fine." She put her guitar in her case, slammed the latches in place and turned to find Duncan. He had his back to her, drinking what she was sure was ice water. She could see his face in the tinted wall of glass behind the bar. His expression wasn't pain or worry. It was angry.

Duncan drove her to his house. Without even asking. "Maybe I don't want to stay here tonight." It was a lie.

"Too bad." His eyes didn't move.

She forced her arms not to cross. "I don't have my bag." Arms crossed or not, she sounded like a child.

He pulled the car in the garage slowly and carefully. She swore he meant it as overt sarcasm. Like always, he walked around to get her door, but she was determined to do it herself.

He blocked her way to the house. With eyes half closed, he lectured her like she was a child having a tantrum. "Whether you like it or not, you have a drawer filled with the clothes you've left on my floor. And you know what? I'm going to hang them up. With hangers. In my closet. Gloria loves you, her family loves you and you're going to have closet space that belongs to you in my home."

She let her instincts take over and swung at him,

even if she didn't have the nerve to close her fist. He must have been ready for it, because she was damned quick and he caught her wrist as if he was catching a baseball. His eyes were fire. She was going to slap him. She'd never slapped anyone in her life. Punch, yes, but slap? She barreled forward, forcing him to stumble on the few steps that led up to his service entry. With her free hand, she pushed him against the door and covered his mouth with hers.

Against his wishes, Duncan went instantly rock hard. He didn't know what all was going on in that head of hers, but he was done kidding around it. He'd intended to make her talk, to make her sit down and talk. Somewhere in his head, he remembered that plan, but other parts of his body had taken over.

She tortured him with the way she squirmed against him, leaving him sandwiched between her female body and a cold door. Her lips were more than angry, more than demanding, they needed. And she took.

Reaching behind, he turned the knob and let them tumble through to the floor. He broke her fall as clothes were yanked free and buttons skidded across the carpet.

She had damned strong arms for a woman and used her strength to pin his shoulders to the rug that covered the hardwood floor. Her lips attacked his with a vengeance, her tongue a challenge.

Taking her torn blouse, he slid it over her shoulders, trapping her arms as he flipped her over and beneath him. The sounds she made were like an animal. Her back arched madly, and he leaned low, taking her into his mouth, nipping one side, then the other and pulling with his teeth. She screamed with what sounded like part frustration, part pleasure.

Twining the single boot she still wore around his calf, she twisted until he was forced to release her or end up with a broken leg. She straddled his chest with one leg in her jeans and her blouse hanging from an arm. Reaching behind her, she grabbed him, forcing out his own set of frustrated growls. His fingers dug into her hips as she moved, somewhere in his head, he knew he would leave marks. Before she caused him to fly over to a place he wasn't coming back from, he sat up, making her slide off his chest, landing heat to nothing but heat.

She blinked rapidly, and he took the moment of surprise to dig his fingers into the warmth.

CHAPTER 22

———— ➤ ◆ ◆ ◀ ————

Somewhere in her head, Nickie knew her body shook with desperation of many forms. But for now, there was this. There was him. His fingers assaulted her inside and out. In her drunken lust, she sensed his other hand lacing through her hair and pulling her head back, so he could reach her jaw, her neck, her collarbone. Teeth grazed over her.

The crest was brutal, shaking her from head to toe. The hand that fisted her hair went from demanding to stabilizing as her body shuddered and released. His arms were the one place she felt safe. She let herself go, body, voice and heart. The exhaustion that followed left her completely limp.

"Oh, no you don't."

He guided her to the rug more carefully than she would have liked and began moving his lips and hands in ways she wasn't equipped to stop. She climbed a mountain so fragile she would surely break. The peak threatened her. She was too weak to do a damned thing about it.

He gave and gave. Enough for both of them. Her arms and legs were weights holding her to the rug. He took her over, her eyes rolled and noticed him watching her with a heart-breaking intensity. The convulsions rocked her, and she thrashed with the weight of him keeping her grounded, keeping her protected.

Her fingers inched their way around the muscles in his sides and held on. Opening to him, he poured himself over her and into her, pausing for a mind-blowing moment when completely joined. She cried out in need as lines of tears dripped down the sides of her face. Digging her nails in his sides, she pulled him to her, moving with him in perfect sync.

"I love you. I need you," she choked as they moved faster. He was close but in control. She forced her eyes to focus deep into his chocolate brown. Flecks of gold flashed in his irises as Nickie and he moved and pulled, grabbed and arched. They went over together, sweat sliding their bodies against each other. Neither could stop and worked every ounce of the last push.

Somewhere she heard her heels thump against the wood floor and sensed her arms dropping to her sides. He was heavy and warm, and she didn't want to move from this spot for days. He lifted on an elbow, causing her to open an eye in one last pitiful attempt to seem intimidating—as if she could ever intimidate Duncan Reed.

With one boot still on her leg and Duncan's shirt still over his shoulders, he slowly and gently brushed the hair from where it stuck on her forehead and cheeks, slyly wiping away her tears.

"My eyes were watering."

He kissed her temple where he had dried her face and whispered, "Of course they were," before turning her head to kiss the other side. "You're all I want. You have every piece of me."

More water escaped, and a flood of guilt poured

from each surface. "I'm so sorry—"

He placed his fingers on her lips. "Shh. I know you are."

Nickie slept next to him without moving, tucked into him as she rarely did. No dreams shook her or caused the whimpers that made him realize how helpless and useless he could be. He'd woken a dozen times throughout the night, checking on her, ensuring she was still there and was still his.

Deep sleep must have eventually found him, because for the first time he could remember, he woke to find her sitting on the wooden stool in his painting studio, writing on a piece of chart paper he used for practice and samples. The moon still shone through the skylights with a haze of cloud cover making it a soft light.

With brows tucked closely together, she wrote feverishly and didn't move when he rose. He slipped on a pair of workout pants and headed to the bathroom. As he passed his closet door, he noticed his shirts had been pushed together.

He leaned in and his heart skipped a beat. The clothes she had worn the night before hung in the space between the wall and his shirts. He brushed his teeth and set the coffeemaker before making his way to her. Careful to walk around the back side of his easel, he lowered himself onto the settee near his stool.

"Good morning," she said as she drew, crossed out and wrote. She wore one of his shirts and a pair of purple panties he remembered putting in her drawer.

"Good morning." He leaned over and kissed her once on the lips. She tasted like mint and Diet Coke.

She turned the easel so he could see. The fact that she was ready to share this made him nearly as happy as the closet space.

It was the same sheet he had used to list the names of the five men who were involved in her past: Jun Zheng, ex-Police Captain William Tanner, ex-Fire Chief Brian McKinney, James 'Slippery Jimbo' Spalding and Thurmond Moody.

Beneath, she had written a chronological list of events. "I'm done ignoring, done suppressing. I'm writing what I remember, making notes of what I don't. Some of this I don't remember in my head, but I remember NYPD discussing it."

Her timeline started with the day she was abducted from her home. Although he could see fine from where he sat, he leaned in to get a closer look. It was in the night. Everyone had been asleep in her home, including the help. She was in a second-story bedroom. Her window had been closed. The man took her at gunpoint.

Duncan didn't know any of this before now.

She wrote the name Jun Zheng next to Thurmond Moody. Moody's had a question mark next to it.

Next were the words "Page 2." He yearned to turn the page, but refrained.

The accounts she remembered from the night of her escape were next; the food for the dogs she kept in the pocket of her housecoat, the necktie, the man, fumbling in the cold, climbing the fence and running until she stumbled across the domestic disturbance police investigation.

She wrote about the scene from the picture with Thurmond Moody and Jun Zheng, as he handed her over to her parents and reporters took dozens of pictures outside the police station in Baltimore. She stayed with her parents for a total of eight weeks before the three of them agreed she would be better served as a ward of the state and placed in foster care.

Who does that to their child?

The next line read, 'Page 3.' He assumed it listed the foster homes she remembered, which made him assume page two contained a list of places the men who kidnapped her made her work.

The pain in her eyes from the night before was still fresh in his memory, and he second-guessed whether he was ready to see either list.

Next was the woman who came and removed her from her second-to-final foster home. Nickie had written that she assumed she'd been drugged, then woke in the cold car of the woman she thought was from Child Services.

She listed her eighteenth birthday when she had applied to change her name to Nickie Savage. Her time in the academy, the date of her promotion to Detective and of her lateral transfer to Northridge two years ago.

Following was reference to the photo of Tanner as a detective at a routine press conference. Zheng stood behind him like he was Secret Service.

The next was of Tanner accepting commendations for the arrest of the dozen or so perps involved in the prostitution ring he and Nickie assumed was their competition.

As he read, she added her bust at the Seneca, New York, casino, where a young girl was found dead and handcuffed to a bed in a back room. A second girl had been discovered that night hiding in a janitor's closet and gave up the location of where they were taking the rest of the girls. Las Vegas, Nevada.

She jotted down that he saw Zheng there. A sharp pang of guilt raced through him as he thought of how long he took before he shared that information with her.

She wrote that Slippery Jimbo spotted Zheng in

Northridge, that Zheng had been asking about her, that he was probably the driver in the crash that took down Tanner and McKinney and that Zheng was involved with Thurmond Moody.

Finally, she spoke. "For years, I suppressed my memories as a way to move forward."

He contemplated that statement for a few minutes while she wrote about how Moody was involved to this day and how they now waited for the feds to call, saying they had a bite from the bugs Duncan had placed around the white house. "Some would say suppressed memories are a protection from events too harsh to remember."

"Those people don't have knowledge that could help rescue young girls from captivity and forced prostitution." She crossed her legs on his stool, making him wonder how she could do that on such a small space. "I'm going to talk to Gloria."

She must have sensed he was going to protest, because she held up a hand. "I believe in her, in them, but I need to know what they know. They never took another foster child after me. Why? Who contacted them to say I was coming? Do they remember a name? A face?"

Taking his hands, her gaze lifted to his. "Mostly, I want to find the missing file from my disappearance. I don't want to shove any more of this away. I need to know. I'm ready to know and want you to…do what you do to find it."

Nickie sat in the perfectly shoveled drive of Gloria's home. It was mid-morning, which meant the regular myriad of parked cars in the drive and along the curb was absent. The snow was at least eighteen inches deep with drifts over three feet. She couldn't remember a time when Gloria's drive and walks weren't manicured to perfection. The multitude of loved ones who helped her seemed endless.

And yet, here Nickie sat, and for some reason, she couldn't convince herself to open her car door. What if? It was a question she didn't want to consider. Gloria was the only true family she'd ever had. But it wasn't possible that a licensed foster parent wouldn't know a child from across state lines was placed in her care. Nickie ran her hands over the top of her hair.

The front door was open, as it generally was. The glass had been pulled up over the screen on the storm door months before when the chill in the fall air hit. The glass was steamed, maybe frosted. She couldn't quite tell from her car. Turning her eyes down, she considered the file she held in her hand.

Noticing movement, she turned her gaze to the front of the house. Gloria stood with the door opened wide. Nickie clicked the ignition far enough to roll down the passenger window.

"How long are you going to stay out there?"

It made Nickie smile. Rolling up the window, she took a deep breath and got out.

She found Gloria in the kitchen, making coffee and tea, one for each of them.

She slithered into one of the mismatched chairs she'd learned to love. The table in the middle of the kitchen was small and made their proximity uncomfortably close. She noticed Gloria's eyes land on the file as she lowered to her chair. She didn't inquire, but instead cupped Nickie's cheek with her warm, plump hand, causing Nickie's eyelids to close unintentionally.

"Tell me about the day I came here." She hadn't even said, 'hello.'

Gloria didn't flinch, not even a blink as she released Nickie's cheek. A small smile curled at her lips, and she dipped her head to the side. The ancient teapot on her stove sang. Rising from her chair, Gloria pulled down two mugs that were as mismatched as the chairs.

"I started as a foster parent when my husband died, rest his soul." Her back was toward Nickie. She had no face to read. "I needed the money, but mostly needed to feel needed." She mixed a spoonful of instant coffee in one mug and dunked a tea bag in the other. Carrying them to the table, Nickie watched as she took a deep breath.

"I always wondered when you would come to me with this. It was silly of me, really. To become a foster parent. I had my own children to care for, then their children. It wasn't long until I was overwhelmed and had Child Services place me on its emergency-only list."

Nickie hadn't realized there was such a thing and assumed she was at the top of that list a number of times in the Maryland system.

"I took in a child or siblings once or twice a year, usually for a day or a few days." The memories seemed to make her shake her head. "It was very sad. Then, a man came to visit me. I'd always had a phone call before, but this man had...what do you call it?"

"Credentials?"

"Yes, that is it. I let him in."

The hairs on the back of Nickie's neck woke and prickled.

"We had a short talk, me and this man. He emphasized the need but didn't share the emergency. The next day, a woman brought you to me. You were a dirty, skinny white girl. You slept in her car for over an hour in my drive. The woman said your emergency had kept you up through the night and that we should let you rest."

Gloria took a drink, and her eyes told Nickie she wasn't here, but back in time over a decade ago.

"You were such an angry child, pushing me, threatening to leave and oh, the language." She covered Nickie's hand with hers. It was warmer yet from her mug of coffee.

"But your eyes were tortured, tortured and wanting. You wanted to live here. You just had no idea how to do it. I have enough of my own children to know patience, and so patience is what I offered. One day you came to me. Do you remember that day?"

She did.

"You stepped next to me at the sink and said you were sorry. Not for anything in particular, but you apologized. Then—"

"I picked up a damp dish towel and starting drying dishes. We never spoke of it again."

"There was nothing more to say." She took a sip and her brows furled. "You never spoke of your home in Maryland or anywhere. Mr. Li called—"

"Mr. Li?" Sweat formed instantly, misting her upper lip. She gripped the untouched mug of tea and let the heat burn her hands.

"The man who came to me. He called once a week at first, explaining there was no other placement and asking if I would keep you a while longer. Then, the calls changed to once a month, and by that time, I knew. I knew I would keep you, wanted to keep you, as long as they would let me. The last six months of your stay, I received no phone calls."

Painfully, Nickie lifted the corner of the file folder, bypassing the picture of Thurmond Moody and William Tanner as she had planned and slid out her best close up of Jun Zheng.

Gloria sighed heavily, the corners of her mouth turned down. "That is him."

Nickie's mind spun with dozens of realizations and connections. It terrified her and angered her. For him to have come here. To bring Gloria and her family into this...

Zheng was going to pay.

"I knew this day would come," Gloria said again before she calmly took a sip. "I expected it before now."

"I don't understand."

"It was shortly after your eighteenth birthday. You were in college. You started talking about Maryland...never New York. I thought that maybe your birth family had moved to New York. I never pried into the lives of any of the children I served, asking them about their past. This was to be a refuge. But I had my suspicions. Then, one day I called and discovered there was no Jimmy Li who ever worked at child services. That was the day I signed up for shooting lessons."

Nickie nearly choked on nothing. "Gun shooting lessons?"

"Of course. What other kind is there?"

"Do you own a gun?"

"Two guns. One I keep in the cabinet over the sink next to my cookbooks and one I keep locked in the nightstand next to my bed."

Nickie took a sip of the tea. She hated tea but she had to do something with her hands. "I know who this man is, Gloria."

"I thought you brought me his picture for a reason."

"He's a bad man."

"I thought that too. He hid you in my home."

"I have something I need to tell you, something I haven't told anyone before. Except Duncan."

Gloria turned her chair to face her, and placed both her hands on Nickie's cheeks. "It's time, my Nickie. I always knew."

"How—?"

"The dreams. The horrible dreams that made you cry and thrash. I never woke you. Your mind would bring you to this when you were ready. You don't have to tell me if you—"

"I want to."

Gloria's warm smile soothed her. She told her of her abduction, her time in captivity, her escape and waking in the cold car as it sat on Gloria's drive. Nickie left out nearly every violent detail, but the tears still flowed freely down Gloria's face. "This is the man, Gloria. This is the man who kept me. I don't remember if he was the one who took me, but he is the one responsible for my scars. That, I haven't told Duncan."

Nickie's eyes were watering again as she pulled away from Gloria's drive and headed for the station. Damned cold weather. A new sense of determination followed the foreign stir of the need to protect someone she loved.

The drive was short, but it gave her enough time to sort through this new sensation. For most of her life, she had a need to protect strangers—the girls with her in captivity, victims of the crimes she investigated—but this was family and the rage was blinding.

She parked in her spot in the gravel lot she preferred and took the stairs, welcoming the endorphins produced from the climb. Nodding greetings to the desk clerks in the common area, she stopped when she reached her office. Without turning on the light, she hung up her coat and headed for Eddy's office.

He was there, beating furiously on his keyboard. Lifting his eyes, he froze expectantly when she stood without speaking. Right, right, right. She hadn't come to his office in weeks without barking that the captain needed to see them, or about a lead she had or a question, but he didn't need to make a thing about it.

"You coming in?"

"Sure." She plopped down in his chair and looked around. It was the first time she'd ever really done so. What a big place compared to her office. She'd been offered this space when Tanner went to prison. She turned it down. His chairs were even better, newer and with cushions.

She turned up her eyes to see him leaning back in his chair, staring.

"So, what are you working on?"

"What am I working on." He said it as a statement.

"Yeah. I hear beat patrol had a call about a shooting. Could be we're outta here soon."

He seemed to warm to the idea of her making a random visit and folded his hands over his lap. What he didn't know was that she was simply avoiding her laptop.

"Is this your way of saying you're sorry?"

For what? No. "It could be my way of saying let's let bygones be bygones and get on with working together. We're a good team."

He smiled. "True."

She stood as he squinted his eyes. "I'm going to hit the paperwork. Let me know if you get that call."

She was acting like an idiot. Stomping to her office, she flicked on her light. She considered picking up the place. It was a disaster, then realized that was lame. Reminding herself of her new determination, she plopped down in her desk chair and booted up her laptop. Ignoring her shaking hands, she entered two words into her search engine she had never entered before, 'Nicole Monticello.'

CHAPTER 23

There were two pages of hits during Nickie's missing year and a half. Most missing children had dozens. The earliest links were to English riding competitions and recitals where she was forced to perform. The period after her abduction provided a handful of reports from the media. Prominent Monticello Daughter Missing. She found a single picture of her parents at a press conference. The attached article read how they pleaded for her return. Then, nothing. Nothing for eighteen months.

She found reports of her father's business deals that mentioned the names of his family, ones of his fundraiser gatherings but nothing about her. It wasn't upsetting, and she questioned whether it should be.

The day she was found earned a few hits. There was the picture of her clinging to the police officer standing next to her, her parents on her other side. She hadn't noticed Zheng standing by the car at the time and somehow realized it was useless to kick herself about that now.

It brought back the memories of her few short months at her parents' home after her return. She had always considered their actions as embarrassed, but it was more than that. Turning away from the image on her monitor, she stared at nothing and realized their actions were those of frustration and anger. It made sense, she shrugged. A Maryland Monticello wouldn't want a daughter who had done what she did to survive.

And there it was.

A press release announced a runaway. Nicole Monticello. Except it wasn't from when she was fourteen and taken from her bedroom. It was when she was sixteen and had already been through several foster homes. Suspected runaway, it read. She must not have earned milk-carton status. It was right before she landed on Gloria's doorstep.

Zheng had been keeping tabs on her all this time.

"The Audi would have gotten better gas mileage," Duncan whined as he rode shotgun in his brother's Jeep.

"I doubt that," Andy responded. "Although our chances of staying out of a ditch have increased exponentially."

It was cold inside no matter how high they cranked the heater. The Jeep bumped down the highway enough to keep Duncan from checking his appointments on his tablet. Andy always insisted on traveling out of town when they did their more intensive hacking. Today it was an upscale coffee shop in Rochester. And the hacking would be one of their most difficult.

They'd hacked into school systems, police departments, overseas bank accounts, the damned FBI and even the government of Nicaragua. The recent hype surrounding the U.S. hacking into its citizens' personal information should make Duncan wary of what they were about to do. *Should* was the operative word.

He knew better than to allow himself to become overly confident, but the facts were that between his eidetic memory and Andy's talent for constructing safe pathways, they had a full-proof system. Still, Andy insisted on jumping around from free Wi-Fi spots in addition to chasing an electronic trail through several states before they got started.

They pulled into a spot beneath a wrought iron lamppost. The place was in an upscale strip mall, the walks shellacked aggregate stone. Back-to-back security cameras stood at the corners of the buildings on the outside, but inside the coffee shop there were none.

The place must have been shooting for cozy because half was lit with natural sunlight from floor-to-ceiling glass walls, and the other dimly lit booths and cushioned seats at small tables. Hazy lights hung low over hardwood tables. They chose one that was away from the front windows and booted up both their laptops and tablets. It was Nickie's lost file they were searching for today.

Although Duncan would tap into his constant feed linked to the bugs at Moody's white house, he had done a shallow search for the missing file already. It had been part of the official Baltimore, Maryland, police report. The details regarding Nickie's missing persons report were there, the parts about the pitiful search, her parents admitting they thought she had run away and all the information regarding her return. The piece missing was the forefront of the reports, the part that would come chronologically before the rest.

Duncan assumed what was missing. There was nothing to be found regarding the crime scene of the night Nickie was abducted. But he could see it, an empty space like a bottle of shampoo that had been taken from a perfect row displayed on a drugstore shelf. Something had been deleted.

But everyone knew nothing was ever permanently deleted. It would be difficult to find something this old. The rush of such a challenge generally excited him. This was different. It wasn't an excitement but more of a determination. Nickie had given him the green light to find it, and he was obsessively determined to do exactly that.

They went at it from every angle. Department historical files, the personal system of every police officer involved. He was going to owe his brother big for this. Andy had his business to run. He elbowed Duncan soundly in the ribs.

"I think I have a name. A name or a business. Look." Duncan craned his neck, checking out what Andy referred to. He tried to remain cautious, not up for another letdown. Andy found copies of old microfiche files. The one they were searching for was still missing, but the copies of the subsequent entries were all labeled with the name L. Schuster.

They turned their search to anyone with that name in a sixty-mile radius of Baltimore. There was only one L. Schuster in the area. He turned out to be a Larry Schuster who had worked as a second grade teacher for the local public school system for the last twenty-five years. They moved their search to fifteen years prior.

That brought up a Leslie Schuster, who, at that time, worked for a company called IEM Import and Export Moving Services. She'd changed her name back to her maiden name of Jacobsen five years ago and still lived in Baltimore, working for the company.

IEM. Why did that ring a bell?

His heart rate took a jump as he and Andy turned to

each other. Both had caught the possibility. They hacked both her personal and work addresses and phone numbers, then did a thorough background check.

Single, lived alone in a highly upscale apartment condo. Work title was executive assistant, latest term for secretary. They hacked into her credit cards and found she liked to travel. Maui, Alaskan cruise, three weeks in Ireland. Plane tickets said she was leaving in four days for a two-week trip to San Juan.

"I won't ask you to come with me," Duncan whispered.

Andy seemed irritated. "I want to. I feel invested."

"I thought you would. You've done enough, though. See if Rose and the baby are up for dinner at my place. I'd like to repay you for your time."

"I'll take you up on the dinner invite, but you've taken your share of time with me, brother. No need for paybacks. We don't work that way."

Duncan stood with his feet apart, left arm outstretched. He focused down the sight of his Beretta and gently squeezed the trigger with his right forefinger once, twice, three times. The headphones helped, but his mind itched to take him back to the desert. Back to a time when he never knew if the sound of gunfire would be the last thing he heard.

He was an excellent shot. If not, he would be dead by now. Explosives experts were put on the front line. He'd signed up for service after college, which was backward to everyone else in his platoon. He did it because he had needed to do something with this memory he was given, something more than paint pictures for people who didn't need them.

Nickie stood next to him, shooting rounds from her Smith & Wesson. Shooting off one after another, she emptied her magazine, dropped it to the floor, reloaded and shot three more bullets in seconds. Semiautomatic carried a negative connotation. Nearly ninety percent of guns were semiautomatic, but that term didn't mean rapid fire. That is, unless you had a fast enough trigger finger.

She stopped and turned, the corners of her lips lifting when she caught his glance. Pulling off her hearing protection, she strolled to him where he took a break and leaned against the back wall of the shooting range.

They were the only ones there at this time of the afternoon. Business would pick up toward the evening hours.

She moved her eyes from her target to his before she commented, "Nice shooting, civilian."

He didn't leave his position against the wall, arms crossed with one ankle resting over the other. Tilting his head, he judged the two targets. They weren't bull's-eyes this time but silhouettes of people. Her aim was markedly better than his. Shrugging, he pushed from the wall and reloaded but didn't replace his headphones.

"I have a lead." She would know what he meant. He knew he needed to tell her. He'd learned that lesson well enough. But he did his best to brush it by her casually. Still, he sensed her tensing and waiting impatiently for him to continue.

"It may be a wash, but I'm flying out to Baltimore in the morning to look up a person whose name may or may not be attached to your missing file."

"No file, though?" She didn't sound hopeful.

He shook his head as he checked the safety on his gun. "I didn't just come for shooting practice. I came to invite you to come with me." He lifted a brow and cocked his head.

"I didn't think you were here by coincidence, and I can't make it. I have a meeting with the feds. They want to know about my little one-on-one with Tanner. After all, they were the ones who granted his isolation. I discovered two boxing matches this month that may likely have an *entertainment* schedule."

He turned to face her fully, leaning a hip against the low wall separating them from the shooting area. "Tell me."

She slid her gun into her holster. "One next weekend at Madison Square Garden, and the next at Broadway Boxing. The feds mentioned Madison Square before, but I can't imagine taking the girls there when Moody's place is so close. I need to tell them this, make sure they let me in."

She meant only her. He wouldn't be allowed to take any part this time. Why hadn't he realized that before? Keeping his face relaxed would have been a lot easier if he'd had some warning.

"Moody has cameras in each room. I didn't tell you before."

There was a lot she had yet to share with him, he knew.

"I think he records the johns, probably for blackmail. Or possibly as insurance. Who knows? And maybe he doesn't anymore. Fifteen years is a long time." She wandered off subject, staring blankly over his shoulder. He didn't want to consider where her mind was going. "Regardless, that fact alone is enough to lean toward him bringing them to his white house."

"Will you share this with Strong and Lewis?"

"The cameras? No. I know they know of my past, but I'm not ready to have the show and share that I was in that house."

He slipped his gun into the back of his belt and

stepped to her. "So, tomorrow is booked, next weekend is booked, as is the next. How about dinner with my brother and Rose at my place this weekend?" He traced the backs of his fingers along the side of her face.

"Dinner? I don't cook. I grill. I can grill."

"This is the turn of the twenty-first century. I invited them. I can cook. Grill, actually."

"I'll bring a dish to pass. Domestic me."

Duncan and Andy took a cab from the Baltimore airport. How was it that an hour flight south took away two feet of snow? The ground was bone dry. Traffic was heavy as they crawled between buildings that rose higher and higher. It wasn't L.A., but it served as a sinking reminder he had a short trip there the following week.

The IEM building towered above its awning, complete with a section of no parking in front. Duncan thanked the cabbie by name, tipped him and he and his brother stepped out. A valet stood to the side and a doorman to the front of them. Somehow, Duncan realized they were staring, silently questioning the awestruck stance of both him and Andy.

The awe was not from the size of the building or the pricey décor. In deeply etched glass read the name of the business, but it didn't only read IEM, Import and Export Moving Services. Beneath, it read Ivanna and Edward Monticello.

CHAPTER 24

⎯⎯⎯ ◆ ◆ ◆ ⎯⎯⎯

They were in *her* station in *her* office. Those facts alone made Nickie feel better. The pissing contest with the feds was getting old, but she needed them and she guessed they needed her.

She imagined their closets with rows of suit jackets and boring ties and wondered if they wore them during takedown operations. She wanted to address them as Mr. and Mrs. Man in Black but thought that might strain relations. "Can I get you some coffee, water?"

Strong shook his head.

Right to it, then. It seemed too much rode on this conversation. She had nothing she could bring to them except hunches and gut feelings. Damn and shit.

"As you know, I met with the former captain of police during his stay at the United States Penitentiary in Terre Haute, Indiana."

No nod. No sign they were going to acknowledge her start of the conversation.

She wondered if this was somehow connected to the source of their tip about the Madison Square Garden fight. "What I got out of him supports your boxing match theory. However, I must say it doesn't seem feasible to have this elaborate white house for paid and forced prostitution—"

"Alleged paid and forced prostitution, Detective. We still have only your word on this."

She wasn't willing to trust these guys enough to tell them she had been in the house or about her knowledge of the possible surveillance cameras. She also couldn't tell them she knew they dug up her past. "But isn't that why you involved me in the first place? Look, there is the match next weekend at Madison Square Garden," she said like she didn't know they knew. "And another the following week at Broadway Boxing. It's possible Moody might arrange for the girls the night before, but men are going to want...sex after they've beat their chests at a boxing match. I think he'll bring them back to his place."

"Or he'll arrange to service the men on-site like he did at both the Seneca Casino and the one in Vegas. We have this under control."

Panic settled in her spine. "You're shutting me out."

"This isn't your jurisdiction, Detective." A spray of spit erupted from Strong's mouth as he said the last word. The finality of his statement was a swift slap in the face.

"I was lead detective seven months ago when the dead girl was found in a back room at our local casino. I was the one who found the additional girl, hiding in the janitor's closet, and I was the one who got out of her where they were taking the girls." She would leave out the part about Duncan's role in it. "You can't shut me out, Strong." She sounded like a whimpering adolescent. It sickened her.

"I found these guys in Vegas. Me." And Duncan. "I know their habits." She nearly jumped from her chair. "With three measly beat cops from Vegas Metro, we were able to save four girls and arrest three thugs and six johns. Lewis—" She tried for the softer of the two. "—you need me."

Strong answered for him. "Do you want us to have a truck full of SWAT doing a stakeout in front of Moody's place each time a big event is anywhere within an hour radius of his place? We feel you're not looking at this objectively, Detective. Unless you have any new information for us, we'll see ourselves out."

They left her sitting there, humiliated and deserted. She gave herself a full ten minutes before she peeled her numb fingers from where they clutched the sides of her chair. Opening and closing her hands, she loosened them and turned to her desktop computer. She used her preferred search engine to find agencies within the states that worked to fight child sex trafficking.

She found nonprofits such as Child Rescue and Slavery No More and even read about the FBI's Innocence Lost National Initiative, which it started in 2003. Rarely did she bother with the comments left beneath online news articles, but there was one on top that caught her eye, directly below where she was reading.

The article was about Child Rescue. The founder was the last in generations of women forced to sell their bodies, often as early as the age of twelve. The founder broke the cycle, severing ties with her relatives to keep her daughter protected from the life.

The comment made mention that some women use their sexuality to land a guy. That's right, asshole. Twelve-year-old girls like to use their sexuality to land a fifty-year-old man.

She pushed away from her desk, letting the feet of her chair scrape against the linoleum tiles. She hadn't felt this helpless since she was forced from foster home to foster home at the age of sixteen.

Connections rang in Duncan's head. Nickie's parents had something to do with her missing file. Were they truly so embarrassed from what she was forced to do? Remember their introductions at his art show, it didn't seem like such a stretch.

Duncan had a good father, followed by an uncle who served as a good father figure. His biological dad was loving and attentive. He wished he could pick up the phone and tell him he remembered how he used to play Candyland with him and read to him and Andy at bedtime. Duncan could see it like he was watching a home movie. And his uncle had sacrificed his job and his first home to be a good parent when Duncan's had died.

The thought of dismissing your own flesh and blood after what Nickie had been through was incomprehensible as it was, but this? This was no coincidence. Edward and Ivanna Monticello had something to do with the missing file from Nickie's past.

A small nudge in the arm made him focus on the scene in front of him. The doorman held his hand on his walkie like he was ready to call Security as he and Andy blocked the path of the valet driver and the next group of businessmen who piled out of a Lexus. "Come on, man," Andy said in his ear. "Let's go find this Leslie Jacobsen."

Giving his head a single, small nod, Duncan moved his feet. "Good day," he said to the doorman as the man held the door for them. "Thank you."

The lobby was marble. Marble floors, marble pillars and marble-backed benches lining the center. An enormous marble reception counter was centered in the area. He and Andy passed it to the left and headed for the elevators. They didn't need directions. They were going to the top floor. There were three sets of elevators, each the color of gold-plated metal.

They stood stoically in the quiet elevator. Both fit into their surroundings with their designer suits. Andy had to borrow a pair of Duncan's shoes and a tie. He didn't have ones to match the brown or black velvet hats they wore to conceal as much of their faces as they could. They waited until all but the last person exited on the way up to push the button that selected the top floor.

They left the elevator and Andy walked right up to the first desk that held a younger woman. He whispered in her ear before he smiled and shook the woman's hand with both of his. This would not be a good time for anyone to recognize Duncan. Andy had always been the thicker of the two of them. Not nearly as tall as Duncan, but Andy was a brick. In high school, the girls called him the boy with the million-dollar smile. The woman who beamed at him as he walked away seemed to agree.

They walked quickly and with purpose. "Last office before the corner office. On the right," Andy said to him.

An assistant in a suit dress stood at a file cabinet just outside of a door that read, 'Leslie Jacobsen.' Four plush guest chairs lined the wall outside the office. The upper half of the door was opaque with frosted glass.

Andy walked to the woman like he owned the place. Holding out his hand, he said, "Sylvester Andrew here to see Ms. Jacobsen." His full first and middle names. No one could accuse him of false impersonation.

The woman had only slightly the same reaction as the one who gave him the directions. She accepted his hand and gave her regrets. "I'm sorry, Mr. Andrew,

Ms. Jacobsen is gone for the day. Can I leave her a message?"

Duncan could have kicked himself. It was a Friday. He never considered checking to see if Jacobsen might take off a day early to prepare for her vacation. Without a second's consideration, Andy retorted, "Yes, her trip to San Juan. Her plane doesn't leave until Sunday. She's making a special stop to meet with us."

It looked as if Andy planned to break a lock. Duncan's coat lay over his arm. Digging in the inside pocket, he ensured his vials of mini-explosives were within easy reach.

The woman blinked at Andy's knowledge about the trip and the date of the plane tickets, and awkwardly gestured for them to wait in the guest chairs. Now what did they do? As much as he wanted to, Duncan wasn't about to turn his eyes to Andy and give him the look that asked exactly that.

They sat stoically, hands on their knees, as the woman went back to her filing. She made two phone calls, and Duncan could see she was working on a document. Control + P. He checked the area. No printer. Without moving his eyes from his forward gaze, he tapped Andy's shoe with his own.

As if on cue, the woman walked to the center of a group of cubicles. The printer must be there. Duncan took his chance and grabbed one of the miniature vial of C4 from the pocket of his coat. He rushed the door that read, 'Leslie Jacobsen' in stenciled letters across the opaque glass. Grabbing a lighter in his other hand, he wiggled the knob on the door. It was open. He glanced over his shoulder just as the woman turned with papers in hand.

He clicked the door shut as she stood in front of Andy. Her expression must have asked some unspoken question because he heard Andy say, "Bathroom. It was a bumpy cab ride."

Duncan stayed low and went first to Jacobsen's computer. He doubted she had fifteen-year-old files stored on it but copied her hard drive onto a mega-flash drive anyway. As the documents uploaded, he combed through her drawers, not knowing what he might be searching for. Three tall, cherry wood file cabinets stood in the middle of a side of her office. Each had a lock. This time, he checked to see if they'd been left open first. They hadn't.

The C-4 putty was a last resort. Instead, he searched the desk for the keys. In the drawers, beneath and on the sides of the desk. Any small hooks? Nothing in the canisters for pens or paperclips. But the matching black metal canister that held binder clips. Bingo.

Pulling out the tiny keys, he heard Andy's voice. "No worries, Ms. Jacobsen. We just got here. Take your time. That sounds lovely," he said. Andy was pretending to speak into his phone.

The file cabinets held neatly stacked folders, crisp like they'd hardly been used. The first file cabinet was A through H. At a whim, he checked the middle under M for Monticello. Nothing. Sighing, he flipped further to N for Nicole. Nothing. The ding of the computer signaled the uploads were complete as he heard Andy speak up expectantly. "No! No need, thank you. I'm sure he's fine. He gets car sick and the traffic…"

Duncan hurried to eject the flash drive. He unlocked S through Z and decided to check Savage for the hell of it. The file was yellowed, but the corners just as crisp and untouched as the others.

He heard the female voice from outside the door. "I'll call and let her know I'm taking my morning break soon."

"You know, maybe you're right. I'd better check on

him. Can you show me the way to the nearest bathroom? Women can be so much more insightful than men." Duncan imagined the smile on Andy's face as he said so.

"Down the hall on your left. You'll see a side hallway."

She wasn't leaving. He cracked open the door enough to see her.

Andy scratched his head. "Where?" He took a step, placing his hand on her elbow and craning his head down the hall.

Duncan stepped out with the file draped under his jacket.

She turned before he barely cleared her desk area.

"Is that the faster way to the bathroom, then?" Duncan asked the both of them. "I certainly took the long way." He reached in his pocket as he sat in the guest chair and blindly hit speed dial number three.

Andy's phone rang. He answered, and Duncan hoped he heard the telltale signs of rustling in a pocket.

"Oh, that's no problem. Certainly, we'll see you there."

Andy stood and Duncan followed. "It seems we are rescheduling locations to that wonderful bakery down the street."

"Marsella's? She loves that place." The woman nodded as if it made perfect sense.

"Have a nice weekend," Andy said, and they headed for the elevator.

"You bought a dining table for tonight?"

Nickie stood in the kitchen's east door that led to the dining room. She stood with her legs locked, slightly spread. Duncan liked to think of it as her rock-star stance. Next to the kitchen door to the north sat his perfectly acceptable kitchen table. Except he decided this was a dining room event and purchased a circular, glass table with wrought iron chairs. The kitchen table was enormous. It reminded him of home, and really anything smaller would seem out of place in a kitchen this size.

In the middle of the kitchen table was the bouquet of assorted flowers he chose when he picked up the steaks and potatoes. On one side of the bouquet was the single brown paper grocery bag she brought with her. On the other side was the plain manila file folder labeled with a computer-generated label that read, "Nickie Savage." Not her birth name, Nicole Monticello. It was that fact that bothered him more than the contents. Her eyes went right to it when she arrived. He would let her take lead with it.

CHAPTER 25

"Mmm," Duncan nodded regarding the dining room furniture, "and a grill." He stabbed the potatoes with a fork. "I'm thinking of making the final area in the basement into a wine cellar. A certain cop ruined my dreams of a shooting range."

"Sheesh, Duncan. It wouldn't be like an illegal cable line or pirating songs from the Internet." She moved toward him with her glass of Old Vine Zinfandel as he wrapped the bakers in foil and placed them on a plate.

When he returned from starting the potatoes on the grill, she had moved the grocery bag and was ripping lettuce into the large bowl, which he also purchased that afternoon.

"When are we going to discuss what's in there?" he asked.

She stopped what she was doing, set her hands on the edge of his tall granite counters and locked her elbows. Dropping her chin to her chest, she sighed. "I think I want to wait."

He slipped behind her, sliding his arms around her waist as he tucked his lips beneath her ear. Her shoulders relaxed as her head lifted.

She continued. "I've thought about it and realized the last time we ate with Andy and Rose we had to deal with my drama."

As he turned her to face him, she opened her knees so their legs scissored. He brushed the hair that hid her face over her ear and shoulder. "Drama is when a person or persons exaggerate a scenario for the sole purpose of...well...drama."

Her eyes lit and she smiled. "You read that in Webster's, did you?"

"Yes, I did," he lied and kissed her forehead, then her cheek. "And I was asking when we were going to discuss what was in your grocery bag." He kissed her other cheek.

Her chest expanded against his. Her heartbeat was steady and strong.

Rotating beneath him, she returned to her lettuce and answered his original question. "Strawberries, craisins, sesame seeds, tomatoes and dressings." She pressed her knuckles to the side of her jaw, cracked her neck and then repeated the procedure on the other. "Let's keep this where it belongs, in the station. Can you come early, before you go to work?"

Sticking his hand in the bag, he started pulling out the items. "This is female salad stuff, just so you know. And, yes, I can follow you in first thing."

Duncan didn't follow her in that morning. He told her he was stopping at the only bakery he deemed worthy enough to brew an acceptable cup of coffee. Nickie's caffeine was less maintenance. She could get it from the machine at work or stop at her favorite convenience store. Today would be a 20 oz. bottle from the machine at work.

Her joints were pleasantly pliable from their night of sex, her muscles loose from her morning swim.

And yet, the thin file weighed down the briefcase in her hand as she headed for the stairs. She hadn't seen Duncan's Audi when she parked.

One of the first ones there, she flipped the lights in the common area and noticed Eddy had beat her in. He stood when she popped her head in his door. "Don't get up. I just stopped by to say, 'Good morning.'"

He came around his desk anyway. "Is everything okay? I heard about the feds."

"You heard?"

His head dropped as if he was embarrassed for her. "Everyone knows."

Everyone except Duncan. "You need anything? I'm getting a soda."

He smiled and shook his head. She must be forgiven.

She had to pay the damned machine twice for her Diet Coke, but she had bigger things on her mind. The sound of the sizzling release of carbonation was a good start. As she left the break room, she saw that Duncan had arrived...and was in Eddy's office. And right when she had been forgiven. Oh boy.

As quick as a snake, Duncan's hand jutted out in a tight jab that landed centered on Eddy's face. Her shoulders lifted involuntarily as she winced. She knew no one else was here yet, but her head dropped and she looked from side to side anyway.

Assaulting a police officer at the station. What the frigging hell was he thinking? Eddy returned the jab with a reflexive push that did little to waver Duncan. She didn't know whether to intervene, whether to pretend she didn't know what was happening or whether to give each of them a taste of their own medicine.

She couldn't hear what Eddy said to him. It sounded

like growling profanity. He grabbed a tissue as the blood started to drip. It was comical, Eddy sticking his chest out, holding the tissue to his nose and arguing about what she could only assume was the fact that Eddy had taken the sketch of Zheng from Duncan's personal printer.

It didn't seem that it was going to be one of those short, testosterone things men did. They were nose to nose and getting louder. Eddy jerked his head forward, head butting Duncan in the forehead. That was effective. Catching his balance, Duncan faked a second jab before he rounded a hook to Eddy's jaw. Both would be on the floor and bloody if either had truly wanted to do honest damage. She stepped forward to intervene when Eddy noticed her. He snarled at Duncan, turned his eyes down and took a step backward.

Duncan must have sensed the reason for his retreat and glanced over his shoulder.

"If you boys are done with your male posturing, can we can get started, Duncan?"

The sneer from Duncan to Eddy was one she'd never seen before.

"Isn't a fist to the face enough? Do you have to mock him?" she said as they entered her office.

"He asked for it. Are you sticking up for him?"

"Yes."

Duncan's feet stopped but only for a moment. She shut her door but kept her blinds open. Pulling one of her guest chairs around her desk, they sat together as she booted up her desktop computer. She noticed Duncan's coffee steaming from the far side of her desk. He must have dropped it off before he went to pick a fight with Eddy.

"You better hope he doesn't press charges."

"Pft. He's more of a man than that," Duncan said as

he picked up his java.

"I want to go first," she said, ignoring her briefcase for now.

He sat back, signaling he was ready.

"I can't tell if the feds listened to what I had to say or not. They acted like they didn't. They said there has been no suspicious activity at the house. We know that to be true. They shared a lead they had on the match we've been looking into at Madison Square Garden. But only because they wanted me to be forthcoming with what Tanner told me. It's like a game of frigging Ping-Pong. They won't tell me they dug up my past. I can't tell them I know because they'll suspect about the hacking into their database. I won't tell them I've been in the white house, because it's none of their damned business. Which means they don't know Moody has cameras in each room. Or did, at least." She took a long swig of soda. "Regardless, they're shutting me out."

His head jerked toward her. "What do you mean, 'shutting you out'?"

"I mean they don't want me to have any part of their infiltration of the boxing match at Madison Square. I can't figure out what to do about it."

"You can do something about it?"

"Your turn. I'm ready." Somewhere she knew she should have asked if he was ready, but right then, she was in survival mode and it was all about her.

He accepted her change in subject and answered, "We found the person whose name was listed on the files chronologically entered before and after the missing one. A Leslie Jacobsen. Or, we found her office. She was out of town, but Andy and I…worked around it."

"You broke into the woman's office? Were you seen?"

"Yes, but what are they going to do? I hid the file in my coat. Unless she has secret agent cameras hidden in her florescent lights, no one knows I took anything."

"Except you were seen at her office, and now she has a missing file. How did you get in? Weren't there people watching?"

"A file that was illegally hidden and secured. How are they going to get me for it? And Andy is a smooth, fast talker. He got me in."

She rubbed her hands over her face. "Okay, okay." She slid the file from her briefcase as it sat on the floor. The file was old and labeled with her new name. Placing it on her desk, she continued. "What else?"

"You haven't opened it, have you?" It was a rhetorical question.

She shook her head.

He took her hand. She pulled it away. She knew it was cold, but she couldn't keep it together if he coddled her.

"Before I open this, I need to tell you where I found it."

He spoke softly. "Jacobsen works for IEM."

Her eyes widened as they darted to him. "What the hell are you talking about?" She wasn't dense. She knew what initials he was referring to. "You think? Don't give me a hunch, Duncan. I need the facts. I can't take hunches right now."

She squirmed in her seat. She hated that she was losing control, especially when it had to do with her parents.

None of this made sense. "But the tab on the file folder says Nickie Savage, not Nicole Monticello. My parents never acknowledged my new name."

She saw his chest rise and fall deeply, the agony in

his face. He placed his hand on the file without opening it. "Inside are the police reports from the night you were taken. They detail the scene of the crime, through to the subsequent Amber Alert."

Her fingers still wouldn't move to open it and see for herself no matter how many times she told them to. Thankful Duncan knew her well enough to sense this, she nodded to him as a signal to continue.

"No prints were found. A few items in your room were broken or disheveled, showing signs of a struggle."

She'd never remembered much of that night. Had she fought? What had she worn? How was she taken? She waited impatiently, afraid to speak.

"All seemed to be expected except for two things. Nickie, your screen wasn't cut. Your alarm was intact. There were no signs of a forced break-in."

Nickie insisted on riding in a commercial jet like normal people. It was petty, she knew. But for now, she needed as much familiarity as she could get and thought riding in Duncan's plane or even in first class wouldn't do that for her. She was simply confused. Duncan rode in coach with her. He had his stubborn side, his introverted side and the side of him that loved big, expensive things. But when it counted, he was the most giving and flexible person she'd ever known.

"Are you sure about this?" he asked from the two inches the economy seats provided between them.

"I need to put an end to this, Duncan. Once and for all. I want to know. I'm finding myself suspicious toward everything and everyone. Was it my parents who had my file listed with my new name? They're the ones who want nothing to do with this part of my life. Or has Zheng or Moody infiltrated their files and employees? Or maybe this Leslie Jacobsen made the decision on her own?" She was thinking aloud. A man of few words made for a good listener.

"The FBI has the chance at taking them all down. I'm positive they have eyes on the bugs at Moody's white house, but if they're waiting at Madison Square..." Her thoughts became jumbled. It was all confusing. She yearned for clear vision.

They touched down in Terre Haute as the sun came up. Midwest land was flat for miles. She took a short moment to see the sunrise from such a distance away.

They took a cab from the airport to the penitentiary. He did it for her and her need for familiarity, and it all made her wish he'd rented one of his ridiculous cars. They let him work on his tablet but only in the first waiting area. She left him there as they escorted her back.

Tanner was in much better shape this time. Still thinner, but his face was clear of the swelling and bruises. The defensive wounds on his hands were healed. He was clean shaven and his face was back to its caramel brown instead of the gray she'd seen the last time she was here.

They had him in a different room, but it was similar. Chair bolted to the floor. Bindings that seemed to be part seat belt and part straightjacket. Except they didn't cuff him this time. He must be acting like a good little boy.

"You look good," she said as she slung a boot over the metal chair that sat at the opposite side of the small metal table.

"Are you planning to make a habit of this, Nick? Because I'm a busy man."

It made her laugh, a guttural icy gut-laugh. "I want to know about Zheng. Zheng and Moody and how far this goes." She slapped down the file labeled with her name on the tab.

He winced at the sound of Zheng's name as he'd done before. "So, that's how this is now? You pull the puppet strings, and I give up information whenever you decide you want something?"

"Pretty much, yeah," she said with a smile.

"You can turn off your sweet-as-a-southern-belle act. I've already seen it. And don't even try the sultry blonde who pretends to be a bit dense. I'm not biting. And your rules? You can take them straight to hell."

"How is isolation, Tanner? No visitors in the shower? No one using you as their pedophile punching bag?"

He leaned closer to her. She saw him check the guard as he did. "You can't threaten me."

"We'll see about that." She lifted from the chair and motioned to the guard that she was done.

"No luck, Detective?"

She clipped on her belt and checked her cuffs, the safety on her gun and her phone. "Patience," is all she said to the guard who had done her pat down. Except patience was a sensation that had been escaping her all too often lately.

Duncan lifted his eyes from his tablet as she plopped down in the chair next to him. Other men would have asked why she was back so soon. Since it was obvious, he didn't. "We have three hours before we need to be back at the airport. Would you like breakfast?"

She didn't want food, but he knew that already. "Okay," she answered.

They found a hole-in-the wall diner. Duncan Reed may like big and expensive, but he had an appreciation and a taste for good, family diner cooking. He ordered a small mountain of food. She had fruit and dry toast. She'd be damned before she let her biological genes take over her pant size.

"I want to be done with this, Duncan."

His nod was slight.

"The girls would have been punished because I ran away."

He set his fork down. "What?"

"That was how they kept us in line. They knew who worked the best under fear and those of us who caved better under guilt. For most of us, it was the latter. If we didn't perform to their standards, they beat the other girls. They forced us to watch and made sure we knew we were the ones who were the cause." The pain was insurmountable. The confusion of Zheng and Moody and now this fucking file, it was all forming into one big ball and rolling straight toward her.

"A few girls didn't care. They were past caring about the rest of us. I get that now. They were beaten if they stepped out of line. I ran away. I'm the only one I know of who pulled it off in the eighteen months I was in captivity. They would punish the girls severely for it. I am likely the cause of someone's death."

"What can I do?"

"I am going to take some days. I never take vacation time. I'm due. Madison Square is this weekend. I'm going to stake out Moody's incognito Friday night. Saturday, too, if I need to." She held up her hand to the expression on Duncan's face. "I know, I know. If I get caught I could be kicked off the force, lose my job forever. But I need this, Duncan. It's why I entered the academy in the first place. Does that make sense? I did it for the girls. I changed my name for the girls."

He slipped his hand over hers and this time she let him.

"I think Moody will wait for the night of the boxing match, but I can't afford to miss him. I'm going to be ready the Friday night before and then the night of the match too. He's going to bring the girls to his white house, Duncan. I can feel it."

"You can't take them all down yourself."

"No. But I can try and keep them contained until the feds arrive. You say you have access to his security system? I am going to ask you to do something illegal. You might get caught. I'm putting you in danger."

He lifted the corner of his mouth in a rare Duncan Reed smile. "What did you have in mind, Detective?"

CHAPTER 26

———— ◆ ◆ ◆ ————

"You don't understand. You mean more to me than anything else in this world. It would kill me to see you in trouble."

"I've hacked into foreign government databases."

Her mouth dropped. She knew about the FBI files. That was astounding in itself. But this? "Where? When?" Instinctively, she looked around, hoping no one could hear them. Other than an elderly man sitting on a stool at the counter, she and Duncan were the only customers in the place. Their waitress made her way over with a pot of coffee in one hand and their bill in the other.

Duncan thanked her for the refill, then leaned in once she left. "I had a customer who wouldn't pay. It was years ago. Said he had recently gone broke and filed for Chapter Eleven. He had filed, that was true. But Andy and I were able to find overseas bank accounts. Large overseas bank accounts. A few anonymous tips, and suddenly he had canceled his Chapter Eleven and was able to pay up. I figure we saved a number of individuals from a scam large enough to cost millions."

She rubbed her hands over her face before lacing her fingers together on the top of her hair. "Oh, jeez. Okay. But that's not government."

"When we were kids—"

"You two did this when you were kids?"

"I had this *ability*. I had no respect for the curse, or my gift as you put it. I used it to my advantage while keeping it a secret. Andy still doesn't know how but he knows I can memorize passcodes, long passcodes. He has this incredible talent for building, constructing if you will. He's the safety guy."

His eyes literally lit as he explained. It was damned frightening. And a bit sexy.

"We can't do anything before he sends out signals to a half-dozen states and sometimes other countries. He knows which ones are lax in their security and how to code our trails so we wouldn't even be able to break the path we leave."

"Countries?"

"Right. Rose's biological father was born and raised in Nicaragua. We broke into the government files and found warrants for his arrest. You know the rest of that pitiful story."

She did. The man was Rose's blood and was ready to kill both her and her mother. "I'd like to see the video feed from Moody's security system. Can you do that?"

"I'm afraid not. It's not satellite. I'd have to be networked to the cable feed on his property. Although—"

"How about the bugs? Can I see them? I know you're keeping an eye on them."

"Wait right there."

She took a bite of his scrambled eggs while he was gone, then washed it down with his juice.

He returned with his tablet, and right there in the

middle of the diner, he logged on and opened the feed. There it was. The feed rotated between the three visual bugs. The audio was constant. She heard wind as she watched. The first was the shot of the parking lot. It was knee-deep in snow. Prints from animals ran in crisscross lines across the sixteen spot parking lot, but no car or human tracks were found. The next image must be from the one stuck to the front door, because it showed the walk leading to the house. Nothing had been shoveled. The last one looked like it was attached to the window on the west side of the front of the house, but it had snow on it and was hard to see through the white.

"We're watching from San Diego right now. See?" He showed her more than she wanted to know. Than she should know. "And see? It changed to Tampa. Andy is a safety freak genius."

She shook her head back and forth a dozen times. "Okay," she said, then repeated herself, "Okay."

"Before we go on, I'd like to revisit the 'lose-your-job-forever' part of the conversation."

"It would be worth it." Saying it aloud cut like a knife, but it was true. "I know there are more organizations that do this, that this is only one group. But if I could get rid of them, Zheng, Moody, free all of the girls, it would be my purpose. It's why I'm here. There are organizations, ones that work on a national scale to free girls and boys in captivity. I've been researching them, and I could...go to work for one of them." It choked her to think of it, but it was time. It was damned time.

Nickie didn't know if her rush was from being this close to taking down these bastards, or the fact that she and Duncan were doing it illegally. Probably both, but the rush was there nonetheless. There was no need to stake out Moody's place across the road. She had the constant feed from Duncan's tablet. She stuffed the thought of the ramifications deep in her subconscious. She was a survivor. It wasn't that hard.

They were staked out in the local bed and breakfast at the edge of Alabaster. It was the same one they stayed in after their first stint at Moody's place. So far, there was no activity, but it was early on the Friday night before the Madison Square Garden fight.

"We might need a lot of caffeine. This could be a long night." She sat on the bed with three pillows propping her up. With her laptop sitting on her legs, she polished her last report of the week for her captain. She'd taken the weekend off. The expression on Dave's face when she requested the time was unsettling, like he thought she might have leprosy. He agreed quickly enough. Had she ever asked for time off before? She couldn't think of a single time. And how awful for Duncan.

She wasn't the easiest person to live wi—around, she corrected, before she caught herself in a self-imposed taboo. Which was one more way she wasn't easy. She couldn't imagine ever turning into *that girl*. The kind you live with, marry and—she physically cringed—have children with. What did she know about commitment, giving or children? She didn't grow up with anything that vaguely resembled a normal family. She was never around children or siblings, and certainly never babysat. Between her childhood, her time in captivity and jumping around foster homes, by the time she reached Gloria's house, she was past the point of learning to nurture.

She checked on Duncan. He sat in a recliner at the corner desk. His tablet rested on the table, facing outward so both of them could watch the lifeless changing feed. He had marriage and children written all over him. It was funny how she would be one of the few people who would think this. The magazine that labeled him *The Taste of L.A.* wouldn't know it. His Hollywood customers wouldn't know it. The fact that she did scared the living hell out of her. He deserved someone who wasn't moody, wasn't broken and didn't need to carry a .45 M&P in order to feel worthy.

Her gun. She would lose her gun over this.

Two in the morning came faster than she expected. The fight was over with. Her anticipation dropped with every passing minute. Yet, she still wore her boots, had her gun safely tucked on her belt and her spare in her ankle holster. Her coat hung from the hook on the back of the door. She was like a firefighter waiting for the bell.

"I wonder what Strong and Lewis are doing," she said to him.

"Maybe the same thing we are."

"Wouldn't that be funny? Strong and Lewis in a bed and breakfast, I mean. Do you think they have backup on hold?" It didn't matter. She wasn't invited. "Hey, do you have a scanner thing? Ya know, to see if they get a bite? They won't be on a regular police scanner."

His hair wasn't long enough to hide his ears, but it did hide enough of them at this angle. He pulled his hair back and revealed a single black earbud. Tapping it, he grinned.

Tossing her laptop on the bed, she swung her feet over the side of the bed. "Seriously? You've been listening?"

"Lewis checked in to say the feed was quiet. I assume he meant the bugs at Moody's. See? They *were* listening to you."

Listening or not, that was all they did through the entire night and the next. Madison Square was a wash.

They drove the four hours back to Northridge first thing Sunday morning.

"We can try again next weekend," he said as he checked his mirror and merged onto 84 West.

She assumed they were the only ones who stayed in the bed and breakfast and didn't have sex. And it was the second time at missing both targets.

The third time was a charm, Nickie hoped, in this case. Her first trip to the Terre Haute penitentiary could have probably been paid by the feds if she hadn't flown in Duncan's plane. The second and third were her idea. Tanner had better be in the mood for sharing. She was fed up with paying for plane tickets and for wasted time. Time asking the feds to include her. Her last time here to pick Tanner's brain. Time staking out Moody's place.

And this time she was alone. Duncan was in L.A., delivering his latest work to his latest Hollywood star. She hated pouting, especially when it came from her.

She didn't call ahead this time. She feared someone would alert the feds. Not that it was any of their business. She could be here questioning him about any cold case in the Northridge database. Luckily, the prison guards recognized her.

They took her phone, her badge, her gun, her cuffs and searched her. It was getting to be mundane. She had to wait this time. It took a full hour to get Tanner in the room and made her appreciate what they went through the two subsequent times in having him ready when she arrived.

Sheesh. She winced. He was a mess. His left eye was swollen shut and his lip freshly cut. She smiled through her wince.

Tanner, on the other hand, was not smiling. His stance, the way he glared at her. The guard sensed it as much as she did, but instead of a grin from ear to ear as she was doing, he chose to use the handcuffs attached to the table and checked everything twice.

"You little bitch," Tanner snarled low through his teeth.

She leaned her chair back and crossed her ankles on the table. "You already knew that."

"You knew what they would do to me. How could you lead me into a situation like that?"

"You're joking, right? You mean a situation like raping girls too young to have had their periods? 'I've been winning for thirty years.' Isn't that what you said to me? And you're right." She let her legs drop and inched her face forward, just out of reach in case he decided to head butt her. "This is how it's going to be. You tell me what I want to know and you go back to the safety of your isolated, pathetic life. If you don't...if I even think you're lying to me, I'll feed you to the wolves and come back later just to see their handy work on your pretty face."

Slapping the file down on the table, she growled, "Zheng. How far does this go? How far does he go?"

For a moment, she thought he might spit in her face and she really hated when perps did that. Without flinching, she stared at him from one eye to the other. The noise of his cuffs broke their silent standoff. He pulled the file toward him, bending the corner on his cuffs.

He took his time reading every word. She could see the cop in him as he did. It made her remember the time she respected him.

"Did Mommy and Daddy want to hide the disgrace of their daughter?"

"Careful, shower boy. You don't want to piss me off."

"It wasn't my idea to transfer you. Someone had to

keep an eye on you. I drew the short fucking straw."

It was…staged? The words were a sucker punch to the gut, but she carefully kept her face even. "Go on."

"You were clueless. And you made it obvious you had no intention of turning over old stones. I kept an eye on your computer. You never searched your past, nothing that could remotely be connected." He leaned in, and for the first time since the night he was captured, he ogled her like a juicy steak. "Why is that, I wonder? Then you got involved with the Reeds. What a cluster fuck. The fire chief had this thing for the aunt. You started getting warm to it and everything went to hell."

"The file. What does this all have to do with the file? Why was the scene of the crime secured, as was the subsequent Amber Alert? Why was there no evidence of a break in at my parents' home?" She hadn't meant to ask that last question.

"You might want to ask Edward and Ivanna that question."

There was no need. She already knew the answer. They were disgusted with her. Had been since before she was abducted, but after…Why couldn't she accept it and move on? She had before.

"Why not just take me out? Why the theatrics of a transfer?"

"Take out Nicole Monticello of the Maryland Monticellos? You don't know how important your father is, do you?"

"I'm asking one more time. Zheng. How was he involved?"

"I answered to Moody. Zheng is beyond me."

CHAPTER 27

————◆◆◆◆————

"You want another weekend off," Nickie's captain said as a statement. He stood from his chair and walked around his desk. His six-foot-four body towered in front of his desk. Leaning back, he crossed his arms in front of him.

It was like sitting in the principal's office all over again. "I know, I know. It's weird. But, yes. I have time enough to take the next two dozen Friday's off."

"Nick, it's me. You can talk to me. Are you...ya know, expecting?"

Her body leaped from his chair before her mind told her not to. "Holy shit, Dave. Are you joking? No, I'm not pregnant. What do you take me for?"

"A woman who is involved with a guy?"

"And that means I'm knocked up? Chauvinist, much?"

"You know that's not true. But you never come to me anymore. You're holed up in your office with your nose in your computer. You come in early. You stay late. You have pictures taped to your desk computer— yes, I looked—and now you want Friday off. Again."

When he put it that way, it did sound like something

huge. "I'm fine, really. You've been a great captain. You were an amazing mentor when I came here. I wouldn't be who I am today if it weren't for you. Thank you."

"Then why are you talking like I'll never see you again?"

The pain in her gut was real, as real as the possibility that after this weekend, she wouldn't see him again. She didn't think she would do time, hoped she wouldn't. But she most certainly wouldn't be allowed to work as cop ever again. Expanding her chest, she lifted her chin. "That's ridiculous. I'll see you at the team meeting this afternoon."

For the third time in less than month, Duncan lay holding Nickie at the only bed and breakfast in Alabaster. They were in a different room. This one smaller but with more windows. It was floral with pastel colors and eyelet lace curtains and pillow covers. They lay together, fully clothed, on top of the sheets and blankets, the thick comforter folded at the end of the bed. Her guns were in her briefcase, and her boots were stacked neatly at the side of the bed. She never stacked anything neatly.

Something happened in Terre Haute. He wanted to kick himself that he wasn't there. Something happened that changed her. Something happened or maybe it was the last something one person could handle. The straw that broke the camel's back. She knew her father never accepted what happened to her in captivity. But to discover he went to great efforts to hide it, to withhold information about the scene of the crime that could help find her captors, he didn't know how someone came back from that.

As a cop, she had stumbled upon a group of girls taken from the same organization that had taken her fifteen years ago. Found Zheng. The FBI didn't trust her. They used her, and then shut her out.

Her head tucked tightly beneath his chin, resting on his shoulder. The faint smell of lavender filled his senses, as familiar now as the back of his hand. She was silent, much like she'd been for the last several days.

Tonight was their last chance. Madison Square Garden turned out to be no more than willing adult prostitutes who were stationed in back rooms behind the scenes of the boxing match. He imagined their surprise when they were crashed by the FBI and a full tactical SWAT team. Duncan sensed Strong and Lewis were fed up. They had nothing concrete from Moody's white house, and no child prostitution rings emerged from their boxing tip. The last thing he'd heard on the FBI police scanner was that Strong and Lewis had returned to Langley.

Movement from his chest caused him to lift his arms. She rolled to the side of the enormous bed, grabbed her shower bag and walked out the door. He couldn't remember the last time she'd eaten.

He eyed his tablet. The visual stream at the white house showed no movement. The snow had melted, exposing the centers of the drive and the walks. He slung his legs off the bed and set his forearms on his knees. Tonight was their last chance, he repeated in his head. And if not, then what? He'd never considered what they would do if Tanner had misled them.

Them. Who was he kidding? He was the civilian.

He wasn't sure how long he sat as he did, but when the door reopened, he was surprised it was her already. Uncharacteristically, her hair hadn't been dried or styled. She wore no makeup. A short peach-colored towel wrapped around her body and tucked beneath her arms. She walked through the hallway of the bed and breakfast like that?

"You need to eat," he said as he studied her face. It was gaunt and he could swear it seemed thinner.

She stepped in front of him and dropped her towel. "I'm not hungry for food."

The air left his lungs. His eyes darted to hers. In them, he didn't see want or desire. He saw need. He placed his palms low on her hips and wrapped his fingers around her flesh. It was cool to the touch from her shower. As he pulled her to him, she placed a knee on the bed. Asking. Inviting.

He answered and trailed his fingers around her hip and over her skin until he found her. Her eyes rolled to the back of her head before her lids closed and her head fell back. He moved for her in the way he learned she responded, holding onto her back to keep her from stumbling. She shuddered beneath his hands and lifted her arms, resting them on his shoulders. He feathered his fingers from her firm stomach over her silky waist and up her ribs. He cupped her, taking her into his mouth. Fingers dug into his shoulders as he circled with his tongue, then pulled.

He caught her as her knees buckled. Taking her into his arms, he laid her on the blankets and stood back, taking in the shape of her. He released the buttons of his shirt as he ran his eyes over the curves of her hips, the way her waist tucked in tightly beneath her ribs, all the way to her eyes, opened wide and watching. He tossed his shirt over the end of the closest chair and then followed it with the rest of his things. Her eyes were a deeper gray, darker, sadder.

Lowering himself to her, he nudged between her legs.

Nickie knew she was acting selfishly. His tongue was warm, yet left a cool breeze in its wake. The spot inside her knee, lazily along the length of her inner thigh too. "Oh." She shuddered and laced her fingers through the back of his hair.

He knew every piece of her. Inside and out. Rarely was he gentle, were *they* gentle. But he knew. He always knew. His hands were everywhere, his mouth, his tongue. Carefully, slowly. He took her away from this place. It was exactly what she'd asked, and she didn't even need to ask.

The rise was slow and steady, building like a ballad anticipating the bridge. Every inch of her trembled, but she hung on. He would keep her safe. Keep her grounded. She trusted him completely and took down her restraints. The peak was long and hard, her heels digging into his sides. And more. More until the bridge of the ballad turned into the culmination at the end of a melody.

His kisses trailed a line up her trembling stomach. She came down from the high as the sensation of rough whiskers ran over one breast, then the other sending her again on an upward journey. Her arms and legs were still terribly weak, but she grabbed hold of his perfect backside with both hands, leading him to her. She trailed a hand around to find him and relished in the way he froze, then squirmed. The guttural sounds coming from deep in his throat satisfied her nearly as much as his teeth as they grazed her skin.

Digging her nails into his perfect butt, she guided him deeper before releasing him. He paused and brought his eyes to her. They spoke more than any words could. She could feel him there. It took every ounce of restraint to let him lead. Her body shook with needs of more kind than one.

His entry was quick, filling her completely. Her body took over. She dug her fingers into flesh and muscle, lifting to him, coupled and loved. This wasn't slow or gentle. It was two people who needed, needed more. More than this and more than each other. At that moment, it had to be both.

He grabbed hold of the sides of her face, moving with her. "There you are," he said with eyes as black as night.

Cries erupted from her lungs, her body, rushing to her core where they exploded, sending them over to an isolated place only they occupied. His body shook over her and hers beneath him. Sheer will kept her spent body moving until the last united push. He paused, shivered once more, then fell and covered her with the warmth of his body and of his heart.

They lay there much longer than they normally would. She was relieved. The weight of him was something she needed that she couldn't quite explain.

"They staged my transfer to Northridge." She didn't know where that came from, but a small piece of her fear disappeared as she said it. "Zheng pulled the strings, or maybe it was Moody." She shrugged as Duncan moved to her side.

He lifted on an elbow as it all came out.

"Tanner told me someone had to keep an eye on me and that he drew the short straw. It was like he was glad to finally be able to shove it in my face. I thought I was transferred because I was a good detective, a good cop. Now, I don't know."

She hadn't consciously thought of it before, but it was true. Was she even a good enough detective to keep around? Or was her only purpose in Northridge so one of Moody's men could keep an eye on her?

"Nickie, look."

She turned her focus to him and saw that he noticed something on his tablet. Bolting upright, she watched as a truck plowed the parking lot to the side of the white house.

"What time is it?" she howled, lunging from the bed and turning in a circle as she looked for her clothes.

"Whoa," he said with hands outstretched. "The fight doesn't start for another two hours."

He came to her and grabbed her wrists. Her heart was beating so hard, she could feel the rapid pulse in her head. "Okay," she said and bent over, putting her hands on her knees. This was going to be her last night as a detective. Four years in college followed by one in the academy. "Okay. We have time. Let's get ready."

She took a second shower, and this time he joined her. They went over their strategy for the hundredth time as he shampooed her hair and she washed his back. When did she become the type of person who could be this comfortable with any human being?

When they returned to the room, the sidewalks had been shoveled as carefully as a manicure. She affixed her belt, her cuffs, her phone, and finally, her gun. Checking the safety, she reached for her ankle holster. It was going to happen.

Duncan tucked one black earbud in his ear and adjusted a tiny box before sticking it in his shirt pocket.

"Are you going to contact Strong and Lewis?" he asked.

She stopped at the question. "If I tell them, they'll know we have access to the classified feed from the bugs you planted."

"That seems highly ungrateful."

She nodded. "I'd like to give them some time to respond." They had to be watching. Duncan said they were last known to be headed to Langley. She shook off the thought.

"How much time is time?" he questioned.

"They can call locals to cover for them if they need to." She could only hope she was making the right decision.

Stuffing her shower bag into her duffle, she zipped it quickly and reached for her coat at the same time he clicked his briefcase closed.

"Let's go."

Duncan parked in a spot he said Moody's cameras couldn't reach. How he knew that she didn't want to know. She was completely psyched. This had to work. The only glow in or out of the car was from the dimmed tablet light as they watched the white house. The place stood as quiet and somber as a graveyard.

She saw an Expedition drive toward the exit gate. They slouched low in Duncan's SUV as it approached. But it didn't take the road to Moody's manor. Instead, it turned south and headed down the road that led to the warehouses and the white house. It must have stopped somewhere, because they didn't see it in the feed from Duncan's tablet for nearly twenty minutes. Nickie's blood boiled with anticipation.

Two men parked crookedly in front of the white house. The taller of the two used keys from his pocket to open the front door. She and Duncan couldn't see inside and had no idea what they were doing, but they were still in there when three white station wagons pulled up to the gate. On the side of each, it read, 'Elegant Catering.'

She could vomit.

It was close to eleven o'clock, and the boxing match would be nearing the end. The men from the SUVs did not emerge as the caterers carried boxes of food and bottles of liquor, long folding tables and linens Nickie assumed were for the tables.

"Anything?" she asked Duncan. He would know she

referred to the FBI police scanner feed he had coming through his earbud.

He shook his head and time carried on. The car's digital clock seemed stuck.

"You have your jammer thing?" she asked for the tenth time.

"Yes. If anyone is watching, they might be confused for a few moments, but they won't see that we've broken in. Are you going to call Strong and Lewis?"

That meant he hadn't heard anything. But she hadn't seen anything definitive either. This could all be about adult prostitutes like what happened the weekend prior at Madison Square. "Not yet."

And then it came.

CHAPTER 28

A large, white box truck turned down the road. Nickie craned her head away from it. More because she could hardly bear to see it, knowing what was inside than to hide from the view of the driver. She had been in a truck like it, time after time after time. It would be empty on the inside. Empty other than nearly a dozen young girls and a few men with guns.

Maybe a single bed to threaten the girls in case one of them got out of hand. The walls would be lined with handcuffs, but they were rarely needed. Many of the girls would be drugged.

"Are you going to call Strong and Lewis?" Duncan's tone was turning impatient. He knew as well as she did that on their own, they would be lucky to get out alive, let alone rescue any girls.

"And tell them what? A box truck went onto Moody's property? They can't know we have access to the feed from the bugs you placed. I have to wait for the first john to show up. We can't be seen. How long does that jammer thing of yours work?"

"I adjusted it to thirty seconds. It's the best I could get."

She smiled now, as ready for this as she would ever be. "How fast does this car go?"

His returning smile was like a shot of adrenaline.

They watched his tablet while slouched in the buckets of his SUV. The anticipation scratched the surface of her will like an animal caught in a trap, digging its way out. To see the truck park in the lot, the girls tumbling out like herded cattle. They were cleaned and showered similarly to washing a dog before an AKC show. Images, memories flooded her mind. The smells. Duncan always told her the sense of smell was the one that brought back memories and sensations more than any other sense. At that moment, she smelled bodies, metal, and fear.

She hadn't realized her hand had drifted to cover her mouth. The sensation of Duncan's long fingers around her wrist shook her awake. A canary yellow Porsche Panamera turned the corner at the end of the street. She nudged Duncan and gestured her head toward it.

He turned to look, then moved his jammer device to his lap and said, "My aunt's sister calls these 'sorry-about-your-penis' cars."

She was completely taken off guard by him, something that rarely happened anymore. Her shoulders started shaking in laughter. She laughed all the way through the gate. Then, hung on as Duncan floored it. They didn't go south. Not toward the white house. Not yet. Patience, she reminded herself. First, they had to deal with the cameras. And they needed to get to the manor before the jam on the surveillance cameras unfroze.

"Are you sure you know where you're going?" she asked as she hung on to the dash. Fifteen seconds. He took the weaving road with one hand and grinned as he tapped the side of his head with the other. The roads were clear and dry on the way to Moody's house.

The place was ridiculous. And she thought Duncan liked big. It was like a hotel. He drove to the south of the building. Twenty seconds. He backed into a spot next to a garage door that was tucked into a lower level.

His chest rose and fell. His fingers gripped the steering wheel at ten and two, but he was smiling. "The cameras don't reach down here."

She checked the feed streaming through the tablet one more time. The box truck was gone, and the only cars in the lot were the black Expedition and the yellow Porsche. If just one more 'sorry-about-your-penis' car showed up, she would make the call.

"Here." She handed him a pair of thin, plastic gloves and noticed he was checking the pockets of his jacket. Did she want to know what he had in there? It made her check her own pockets, which was ridiculous. She'd already done that a dozen times. Ignoring the gun at her belt, she pulled the one from her ankle holster.

"Are you going to tell me not to touch anything?" he asked sarcastically.

Damn, how could he make her smile at a time like this? She'd told him those exact words before. More than once. "Let's go, smart ass." Nice ass.

Guns drawn, safeties off, they slinked tightly along the side of the house. He held up a fist and signaled for her to stop. She guessed hand signals in war were much the same as ones in a bust. He pointed up. She saw it.

Lucky for her, she had a guy who could memorize the locations of each security camera. He was like a human GPS. The one in question rotated toward the door they were going for. He had explained in their planning that the ones on the roads were still shots taken in five-second intervals. The ones around the house were constant feed. They waited for it to begin its rotation away and then took off. No dogs in sight. They must all be at the white house, but she was ready regardless.

The door was a service entry. Duncan jiggled the knob with his gloved hand. It was too big to kick in.

He dug in the inside pocket of his coat.

If they shot at it, they would bring attention to themselves. She was ready to try another door when she saw him shake something over the bolt. Curious as hell, she peered around his shoulder only to have him push her back as a small, 'poof,' sounded, followed by a billow of smoke. Holy shit, he brought explosives. The door cracked open, and after checking the camera once more, he held out his arm in a *ladies first* gesture.

Eyes wide, she rounded him and entered. It was a wide stairwell with a landing big enough to fit a small car. Gun close to her face, she checked both sides before motioning for him to lead. They pulled off their leather gloves and pocketed them, replacing them with the thin plastic ones she brought.

They stayed close to the wall as he led them up the stairs. At the top, he checked around the corner and ducked back, placing his hand up, fingers out. She imagined him in desert fatigues executing a similar mission.

After a moment, he checked again, and they hurried down a long hall that led to a plush burgundy-carpeted hallway. Thick, red-tinted wood lined the floors and ceiling. They passed occasional doors as they went. All were closed.

Waving her forward, he ducked around a corner and stopped at a door. He pointed. She motioned to him that she was going first. He dug his brows but backed away, giving her the lead.

She placed her hand on the knob. It moved. Slowly, she turned it completely before swinging the door open. A blond man that looked to be in his mid-twenties spun in a swivel desk chair. One look at the end of her gun, and a large, wet spot appeared between his legs.

She lowered her gun to his shoulder and pulled the trigger.

A hard grip circled her upper arm and jerked her out of the way. Duncan looked at the tranq stuck in the boy's arm. It flopped around as the boy turned his eyes down at it.

"I thought you shot him! You said those were for the dogs."

She shrugged as the blond slinked to the floor. Behind him were four rows of flat screens, at least a dozen in each row. The first two were the security feeds, the top row the still shots and the next the stream from around the manor.

Below were constant video streams, each a room. She knew where these were, and they weren't inside the manor. One room was painted and decorated in deep reds, another in royal blues. Hunter green, pearl white, each a color as the room would be named.

A few of the rooms had two-by-fours hammered to the walls with chains or leather straps dangling in wait. Normal people who noticed the rudimentary two-bys slapped up with a handful of nails would think there was a mistake, placed in such an exquisite room. But she knew. Some liked it that way.

She turned to find Duncan, his lips pursed as he scanned the cameras like he smelled rotten eggs. "Can you do this?" she asked.

He nodded and got to work. There were three keyboards. He used the one in the middle, fingers flying over it like he was on speed.

"I'm taking a screenshot of each room and saving it for later."

She knew better than to ask and kept an eye on both the door and the security feeds.

"Now, I'm rerouting each stream to the dummy site Andy and I prepared. Constant recordings of each will begin as I load them."

He explained he would need to do each separately. It would take time. She watched as more cars arrived. Reluctantly, she took out her cell. It would be the call that began the end of her career.

Duncan lifted a hand and held it over the ear with the bud. "They're coming."

She scanned each flat screen, then asked, "Who's coming?"

"FBI saw the girls. They're organizing."

Relief was mixed with the worry that they might not make it in time. Alabaster was far from any SWAT tactical units. Langley was a five-hour drive. The local black and whites and two detectives would do little to catch everyone. To save everyone. Which was much of the reason she and Duncan were here.

For safe measure, she jiggled the door to make sure Duncan locked it and mentally went over their plan. Moving the blond a few more feet out of sight, she assessed his size. The tranqs were said to put a hundred-pound animal to sleep for approximately four hours. If he weighed one-sixty, she hoped for three. She turned to wait and found Duncan, hands on his thighs, his chest rising and falling deeply.

On the monitors, young girls were led, dragged and carried into the rooms. Her heart ripped from her chest, knowing what was going through the minds and souls of each of them. Some were drugged, some were resisting, some nearly unconscious. All a matter of preference, she knew.

Desperately, she ached to sprint all the way to the white house and open fire. Save the girls from one more night of this. Patience, Savage. Step by step.

A few were posed in the center of the beds and stayed there, swaying as their eyes drooped. Some had one of their wrists handcuffed to one side of the headboards.

Forcing herself to refocus, she noticed the way Duncan's fingers clung to his thighs, the tips white from lack of blood. Carefully, she placed a hand on his shoulder. "Duncan, we need to go."

His fingers moved to the keyboard and flew faster, harder. She hoped he wouldn't make a mistake. The monitor was imbedded in the long table beneath the flat screens displaying rows of files. His fingers stopped as he scrolled through, opening some, closing those, and then opening others.

She'd seen Duncan lose his temper. And although she was at times the only thing that could bring him back, she didn't want to see it again at this moment. He pushed away from the table. Each screen that displayed a room in the white house was back to empty. He'd used the earlier screenshots of the empty rooms and froze them on the feeds. It was genuine and it was time to go.

"How many of those things did you bring?" Duncan asked, referring to Nickie's tranqs as he stepped over one of Moody's grounds crew.

"The case holds a dozen. They're coming in handy."

She was too calm about this. He'd never been handcuffed in one of those rooms, and he was the one who couldn't get his hands to quit shaking. The images of the young girls. Could any of them be older than fifteen? He hoped she ran out of tranqs, so he could take out the johns the old-fashioned way.

"I know you've got your gun on you, Duncan, and you need to keep your head on. You're not a cop."

He lifted a brow as they took the road. Had she read his mind?

"We've talked about this. You're going to see things. Bad things. You won't be of any use to me if you lose it. I assume you would tell me, but any word from the feed in your earbud?" She grabbed the dash when he left the road.

"I'm going to leave it. I think they moved to a new feed. It's dead."

"Let's hope they're using the Alabaster PD. They would be closest."

He parked in the woods. The bright light at the corner of the parking lot was visible. He picked a spot behind a mature evergreen and turned off the engine.

They'd barely made it to the front of the car when they heard the dogs. Nickie pulled her tranq gun, dropped to one knee and waited. Ninety feet, seventy feet, fifty. She let out a shot. The first dog yelped and stopped, then started toward her once more before dropping. The next dog paused to sniff the first as it lay in the snow before charging. Bam. A third emerged, trailing far behind the others. Soon, they had three dogs falling asleep in the snow.

She sheathed her gun as she shook her head. "I really hate it when people take a dog and train it to be evil."

They were Rottweilers, all three of them.

She looked around for what, he wasn't sure.

"They're going to be too cold."

She was worried about the dogs?

He put a hand on her upper arm. "No, they're fine. It's not that cold. Their bodies will warm the snow. Let's go. Someone's going to miss them."

"I'm taking an east path. You go west," she said.

Was that a joke? "I'm not leaving your side."

Dipping her head, she sighed. "We've got to be partners on this, Duncan. It's smarter if—"

"I'm not your partner, and I'm not leaving your side."

"Fine."

The house came into view within the first fifty yards. None of the windows had screens. The blinds were drawn on each. Silently, she jiggled the first back window in the northeast corner. As she checked the type of lock, he took out his glass cutter.

Nudging her, he held up the miniature contraption and was shocked that she had it in her to roll her eyes at a time like this. He secured the central suction to the lower pane and drew a tall, slow oval. Releasing the blade, he then pulled just enough to loosen the glass.

He heard crying. His hand started shaking. He didn't want to move the cut oval of glass completely away from the window. The wind might howl in. But the cries. Cries and grunts.

Nickie squeezed his arm, the steel gray of her eyes staring into him.

He whispered, "I'm afraid to remove it completely. The wind might disturb the blinds. I need two sticks. Pencil size."

He didn't sense any wind, but he wasn't sure. His eyes clamped shut like that might make the sound of what was going on inside disappear. Nickie didn't ask or even blink. She picked up the sticks and passed them to his free hand. "We won't have much time," he said. "Here, you take hold."

She stepped in his path and took the oval piece, hovering it near the window.

"You're going to remove the glass. I'm going to prop

open the wooden slats. Then, you shoot." She'd used five tranqs. That was seven left. The fucking backup had better be on its way.

She pulled her gun with her free hand and nodded. The oval left enough space for the barrel of the tranq gun at the bottom and room for her to aim. He couldn't see what was in there. Only the green color of the far wall. The sounds didn't stop. The people inside must not have heard them. She took the shot.

He froze waiting for a gasp or a scream from what just happened. Nickie held up a finger as she peered with her eye close to the hole.

Duncan took a second to check their surroundings, and when he turned back, she had her arm in the hole and was reaching to unlock the window.

"Come on, honey. We're here to get you out." She put a finger to her lips as she spoke into the room. Slowly, she lifted the window. A girl sat on the bed, her mouth open wide in shock as the man lying next to her mumbled in his last few moments of consciousness. As if waking from a dream, the girl scrambled from the bed toward the window.

"The chair. Can you get the chair to the window? Bring a sheet. It's cold." The girl ignored Nickie's first suggestion, grabbed a sheet and pulled herself up and through.

Setting one knee in the snow, Nickie peered into the girl's eyes. "We have a car." She pointed. "Follow the footprints."

"I'm scared of dogs," the girl said. Her voice sounded even more like a child.

"I took care of the dogs. They are sleeping. You'll see them when you run. Now go."

The girl took off, and they went to the next window. They repeated the procedure with the glass and the tranq gun. This girl was handcuffed. Duncan cupped his hands and gave Nickie a boost. She used the handcuff keys from her belt and wrapped the girl in a blanket as she spoke to her quietly.

Blue eyes as wide as saucers darted to the window and froze on Duncan. He tried to smile reassuringly, but he was a man. Nickie copied his movements by cupping her hand, and Duncan helped her through the window. The girl took off along the path of footprints as they went to the next window.

They repeated the process and were able to free three girls before they needed to turn the corner to the west side of the house. They would be exposed to anyone driving by. They had a system and were getting faster. As quickly as they could, they cut the window, removed the glass and shot. Nickie lifted the window to a man who was face down on the floor.

This girl was so drugged, she hadn't noticed the man had gone down. Duncan boosted Nickie into the window, checking their surroundings as war taught him to do. He waited by the window and helped Nickie lift the girl through. She wore red lace underwear and matching bra. They were disturbing on her small body.

"You have to carry her to the car, Duncan. Check on the other girls."

"I'm not leaving your side," he repeated.

"Duncan, we don't have time. I've got this. I've only got one more tranq anyway. Then, we wing it. Go."

He picked up the limp girl and ran. Her head bobbed over his shoulder, but her eyes rolled. She was still conscious. He saw several sets of footprints and was surprised none had decided to make a run for it on their own. The dogs still lay on their sides. The windows in his SUV were steamed.

He set the girl on her feet, holding her up with one arm as he cracked the door. Gasps and cries erupted as he opened it.

"It's okay. I brought another girl. Just like you. See?" He opened the door completely.

"Gabby," a few of them cried out.

"Detective Savage and I are going to get more of your friends. Take care of her. Share your blankets."

His feet weren't fast enough. He had to see her. When the house was in sight, there was nothing but a slew of their footprints and quiet windows with holes in them. The woods were clear. The corners of the house were clear. He sprinted to the window she would be in.

There was no cut oval. No. He whipped his head and dug his temple into the barrel of a gun.

CHAPTER 29

The same man who brought him his drink when he solicited Moody for work buried the gun into Duncan's face and forced him to turn around. In front of him stood Moody. His gun was pointed at the side of Nickie's head, his other arm possessively wrapped over her shoulder. She looked like she was going to be sick.

"Hello, painter," Moody crooned.

"What did you do to her?" he yelled. The man took Duncan's Beretta and sucker punched him to the side of the head. Duncan saw stars, but he'd been through worse. His head buzzed with adrenaline as he assessed everything around him, the position of Moody's arm, the balance of weight between his legs, the size of the man who put his gun back to Duncan's head. But mostly, Nickie's face. Something was off, even for someone with a gun to her head.

"What did you think the two of you were going to do here, Mr. Reed? You should know I have cameras over every inch of my property. It will be only been a matter of minutes before I am contacted about your arrival. In fact, there will be consequences that you were able to get this far without my notification." He dipped his head to Nickie and licked her cheek making Duncan shake hard enough for the gun to dig a bruise in the side of his face. "And what did I do to our precious savage? We're having a small reunion."

To *our* precious *savage*? His eyes darted to hers in question. She knew the question and nodded. He'd had his hands on her. He may very well have been responsible for the marks on her back. He'd had his hands on her.

An explosion blasted from the east, followed by the sounds of engines coming from the west.

In her signature move, Nickie ducked her head forward, feigning a scared girl whimper, then threw it back, bloodying Moody's face. Duncan took the opportunity to flip Moody's man over his shoulder, following him into a roll before landing at Moody's feet. Moody threw his fist down, landing a solid punch to the side of Duncan's jaw. Duncan swept Moody's legs from beneath him and watched as the side of his face landed in the snow.

Nickie grabbed her real gun from Moody, and Duncan heard her screaming orders to the dude on the ground.

Duncan straddled Moody and used his body weight and momentum to plant a hook to the side of Moody's face. Then another. And another. He'd had his hands on Nickie. He lifted him by the shoulders and slammed his head back on the ground. He had his hands on Nickie when she was a little girl. He punched him again and saw the blood from his knuckles leave lines on Moody's face.

"Duncan, the girls in your car." Moody was unconscious. The other man cuffed. Backup was arriving, and they weren't part of this takedown.

Two men dressed completely in black and one only

half-dressed came in low, running around to the back of the house. No tactical gear. Thugs and a john. Duncan promised Nickie not to use his Beretta unless he absolutely had to. The bullets could be traced back to his gun. He didn't have to use the bullets. Taking the butt of the gun, he swung to the side of the first thug's head. The man hadn't even seen it coming. The second drew his gun as Nickie jumped and used her body weight to come down strong with a full-force punch to the face. She gave one, two more for good measure.

The john stood frozen and lifted his hands. Fight back, Duncan wished, as he watched Nickie waste her cuffs on him. They heard car doors open and a van door slide. Loud voices ordered men to surround the property.

"Duncan. The girls."

Together, they took off running before they ended up cuffed like the john. The path was well worn by this time. As they ran, Nickie couldn't help but consider the possibility that she might get out of this. That was SWAT she heard and not just a few of them. They'd gotten the four who almost escaped. The feds would most certainly get the rest. Where was there to hide? They might be able to get the girls in the SUV to safety and slip out just as they had slipped in. The idea of both taking down this operation and keeping her job made her legs run all the faster.

They passed the dogs and ran to the completely steamed car. Yanking open the doors much too fast, the girls screamed and huddled next to each other.

"It's okay. It's okay. It's me. Does anyone need medical attention?"

They turned to each other, then shook their heads.

"I'm Detective Savage. This is Duncan Reed. The of the police are here. They are gathering the rest of the girls. We're going to drive you—"

"Nickie," Duncan said quickly.

She jerked her head to him, then followed his line of sight. The shadows of two people ran through the woods toward the exit.

Without thinking, Nickie slammed the door and took off running. Her legs were tireless, her arms swinging for momentum. She heard Duncan yell something, but she didn't slow. His quick steps were close behind her.

One of the men checked over his shoulder as he ran and spotted her. He ducked behind a tree. She saw the gun wheel around from the trunk, and she ducked behind the nearest cover. The aim was good, too good, as it grazed the bark next to her head. To the side, Duncan had found shelter and was unharmed. He had his Beretta and let off a few rounds. She waited for one more shot before she flew her hand around the trunk and shot at any sign of movement.

Silence ensued. She watched Duncan. He was the one with what seemed like super human hearing. She couldn't make out his face but analyzed his movements nonetheless.

Certain she hadn't seen any bodies tumble over, she decided to be the one who flinched first and rotated, letting off another round of shots. Duncan followed suit. The answering return fire was just as aggressive. She took the time to change magazines when she heard a single shot.

"Ah." It was Duncan's voice. Her shoulder against her cover, she saw him drop to his knees. Away from his tree. Several more shots danced the snow in front of him.

"No!" she screamed as she left the cover of the tree and ran forward shooting, rolling in the snow and shooting again. She could see everything now. An arm came down from around a tree and before the man had a chance to get off the round, she shot him at his exposed side. Ducking to the ground, she waited for number two to show himself. He took off running and with one clean shot, she got him in the leg.

With less than a second to assess her targets, she lifted from the ground and took off toward Duncan. He was upright again, but not of his own will. She half-walked, half-ran in low with her gun pointing at the man who held him up. Moody.

He held a gun to Duncan's head. Blood stained Duncan's arm, a large hole in the shoulder of his coat.

Moody's face was swollen and cut, blood dripping from his temple and cheek. He opened his mouth and sneered. "Drop the gu—"

She shot him dead center in the forehead.

Duncan expelled a heavy breath he had been holding and dropped to a knee.

"Are you okay?" The panic was worse than the sick sensation of Moody's tongue on her or even the memories it brought back. "Let me see." She tried to pull his coat to the side, but he shook his head and plopped in the snow.

"What about, 'Put down your gun, Moody?' or 'We can talk about this, Moody?'"

Her cheeks expanded, and her smile spread from ear to ear. "I had a good shot."

"That's not what they do on television. You need to watch more television." His voice almost cracked as he let his head fall against the tree he used as a backrest. "You scared the shit out of me."

She sat in front of him, gently spreading his coat to assess the wound. "I scared the shit out of you? As opposed to having a gun pointed to your boyfriend's head?"

"I don't have a boyfriend." He winced as she

examined the hole.

"It went clean through. That's a good thing." She took off her coat and, ignoring the buttons, pulled her shirt over her head. She replaced the coat and ripped her shirt in strips. With no time for careful, she stuffed a piece in the front and back of his shoulder, then wrapped the remaining strips over his shoulder, around and under his arm.

"You make a good field dressing, Detective."

"Can you walk? We need to get the girls."

He nodded and lifted to his feet as blinding flashlights came at them from four angles. She dropped her gun and reached for her badge.

"Hands in the air!"

"See?" Duncan said as he lifted his good arm. "That's what cops say."

"Man down," she yelled. "I'm a detective. I have identification." She held her arms up high. "The man next to me is civilian. He's been shot. He can't lift his left arm."

Men in full SWAT gear rushed them but didn't take them to the ground. They had a dead man lying three feet from them. Rifles pointed at their heads, but they didn't tackle her and Duncan? Then, Lewis and Strong came around from the cover of two of them.

"Detective Savage. Mr. Reed," Strong said in sarcastic greeting. "Funny meeting you here. Continue the search," he added to the team.

"We have a car…an SUV—"

"We found it. The girls are all accounted for. We got everyone except three or four men who ran. I assume this is one of them?" he said, referring to Moody.

"Yes, sir."

"They'll find the others." Strong referred to his team.

"They've both been shot," she confessed. "One in the leg and one in the side. I left one twenty yards due west of here and the other ten yards north of that."

Lewis called it in to the walkie on his shoulder.

"You have a lot of explaining to do."

"I'd like to get Mr. Reed to a doctor first."

He seemed like he was considering it? "Agreed."

Much to the doctor's disapproval, argument and threats, Duncan refused overnight observation. Since they got to the hospital at 4 a.m., she supposed overnight was a gray term anyway. He was fully dressed, and she waited with him for his release papers.

The sun was rising, and she was going to start her new life. The idea of getting away unnoticed was squashed with the minor detail of her shooting Moody dead. It was worth it. No more chasing his ring of guards, thugs and girls. Each was either in jail or in protective custody. The dozen johns who were taken in were the cherry on top.

She wasn't scared. That surprised her. She was ready to go to Child Rescue and see if they could use her there. There were plenty of organizations who might be able to use her.

He was watching her. Duncan's beautiful chocolate brown eyes looked through her and into her soul.

"They're going to want to talk to us separately," she said as she placed his coat in her lap.

"Of course, they are."

She lifted from the seat next to him and laid her lips on his.

"Just so you know," he said, "not all of my parts are broken."

Strong and Lewis stepped in front of the nurse who carried the discharge papers. They were still in their tactical gear, and she assumed came straight from Moody's property. "I'd like to speak with Mr. Reed before he leaves," Lewis said, taking Nickie's seat as she stood.

"Follow me please, Detective Savage," Strong ordered. Nickie would miss the title.

She and Duncan knew what to say. Keep to the truth as much as possible. Well, keep to the truth that wouldn't put them both in jail for twenty to forty.

Strong had somehow reserved a patient room in ER. She wondered how he was able to pull that off.

"How did you know tonight was the bust?"

So, no greeting, no niceties, no concern for her health. "I didn't."

He seemed exasperated, and she had to remind herself they were both exhausted. "Tanner told me to look into boxing. You, yourself, said you had a tip. You had Madison Square covered. So, I decided to take some time off and picnic in a car on a public street."

"And you just happened to have the right night? Where are you getting your information, Savage? Who is your source?"

"I didn't have the right night, believe me. I sat for the entire Friday night before the Madison Square boxing match, the entire Saturday night of the match, and then did the same this weekend."

"I can talk to your captain to verify that."

"I didn't tell him where I was going, but he will verify that I took these last two weekends off. They were my first vacation days since I started at Northridge."

"You were told to terminate your involvement with this case. We told you we would call you if we needed you."

"Another half hour and they would have been gone. The men were...finished when I got to the girls." Duncan would never have been able to handle what she saw through the blinds. Duncan. She wanted to be with him. Strong went on like this for over an hour. She wanted to at least ask about him. Duncan was going through this with a hole in his arm. But asking would have been useless. She told Strong about the cameras they *noticed* as they helped the girls. How they were able to break into the surveillance room and route each and every file they had for the white house to a separate site. Instead of acting like a cop who was just handed the goods on potentially hundreds of high-profile citizens, he barely blinked. Patience, Savage.

He seemed to be tying loose ends together. Or else twisting the knife a little. "You'll lose your badge over this stunt."

"I know."

"I hope it was worth it, Savage." He was already dropping her title.

"You're welcome."

CHAPTER 30

Eddy came into her office as she packed. He sat a hip on the back of one of her chairs...one of the department's chairs. She didn't really have much. No family pictures. No trinkets.

"Maybe I'll put in for a transfer," he whined.

"That's ridiculous," she said as she cleared the crap from her desk.

"Maybe." He lifted from the back of the chair and walked to her, placing his hand on the side of her neck. "It won't be the same." He reached over and kissed her on the cheek. It wasn't romantic, not expecting. Just...kind.

"Ahem." The captain stood in the doorway.

Eddy winked and waited for him to get out of the way. "Captain." He nodded his head.

"Was it worth it?" Dave asked.

She laughed. "That's what Strong asked me." Stopping what she was doing, she stared at him eye-to-eye. "Yes. It was. I can't believe the burden that's been lifted from my shoulders. There are hundreds of rings of girls where this one came from. But this one...well...it was worth it to take this one out for good."

"I guess I'll see you at the annual July Fourth celebration at the Reeds'. Don't be a stranger."

She couldn't imagine coming back here. For what? A visit? "Sure thing," she lied.

Two men dressed in pants and polos knocked on the doorjamb.

She and the captain looked to them, then to each other, then back to the men. "Can I help you?" she asked.

"We're looking for a Detective Savage?" They peered at the door where her nameplate used to hang. "We were told it was this office."

Uh-oh. "I'm Ms. Savage."

"We'd like a few minutes alone," one of them said to Dave.

"I'm the captain of this station. How can I help you gentlemen?" Always part father figure. How could she not miss this man?

"Our apologies, Captain. We didn't see your badge." The first one, the one with sandy brown hair stuck out his arm. "I am Special Agent Goodrich and this is Special Agent Hurst."

Feds? Holy crap. They didn't dress like feds. She didn't care what it looked like, she let herself sink into her chair.

Another knock came at her door. "Why not?" she said aloud to the fifth visitor. "Come on in." She didn't know or care who it was.

It was Duncan? They hadn't discussed his coming in as she packed. Of course, he would. Her tiny office was barely room enough when she had two suspects or meetings with witnesses. There were six of them, including her, and Dave could easily count as two.

"I'm sorry, sir, but we'd like to talk to the detective alone. We'll have to ask you to wait in the common area."

Duncan's eyes said he thought she might be cuffed at any second. She shook her head, assuring him, but she wasn't all too sure if she should. He dipped his head and stepped back only enough to allow Dave and Eddy room to exit. Overtly, he locked his knees and folded his hands in front of him.

The special agent with sandy brown hair sat down first. She already couldn't remember his name and she never forgot a name.

"We'd like to thank you, Detective."

"Excuse me?" Was this a joke?

"We'd like to thank you for your work with the Moody case. We've been following it, and feel you were the core to getting these guys."

So, this was a joke. She lifted her brows. "What are your names again?"

They gave approving glances to each other before answering. "I'm Special Agent Goodrich, yes, like the tire." His partner snorted. He snorted?

"I'm Special Agent Hurst."

"Where are Lewis and Strong?"

They glanced at each other again. Yep. These guys were feds. That was the creepy thing feds did.

"They've been...uh...reassigned. Langley would like for us to try and work with you instead."

"Work with me? I don't know if anyone told you this, but I've been stripped of my badge. I'm no longer a detective. I'm sorry you wasted your trip."

"I don't think you understand. We are here to tell you that was all a misunderstanding."

"A misunderstanding," she repeated as a statement. She disobeyed a direct order from the FBI, from these guys' colleagues, and there was a misunderstanding?

"We know about your past, Detective."

She lifted her chin. At least they had the decency to say it aloud.

"Your record speaks for itself." Hurst spoke this time. "Your work is clean. You have the best conviction rate in the state. And your history gives you an incredible advantage. You recognized details in the death of the girl in your jurisdiction ten months ago. Were able to track the perpetrators to Nevada and practically single-handedly took down a number of them. You scared them enough to cause them to abandon the house they'd been using. You found Moody. That alone was impressive. You have a sixth sense that we want to use."

She knew all this, but it sounded surreal hearing it aloud nonetheless. She had just come to a point of closure in her past. In her present. She paid her debt to the girls she left behind. To the girls who took her place. She was ready to start new.

And did she want to have to get used to the annoying way they looked at each other like they were at that moment?

"Are you offering me a job?"

"If it were up to us, we would. But, no. The reason we're here is to tell you that your title has been reinstated and that we'd like to count on you from time to time when we need expertise in related investigations. If you choose to agree, you'll have to take mandatory psych time. You did kill a man."

"Hold on a minute." She lifted from her chair and walked to the door, then opened it wide. Duncan was still standing there fuming. She squinted her eyes and smiled at him. The expression of confusion on his face was priceless, but his words were the three that had meaning to only them. "There you are."

She winked and said loudly, "Come in here, if you would, Duncan." She didn't wait to see him in and, instead, turned and walked back to her desk. She left her chair open for him on purpose and leaned a hip on the corner of the bare desktop. "Sit down, please." She gestured to her desk chair. She was making a point.

Her blood flew through her veins, but she knew exactly what she was doing. "This is Duncan Reed."

"Your boyfriend." Hurst said it like he could choke.

"Yep." She popped the P. "He has been given status as a civilian consultant on a handful of my cases." His gorgeous, confused eyes darted between the three of them. She hadn't even introduced them yet. "He was the one who noticed the telltale scarring on the girl's back in the casino that was in my jurisdiction ten months ago. He was the one who discovered the bracelet found in the abandoned house in Nevada as the one belonging to Thurmond Moody. And he was the one who was able to transfer Moody's long list of extensive files, recording—who was it?—several politicians and CEOs as they paid to have sex with minors. If I agree to this, I want to know that I can use him when I need to."

They leaned back. She didn't care if they said yes or no. She was ready to start her life over. Now, as they did their creepy look-at-each-other thing, she was second-guessing her confidence.

"We can't guarantee him access to—"

"Just your word that I'll be able to use him...when possible," she added as a disclaimer.

Hurst stood first, followed by Goodrich. Hurst held out a hand. "Mr. Reed, I'm Special Agent Hurst. This is Special Agent Goodrich. Welcome aboard. I imagine you and the detective have much to discuss. We'll be in touch."

And they left. They shut the door and left. She waited stoically until she was sure they were gone. Then, she spun her butt on her desk, her glorious, tattered, splintered desk and faced Duncan. He was wide-eyed and staring at her with his head turned slightly away, his brows dug deep.

"What just happened?"

"We just got ourselves into a load of shit," she said with her biggest smile. Breaking her own hands-off-at-the-station rule, she slid onto his lap and brought her lips to his.

THE NICKIE SAVAGE SERIES

Turn the page for an

excerpt from

SAVAGE
RENDEZVOUS
The Nickie Savage Series
Book Two

R.T. Wolfe

Stuck at a dead end, Nickie pushed her laptop away. "Police work should be more like television," she whined. "Every case solved with fast action, loads of obvious clues, and all in a half hour." Before her eyes crossed from staring at her screen another moment, she closed them and rested her head on her desk.

Even sealed, her eyes betrayed her. She saw the leads that still needed to be followed and reports yet to be completed.

Strong hands slithered over her back, kneading the knots as they traveled up her neck. The reaction from her body wasn't what she assumed Duncan was aiming for. He laced his fingers through her hair, massaging her scalp, making every muscle in her body a puddle of mush.

There was only so much a woman could take.

She lifted her head and swiveled her chair 180 degrees. Straddling his legs, she locked the tops of her boots behind him and pulled him closer.

"You're not sleepy anymore?" he crooned low and sexy.

She didn't answer with words but slipped her fingers in his waist band. He tucked his hands under her backside and lifted, wrapping her legs the rest of the way around him. Heat found heat.

"You promised me a painting," he said as his teeth grazed her neck.

How could she possibly argue when he did that? Regardless, her nerves lifted. Glancing down, she noticed she'd chosen her raspberry pink blouse that morning. It still held creases from wearing her gun holster all day. Her pants were too tight, her boots too tall. She liked it that way, but for a Duncan Reed painting? It made the differences between the two of them much too real. He was Duncan Reed. His paintings hung in the homes of politicians, the dripping rich and people so famous even she knew who they were. She, on the other hand, was just…Nickie.

"Now?" she asked. "Wearing this?"

His head lifted quickly, looking at her through squinted eyes nearly as dark as his chocolate brown hair. A smile, evil and glorious, slowly spread across his face.

Her phone buzzed on her hip. It was the ring tone for forwarded calls from the police station. Giving him the most apologetic look she could muster, she pulled it from her pocket and answered. "Savage."

"Savage," the voice on the other end repeated.

She didn't recognize it or understand why the nerves at the back of her neck came alive and pricked her.

"Nickie Savage. You changed your name. How appropriate."

No. Her eyes darted from one side of Duncan to the other. Her legs dropped from around him and hit the floor with a thud.

"You were never a Nicole Monticello. Nickie Savage suits you."

Now, she remembered. Sixteen years couldn't erase the memory of the voice. She couldn't speak, couldn't

move.

"I see you recognize my voice." He laughed. It was the same laugh that haunted her dreams for years. The laugh he once used as he put the scars on her back.

SAVAGE RENDEZVOUS

**available in
print and ebook**

MEET THE AUTHOR

It's not uncommon to find dark chocolate squares in R.T.'s candy dish, her Golden Retriever at her feet and a few caterpillars spinning their cocoons in the terrariums on her counters. When R.T. isn't writing, she loves spending time with her family, gardening, eagle-watching and can occasionally be found viewing a flyover of migrating whooping cranes.

R.T. enjoys hearing from readers. You can contact R.T. through her website: www.rtwolfe.com

way around him. Heat found heat.

"You promised me a painting," he said as his teeth grazed her neck.

How could she possibly argue when he did that? Regardless, her nerves lifted. Glancing down, she noticed she'd chosen her raspberry pink blouse that morning. It still held creases from wearing her gun holster all day. Her pants were too tight, her boots too tall. She liked it that way, but for a Duncan Reed painting? It made the differences between the two of them much too real. He was Duncan Reed. His paintings hung in the homes of politicians, the dripping rich and people so famous even she knew who they were. She, on the other hand, was just...Nickie.

"Now?" she asked. "Wearing this?"

His head lifted quickly, looking at her through squinted eyes nearly as dark as his chocolate brown hair. A smile, evil and glorious, slowly spread across his face.

Her phone buzzed on her hip. It was the ring tone for forwarded calls from the police station. Giving him the most apologetic look she could muster, she pulled it from her pocket and answered. "Savage."

"Savage," the voice on the other end repeated.

She didn't recognize it or understand why the nerves at the back of her neck came alive and pricked her.

"Nickie Savage. You changed your name. How appropriate."

No. Her eyes darted from one side of Duncan to the other. Her legs dropped from around him and hit the floor with a thud.

"You were never a Nicole Monticello. Nickie Savage suits you."

Now, she remembered. Sixteen years couldn't erase the memory of the voice. She couldn't speak, couldn't move.

"I see you recognize my voice." He laughed. It was the same laugh that haunted her dreams for years. The laugh he once used as he put the scars on her back.

SAVAGE RENDEZVOUS

**available in
print and ebook**

MEET THE AUTHOR

———◆ ◆ ◆ ◆———

It's not uncommon to find dark chocolate squares in R.T.'s candy dish, her Golden Retriever at her feet and a few caterpillars spinning their cocoons in the terrariums on her counters. When R.T. isn't writing, she loves spending time with her family, gardening, eagle-watching and can occasionally be found viewing a flyover of migrating whooping cranes.

R.T. enjoys hearing from readers. You can contact R.T. through her website: www.rtwolfe.com

www.ingramcontent.com/pod-product-compliance
Lightning Source LLC
Chambersburg PA
CBHW020554260626
47157CB00003B/693

CHAPTER 1
Mama Calls

AKWELE OKINE SWUNG her white Sorento into the parking lot of the Star Tower, a ten-story building that housed several businesses in Kumasi.

Her brown high heels *click-clacked* as she sauntered across the parking lot to the first-floor elevator. The clock had barely made it to 8:00 a.m. and her day was already packed. On her agenda were project review meetings with junior software engineers and budget meetings with the partners of Peprah & Anderson.

The elevator dinged as the steel doors swung open. Akwele's attention was drawn to two ladies staring at her as she entered.

Her hand fumbled as she pressed the seventh-floor button. *Why all the staring?* She checked her reflection in the mirrored wall of the elevator; her light makeup was flawless, her thick black curly hair was neatly set in an updo, and her navy blue dress fit her like a glove. Nothing was amiss.

What's going on?

Even though the elevator was crammed with people, they'd deliberately left space around her.

The stares burned Akwele from all sides, and her stomach twisted slowly. She reached for her phone to text her husband, Kwame, her go-to person. As a news anchor at CableOne, he would know if anything about her was buzzing on the news.

Unfortunately, the phone had barely any signal bars. Her lips twitched into a frown as she slipped the useless thing back into her handbag. She waited for the elevator to get to the seventh floor, praying her secret was still safe.

When the elevator opened she dashed out, the people in the corridor silently making way for her. She crossed the short walkway connecting the elevator to her company and stopped in her tracks at the sight of multicolored streamers and balloons hanging from the ceilings. Her typically stoic coworkers paraded around with yet more balloons, and Akwele's jaw fell open. Faces usually glued to computer screens wore beaming smiles and expectant expressions.

She'd never seen the office like this, not even at Christmas. *Was there some party notification I missed?*

She stepped into the company's lobby, and her coworkers burst into thunderous applause.

The company's partners, Daniel Peprah and Michael Anderson, came to meet her, clapping wildly.

Daniel rocked a headful of gray hair and always wore the widest smile she'd ever seen. "You won the Africa Award for Engineering Invention. It was

2

announced this morning!" He hugged her. "I even got the billboard outside updated."

Surprise and delight rolled over her as she laughed. "Ha! I thought I was losing my mind." Akwele returned his squeeze and stepped back. "This is wonderful news." She squinted through the glass walls, trying to catch a glimpse of the company's billboard right outside the Star Tower.

Eager to call her husband, she dug her hand through her handbag for her phone. They'd celebrated her nomination for the $20,000 prize, though, at thirty-two years old, she'd thought herself too young for it.

Michael, the other partner, hugged her next. "I know what you're thinking, and let me tell you, you're more deserving than anyone I know." He patted her firmly on her back.

"Thank you, Michael."

Applause continued around the office.

Half-dazed, she pressed her palms together in appreciation, then quickly made her way to her office. She'd never been a fan of the spotlight, and she'd received enough stares to last the week.

Once inside her office, she breathed a sigh of relief. The news thrilled her, but it was overpowered by the relief that all the stares had nothing to do with her background. Her secret remained safe—no one knew she was from a prominent family. She walked to her mahogany desk, past a tall shelf that already held several awards.

As the cellular network finally kicked in, her

phone beeped with notifications for missed calls and messages. She turned on her computer and opened the prize email; she'd been awarded for her work on *Ispa*, a software platform for optimizing business operations.

Her phone buzzed again, and her husband's face flashed across the screen.

"Hey, dear." Phone to her ear, she continued reading the email. "You wouldn't believe the morning I've had."

"Congrats, Kwele!" He called her by his nickname for her. "I'm over the moon with pride," he gushed. "I've been trying to call you all morning." As the news anchor for the 7:00 a.m. program, he was usually at work by dawn.

"Poor network, nothing was coming through. This prize feels…" She let out a long breath. "I feel like I made the right decision—career decision, I mean."

"Yes, of course, I knew that from the first day I met you."

Akwele fell back into her swivel chair and spun around until she faced the glass wall overlooking central Kumasi. The colorful reflections dancing along its surface told her the celebration was ongoing. She could hear the beats of the latest hiplife song through the door. "You should see the office now. It's a jungle." She laughed.

"Yes, I can hear the music. Well, this is a career victory for you and major publicity for the company. You're going to have a lot of networks lining up to interview you, but hubby gets first dibs."

They both laughed.

"Also, Kwele, with this major career victory down

pat for you…maybe we can now work on our family. Maybe a baby? What baby wouldn't want an award-winning mother?" Kwame didn't waste any time jumping into his latest obsession.

A thin smile crept onto Akwele's lips. "Haha, I see what you're trying to do, Kwame." She couldn't fathom adding a baby to her life now, although she empathized with her husband; he was over ten years older than her and all his colleagues had kids.

Her phone vibrated in her hand as another call came through. "One second, Kwame." She pulled the phone away from her ear to see who was calling and arched an eyebrow. She couldn't remember the last time her mother's name had lit up the screen. *Trust a big prize to bring Ma around.* "I have to take this, Kwame. It's my mom. I love you!" Akwele gave Kwame a second as he returned his love, then straightened in her seat and picked up her mother's call. "Ma?"

"I'm surprised you picked up my call. You seem determined to keep your family out of your life. I've been trying to reach you for weeks."

"Hi…Hi, Ma, I'm so glad you called. It's been quite a day with the big announcement about the prize."

"I wanted to ask you—are you coming for your brother's wedding?"

"Brother?" Akwele scratched her head. Who was this brother? She had no brother. Her twin sister, Akuorkor, was her only sibling. Or was her mother using the Ghanaian jargon where close non-family members were regarded as family?

She'd assumed her mother had called because of

the prize and had been expecting to be congratulated. Instead, she was being asked to show up for a wedding.

"Tetteh has grown very close to me. He's become like my own child," her mother said. "You do remember him, don't you? The gardener's boy?"

Akwele clenched her hand around the phone as a knot formed in her stomach. How could she forget the gardener's boy? The mention of his name invoked the hurt from their breakup years ago. "Yes, Ma, I do remember him."

"He's been taking care of the house, our properties. Your father and I are getting old, you know. He has been our child when we really needed one. He's leaving the house after his wedding, to start a new life with his wife. Let's give him the farewell he deserves. We are his family. His parents served us, but they're dead now. He has no one else but us. Akwele, I'm just asking for you to come for a family event for a few hours."

If only her mother knew what she was asking. The knot in Akwele's middle tightened. "Ma, please…"

"We need to see you home, Akwele, even for a visit every now and then. I mentioned to Aunty B, your nanny, remember her? I mentioned I was going to invite you home for the wedding. You should've seen how emotional she got. That woman loves you more than her own life."

Akwele squeezed her eyes shut; her mother knew all the right strings to pull.

"It's been thirteen years since you left home. It's time to come back. We're going to come together as a family for Tetteh's wedding this weekend. A lot of people have been invited, and there will be many eyes on us and our home. It'll be a wonderful opportunity for everyone to see you again." There was a long pause. "I'm putting my foot down on this one, Akwele. You *are* coming home this weekend."

Akwele shook her head. Ma will always be Ma, pulling her strings like an expert, never mind that Akwele was a top software engineer and had just nabbed a big prize. "Yes, Ma."

She'd always known the time of reckoning with her past—and the reasons she'd left home—would come. She'd just never counted on that time being now, when she'd earned her greatest achievement.

When she finally hung up, Akwele was shaking. She threw the phone across her desk. Her stomach churned uneasily.

She stretched her hands across her desk and let her forehead touch the cool surface. Gone was the confident and celebrated engineer who'd stepped into the office that morning, now replaced by a broken teenager who'd left her home.

CHAPTER 2
The Interview

"You know, it's funny." Kwame sat up in their king-sized bed, took off his reading glasses, and stared at Akwele as she rummaged through their closet. "I never knew you had a brother."

"Well, neither did I," Akwele muttered as she flipped through the hangers in the closet, dressed in a faded, red-checkered bathrobe, a stark contrast to her usual classy attire. She turned to her husband. "He's more of an adopted brother. His father was my family's gardener, but apparently, he's become more like family since I left home. We have to be there for him on his wedding day."

"It's incredibly short notice and nobody sent us a proper invitation." Kwame shook his head incredulously.

Akwele gritted her teeth in irritation. She continued flipping through her clothes, trying to find a dress she could wear to the wedding.

"From what you are saying, he grew close to your family *after* you moved away from home—over *ten* years ago. I don't recall you ever mentioning a call or a visit from him. So why is his wedding such a big priority for us?"

Akwele wanted to crawl under a rock. She hadn't been herself since her mother's call. Kwame was driving her crazy with his questions and she couldn't find a dress she wanted to wear, despite the many options hanging before her. She turned to Kwame's section of the closet and wondered which suit she should pack.

"Honey," she said, turning to him as she held up a silver-colored suit, "do you want to wear this one? I thought it looked very good on you at the journalists' banquet last month."

Kwame reached out and smoothed the black lapels. "You don't think it's a bit over-the-top?"

Akwele shrugged as she looked at the garment. "No, I don't think so. It looks great on you, and I want us to look like we are doing okay." Her voice trailed off as she put the suit back in the closet.

"Really?" Kwame raised his eyebrows as he eased himself into bed. "Kwele, you just won best engineer. You are a senior program manager at a top software company. You live in a nice community, and you are worried about looking okay?" He closed his book and placed it on the nightstand. "What is it with you and this wedding? I am not even sure if I can make it. You know I have an interview this Saturday morning."

Akwele climbed atop the bed and sat next to her husband. "You can catch a plane after your interview. The flight is less than an hour long, and the wedding doesn't start till two. I will drive there the day before the wedding—"

"Drive five hours when there is a flight to Accra that takes less than an hour?" He scratched his head.

"The drive is not too bad."

"I'm sorry love, but the notice is too short—I can't make it." He turned off the lamp on the nightstand and pulled the sheets up.

"No, you have to come, Kwame. I need you to come home with me." She couldn't emphasize how badly she needed him there. Her mind raced with ways to convince him. He'd been obsessed with starting a family lately and had been trying hard to get her on board. "Maybe," she said in a sultry voice as she leaned over and kissed him, "we can get this wedding thing done and then focus on other very important things. Like growing our family."

He stared at her, clearly sensing her manipulation but desperately wanting what she was offering. "Fine, we'll go." He pulled her closer and kissed her back.

"Yay," Akwele said and then pulled back. "But we first need to find you a suit."

Kwame shook his head as she slipped out of bed, tightened the strings of her bathrobe, and walked back to the closet.

KWAME DREW THE covers over his ears to block out the *clang-clang* sounds of Akwele shifting hangers as she raided their closet.

Why is she so obsessed with the clothes we'll wear to the wedding?

11

Sometimes he felt like he didn't know her at all, despite being married to her for three years and dating her for four before that. In all those years, she'd barely mentioned her home.

In the months leading to their wedding he'd begged her to arrange for them to visit her family, but she ignored his request. He finally met her father and sister on the wedding day. Her mother was unable to attend because of ill health, he was told, but he still found it strange that she had never called to congratulate them or visit.

Now, Akwele had just told him someone close to her family was getting married and insisted he come to the wedding. *Why hasn't she ever mentioned him?* And why did it seem like she was calling in the cavalry because of the wedding?

Her insistence on having him come with her made him wonder if she was worried about something or someone she would have to confront back home. That surprised him because she was the strongest woman he had ever met.

The clanging sounds continued—Akwele clearly hadn't found their finest clothes yet. *Does she want to show us off to her family? Is that why we have to look our best?* He would never have guessed that the girl he met seven years ago—he could still remember her faded, oversized jeans, stretched-out T-shirt, and hideous spectacles—was a show-off. He always thought he was the one who had encouraged her to come out of her shell; now, he wasn't so sure.

Who exactly am I married to?

Seven years ago

KWAME LOOKED AT his watch as he waited at the Computer Engineering Department of KNUST. He then peered through the glass window of the office in front of him and darted his gaze around the empty room. Where was the professor? Kwame's meeting with Dr. Sekyi was supposed to have started thirty minutes ago.

He checked the black nameplate on the office door. It read: Professor Yaw Sekyi, Head of Computer Engineering. Kwame was certainly at the right place. He rolled up the newspaper he had in his hand and tapped it against his thigh.

Students in jeans and T-shirts briskly walked past him and threw the occasional curious glance his black, tailored-suit's way.

A girl who looked like she was drowning in oversized clothes almost bumped into him. "I am so sorry," she said, looking up at him with a brief glimmer of recognition before scooting along.

"No worries," he reassured her retreating back. He paced in front of Dr. Sekyi's office, but noticed the girl's retreat had slowed as she kept glancing over her shoulder at him.

Finally, she turned and walked back. "Are you looking for Dr. Sekyi, the head of the department?" She looked up at him through huge, goggle-like glasses.

"Yes, I am. I was supposed to meet him this

morning, but he is not in his office. I host the show *Science Today*, and I have to practice an interview with him."

"He had a family emergency and left for his hometown," she told him. "Sorry if you've been waiting long."

Kwame shook his head. "I hope his family is okay. Will he be back soon? The interview is scheduled for this evening."

"I'm not sure when he will be back. I'm one of his teaching assistants and part of his research group. We just got an email that he had to leave on short notice. I think you'll have to reschedule the interview. I will let him know you were here." She shrugged and turned to walk away.

"Please wait," he called out as he unrolled the newspaper in his hand and glanced at it quickly.

Her eyes lit up with recognition. "Is that the recent news article on the *Ispa* software platform?"

"Yes, Dr. Sekyi is listed as the head of the group working on the platform and…" He scanned the paper. "Someone named Maria works with him. Do you know who she is or where I could find her?"

"Maria Okine?"

Kwame skimmed the paper again. "Yes, Maria A. Okine." He nodded and then repeated, "Do you know her?"

She extended her hand. "I am Maria Okine. I go by Akwele, though."

Kwame's eyes widened. The girl before him looked

like she was twelve, and the article was an important one. "I am referring to the name listed here." He indicated as he showed her the paper.

"Yes, that's me. The *Ispa* platform is my project, and Dr. Sekyi is my advisor," she said smugly.

Kwame was not quite convinced, but there was something about the confidence in her voice. "My apologies. It is a major piece of work, and I was expecting someone older."

She chuckled. "That's okay; I get that a lot. I started university a year early and did an accelerated graduate program, finishing in record time. I am actually twenty-five, though people often tell me I look no more than twelve."

Kwame gaped but extended his hand to introduce himself. "My name is Kwame, Kwame Marfo—not sure whether I introduced myself. I am a news anchor for CableOne and host of *Science Today*. It's nice to meet you, Akwele. You must be a twin." Her name was popular for twins from the Ga tribe.

A shadow crossed her face, but she quickly recovered. "Yes, I have a twin sister." Akwele shook Kwame's hand. "It's nice to meet you, Kwame."

"So, how long have you known Dr. Sekyi and worked with him?" Kwame pulled out a small notepad and pen from his front pocket and started scribbling.

"Since I arrived at the university—about eight years ago. He guided me with my scholarship application. I then went on to become his teaching assistant, which provides some accommodation benefits and an allowance. He's great to work with—we share similar interests."

"Tell you what," Kwame said as an idea came to him. "Let me interview you tonight. Dr. Sekyi's cancellation is tough for a show that's supposed to go live." In fact, he knew interviewing Akwele would be even better than the original plan. The audience would be expecting a graying professor but would be getting a whiz kid instead.

"I am not sure that would be a good idea." She checked out Kwame's clothes and then her own baggy ones.

Kwame read her thoughts. "Oh, we have people who can get you ready. They have clothes in all sizes. Cindy, my stylist, is the best at getting people ready for interviews."

"Okay." Akwele shrugged. "I can email Dr. Sekyi and let him know that I will be filling in for him. And all you'll be talking to me about is the *Ispa* platform, correct?"

Kwame briefly checked the newspaper for details of the software platform. "Um, yes, that is correct." He was tempted to include more personal questions. "We can practice this afternoon. You know, to help you get ready."

"No, I don't need to practice. I know everything about the platform," she said.

Usually, Kwame would have insisted on practicing. But the girl, despite her disheveled appearance, exuded confidence. He handed her a card with the interview location.

"See you later tonight," she said as she zipped away.

Kwame watched Akwele walk away. He was certainly glad she had agreed to come on his show. It promised an interesting evening.

He tapped his phone screen, browsed through his contact list, and called his stylist. "Cindy, this is Kwame. You may need to do some major work on a girl I am interviewing tonight, dress size six, ebony skin color, yeah she needs total work."

Several hours later the set of *Science Today* was, like every Thursday night, bustling with activity in preparation for the show airing. Kwame sat in the host seat, tea mug in hand. On the wall behind him hung a huge sign reading *Science Today*. Several cameras perched on stands in front of him.

He had switched his black suit for a navy one, put on a white shirt and a red tie, and had a white bib-like cloth on his chest to prevent any of his tea from staining his clothes.

He took another sip as he went over his questions for the interview, wondering whether to update or tweak any of them, given he was replacing Dr. Sekyi with Akwele. No easy task, considering he hadn't even practiced with her. This was probably going to be a tricky interview. He would have to adapt as he went along.

The room descended into sudden quiet and Kwame lifted his eyes to see a lady who looked like one of the network executives striding toward him. He could usually tell who the network executives were by how confidently they marched onto the set, as if to remind him they could pull the plug on his show as easily as plucking a stray eyebrow hair. They were also elegantly dressed, which made it clear where all his show's revenue was going. They were not his favorite people, but Kwame welcomed the intrusion, for this lady in her ruby red sheath dress and silver high-heeled sandals froze the tea mug mid-tip at his lower lip.

"Hi, Kwame." Her voice sounded eerily familiar to him. "Do you still want to interview me?"

He choked on the hot liquid trickling over his tongue and couldn't be more thankful for that white cloth he had on his chest. "Akwele?" He dabbed his mouth with the bib while struggling to absorb the transformation. Without the hideous goggles and framed by beautifully defined curly hair, her face was pure perfection. The red dress against her ebony skin was a complete winner.

He needed to stop gawking, as did the rest of the people on the set. "Please, have a seat." He gestured to the chair opposite him, then cleared his throat and ripped off the soiled bib. Behind the cameras, Cindy gave him two thumbs-up. The stylist had outdone herself. He winked at her and turned to Akwele. "You look great." An understatement.

"Thank you," she said as she eased into the stuffed armchair next to him and crossed her legs.

He had interviewed a lot of people and had seen a variety of reactions before interviews, but she was by far the calmest. She looked around the set and noticed the eyes fixed on her, but just sat there completely at ease, which fascinated him. Cindy had done a stellar job, but the elegance and grace Akwele exuded blew him away.

A hush fell over the set a few seconds before 8:00 p.m., and the house lights dimmed as the spotlight above them brightened. "Good evening, welcome to *Science Today*. I am Kwame, your host, and I am pleased to have with me Akwele Okine, a computer engineer at KNUST. She'll be discussing *Ispa*, a project she's working on with Dr. Yaw Sekyi, the head of the Computer Engineering Department at KNUST. Welcome, Akwele."

"Thank you." Her reply emerged confident and crisp.

Then, over the next thirty minutes, she blew him away a second time as she discussed the work. She blossomed like a flower in front of him. She was a master of the work she spoke about, and she didn't use obscure scientific language but told him a story with the grace of a ballerina, fluid and flawless.

She owned the interview, and as for himself, not once did he look at his questions. He didn't even pause for a commercial, as he should have, for he was completely entranced and enamored by her.

Kwame barely felt the time go by and was hesitant to close the show, even as one of the technicians held up a sign indicating they had only five more minutes. Like the final act before taking a bow, she grew more intense, and her answers became more passionate.

He looked up at the time: exactly 9:00 p.m. He closed the interview with the usual pleasantries and ended the show.

Most times, when the show closed, the set erupted into activity. A few times it ended in applause. Today, it remained dead quiet. He looked at Akwele, and he could tell without a doubt she knew she had mesmerized everyone, that this interview would be one to remember. "That was really great." Kwame was eager to continue the conversation. "Can I take you out for a drink? My small way of saying thanks for coming on the show tonight."

"Thank you, but I do have some work to catch up on."

He gave her a ride back to the university, but was reluctant to let her go.

Before Akwele could swing the car door open, he said, "I came here this morning for an interview rehearsal with Dr. Sekyi. I've heard him discuss his work a few times." He turned to her and looked her squarely in the eyes. "But your knowledge of your work is astounding. You own it. *Ispa* is your brainchild, and you are the real deal. You will gain nothing by playing small and hiding in his shadow."

She released a sigh of annoyance but said nothing, fidgeting with the door handle and staring at the time on the dashboard.

"I have a friend called Michael Anderson. He's a co-founder of a software company. They do some very interesting work, and I see you fitting in well there. I think you should call him."

Interest flickered in her eyes, but she blinked it away. "I will think about it," she mumbled as she opened the car door.

Kwame wasn't convinced. "Not much to think about, is there? Just give it a try, and if you don't like it you can come back here."

"Okay, I will give your friend a call." She had one foot out of the car.

Kwame smiled. "I have a call with him later tonight and could mention you, if you want me to." He was lying, but he wanted to make sure she would give the opportunity a chance.

"Sure, you can," she said. "I will also find a way to return your set's clothes."

"Please no, keep them." He also wanted to tell her to throw away the baggy, worn-out clothes, but he held back. *Everything in good time.* Besides, there was something about Akwele that told him fine things weren't new to her, that she could comfortably switch from the girl in near rags to the lady in red. He glanced at her and wondered whether the ratty clothes were a choice, a way to hide. He'd done a brief background check on her prior to the interview and didn't find out more about her than she'd told him—her name was so common, and she wasn't on any social media pages.

"Thank you," she said. And then she was gone, disappearing into the building. Moments later, the lights on the third floor came to life, where he had met her earlier in the day.

Kwame reached for his phone and commanded, "Call Michael." After several rings, he left a message. "Michael, its Kwame. I don't know if you saw my interview tonight, likely not since you don't like to watch me," he said as he chuckled. "The clip is available on the network site. Watch it and give me a call. The lady I just interviewed would be a wonderful addition to your company."

CHAPTER 3
Homebound

Present day

"WILL SHE MAKE IT?" Akwele asked the man in grease-stained blue overalls standing next to her. "The journey is long, and she hasn't moved much in thirteen years."

"I think she will." The man wiped black grease off his hands with a dirty napkin. "She's worn but strong, stronger than she looks." The man turned to Akwele. "Sounds like you really want to take her."

"I do." Akwele stared at the old, gray 2000 Toyota Corolla parked in the corner of her garage. "She has never really had a place here. It's time for her to go home."

The man knelt to collect his tools from the ground. "Is the road good?"

She gave the man a thin smile. "Yes, the road is good."

Akwele and the man stood silently for a few more seconds, staring at the old Corolla. The car didn't look too shabby, but it stuck out like a sore thumb between the two modern cars she and Kwame owned.

The man next to her was named Seth and had served as their car mechanic for years. However, this was the first time Akwele had asked him to work on the Corolla. As they stared at the car, she was sure he wondered—as did she—why she was bent on taking it on her trip; but he didn't ask, and she was grateful.

"If the road is good," he said as he picked up his toolbox, "then she will make it. Travel well, madam." He nodded to Akwele and left the garage.

Akwele stood in that same spot with her hands folded over her black-and-white striped top, which she had paired with navy skinny jeans. She recalled how dismayed Kwame had been earlier in the day when she told him about her decision.

"Are you serious?" he had asked. "You want to take a five-hour trip in that old banger?"

She had softened the truth by telling him the Corolla was her mother's and she needed to return it, but he didn't seem satisfied with her answer.

"There are companies that will move a car for you, you know. Do you think your mom still misses her car after thirteen years? Have you even asked her if you should bring it back?"

Kwame had kept asking questions, some of which she answered and others she ignored. How could she tell him the truth: that she had stolen her mother's car when she ran away? Would he understand she hoped driving back home in the car she fled in would somehow bring her closure?

Gingerly, she walked toward the old Corolla, dragging her suitcase behind her.

Thirteen years ago

"I NEED YOU to get Ma's car keys for me, the Corolla keys," Akwele said to her sister Akuorkor as she hastily pulled clothes out of her drawers and stuffed them into her backpack. She turned to her sister and folded her arms across her green pinafore school uniform. "I have to go, Akuorkor. I just can't stay."

"Is leaving like this the only choice? Where will you go? You are only seventeen. Where will you live? What will Ma and Daddy do when they return from work to find out you've left without telling them?" Akuorkor pleaded as she looked at her sister in dismay. "Whatever it is, we'll fix it. I promise."

Akwele shook her head as she zipped her overstuffed backpack closed and swung it onto her back. "It can't be fixed, Akuorkor. If you want to help me, then get me Ma's Corolla keys, please."

Akuorkor simply stared at her in disbelief.

Akwele stared back. She usually rebuked Akuorkor for being wayward, but today she was asking her to steal their mother's car keys.

"Wait here; I will go get them." Akuorkor slipped her hands into the pockets of the red-checkered bathrobe she was wearing and left Akwele's room.

Akwele peered through the slightly open door of

her room as Akuorkor walked across the hallway to their parents' bedroom. Clearly, Akuorkor's loyalty to her twin trumped that to their parents. A few minutes later, she returned with more than the keys.

"You were only supposed to steal the car keys." Akwele took them off her but frowned at the wad of money still held out.

"We are already thieves. Adding some cash doesn't make us any worse." Akuorkor stuffed the cash into the front of Akwele's backpack, but not before she slipped a few of the notes into her bra. "In fact, I am sure Ma will be glad you at least had some money on you when you ran away."

"What a way to rationalize theft!" Akwele sighed but smiled at her sister and hugged her. They were as different as night and day, but they loved each other fiercely.

"So, where will you go? You don't have many clothes in your bag." Akuorkor hastily looked around her room and then pulled off her bathrobe. She gave it to her sister. "Take this. I am not sure how useful it will be, but it's my favorite; it might come in handy."

Akwele took the bathrobe, gaze downcast. She couldn't look at her sister, and she couldn't tell her where she was going. She just dashed down the stairs and out of the house with their mother's jingling car keys in hand.

Present day

AKWELE SIGHED AS she sat back in the Corolla after so many years. Dust coated the interior, and the ancient dashboard, a far cry from the Sorento she drove now. The scent of old leather lingered, and the seats felt rough.

Maybe Kwame was right. Maybe driving this car all the way home was a bad idea; perhaps it wouldn't even start despite all the checks by her mechanic. She exhaled deeply, turned the key in the ignition, and the car roared to life. The time on the dashboard read 5:30 p.m.

Now or never.

She slowly lifted her foot off the brake pedal, and the car moved forward steadily. The automatic garage door opened, and the yellow-orange rays from the sunset flooded her sight as Akwele began her journey home.

As she drove away from Kumasi, Akwele felt she was leaving the safety and certainty of the life she had built for herself, heading into a world she had no control over, especially over her own self.

"Tetteh is getting married," her mother had said. *"You do remember him, don't you? The gardener's boy."*

If only her mother had known how much those words had dug up her memories. She looked out at the scenery to distract herself from remembering her mother's words.

The terrain ahead loomed, with tall trees flanking the road. The more she drove, the more they emerged. She felt they were going to engulf her. Deep down, she knew her uneasiness was not about the trees but about seeing Tetteh again. Hurtful emotions from their last meeting rose up her throat like bile.

She sighed as the city shrank further in the rearview mirror, and the tree ranges loomed higher. *What if I can't turn back to the life I have built here?* Hadn't she learned from the steep price she had paid for acting out of character thirteen years ago? She glanced again in the rearview mirror—the city behind her was barely visible.

Maybe now was the time to turn back, before it was too late. But, somehow, her foot weighed on the accelerator until the city was no longer visible.

Thirteen years ago

AKWELE WALKED PAST Tetteh often on her father's compound, but barely made eye contact with him or any of the other house helps.

Unlike Akuorkor, who chatted and laughed with the help, Akwele spoke only to her immediate family and Aunty B, who doubled as the nanny and chief cook.

Akwele would sigh when she caught the house helps staring at her or whispering that she was the favorite daughter. Their whispers caged her, and she wondered if she would ever be free to live her own life. At only seventeen years old, the weight of her family's status was crushing her.

She'd never heard any of those whispers from

Tetteh. Other than walking past him on the compound, she'd see him watering the flowers from the window of her room or pulling out weeds from the garden with his father, the gardener. A few times, she'd seen him staring dreamily at the main house. His father would then nudge him to focus on the work. They both had the same tall, lanky figure and dark skin color. Tetteh looked no more than three years older than she was.

The first time she spoke to him was a June afternoon, and the rainy season had just started. As Akwele walked home from school the sky grew darker and the winds stronger, and around her people ran out of their homes to remove their clothes from the drying lines.

A driver was usually sent to pick her up from school but she often sent him away, preferring to stay longer at school to work on math problems. Besides, she'd rather be known for her math prowess than for the sleek car that pulled in to pick her up.

Akwele walked faster, furiously wondering why the driver didn't come back for her given the sudden change in the weather.

Loud thunderous booms shook the sky as merciless rain started to pour down, and without an umbrella or a raincoat Akwele was soaked by the time she made it to the tall front gates of her home.

She expected Adamu, the gateman, to be at his office next to the gate, but he wasn't, which infuriated her even further. She squinted through the iron-bar gates and pounded on them, hoping someone would hear, but the main house was far across the yard and the rain was drowning out the sound of her pounding.

She almost gave up when she heard someone call out her name from the other side. "Sister Akwele?" The house helps referred to her as Sister, a local terminology for showing respect. It was hard to see who it was through the rain, but she could discern a tall and lanky figure running toward her with a huge black umbrella.

"Open the gates," she screamed. As the figure drew closer, Akwele recognized him as the gardener's boy, Tetteh. "Isn't Adamu supposed to be at the gate?" She demanded as he let her in. "I will need your umbrella to get to the main house."

"Come to our home, Sister Akwele. It's just behind the gate." He gestured at the quarters close by. "Stay till the rain passes. The main house is far. It's better to wait in our home till the rain stops."

Akwele peered at the quarters through the rain; she had never been to that side of the compound and was hesitant to go there with Tetteh. "No, it's fine. I will just walk quickly."

Tetteh caught the sickened look on her face as she looked at their quarters. "I promise you won't die there," he snipped. "In fact, you will die faster walking in this rain than waiting in my quarters."

Akwele frowned at his sarcasm; none of the house helps had spoken to her that way before.

"Seriously, Sister Akwele, your mom will kill us both if I allow you to walk through this rain," he pointed out as lightning flashed across the sky, followed by loud claps of thunder. The rain continued to hound them, with water rushing past their feet and soaking their shoes.

There was no arguing his point as the entire town knew of Tina Okine's wrath, and not even her twin daughters were spared of it. "Ok, fine!" Akwele was angry; first at the driver for not coming to pick her up, then at Adamu for not being at the gate to let her in, and now at Tetteh for not giving her his umbrella and insisting very rudely she wait in the servants' quarters. What was the purpose of having help when they wouldn't help you?

Tetteh took Akwele's backpack, which was dripping with water, and held his umbrella above her as he led her down a narrow, pebbled walkway to the servants' quarters. Three small homes with front porches stretched along the lane. Tetteh's home was the first, nestled in the shrubs and painted light blue. He opened a small gate to the porch and led her in.

Akwele stepped onto the porch and out of the rain. "I just don't understand why Adamu wasn't at the gate to let me in. How difficult is a job where you only sit in an office by the gate?" Her clothes and hair were dripping wet. She fumed but suddenly calmed down when she saw a board that was propped on one side of the porch wall. The board had math problems on it, and it looked like someone had been trying to solve them. It immediately drew her in.

"Come in, Sister Akwele." Tetteh held open the front door that led from the porch to the living room.

She picked up a piece of chalk from the ground. "You are solving these problems wrong," she said as she began writing furiously on the board, oblivious to him, to the sound of the rain pounding on the shrubs around them, and to the fact that water dripped off her chin and her clothes still clung to her.

"I know you are good with this stuff, but this is senior year math." His voice trailed as he watched the ease with which she was solving the problem.

"Funny, I was just working on a problem like this. That's how I missed my ride and got stuck in the rain." She looked up for a second and saw the confused look on his face. "You know what it's like when you are solving a math problem and you get so lost in it."

"No, I really don't," he mumbled while still holding the door open for her.

She turned to the board, rubbed off his solutions with the duster, and continued writing. "Done!" she announced as she turned around to face him. "X equals seven."

"How do you know that's right?" He scowled at the board, irritated by the ease with which she had solved the problem.

She tossed up the chalk and caught it without looking up. "I know it's right, go ahead and check. Do you want me to explain to you how I got the answer?"

"No, I don't. Because I don't care about what's on the board, and even if you explained it a thousand times I still wouldn't care. Now, can you please get inside before you catch a cold!"

His rudeness jutted her head back, and she wondered if he had forgotten who she was. She stepped inside the room, which was smaller than her bedroom and painfully simple, with three wooden chairs arranged around a small wooden table in the center and a door at the back. The ceiling hung so low it tightened her chest with claustrophobia. The extraordinary thing in the room was what looked like a giant black guitar case propped against the wall in one corner of the room. "What's that?" she asked

"That's my cello," he announced with shoulders thrown back and smiled. "I am actually very good at playing it."

"Really?" She giggled. "Who in our part of the world plays that?" She also wondered how a house help could play such an exotic instrument, but she didn't ask him that.

He briefly disappeared through the door at the back of the room and came back with a clean gray T-shirt and a pair of shorts. "Go in there and change," he ordered, pointing to the room he had just come from.

She stepped into the room and was again surprised by its sparseness. A twin-sized bed lined one wall, and a sleeping mat stretched on the ground beside it. On the mat lay several music sheets; maybe he was passionate about music. She hurriedly peeled out of her wet school uniform and into the clothes he had given to her. They felt rough and stiff against her skin compared to the soft and comfortable fabrics she usually wore.

"I don't suppose you've had anything to eat this afternoon," he called out. She followed his voice down the hall to the kitchen and found him standing next to a tabletop stove, dishing rice onto a plate. Like the other rooms, the kitchen was tiny. In addition to the ancient-looking tabletop stove there was a mini fridge, a small sink, a small cupboard, and a dining area with two chairs. The final feature, a small drying line in the room's left corner, was where she hung her wet uniform.

He placed a plate of rice and stew on the table. "Sit."

His tone infuriated her so much she wanted to explode. "You shouldn't speak to me that way." She yanked the chair out from under the table and sat, clenching her jaw to contain her anger.

He shrugged. "Because...?"

She lost control of the vitriol boiling a path up her throat. "Look. I may be in your cave and wearing your rags, but let's not forget who the boss is here."

"You are not my boss. Your father is." His tone lashed as sharply as hers. "By some stroke of luck, you were born in the main house and I in the quarters. That doesn't make you any better than me."

She sat frozen, staring at him and unable to believe what he had just said. She was definitely going to report him to her father.

"Now eat." The bite remained in his tone. "The food is not as great as Aunty B's, but I am not a bad cook."

"You are not humble either." She took a forkful from the bright yellow plastic plate. She found the rice a bit hard and the sauce heavy on the tomato side, but she was hungry so she ate. "Thanks for the food. It's, um...nice," she lied.

Without looking at him, she could feel his eyes searching her face as she ate. Why was he looking at her like that? Was he about to make another rude outburst? She shifted her mind from him and instead thought about the math problem she had solved on the board outside.

"Okay, I am full." She pushed the half-empty plate away from her.

He pulled it toward him, rolled up his sleeves, and started eating her leftovers with his bare hand. She found it weird, but somehow intimate. Like they had done this before, like they had done this several times. She watched him wolf down the food, seeming hunched over as he ate, but perhaps that was because he was very tall and the table was short. His shirt clung to his lanky frame as if it were too small for him, and sitting this close she could see how threadbare it was; it looked like a hand-me-down.

"Your first name is Maria," he said without looking up from the food he devoured.

The out-of-place question fumbled her tongue. "Um, yes, it is."

"Maria is a nice name. I like it," he said. The red sauce he fingered from the plate held his full attention.

"Okay." It was the first nice thing he'd said to her. "Um, thanks."

He said nothing else until he had picked every grain of rice off the plate and cleared the table. He looked outside. "It has stopped raining."

She turned toward the window. "Oh, I didn't even notice. I should go home. Thanks for taking me in." She picked up her backpack and swung it over her shoulders, then removed her wet pinafore from the line. "I will make sure you get your clothes back."

"No problem. Will you come back?"

Certainly not, she inwardly snorted, as she found him rude and insolent. "I don't know. I am not really the friend-making type. You can try my twin. She's buddies with *everybody* in this town."

He shuffled his feet and peered at her from the tops of his eyes. "I was hoping you'd help me with my math."

She paused. His pride surely wouldn't allow him to lie about needing help—and he clearly did need help—but by his sudden awkwardness she wondered if there was more to the request.

Hands shoved into his pockets, he gave her a sheepish smile. "I have already repeated senior year twice, and I don't have many options left."

Oh. "Of course. I love teaching, and you clearly need help. Are you free tomorrow afternoon? I can come by, but let me warn you I am a tough teacher."

He grinned and opened the door for her. "Yes, I will be here. I will be here waiting for you anytime you come back."

CHAPTER 4
Home

Present day

As Akwele steered the Corolla off the highway and onto the road that led to East Legon, she could feel her home beckoning. Earlier in her journey she had wondered if she would be able to remember her way back, and was surprised by how easily it came to her. Her hands turned the steering wheel, and her foot hit the accelerator, without even thinking.

The unsettling feeling that had weighed on her mind gave way as she ached for home and for the familiar. She yearned to be hugged by her father, kissed by her mother, and fed by Aunty B. Mostly she yearned for Akuorkor, and remembered how they used to dress in matching overalls when they were younger and run after each other.

She relaxed her grip on the wheel, allowed her shoulders to drop, and rolled down the window. The air felt lighter, and her breathing came easier. Lingering scents of *kelewele*, spiced fried plantains, and *kenkey*, fermented cornmeal, wafted into the car. The sellers were long gone, as it was late in the evening, but the air still held on. It amazed her that so much time had passed since she'd left, and yet so little about her and her home had changed.

The tall black iron gates came into view, and she pondered the welcome she would receive. She slowed the car and inched ahead, wondering if Adamu, the gateman, still worked at the gate. No light shone through the gateman's office window, which made her consider turning back to find a hotel nearby. It was almost 11:00 p.m., and the last thing she needed was for everyone to wake up upon her arrival.

She didn't have to consider the hotel option for long as she caught sight of Adamu fast asleep on a plastic chair next to the gate, with his head rolled so far forward it appeared close to falling off his body. Neither the sound nor lights of her car had woken him. This was the man in charge of watching the main gates?

More surprisingly, he looked like he hadn't changed at all. Even the blue-checkered shirt he wore looked familiar; she wondered if it was the same one he'd worn so religiously years ago. The only difference about him was his fuller and rounder belly.

Aware of how her interaction with him would go, she reached for her handbag and pulled out two hundred GHS from her purse. She folded the money and honked.

Adamu staggered to his feet, shielded his eyes briefly from the glare of her car lights, and then rushed over to her.

As he approached her window, she lowered the glass farther. "Adamu, *te oyɔɔ tɛŋŋ*?" She hadn't spoken Ga for quite some time, but it rolled easily off her tongue.

"Sister Akwele, we are well, *wɔyɛ jogbaŋŋ. Bianɛ onukpa ji bo.*" He smiled as he commented on her being an adult now. "*Wɔ mɛi bo haahu kɛjɛ leebii nɛɛ.*"

Her brow rose, guilt twinging. The help had been waiting for her since *morning*?

"*Mɛni okɛba hami?*" he asked.

"This." Akwele reached out to give him a handshake and slipped the money into his hand. "I brought you this."

Adamu's smile widened as he felt the notes. "*Oyiwaladoŋŋ*, thank you. Aunty B *mii mɛi bo.*"

Apparently, Aunty B was waiting for her. Akwele waved at Adamu and drove past the gates. She deliberately kept her gaze away from the servants' quarters and stepped hard on the accelerator.

Thirteen years ago

"I'M REALLY GLAD you agreed to tutor me," Tetteh said as he toyed with his pen. He was seated at a table on the front porch of his quarters with an unopened notebook in front of him.

Akwele wrote on the board next to the table. "It's no problem. Did you do the homework I gave you yesterday?" She looked at the mathematical figures more than at him. Any time she turned around he was either fiddling with the stationary, scribbling music notes, or flatly staring at her.

"No, I didn't do it." He spun his pen on the table playfully.

"You've never done any of the homework I've given you. I have been coming here every day for the past two weeks, and you don't seem interested in learning." Akwele shook her head in dismay. It baffled her that he had asked her to tutor him when it was crystal clear math was the last thing on his mind.

"I am interested in learning. I clearly need help." He held up a math sheet with an F written in red ink on it.

"Good, let's make each other's time worthwhile then." She sighed loudly. *Why can't he be more serious about his studies, since it will help him in his future?*

"I think these sessions really give us a chance to get to know each other. Before you started coming here, I always thought you were spoiled and privileged."

"What?" She spun around to face him.

"But you are not at all," he threw on. "You are very intriguing. For example, your eyes, at first pass, seem unfocused. Like you are staring at nothing. But upon a closer look, I find them strikingly focused, not at what is before you but rather inwards, like you are constantly calculating something or playing with something in your head. Now I know you are constantly playing with numbers in your head."

Akwele gritted her teeth as she turned to the board. "You should give up school and be a poet."

"Tell that to my father, who doesn't think highly

of being an artist. Another thing I find very intriguing about your face is that from a distance it's porcelain smooth, but up close there are very faint lines under your eyes, and then right there"—he pointed to her cheeks—"a few tiny black spots are scattered at the top of your cheeks. I feel like those lines and spots, those imperfections, are telling me a story. I desperately want to know that story."

Wow. "How about I give you a picture of my face, pack up my books, and go home?"

"Oh no. Have I said too much? I'm sorry. Let me make it up to you."

"Just open your book and solve the problem. Not one more word from you unless it's related to math." Akwele turned back to the board with a loud sigh.

"Do you like music?"

She rolled her eyes and resisted the urge to snap at him. "I do." She wished he would ask her about the chalked math problem. "I like to have a little music in the background while I am trying to figure out math problems. It can make problem-solving a lot of fun. You should try it," she said, trying to refocus the conversation on math and remained glued to the board.

His chair squeaked and footfalls led inside the room, but she didn't turn around. The door slammed shut as he came back shortly after, sat back down, and opened a case.

Then came a soulful sound so fascinating it compelled her away from the equations. He sat with the cello between his knees. His body seemed lankier around the huge instrument but he played it so well, with his right hand moving the bow back and forth while the fingers of his left hand held down the strings. *How and where did he learn to play that exotic instrument?* He may have anticipated her surprised reaction, but he was so focused on playing that it didn't seem he could even see her. He was an extension of the instrument. His body swayed with it as he coaxed a haunting melody from the wood, and another time and place floated across his faraway gaze.

She remembered how she had almost laughed when he told her he played well. She now regretted that reaction, but still wondered how Tetteh was so gifted with such an exotic instrument. Seeing his mastery with the cello explained to her why all the math on her board was Greek to him. There was only room for one love in his life, his music.

The sound of Tetteh's music inundated Akwele's senses in ways she never imagined possible. This was the first time in her life anything had turned her away from her board. With that music she couldn't think, let alone solve math problems. No one could.

She put down her chalk and sat next to him while his bow caressed the strings. When he'd asked her whether she liked music, she had expected him to turn on a radio or some other device. She hadn't imagined he would pull out his cello. As she told him earlier, she was used to having music in the background while she worked math but now, for the first time, the math was in the background.

Above all his song choice broke her, for she was in the melody, in the poignant strains of "Ave Maria."

Present day

As AKWELE DROVE up to the main house, Aunty B's big, towering figure waited for her at the top of the staircase that led from the driveway to the front door.

Aunty B had a white scarf tied around her head and a loose blue African-print cloth draped around her yellow-flowered nightgown. She held a lantern in her hand, despite how well-illuminated the front of the house was. While growing up, Akwele was convinced that Aunty B carried the lantern purely out of habit rather than necessity, and the sight of it now almost made Akwele laugh.

She parked and raced up the staircase to meet her. When Aunty B saw Akwele, she broke out into a local gospel song and headed down the staircase. Aunty B's steps were slower than Akwele remembered, and despite Aunty B's strong-looking figure, age was starting to take a toll on her nanny.

They met at the middle of the staircase and hugged for a long time. Akwele never wanted to leave Aunty B's big, warm embrace. She breathed in deeply the scent of Aunty B's familiar dusting powder while being lulled by the gospel song.

"I prayed every day I would still be alive when you returned home." Aunty B took a step back to study Akwele. "Look how much you've grown, how beautiful you are," she exclaimed as she hugged Akwele again.

"I am sorry I didn't call you more," Akwele said, still wrapped in the embrace.

"No worries, daughter. It is all in the past."

A flicker of light caught Akwele's eye, and she looked up. The light in her parents' bedroom had been turned on. Her parents' bedroom was at the left corner of the second floor, and had a clear view of the front driveway and the staircase. The window framed the silhouette of her mother's body. Despite being away for so long, Akwele could still discern her mother's petite figure anywhere. Then the silhouette went away, and the lights were turned off.

Akwele had half-hoped her mother would come out to meet her, maybe even give her the kiss she had yearned for, but no. Clearly, not everyone at home would be as excited to see her as Aunty B was.

"Your mother is resting," Aunty B said as she also saw the lights being turned off. "She's had a long day, organizing this wedding…" Aunty B's voice seemed to trail off. "But she is very happy you are home."

Her nanny was trying to protect her feelings. "Of course, I understand."

"Akuorkor is out now. I believe she is at a bachelorette party. Your father had to make a quick trip to take care of some work-related matters. Your workaholic father hasn't changed his ways, but he will be back early tomorrow for the wedding. Come in now, my daughter." Aunty B headed for the front door.

"I will just get my bags and, um, park properly." The return of the Corolla would surprise many in the household. The least she could do was not leave it sitting glaringly before the main house.

"Oh, don't worry about that." Aunty B blew out

the lantern and opened the front door. "I will send someone to take care of all that. Are you hungry? I could fix you some dinner."

Akwele didn't remember when she last ate, but she didn't feel hungry at all. "Thank you, but I am okay…" Akwele's voice trailed off as she entered the house. Her senses roared. The room faintly lingered with the rose-scented air freshener they had used in the house for years. Most of the lights were off, but the organization of the living room furniture hadn't changed.

As she walked up the staircase to the second floor where her room was, she touched the cool and rough-textured wood of the staircase handle. Her childhood memories came to her fiercely, and even in the silence, she could hear her and Akuorkor's shrieks as they played, up and down the stairs and around the house. Aunty B followed her up the staircase quietly, her presence barely felt.

On the second floor, Akwele passed Akuorkor's door and finally reached her own. The door slightly creaked as she opened it. She found the light switch exactly where she knew it would be. White sheets covered the few chairs in the room. Her desk still held her notepapers and books. Someone had dusted and cleaned, but left every paper and pen exactly where Akwele had left them. Her chalkboard still stood in the middle of the room. It was as though she had never left.

Her room hung thick with emotion, and the enormity of the moment weighed heavy on her; the realization she was home after so long. The same home she had run from. She walked toward her full-size bed, which was next to the window that overlooked the front of the main house. She drew aside the lace curtains and found the view hadn't changed.

Akwele suddenly felt exhausted from the long drive, from the onslaught of emotion and from the anticipation of how home would be after thirteen years. She sank down onto her bed and her heavy eyes caught sight of Aunty B as she pulled the white sheets off the chairs. The lights then went off and the door squeaked closed.

As sleep started engulfing Akwele, she wondered if she should have gone to greet her mother upon her arrival. She also wanted to call Kwame, to let him know she had safely arrived and couldn't wait to see him in the morning. She did none of those things, as she fell into a deep sleep.

Down the hallway from Akwele's room, Ma Tina had cracked opened her bedroom door to watch her daughter come up the stairs. She continued watching Akwele as she entered her room, with Aunty B in tow. When Aunty B shut Akwele's door, Ma Tina went to her bed and sat down pensively in the darkness.

Moments later, there was a gentle knock on her bedroom door. "Come in B," she murmured.

"Ma Tina, Akwele is home," said Aunty B as she entered. "She looks well, letting you know as you asked."

"Thank you, B. Before you go to bed, call my seamstress. Tell her my daughter has returned home and she will need to finish her dress."

CHAPTER 5
Twinnies

AKWELE WOKE UP to the sounds of banging pots and clanking dishes from the kitchen downstairs. *Is someone actually cooking or just fighting with the pots?* Groaning, she pulled the bedcovers over her ears.

It seemed like the big wedding day was already in full swing. She imagined the caterers and servers putting their finishing touches on an impressive array of dishes in the kitchen. Her mother's fine plates and glassware were probably being wiped till they reflected light; one speck would be all it took for Tina Okine to throw a fit.

Akwele ran her hand over the bedsheet. It felt soft, like she remembered, and was even her favorite blue color. She felt so good being wrapped in the covers that not even the jeans she still wore from the day before, which were not the most comfortable to sleep in, could spoil the moment.

A loud engine revved outside her window as a truck pulled up. The clinking of glass bottles suggested crates of drinks were being unloaded. Akwele sighed loudly—there was no way she was getting any more sleep. *I can't wait for this wedding to be over*. All the activity was making her want to pull out her hair, and she shuddered as she anticipated other activities yet to come during the day.

She sat up and picked up her phone from the nightstand. She had already missed two calls and a text from Kwame.

Kwame: call me Kwele, wondering if you got home ok, love Kwame.

Before going to bed, she should have called to let him know she had arrived.

The digital numbers on her phone switched to 9:32 a.m. Kwame was probably in the middle of his interview. She decided to wait on calling till after ten, when his interview was over and texted instead.

Akwele: Got home safe love. Call back when your interview is over, love Kwele.

As she placed her phone back on the nightstand, she noticed her suitcase and purse had been brought to her room and placed at the foot of the bed—Aunty B was a godsend.

Akwele cast her eyes around the room, seeing more of it with the sheets removed from the furniture and sunlight streaming in. To the left of her bed stood the door to the bathroom she shared with Akuorkor. Their father, a stickler for little things he thought promoted unity, had insisted they share a bathroom even though there were several in the house.

She and Akuorkor shared a room till they were ten

years old and their parents realized they were incompatible roommates; Akwele was organized to a fault while Akuorkor thrived on mess. Despite moving to separate rooms they had stayed close, with the bathroom they shared providing easy access to each other's rooms.

The more Akwele looked around her room, the more poignantly she remembered her last hours there before she left home.

Thirteen years ago

IF AKWELE'S EYELIDS could speak, they would complain about the many times she had blinked just to keep back tears and shut out the mental picture of Tetteh etched in her mind. Her face wore a heavy frown, and she kept her hands folded as she stood in front of the chalkboard in her room.

She still wore her uniform, even though school had been over hours ago. Everything about her demeanor showed she was upset, but she was also trying hard to shut down those emotions by attacking the numbers on the chalkboard.

Munching on a meat pie, Akuorkor walked in through the bathroom door. Her red-checkered bathrobe, which was open in the front, showing her hot pants and tube top. "Aunty B just made meat pies, and they are so good. I am telling you, that woman has dwarfs in the kitchen." She looked at Akwele and frowned. "Why do you look so weird?"

49

Akwele kept her eyes on the board; she couldn't look her sister in the eye. She couldn't tell her the reason she was upset. "I…" She choked with emotion. "I am j-just trying to figure out my homework."

Akuorkor eyed her suspiciously and blinked hard at the board. "Okay, talk to me about it. That might help you think through it."

"Um, I don't understand why this and this number don't add up to that number if they are necessary and sufficient in this equation." Akwele knew the numbers on the board, and all she was saying was probably Greek to her sister, who didn't care much about academic work, let alone math. She also knew that Akuorkor was just playing along and feigning comprehension as she was concerned about her. That concern—and the meat pie—were probably the only things keeping her sister awake through the explanation.

Tears stung Akwele's eyes. "These two numbers are supposed to add up." She bit her lips to keep them from quivering. "So why won't they?…Why can't they? Unless—" Akwele paused suddenly. "Maybe it's because we don't know the nature of the numbers. We need to know as much as we can, so we can make the most informed decision." The words rushed out of her mouth as she hurried to her backpack and frantically dug through it. She grabbed an envelope and dashed toward the door.

Akuorkor raised her hands in frustration and followed Akwele. "What is going on?"

"Just wait here. Don't follow me!" Akwele said as she ran out with the envelope in hand.

Ten minutes later Akwele returned to the room, banging the door shut and leaning against it with the envelope still in her hand and staring blankly at her math board. Before she'd left the room she'd been upset. Now she felt defeated, like she had hit rock bottom.

Akuorkor rushed toward her sister, clearly wondering what must have happened to Akwele in the few minutes she'd been gone. "Akwele, just talk to me! Use words and not numbers."

Akwele took slow, labored steps back to her board. "I just solved the problem. The numbers don't add up because they are mutually exclusive and not mutually sufficient or necessary." Solving the math problem had somehow brought her closer to the reality of her situation with Tetteh. Akwele exhaled deeply as her shoulders dropped. "In fact, they cannot mutually exist. It's one...one or the other."

"What?" Akuorkor had the blank stare now.

Akwele slowly stepped away from her board. "I need to go," she said, staring at the envelope in her hand.

Akuorkor's stiff arms said she wanted nothing more than to shake Akwele to get some answers. She threw up her hands. "Go where, Akwele? Whatever it is, we can fix it."

"Didn't you hear what I said, the numbers cannot mutually exist. It's one or the other!" With that, Akwele grabbed her backpack and carefully put the envelope in the front section. She hastily began pulling clothes from her drawers, stuffing them in the backpack, all while blinking fiercely and holding back her tears.

Present day

BEING BACK IN her room after so long evoked heart-tugging emotions. Akwele wasn't seventeen anymore, but somehow being an award-winning engineer and having a successful marriage wasn't making her feel as strong as she hoped. She rather felt there was a lot more at stake if she didn't check her emotions.

She glanced up at the clock, wondering if Kwame was done with his interview. He was her rock, and she needed him badly. The time now read 10:15 a.m.—his interview should be done.

She called him and sighed when her call went straight to his voicemail. "Hi, honey, it's Kwele. You must be off the air by now. Just give me a call before you hop on your flight, okay. I can't wait to see you. I love you very much, more than you could ever know."

No sooner had she hung up than there came a loud knock on the bathroom door. She knew who it was before a face covered in white cream peered through the doorway. "Is it just you, or are you with your husband?" came the familiar voice.

"It's just me." Akwele sat up in her bed, excited to see her sister.

Akuorkor pounced in, wearing a bright red crop top and a miniskirt. She carried two tall glasses of champagne. Akwele smiled at the familiar sight. "Isn't it too early for that?" Akwele gestured at the drinks.

"We need to have breakfast." Akuorkor settled the glasses on the nightstand and jumped on top of her sister in the bed. "Sorry I wasn't here when you arrived. It's been one party after another. I am not sure if I have had any sleep in the past few days."

"Your life has always been more exciting than mine. What's that on your face?"

"Facial treatment. I have something for you." Akuorkor reached underneath her cropped top for a foil-wrapped package while Akwele looked on suspiciously. "Can you guess what it is?" Akuorkor asked as she handed it over.

Akwele unwrapped the foil and yelled, "Oh my God," as she unveiled a meat pie. Instinctively, she broke it in two parts and handed one half to her sister.

"Aunty B made them, and I saved one for you. You know how fast those go around here." Akuorkor settled in the bed next to her, pulling the sheets around herself.

Akwele took a big bite and allowed her head to fall back on her pillow, savoring the taste of the pie. "Now I know I am really home. How can they be so good? Do you still think Aunty B has dwarfs in the kitchen?"

"At least ten of them." Akuorkor grinned as she bit into hers. They both burst out laughing and then lay down, quietly staring at the ceiling while they ate. "Aunty B hasn't changed one bit."

Akwele giggled. "I didn't think she ever would."

"Remember how serious she was about molding us into good girls. Clearly, that ship sailed with me." Akuorkor mimicked Aunty B's voice. "A girl brought up with good biblical and cultural values should not fool around with boys less worthy of her, otherwise she disgraces herself and her family."

Akwele ate her pie slower. Beads of sweat formed on her brow. "Yeah…"

"Well, enough about her." Akuorkor turned to her sister. "I missed you."

"Me too, but I loved all the times you visited me. You came to my wedding, too, which meant a lot to me."

"Yes. But I missed you here, in your room. I missed eating pies with you and gossiping about Aunty B."

"Yes, I missed that more than anything in the world."

Akuorkor reached over her sister to grab one of the drinks and downed her glass just as fast as she'd picked it up. A beat later, she belched loudly in her sister's face.

"No change I see?" Rolling her eyes, Akwele shook her head. "So, what's the plan for today? Is the wedding going to be at that old, rickety, Presbyterian church and then the refreshments here at home?"

"No, the wedding is in Ma's garden," Akuorkor said.

Akwele flung aside the covers and bit her lip as she continued to listen to Akuorkor.

"Tetteh's father really worked hard on that garden. He tended to it every day. I hear the day he died he had spent the afternoon there. Ma thought it was symbolic for his son to get married in the garden where his father worked. He's leaving after the wedding, and Ma wanted him to take that garden wedding memory with him. Ma can sometimes be such a romantic. Too bad none of us turned out like her. It's also going to be a traditional wedding, followed by a priest's blessing, and then signing of the marriage certificate. After that is my favorite part of every wedding, refreshments and partying. All of that is going to be right there in Ma's garden."

"A traditional marriage is supposed to be in the father of the bride's home," Akwele snapped. "Why is it in our garden?"

"Because Ma dictates tradition as she sees fit. Seriously, they went back and forth on a few options, and this was the best way to have all the marriage celebrations on one day and in one place. Ma's garden has always been a beautiful location."

"Yeah, no doubt," Akwele muttered.

"Plus, you should be the last person to bring up how a traditional marriage should be. Daddy and I came for yours in your living room in Kumasi. That said, you should prepare yourself to answer to Ma on your marriage because you know she will bring it up."

"I have been married for three years. Is she still hung up on how I planned my wedding?" Akwele got up from the bed and opened her suitcase.

"Have you forgotten who our mother is?" Akuorkor drank the last glass of champagne.

Akwele sighed. "The day has barely begun, and I am already exhausted. So, when do we have to get to Ma's garden?"

"The ceremony starts at two, so maybe around one forty-five. Daddy and Ma are filling in as Tetteh's parents, and will likely be running around trying to organize things right to the start of the event. I am a bridesmaid, so I must get there early for pre-wedding photos. Tetteh's bride likes things all timely."

Akwele perked up at this first mention of Tetteh's bride. "So, what's Tetteh's wife-to-be like?" She was dying for information about her.

"She's nice. Her name is Esi. She sings occasionally at the bar where Tetteh plays. I know she's trying to find a more stable job."

"Oh, really." Akwele was sizing up the girl in her mind.

"Here is a picture of her." Akuorkor walked round to where Akwele was standing and handed Akwele her phone.

Akwele squinted at the picture—a blurry nighttime image. "Hard to see, but she looks okay." Akwele shrugged and handed the phone back to her sister. She took her bathrobe out of her suitcase.

"Oh, you still own that," Akuorkor said, and she and Akwele both laughed.

"Yep, would never throw away this gift from you."

Akuorkor hugged her sister. "Okay, I have to go now. Oh, wait." She dashed back to her room through the adjoining bathroom and came back with a covered hanger. "Ma had her designer make a dress for you. I told her you probably have your own taste in clothes now, and you would bring your own, but you know our mother. Akwele, if you don't want to wear it, it's fine. Feel free to toss it somewhere."

"Ma has a flamboyant style, and there is little chance of me wearing what she ordered." Akwele took the hanger and set it aside without even looking at the dress. She could already imagine a hideous combination of colors. "Isn't it great that we are finally old enough to say no to her dress choices?"

"Exactly." Akuorkor laughed as she kissed her sister. "See you in a bit, love."

As Akuorkor left, Akwele realized she hadn't chosen which of the four dresses she had brought to wear for the wedding.

She opened her suitcase and laid them out on the bed. They were all custom made by top designers. She wanted a dress that made her feel secure and confident, and at the same time she wanted to look feminine and beautiful. Where was Kwame when she needed him? He usually had great fashion advice.

She looked over all the dresses again and surprisingly found them all too plain. Hesitant, she unzipped the garment bag Akuorkor had just brought and revealed a dress with a fitted, peach-colored top and a flared peach-and-blue African-print asymmetrical skirt.

Stunning.

She slipped it on and ran admiring fingers over the pleated neckline and the asymmetrical skirt, which was knee length in the front and calf-length at the back. It fit her like a glove, and Akwele wondered how her mother got the size so right.

She couldn't stop admiring the dress as she twirled before the bathroom mirror.

The last time she had been this happy about a dress in that room was on the first evening she went to meet Tetteh.

Thirteen years ago

TETTEH: LET'S GO to the garden.

Akwele: It is late, isn't it?

She was already in her pajamas.

Tetteh: It's just 8. Come hang out with me. It will be fun.

Akwele: I don't know, Tetteh.

Tetteh: I will wait for you just a few steps away from the front of the main house.

Akwele stared outside her window. She had never left the house at this time. Though lights flooded the front of the house, the rest of the compound didn't look as well lit. How would she get past her parents?

As she stood at the window, she listened to Akuorkor singing in the bathroom. Akuorkor went out often, and at any time that pleased her. Maybe she could help.

Akwele headed to the bathroom and found Akuorkor standing in front of the mirror, singing to herself and busily applying foundation to her face with a brush.

Akwele caught her eye in the mirror. "Are you going somewhere?"

"Nope, just checking out this new foundation." Akuorkor raised an eyebrow at her sister—probably surprised Akwele was trying to have a conversation.

Akwele usually spent no more than a few minutes in the bathroom, and then was back to her desk or chalkboard. "It looks nice, whatever you are putting on. You always look nice."

Akuorkor's eyes widened and her jaw dropped. "You usually call me vain, unambitious, and overly obsessed with my looks. Why are you acting so different? What's wrong?"

"Nothing's wrong." Akwele bit her lip. She stared at Akuorkor's face in the mirror, which looked flawless and womanly, and then at her own face—she frowned at her bushy eyebrows. For the first time in her life, she didn't like how she looked. "Do you think that foundation will look good on me?"

"Well, we have the same skin tone. So, yes, probably will."

"I guess, um, I was wondering if you could make me look beautiful tonight, you know, makeup and all."

Akuorkor looked at her sister incredulously. The foundation brush dropped from her hand and into the sink with a thud. "You want me to do your makeup? Are you going somewhere tonight?"

Akwele fidgeted with the hem of her pajama top.

Akuorkor must have realized Akwele was getting uncomfortable with all her questions because she held up her hand. "Okay, you don't have to answer that."

For the next half hour, Akwele obeyed all Akuorkor's instructions; she sucked in her cheeks, smiled, and pouted till Akuorkor transformed her from a geeky girl to a beautiful woman.

Even without Akwele asking, Akuorkor undid her cornrows and styled her thick curly hair so it hung long and loose on one side of her face, tucked back with a jeweled hair slide on the other side of her face.

Akwele was lost for words as she couldn't believe the wonder her sister had worked on her.

"You look beautiful." Akuorkor grinned widely. "And I feel accomplished for transforming my geeky sister. Now, we need to find you a dress." She clapped gleefully and ran to her closet. "How about this or this?"

Akwele shook her head as Akuorkor held up one dress after the other. Akuorkor was picking out conservative dresses similar to the ones Akwele usually wore, but Akwele did not want to feel like her old, conservative self. She loved her elegant makeup and hair and wanted the attire to match. She wanted to own the night.

Akuorkor eyes lit up, as if she could read her sister's thoughts. "I think I may have something that you'll like," she said before heading back to her room.

Moments later, Akuorkor came back with a long sleeveless red dress with a neckline that plunged all the way to the waist.

Akwele stared at the dress in awe. "That neckline is *hot*, and where is the back of the dress?"

"It has none." Akuorkor looked long and hard at her sister. "This isn't the kind of dress for a casual event. This is a dress for women, not girls," Akuorkor said with a cheeky grin. "When you wear this dress, there is no coming back, at least not to this house tonight."

"That's what I want," Akwele said as she slipped into the dress. The plunging neckline exposed a generous amount of her bosom, and the thigh-high slit and backless design left nothing to the imagination.

Akwele's stomach fluttered. She didn't quite see herself as young and bookish anymore. She felt elegant, tall and free.

While Akwele was lost basking in her image, Akuorkor changed her own clothes. Akwele turned from the mirror and cocked her head at her sister. "Why are you wearing my pajamas?" Then Akuorkor began braiding her hair into two thick cornrows, and Akwele's eyes widened. "Oh, are we tricking Ma and Daddy?"

"Do you have a better idea of how you were going to leave this house at this time and in that dress?" Akuorkor grabbed Akwele's book bag. "Tonight, I am boring Akwele, and I am going to walk downstairs to the study."

Akwele had been so obsessed with how she looked that she had forgotten the initial reason she came to talk to Akuorkor: how to get out of the house. "You are a genius! Forgive me for all the times I've called you dumb."

Akuorkor opened the door slightly and ducked her head outside. "Ma and Daddy are downstairs watching the news. Wait a few minutes then follow me. Daddy will probably say nothing, but Ma will scream and hurl insults at you. You must keep walking and not turn back. Don't let Ma's insults get to you. Just keep walking."

Akuorkor must have been a seer, for everything she said came to pass. Their mother screamed in fury as Akwele left the house. "Where are you going at this time of the night, Akuorkor? You are only seventeen, and you think running around at night with boys is a good idea? You will bring disgrace to this family after all we have worked so hard for. Why can't you be like Akwele? Twin daughters from the same belly yet as different as night and day. One, my pride. And the other, I don't even know what to call!" Some of her mother's words were harsh, but Akwele thought little of it as she ran out of the house to meet Tetteh.

Present day

As AKWELE DRESSED up for the wedding, she grew increasingly worried she hadn't heard from Kwame. She picked her phone up again to check if he had called her back, but there was still no word from him.

The time on her phone switched to 1:30 p.m. Kwame's flight should have arrived before one. She swiped his name to call him and groaned when the call went to his voicemail again. "Hi, honey, just me again checking if your flight arrived. The wedding is right at my family's house, in my mom's garden. I am going to head there now because it starts at two, but just give me a call when you get here. I will come get you. See you soon, bye." *Hopefully nothing has happened to him. Or has he changed his mind about coming?* She tried to shake off the worry that Kwame wasn't there yet by reminding herself Kwame had never disappointed her. He always kept his word and would show up.

She stared long at her reflection in the mirror and turned her head from side to side to inspect the elegant bun pinned high on her head. Something was missing, *but what is it?* She reached up to pat her hair, but somehow she found herself removing the pins and allowing her thick, curly hair to fall free down her shoulders. She pinned back the curls on one side and let them hang loose down the other side of her face.

She reopened her makeup case, and even though her signature, natural-looking makeup was already in place, she applied more mascara to enhance her eyes, more blush to pop her cheeks, and lined her lips to create the perfect pout. *Much better*, she thought as she stared at her reflection.

She would have given anything to walk to the wedding with Kwame on her arm, but she would have to head there without him. She slipped on her nude high heels, grabbed her clutch, and left for Tetteh's wedding.

CHAPTER 6
My Richer Half

Kwame stood in the domestic flights section of the Kumasi International Airport, fuming that his flight had been delayed. The digital numbers on his phone's clock read 1:32 p.m., and his fists tightened. He should have been in the air two hours ago.

He couldn't bear the thought of how disappointed Akwele would be, given how much she had pleaded with him to come. To ensure he didn't let her down, he'd closed his interview a little early, dashed off the set, and arrived at the airport a full hour before the scheduled departure time. As Akwele had requested, he wore his best suit and looked nothing short of dashing. Despite all those efforts, he had been delayed at the airport for the past two hours.

"Excuse me, sir?" came a hesitant voice behind him.

Kwame turned to find one of the airline attendants gazing up at him, apology etching two little lines between her eyes. He heaved a deep sigh. "Any update on the flight? It's been delayed long enough. When are we taking off?"

"Mr. Marfo, I am really sorry. All flights to Accra are delayed until six p.m."

"Huh? Why?" He could feel his blood heating up. "It's less than an hour flight, and the weather couldn't be more perfect."

"I am so sorry, but the plane is having some technical issues, sir."

"Is there just one plane? How can that be?" He splayed his hands wide, palms up. "I was supposed to be in Accra almost two hours ago, and there is no way I'm dragging this out another five. My wife needs me in Accra." He held up his phone and waggled it at the woman. "I need to call her soon. You see I have already missed several calls and texts from her. When I call her back, I cannot tell her I will not be there in an hour and that I am still at the airport in Kumasi."

"I am so sorry, sir, but there is no other flight we can offer till six," the attendant stammered.

"Please…please keep searching. I'm sure you can find an earlier one."

Ducking her head, the airline attendant scurried away.

Kwame sat down with a big sigh and fidgeted with his phone as he waited. He owed Akwele that call, but his mind kept going back to how much she had begged him to go home with her. This was the first time she'd ever really asked him for anything. And this was how he'd behaved.

He clicked the phone into sleep mode, deciding to

wait for a while more. Hopefully the airline attendant, who was now busily typing at the airline desk and conferring with her colleagues, would find him another flight.

A few nights ago, when Akwele told him that she would be driving to Accra, he'd argued in favor of flying. Clearly, he'd been wrong. If he had started driving after his interview, he would be very close to Accra by now and not glaring at gum mashed into airport carpeting.

As the minutes dragged, his mind slipped back to Akwele's recent unusual behavior and secrecy about her family home. She didn't like to talk about her home, and it had never bothered him until now. The many clues she'd dropped over the last few days niggled his curiosity.

He punched the code on his phone to turn it back on and googled her name. Both her names were so common the search results revealed nothing new: undergraduate and graduate school info, publications, and awards. He really wanted information on her family and life prior to university, but the search fished up exactly nothing—just like the first time he'd searched.

Perhaps he could try another angle. He tapped the browser's search field again and entered her twin sister's name: Akuorkor Okine. He'd met her at their wedding and remembered trying to have a conversation with her, but she seemed more interested in her drink than talking.

Her name came up in the search as Margaret Akuorkor Okine. Several social media pages belonged to her. In Akuorkor's pictures she sometimes sported wildly dyed hair and wore skimpy clothes, and she always had a drink in hand. Kwame could see the resemblance between Akuorkor and his wife—the ebony skin color and dark spots atop their cheeks. However, the difference between their behavioral patterns couldn't be more striking.

He skimmed less-than-kind news articles, one of them titled "Tycoon's Daughter Drinks the Town Away." Shocking, as Kwame would have never guessed Akwele's father to be a tycoon, but at least his suspicions from the last few days were finally confirmed—Akwele came from wealth.

The next inevitable question being, exactly how wealthy? He Googled "Tycoon Okine" next. Her father came up as the owner and CEO of the Okine Industries Limited.

Kwame recognized the company name, but… He shook his head, incredulous. "Akwele's *father* owns it?"

Sweat poured down Kwame's face when he saw that his father-in-law had a net worth of five hundred million USD. Kwame held his phone closer as he counted the zeros—yep, eight zeros.

He stared at the picture of Akwele's father. It was definitely the same man who had accepted the customary marriage drinks in Akwele's house on the morning of their wedding, and who had accompanied them to the city hall to witness their marriage. He had also occasionally visited them in Kumasi, but nothing he said or did indicated that he was so wealthy.

Kwame pulled off his jacket, loosened his tie, and

undid the first few buttons of his shirt. Intense heat crept up his face and neck.

The airline attendant returned and started apologizing profusely about the flight delay, but Kwame barely heard or saw her.

She squinted at him, leaned over, and asked, "Sir, are you okay? Do you need something?"

His voice was hoarse when he spoke. "Water with ice, please?" He settled back in his chair and wiped his forehead with a handkerchief.

The attendant hurried away.

Kwame recalled his recent conversation with Akwele, where he listed all that they owned. She must have found him funny, for whatever wealth he listed was peanuts compared to her inheritance.

It then hit him hard that his wife was an heiress, and he hadn't even known.

Five years ago

KWAME COULD HEAR the honking of car horns and hawkers yelling in the streets as he packed up boxes in Akwele's apartment. "Sweetheart, please shut that window." He let out a long sigh.

Akwele gave him a playful shove. "Come on dear, it's our last day here. You sure you don't want to enjoy all that action one last time?"

"Not at all. Thank goodness you are finally moving." He couldn't understand how Akwele could have been okay living in this rundown apartment in this awful neighborhood for seven years. He had been dating her for two years and her apartment made his skin crawl.

The window screeched as Akwele closed it. No sooner had she done that, than an angry couple next door started yelling loud enough for anyone within a mile to hear.

Akwele giggled as she saw Kwame shake his head. "You know they do this every Tuesday and Thursday night."

"Kwele, you've been at Peprah & Anderson for almost two years and I know you make a lot of money, so I don't understand why it has taken you so long to move."

"This place has sentimental value to me."

Kwame stared around the matchbox-sized apartment, with its peeling walls and frayed furniture, and raised an eyebrow. "What?"

"I know you don't understand, but this has been my only home since I moved here. I rented it with money my sister gave me. I tutored and worked odd jobs just to keep this roof over my head. This roof was all I had as I struggled to settle into a new city and school—I came from a home surrounded by love to a lone room. So, however bad it looks, it's still my home. I am moving to a much nicer place, but this place will always be close to my heart. I'll always think of it when I remember how far I have come."

Kwame took Akwele's hand. "Sweetheart, these are the things you should be telling me, so I can get to know you better." She shared with him many things, but nothing about her home or her family, though he had asked several times.

"I want to meet your family."

"Wh-why do you want to meet them?" Akwele turned toward the closet and started folding her clothes.

"I want to know the incredible family that raised such a down-to-earth, super-smart, and beautiful daughter." Kwame reached for her and kissed her. "And, more importantly, I want to ask your father for your hand in marriage."

Her eyes welled up. "What...you want to marry me?" Tears rolled down her cheeks.

"More than anything in the world." Kwame wiped away her tears.

"My dad was going to drop by the office next week. He's in town for business. If you are serious, come by and ask him then."

"What about your mom? I'd like to meet her, too. Ideally, I'd like to meet them in their home."

"We'll get to do all of that. Someday we'll get to do that." She leaned forward and kissed him.

Present day

Kwame closed the search browser on his phone, which landed him on his home screen where he had a picture of himself and Akwele grinning at each other. How could he have married someone he knew so little about? He was usually good at reading people—a skill that had made him successful in his career—but he had been blindsided by this. Was love that blinding? How could she not have shared any of this with him? What else didn't he know about her?

CHAPTER 7
Mama's Garden

THE MOMENT AKWELE arrived at her mother's garden for Tetteh's wedding, she knew she could not be there. The uneasy feeling had started when she took the shortcut from the main house and heard the soft music coming from the direction of the garden.

On arrival, she found the garden so beautiful it felt surreal. Huge mango trees surrounded the garden and cast shade, yet allowed sunlight to filter through and create intricate patterns on the colorful flowers and lush grass below. Grass carpeted the entire garden floor, with rows of roses, daisies, and sunflowers scattered throughout. Along with the vibrant colors of the plants, the smell of roses and freshly cut grass filled the air.

Tetteh's father had designed and maintained the garden, although the mango trees had been there long before. Ma Tina referred to the garden as her sanctuary and hosted her major events there. When Akwele and Akuorkor were younger, they often played in the garden. In the last few months before Akwele left home, the garden had come to mean more to her.

Thirteen years ago

AKWELE RAN OUT of the house, a wad of red fabric in her fist to keep the dress from dragging on the ground and herself from tripping. She could still hear her mother hurling insults as Akwele darted into the trees in front of the main house, where Tetteh waited.

Her heart thumped in her chest as she looked around; this was the most daring thing she had ever done in her life. She knew Tetteh would be surprised to see her makeover, and her stomach fluttered in antici-pation of his reaction.

She finally found him sitting on a log near the trees, wearing his usual threadbare shirt and jeans. He leaped up from the log when he saw her, and immedi-ately knelt and started to pull weeds from the ground.

"G-good evening, Sister Akuorkor," came his stuttering voice. "I am j-just finishing the last of the gardening."

"It's me. Akwele," she whispered, giving a giggle.

Tetteh's jaw dropped, and his eyes looked like they would pop out. "What? You look so… You are beautiful!" He stood up and stretched out his hands as though he wanted to hold her, but then stared at his hands, which were dirty from digging up the ground, and let them fall back down. "Take that path." He gestured to his left. "It is a shortcut to Ma Tina's garden. Wait for me there."

Akwele squinted at a dirt trail barely visible in the

dark; she hadn't even known it existed. "At this time of the evening?" She was hesitant. The only source of light came from the moon.

"I will be there before you know it," Tetteh said confidently. The shock of seeing her makeover was gone, replaced by his usual confident self. "Wait for me and close your eyes while you wait."

He'd dashed into the trees before he could see her lift her eyebrows, incredulous. She found his request weird, particularly the latter about closing her eyes. *Isn't it dark enough?* She frowned at the trees and darkness surrounding her. She had spent her entire life in the safety of the main house, only zipping by the trees while being driven. Now, Tetteh wanted her to walk down an obscure path and wait alone in the garden with her eyes closed.

"Oh, dear Lord," she said, voice quivering as she walked down the path, allowing the faint light of the moon to guide her as she went. She was amazed by how quickly she got to the garden and wondered again why she had never known about the shortcut. She waited there like he said, hoping he would be able to find her. She hesitated to close her eyes.

The dark pressed in, and the branches of the mango trees rattled like bones. Silence reigned, apart from the cacophonous sound of insects. Her skin, which she had so generously exposed with Akuorkor's dress, lay prey to mosquitoes. She couldn't help but wish she had slapped on some mosquito repellant. Despite these misgivings, she trusted Tetteh, remembered his calm and confident voice, and closed her eyes.

Soon, footsteps headed toward her. "It's just me," Tetteh said softly. "Keep your eyes closed."

A little more at ease now that he was there, she let her shoulders loosen and fall. She kept her eyes closed until the deep and soul-stirring sound of his cello filled her ears. Her eyes fluttered open to find Tetteh, now dressed in a clean white shirt and black jeans, sitting on a tree stump, his cello cradled between his thighs.

The first time she'd seen him play, his eyes seemed far away. Tonight, as he serenaded her, his eyes never left hers. Mesmerized, she began to sway where she stood. The insects' sounds, which she'd found unpleasant barely minutes ago, became the perfect backdrop to the cello's cry. Around them, fireflies lit up and the garden transformed from fearful to magical.

His skill with the instrument took her breath away. Of all the times he'd played for her, this qualified as the most special. When she thought she couldn't get enough of his beautiful music, he transitioned into "Ave Maria"—the same notes and refrains as the first time he'd coaxed it from the strings. Same careful timing. Same mournful strains. But in the closeness of the garden with the scent of roses heavy in her nose, with the warm breeze kissing her exposed skin, and with his eyes doing unspeakable things to her body, it was not the same.

It was as if he was worshiping her, something no one had done before. They both knew she was a math genius, but in the moment, Tetteh, the poor boy who had eaten her leftovers, hailed her with the only gift he had and, in the unique way he could, made her feel like a goddess—his goddess. As Akwele watched him worship her, she wanted nothing more than to be his woman and his bride.

Too soon, the last stirring notes dissipated with the wind and Tetteh lowered his bow. Moments later, they lay on the grass with their arms wrapped around each other. "My Maria," he said as he gazed down at her. "Be mine here and now in this garden."

Akwele was happy to oblige, for she was in love with the gardener's boy.

Present day

AKWELE LOOKED OUT at the white garden chairs neatly assembled on the grass, with a tiny arrangement of pink and yellow flowers on the side of each. With laser accuracy, Akwele spotted Tetteh in the corner of the garden. His back was turned to her and he stood with four other men, all of them in elegant white African kaftans with gold embroidery on the front. The last time she had seen him he was in threadbare clothes, but his frame hadn't changed much in the kaftan. Tetteh turned in her direction and might have seen her if one of the wedding guests hadn't stopped to greet him.

Akwele's gaze shot past Tetteh to the colorfully clothed wedding guests slowly filling the chairs. Some of their faces looked familiar; those belonging to the kids she had grown up with. She was surprised by how little they had all changed despite their pretty adult clothes, fancy hairstyles, and makeup. One could take all those things away and replace them with school uniforms, and they'd all be in high school again. It was as though they were masquerading as adults. Nonetheless, their joy and happiness as they chatted away were palpable, for they were there to celebrate a marriage.

Being in her mother's garden made Akwele relive her fantasy that she and Tetteh could have found a way to stay together. Maybe a small part of her had even held on to that fantasy. As Akwele looked at the garden where Tetteh was about to get married, she realized that fantasy was about to die.

Unable to take another step, Akwele stood at the top of the wooden staircase, no more than ten treads, which led to the garden. Many guests walked past, some looking at her and probably wondering why she was just standing there. Still rooted to the spot, Akwele contemplated turning back and heading to the main house.

"May I?" asked a deep voice next to her.

Akwele snapped out of her thoughts to find a bespectacled, neatly dressed gentleman next to her. "Excuse me?"

He held out his hand and smiled, seeming like a nice guy. "I see your dilemma. If I was wearing heels as high as yours, I would not even attempt to climb down these stairs."

Akwele smiled back him. She wanted to tell him her heels weren't the problem. She wanted to tell him the real problem: that for the past thirteen years she had trained her feet to run in the other direction and away from the man getting married here today. It was, therefore, understandable her feet refused to budge now. But Akwele didn't say any of that. She instead took the man's hand and mumbled, "Thank you." Gingerly, she took the first step down the staircase.

At the bottom, they parted ways. He wanted to greet the groom, which Akwele had little interest in doing. She instead walked toward the rows of chairs.

A girl in a pink dress with a gold feather in her hair walked toward Akwele, waving. Akwele had no idea who she was.

"Hey, hey," said the girl when she reached Akwele. "How come you are here now? Aren't you a bridesmaid?"

Akwele shook her head with a smile. "I think you are mistaking me for my twin, Akuorkor; she's a bridesmaid. I am her sister, Akwele."

The girl raised both eyebrows. "OMG! I know she's a twin, but I've never met her sister. You guys really do look alike; you just look more normal than her." The girl giggled. "Your family is leading the groom's family procession. Will you be joining them?"

"Oh, no," Akwele blurted.

"Okay. The Okines' have reserved seating at the front. I can show you your seat."

"No, no. That won't be necessary." Akwele looked at the seating arrangement, the typical setup of traditional marriages. Two sets of about fifty chairs faced each other for the families of the bride and groom, respectively. Not surprisingly, the seats for the bride's family were nearly filled while those for the groom's family were all empty. Across from the two main sets of chairs was another for friends of the couple. Akwele picked the very last seat in this section. "I am fine right here," she said to the girl, who looked surprised but nodded and walked away.

Soon after Akwele sat down, an elderly lady sat next to her. "So, how do you know the bride or groom or both?"

Akwele wasn't in a chatty mood but smiled. "Friend of the groom." The woman looked like she wanted more details, and Akwele wished she would focus on something else.

"It's so great to be able to come out and support your friend on his big day." She flashed a wide-toothed smile. "*Wɔfrɛ me Grace.*" I am called Grace, she said in Fante. "Grace Kuntu-Blankson. What's your name?"

Akwele gritted her teeth—the last thing she wanted to do was tell Grace her name.

Akwele's phone rang. *Thank goodness.* She had never been happier, not only because it kept Grace's questions at bay but also because the call was from Kwame. "Hey, honey, are you here yet? I can come out to meet you now." Any reprieve from Grace would be nice.

There was a long pause from the other end of the line. "I am so sorry, Kwele. My flight has been canceled. I will be on the next, but I won't be there till seven tonight. I really tried everything."

Akwele's jaw dropped; she was totally lost for words.

"It is about to start," Grace whispered gleefully, a subtle request to get off the phone.

Akwele wished she would go sit somewhere else. "No worries, my dear," she said when she finally found her voice. "Just get here whenever you can, okay. I have to go now." She hung up, wincing at the knots forming in her stomach.

As Akwele leaned back in her chair, the marriage ceremony began with the groom's family procession. A middle-aged woman standing by the wooden staircase that led to the garden shouted, "*Agoo.* May I have your attention?" into a microphone. Akwele didn't know the woman, but assumed she was serving as the spokesperson for the groom's family. Another woman with a microphone standing next to the bride's family and acting as their spokesperson responded, "*Amee.* You have our attention," after which the latest hiplife music boomed from loudspeakers.

Akwele's mother led the groom's family procession, dressed in a stunning pink-and-gold kente *Kaba and slit.* The long wrap skirt and blouse were very flattering, and she wore several rows of gold beads around her neck and a silk pink headscarf. She danced gracefully as she led the procession and didn't look like she had aged a day since Akwele had last seen her.

Her elegant appearance spoke volumes; even though she wasn't the bride, she owned the wedding. Her father followed her mother in the procession, wearing a kente shirt that matched her mother's. His hair had grayed quite a bit since he last visited her, but his figure still stood strong and tall. At the sight of them, Akwele's throat tightened. They danced in unison, and when they reached Akwele where she was sitting, she whispered, "Ma." Yet it was barely audible, and with the booming music her mother likely couldn't hear. Following her parents were several women, carrying wrapped gifts for the bride. Akwele recognized some as house helps on her family's compound; she expected Aunty B to be part of the procession and was surprised to see she wasn't.

Tetteh, now wearing Akwele's mother's kente stole around his neck, followed thereafter with his three groomsmen. He waved at the cheering guests, giving them a beaming smile as he passed by. Grace waved as well, which only annoyed Akwele as she looked down to avoid eye contact with Tetteh. His arrival completed the procession of the groom and his family, where her parents and all the house helps on her family's compound had honored Tetteh. The families of the bride and the groom now sat across from each other, with Tetteh sitting proudly at her mother's right-hand side.

"So nice, eh?" Grace leaned over and whispered to Akwele. "Traditionally, the marriage joins not only the bride and groom but their families as well."

"Mm-hmm," Akwele responded without looking at her.

The dowry was then handed over from the groom's family to the bride's family in a white envelope.

"I wonder how much money is in there," Grace murmured to Akwele. "These Okines are loaded."

Akwele frowned in annoyance and turned away from Grace, who was undeterred by Akwele's body language and leaned closer. "Here's another important part of the ceremony—the *head-drink,* typically schnapps, gin or whisky, is presented from the groom's family to the bride's father..."

Local gospel music began playing, which interrupted Grace's lecture. Akwele heaved a sigh of relief. With the music came a long line of bridesmaids. All wore pink lace dresses and danced to the gospel music. Akuorkor was the third bridesmaid in the line, and quickly leaned over and kissed Akwele when she saw her. Grace looked at Akuorkor and back at Akwele, clearly wondering about the resemblance, but Akwele didn't bother explaining.

As the gospel music reached the hallelujah chorus, Esi, like a vision of perfection, made her entrance in a form-fitting, long white-lace dress. She wore her hair in a goddess braid with tiny gold beads, which matched her gold flower-shaped earrings, nestled within the braids. She gently fanned herself with an elaborately decorated pink-and-gold fan.

Akwele was completely stunned by Esi, as she looked so much more glamorous than in the picture Akuorkor had showed her earlier in the day. Akwele wished Akuorkor was nearby so she could take a second look at the picture. She fumed that Akuorkor hadn't shown her a more representative photo to prepare her for this moment. The guests rose to their feet and many directed their phones to Esi, while others whisked out their white handkerchiefs and began calling out "*Ayefro dondoo*, congratulations to the couple."

While Esi's beauty and majestic entrance had totally stunned Akwele, it was the look on Tetteh's face when he first saw his bride that saddened her. Of all the painful events taking place in the garden that day, seeing such a look on Tetteh's face—that of a happy and fulfilled man—was the most difficult for Akwele.

She surveyed the garden grounds, looking for a

discreet exit where she could slip out, but the layout of the garden was such that everybody, including Tetteh, would see her go. Not that it would surprise anyone, given her reputation for running away. So she sat still and, fearing the other wedding guests would see the thoughts crossing her face, tried not to cringe.

Feeling every minute like she didn't belong and overrun with all her emotional turmoil, Akwele reached for her phone and found comfort in a crossword puzzle. It didn't prevent her from hearing the couple pledge themselves to each other, but it provided some reprieve. She caught Grace looking on disapprovingly at her, but Akwele couldn't care less.

As Akwele waited anxiously for the ceremony to end, she couldn't help but think that Tetteh and his bride had stolen her family. Akwele looked up as the bride walked to her parents to greet them. Her father leaned over to say something to her. Whatever it was must have been funny, for her shoulders fell forward for a moment as she laughed. Ma Tina hugged the bride and pulled her to sit on her lap, showing endearment. The guests cheered.

After the blessing of the couple the marriage certificate was signed, with Akwele's parents serving as witnesses from the groom's family. Akwele had often imagined how it would be to see her parents at home again. This was certainly not what she had pictured. It felt like her parents were giving the wedding they had long planned for her to Esi.

Akwele remembered her own wedding day. It had started out with the traditional wedding in her living room and signing of the marriage certificate at the city hall. Six people had attended in addition to her and Kwame: her dad, Akuorkor, Kwame's parents, and his two uncles. She hadn't worn an elaborate white-lace dress but a simple knee-length cream dress. After they signed the marriage certificate, they'd taken their guests to lunch at a nearby restaurant. It probably wasn't the wedding her mother had in mind for her, but it was the wedding Akwele chose.

Now, as she watched her parents fawn so much over Tetteh and his bride, she couldn't help but feel she had lost her parents.

CHAPTER 8
Love Lost

Thirteen years ago

"Tetteh?" Akwele gently tapped Tetteh's chest to wake him.

They lay on a sleeping mat in his room with a ripped sheet covering them. Her dress—a new one she had just purchased—lay in a heap at the foot of the mat. She'd started buying more clothes rather than borrowing Akuorkor's for her meetups with Tetteh.

"Tetteh?" Akwele tapped him again as she turned toward him.

"Love, let's try to get some rest before my dad gets back. We have less than an hour."

Tetteh's father worked in the garden in the afternoons. Akwele and Tetteh took advantage of that time to be alone together. Her family thought she was tutoring him or still at school—she was careful to change into her school uniform before heading to the main house.

Akwele bit her lip as she lay back down. Tetteh started snoring next to her.

She reached for her book bag from the side of the mat and took out an envelope from the front pocket. She'd already opened the letter earlier in the day, but couldn't help rereading it: *Dear Ms. Akwele Okine, we are pleased to accept you into our computer engineering program at KNUST…*

Akwele sighed as she placed the letter back in the envelope and laid back down.

Why wasn't she happy? KNUST was a prestigious university, and getting admitted there was her big dream. The prior year, while just a second-year high school student, she had taken the early university exams and had been thrilled with the excellent results.

She'd happily applied to KNUST for a place in their computer engineering program. She had done it months before she started her relationship with Tetteh. Now, if only Tetteh could fit in the picture, then everything would be perfect. What would happen to their relationship if she left? Would it survive the long distance? She sighed loudly.

"What are you worrying about?" Tetteh opened one eye. "Let me guess. You are worrying about your schoolwork, which has been piling up since you are spending all your free time with me and not studying."

"I love spending time with you." Akwele looked at Tetteh's face. The old Akwele would have been bothered by the piling schoolwork, but Tetteh had given her life an extra measure of meaning and purpose.

The more time she spent with him, the more she loved him. She loved his free spirit and his confidence and how he pushed himself in his music, combining his talent with persistent practice and progressing so much despite having so little. In some ways, she found it similar to her drive for math, where she combined her talent with rugged practice, determined to make something of her life and not just rely on her family's fortunes. The one difference between them was that she loved to plan and check her boxes while he was free, rolling and riding with whatever came his way until it somehow fit his plan.

"Tetteh? We've been dating for the past three months. I spend more time with you than with my own family." Akwele cleared her throat. "I really want to talk about our relationship and what it means to you."

"We are having fun. What we have is fun, and it makes me happy. Just looking at your beauty inspires the most amazing music in my mind. You make me feel free, like there are no limits to what I can achieve."

"I was thinking more of the future."

"Why ruin the present with future worries?" He frowned at her and huffed.

"It's not worrying. It is planning. Do you think of us getting more serious in our relationship? Maybe consider marriage someday?"

He seemed startled by her question as he sat up. "I don't want to think about that." He got up from the mat, threw on his boxer shorts, and went for his cello. From spending so much time with him she had learned that music was his safe place, somewhere he could block out anything distressing him, like her question obviously had.

Nonetheless, she pressed on for she felt it important to talk about their future, given the offer she had just received from KNUST. "I am really starting to like you, and I want to know if we are serious enough to plan for the future."

Tetteh said nothing and continued playing his cello, but he seemed to be struggling to hit his notes

"Hey, did you hear me?"

He seemed upset and sighed loudly. "Why would you be thinking about things like that now? You are only seventeen!"

Akwele chewed her lips. "Because I love you," she confessed for the first time.

When she looked at Tetteh for his reaction, his jaws were clenched and veins bulged at his neck. That wasn't the reaction she was expecting. Something was wrong, but she couldn't put a finger on it. "We will have to make decisions, life-altering decisions, and I need to know where we stand and where we are going." She sat up frantically on the mat. "All I have means so little to me right now, not this big house, not my family, not even school. I'd give it all up for you. I know our relationship seems like a fantasy sometimes, and will be frowned upon by our families if they found out, but if you're ready to fight for it I will fight with you. Together, we can make it real, but only if you want it."

"I am not ready for this." He abruptly dropped the cello and bow and held his head. "Just listen to what you are saying!"

His rejection stung, and she flinched. "I thought you wanted a future together." What of the romantic gestures from him over the past three months—the music, poetry, and teases? What had they been about? She would have never fallen in love with him had he not done all those things. She pulled the sheet to her chin; she suddenly felt the need to cover herself, like she had already given too much of herself away. For the first time, she felt uncomfortable being with him without her clothes. *Have I lost my innocence to someone who cares so little for me?*

"I don't want to think about the future now." He barely looked at her as he picked his cello back up. "I am your gardener's son. I have nothing but my music and need to focus on it, so I don't spend my entire life pulling weeds from your garden. My music is my only path to the freedom I want. You are daydreaming, but you can afford to do that because your daddy will be around to provide for you. I'd love to daydream about the future, but I can't!"

Akwele had never felt more hurt in her life. She wasn't his world anymore, but rather worlds apart from him. Even though Tetteh had said a lot, what rang out even more loudly was what he didn't say, what he insinuated. He saw her as a privileged kid and out of touch with reality. She knew what she had to do next to protect herself from the inevitable.

"I think we should break up." She wouldn't survive if he broke up with her first. Deep down she hoped he'd say no to the breakup, that he'd jump up and stop her.

Tetteh said nothing but his silence spoke volumes. He just played his cello, pausing every now and then to scribble music notes. If anything, he seemed relieved, as he was now hitting all his notes and creating beautiful music, like their breakup had freed him.

She left his room then, half-hoping he would run after her and half-knowing he wouldn't. He just kept playing a very slow tune as she put on her school uniform and picked up her backpack. She didn't look back as she walked away from the servants' quarters and toward the main house, but she could hear him playing for a while longer. She found it heart-wrenchingly apt she had just broken up with him while he played his music. How could their perfect love story frizzle so quickly?

Present day

As TETTEH'S FORMAL marriage ceremony ended and preparations began for the reception, all Akwele wanted to do was run to her parents. She didn't realize how much she had missed them and her home till that moment. She waited patiently for Tetteh and his wife to leave her parents' side. She would have to congratulate Tetteh at some point, but she wasn't ready to do so just yet—perhaps later during the reception.

As soon as Tetteh and his wife left for their photoshoot, Akwele sprang up from her seat and made her way to her parents, weaving through the guests, who were mingling and helping themselves to finger foods. Throughout the ceremony she felt like Tetteh had usurped her place as the firstborn; now, she just wanted them and her place back.

"Look at that beautiful daughter of mine!" Akwele's dad exclaimed when he saw her. He gave her a big hug. "It's wonderful to have you home, my dear. How are you?"

Delight rolled over Akwele as she kissed him on both cheeks. "I am doing great, Daddy. It's been a long time."

Tears pooled in Ma Tina's eyes when she saw Akwele. She reached out to smooth the pleats on the neckline of Akwele's dress. "I saw my Corolla in the garage this morning," she said calmly.

Akwele wondered if she should apologize for stealing her mother's car, but that was the least of her concerns, given her rampaging emotions. Her mother, on the other hand, continued fidgeting with the neckline of her dress, making sure all the pleats were laying flat. Akwele's eyes welled from being so close to her mother after so long. She blinked away her tears, reached out, and held her mother's hands still. "Ma."

Her mother finally looked her in the eye, leaned closer, and kissed her on the forehead. "Welcome home, Akwele," she finally said.

Akwele shut her eyes for what seemed like the longest time. This was the kiss she had been longing for. Her mother's kiss had made her homecoming complete.

Her father put his arm around her. "Akwele, did you come with your husband?"

Akwele's mother shook her head and sighed.

Despite her mother's agitation, Akwele managed a

polite smile. "Kwame's flight was delayed, but he will be arriving soon."

"Hey, hey!" Akuokor said as she joined them. "My beautiful family all together again."

Ma Tina ignored Akuorkor and turned to her husband. "Let us not bring up this husband business. Did she bring him here to her *family* home to even introduce him to us before she married him?"

"Tina, Kwame is her husband. I accepted the traditional marriage drinks. I was there at the city hall, and I signed the marriage certificate."

"Kaaa kɛ mi nakai," her mother switched to Ga as she insisted her husband not tell her that. *"Maaba ni ekɛ lɛ baaashia kɛha yookpeemɔ lɛ?"*

"Tina, because that is what she wanted. To have the wedding there, not here. *No ji nɔ ni etaoɔ.*" Her father waved his hands in frustration.

"Mɔ ko, mɔ ko le mɔ ni ji lɛ. Okɛ wɔ shika lɛ fɛɛ baaha mɔ ko ni wɔ le," her mother replied, saying, "Nobody knows who he is. You are about to hand all of our money to someone we don't know."

Akuorkor waved to the server carrying the champagne while shaking her head at her arguing parents. She turned to Akwele and whispered, "And you people wonder why I drink so much." Akuorkor lifted two champagne glasses off the tray and downed them both just as quickly as she lifted them. "Why use these tall glasses if you are only half-filling them?" she asked the server, who scurried away with a confused look on her face.

"Akuorkor, there are people and cameras here," her mother said through clenched teeth.

Akuorkor rolled her eyes. "And they can also see you and Daddy arguing about Akwele's marriage when she has been perfectly and happily married for over three years. Continue this pointless argument, and she will run away again. Seriously, let's talk about something else, like how beautiful the wedding was."

"Glad you found it beautiful. That might inspire you to find a marriage-worthy man," her mother said curtly to Akuorkor and then turned to Akwele. "And bring him home to have a proper and beautiful marriage ceremony." Ma Tina finished with a gesture around the garden. "Like this one."

"Oh boy, I am going to need more alcohol to survive today." Akuorkor muttered.

Ma Tina pulled Akuorkor aside as they spoke in heated, hushed tones.

"I don't even want to know what that is about." Akwele's dad said as he put an arm around her. "How is your marriage, my dear?"

"Good. Kwame and I are doing very well."

"That's great. We're still keeping our secret too, eh?" he said with a sideways smile.

"I will tell Kwame more about our family, soon. I know it hasn't been easy for you, too—not disclosing too much about yourself anytime you've visited us, not mentioning me in your affairs or on any media."

"My daughter, I will do whatever you want me to do until the day I die. Just give me the green light when you are ready for me to brag about you. It gets annoying that the media only ties me to your sister's interesting pursuits." He finished with a laugh.

Akwele giggled along.

Akuorkor rejoined them. "I hate to break up this beautiful family reunion, but I need to go mingle with my sister. She's a rare commodity around here. You can have your wife back." Akwele gestured to Ma Tina, who scowled back at her. "Let's go Akwele."

As they weaved through the guests, Akuorkor turned to Akwele. "I am sorry you had to endure Ma's rant about your marriage. I did warn you she was going to bring it up."

Akwele smiled at her sister. "I haven't forgotten how Ma is. Despite how unhappy she is about how I planned my marriage, I really wanted Kwame to be here at my side today. I hoped she would get a chance to know him."

"Oh, Akwele. I can bet you if Kwame was here, she'd be oohing and aahing over him and showing him off as her son-in-law. She would, of course, make up a reason for your quiet wedding and then tell all her friends a bigger celebration is planned. Ma doesn't have a problem with Kwame. She just feels like you denied her the chance to throw a big party."

Akwele laughed. She and Akuorkor now stood a bit away from the wedding guests, under one of the mango trees. The event scene grew more festive as guests chatted and laughed. Akwele turned to Akuorkor. "I thought you wanted to mingle."

"You hate to mingle. Let's just catch our breath a bit before we rejoin the party. It's your first day back, and there is a lot going on."

Akwele was about to thank her sister for being

so considerate when she noticed Akuorkor waving at someone in the crowd. Akwele drew a long breath as she saw the target of her sister's attention.

"There is Tetteh," Akuorkor said. "Let's go say hi to him."

"He's busy with his guests. We can talk to him later." The words rushed out of Akwele.

Akuorkor continued waving until Tetteh finally turned, returned Akuorkor's wave, and started walking toward them. He had changed into a tuxedo, and his tall figure looked lean and toned as he walked.

Akwele held her breath and started to look away. She didn't want Tetteh to see her face. *What if my face shows that I am reliving the past?* At his wedding no less. She grabbed a glass of lemonade from a server passing by and wished it would miraculously turn to wine and numb her from the oncoming emotional onslaught.

"*So* hard to believe he's only the help and not family. He's really bettered himself, thanks to Ma," Akuorkor whispered to Akwele before Tetteh reached them. "Don't you look dashing, Mr. Groom!"

"Thank you, Akuorkor! I can't believe I am seeing Akwele Okine after so long." He opened his arms to hug Akwele.

Akwele accepted the gesture, all the while holding her breath. The hug felt too long and close to her, and she yearned to come up for air.

For years after she'd left home, she wondered when she would see him again, never imagining it would be at his wedding. She could feel her face burning and quickly disentangled herself from his embrace.

Hopefully, nobody noticed how awkward the hug was. Thankfully, Akuorkor was absorbed in trying to get a server's attention.

"I heard you are married now." Tetteh kept one arm around Akwele's shoulder. "Is your husband here? I would love to meet him."

"He's…" Her voice sounded hoarse. Tetteh's arm was heavy on her shoulders. She stepped back so it fell off and then cleared her throat. "He's on his way. He will be here any minute."

She found it interesting he wanted to meet her husband when she did not want to meet Esi, who was standing only a few feet away and had changed into a sleeveless kente dress. "Esi is beautiful, and so is your wedding." She looked at his face up close and again saw how genuinely happy he was, not forlorn and miserable like her seventeen-year-old self had imagined he would be without her. "It is actually perfect."

"Your mom planned and organized everything. I heard you had a super-secret wedding. Hey, I don't blame you. Look what she did for my wedding, and I am just the gardener's boy. Imagine what she would do for *yours*."

Hearing him call himself "just the gardener's boy" almost made Akwele chuckle. Tetteh hated being "just the gardener's boy" and had proved he could rise to be the star of the family. He could now pass for her parents' firstborn and had managed to marry a stunning woman in a wedding that would be the talk of town for a while. Without a doubt, he was not just the gardener's boy. He was the free-spirited Tetteh, able to do anything he set his mind to.

Tetteh continued talking about how grateful he was to her family while she searched his face. She had questions for him. Why did Esi get a lifetime promise while back then she, Akwele, got mere months? How come Esi got the fortress while years ago she, Akwele, got the sandcastle? Akwele swallowed each question—this wasn't the time or place for her questions, nor would there ever be one.

Esi waved at Tetteh, gesturing for him to join her as she and some of the guests posed for photographs. Akwele glanced at her, and their eyes met and held for only a second. Akwele harbored no ill will toward her, but she looked so elegant and confident that Akwele was overwhelmed by a sense of inadequacy.

Tetteh signaled to Esi he needed a minute.

"You should go," Akwele said.

Tetteh nodded and then added, "I am really glad you could make it."

"So am I." She took a long sip of lemonade and swallowed hard as she watched him retreat. She continued to watch as he took his place next to Esi, who beamed at him.

"Hey," Akuorkor interrupted Akwele's thoughts. "You ok?"

Akwele flashed a quick smile. "I am great."

"Come, let's rejoin the party." Akuorkor pulled Akwele toward the reception, where the chairs had been rearranged around pink linen-covered tables and guests were enjoying food, piled high on their plates. The smell of grilled kebabs and pork chops lingered in the air. Ma Tina waved for Akwele and Akuorkor to join her and her husband at one of the front tables.

Tetteh and Esi danced at the center of the dance floor with multicolored lights above them generating colorful circles on their clothes. Esi looked lovingly at Tetteh and glided in his arms, a bride who had clearly found her match. Where some brides would have looked away or been slightly shy, she exuded confidence. All the wedding guests had their eyes on her, but she seemed oblivious to them. Her love for him was palpable. To Akwele, that much was true.

Akwele peeled her eyes away from the couple as a server came by their table with a tray of champagne. She declined as Akuorkor reached for a glass then frowned at Akwele. "You are still not drinking," her sister said as she sighed.

Akwele ignored her. She wanted a drink very badly, but she needed to stay perfectly sober to keep all her emotions in check. She grabbed a goat-meat kebab from the center plate. If she couldn't drink, she could at least eat. The meat was tender, spicy, and delicious. She decided she was going to eat away while the newlyweds basked in their love.

"This party is amazing," Ma Tina said.

"Oh, yes, you have outdone yourself!" Mr. Okine replied. "The only person I haven't seen here is Aunty B. That is very odd."

Akwele nodded. "I agree. Everybody is here except her."

"She surprisingly didn't seem interested in the preparations for the event like she usually is," Ma Tina added.

"Let's check on her when we get back," Mr. Okine added.

Akuorkor swallowed a mouthful of champagne. "Well, it's her loss for missing out on great drinks and food."

Akwele reached for another kebab. "The food is amazing; this kebab is speaking to me."

"You ate all of the kebabs for this table." Akuorkor counted the kebab sticks in front of Akwele. "I never knew you had such an appetite." She giggled.

"Maybe there is no food where she came from," Ma Tina added with a laugh.

"Let her eat in peace." Mr. Okine winked at her. "Pay no attention to them. I bought several goats for this wedding. Eat as much as you want."

"All this eating plus the fact you are not drinking makes me wonder if—" Akuorkor flicked a glance at Akwele's abdomen. "Are you pregnant?"

Akwele glared at her sister, and almost choked on the kebab under her mother's suddenly intent look. Her mother would surely be thrilled with the chance to throw a party to celebrate a grandchild. "Well, Kwame and I are thinking, you know, planning and starting to try, but it's so preliminary…"

Her mother snapped her fingers at the server passing by. "More kebabs for the table." She then picked the last kebab from the center plate and placed it on Akwele's plate. "I was the same way when I was pregnant with you two. I couldn't eat enough kebabs. Have you tried the pork chops yet? It's a winner!"

"No pressure, Tina. She said they were now trying."

Akwele managed a thin smile as she bit more meat off the stick. She was definitely in her mother's good books now; all her past sins were forgiven. She also needed to seriously consider having a baby because of how happy it would make Kwame. As her thoughts traveled to him, she picked up her phone and scrolled through her past calls and messages—nothing from him since the earlier call.

"Happy for you, sis! You know that calls for a drink." Akuorkor picked up a glass from a nearby server and downed it. "And a dance as well. Come on, Daddy, I have worn out all the guys here."

Akwele smiled at her sister and her dad as they strode to the dance floor. When she turned around her mother's steely gaze was fixed on her.

Akwele darted her eyes around the table in search of more kebabs. "Let me go get—"

"Sit down." Ma Tina swirled her drink in her hand. "What did we ever do to you to make you stay away from your own home? Don't even give me that excuse that your father has fallen for hook, line, and sinker. *I want a chance to find myself, prove myself, blah blah blah.*"

"Ma, please."

"Yes, I am your mother. Even though I don't understand you, I have always known of your big need to prove yourself. Your class two teacher once told me that when she asked you to be class prefect you inquired whether she gave you the position because of your hard work or who your father is. So yes, Akwele, I know of your undying desire to prove yourself, but I don't think that's the reason you left. You choose to run instead of dealing with issues—it's your life anthem. You channel your distress into your work, but someday you are going to have to face your issues."

A slow tune started to play as Tetteh and Esi began their final dance. The wedding guests circled around them.

Ma Tina looked out at the dance floor. "Life is so interesting. Some people are born with nothing but are grateful for everything they are given and make the best out of it. Others are born with everything but shun it and don't even want to be associated with it."

Akwele blinked hard. "Ma, I can't rewrite the past but maybe I can make the future better. I'd like to reset our relationship. You, me…Kwame…."

"Hmm?" Ma Tina gave Akwele a long side-eye.

"I will introduce him to you properly, Ma. I will make sure you get a chance to know him."

Ma Tina nodded, then laid a hand on Akwele's and patted it gently.

Akwele let out a long breath. That was the best she was going to get out of her mother.

The reception frenzy began to die down as the couple prepared for their departure. Akuorkor disappeared with one of the groomsmen. Several of the guests, including Akwele's parents, went toward the couple to wish them well.

Akwele grabbed her purse and prepared to leave. She turned around to see her parents and other guests gather around Tetteh and Esi for a photo. They all held their poses, time froze, and the camera flashed. It was one of those pictures that would be displayed on the shelf in the living room. A precious moment etched in history for all to see. Nothing like her hidden memories, which nobody would ever know, which even Tetteh may have forgotten.

Before Akwele left the garden, she walked straight to the bar and lifted a finger to the bartender. "Give me a shot of the strongest drink you have." Now that the event was over, she felt free to have that drink. She downed it in one gulp. It burned her throat, but even that brief physical burn was welcome because, for a few seconds, it numbed the emotional pain.

"Goodbye, Tetteh," Akwele whispered before leaving her mother's garden and walking back to the main house.

Thirteen years ago

LATER THAT AFTERNOON, after Akwele broke up with Tetteh, she tried to solve a complicated math problem to clear her head and to distract her from thoughts of Tetteh. "These two numbers are supposed to add up." Tears stung Akwele's eyes. She bit her lips to keep them from quivering. "So why won't they? Why can't they? Unless…" Akwele paused suddenly. "Maybe it's because we don't know the nature of the numbers. We need to know as much as we can, so we can make the most informed decision." The words rushed out of her mouth as she hurried to her backpack and frantically dug through it. She grabbed the envelope that had the acceptance notification from KNUST and dashed toward the door.

How could she expect Tetteh to know why she was professing her love for him if she hadn't told him she might be moving away soon. She had to get back to the servants' quarters to show him the notification. As she ran out of the main house, she found Tetteh walking down the front steps of the main house and staring at his phone.

"Hey," she called out as she descended the steps toward him.

He turned around and saw her, then glanced about to make sure nobody was watching them. "Hey, I just came to drop off some fruit in the kitchen."

"I know I said we should break up, but there is something I should have told you earlier today."

He looked at his phone, clearly distracted and not very interested in what she was saying.

"I have been admitted to KNUST," she said. He still wasn't looking at her. "It's a really great program, but it is all the way in Kumasi."

"Good for you. You should go." He turned around and started texting.

She was startled at his response. Did he not hear her? How could he not care she would be going to a university that was five hours away? Yes, they had an argument earlier in the day, and she had asked for a breakup, but how could he have switched off his feelings so quickly?

He seemed like a stranger to her. As she walked

back up to the house, she swiveled to look at him. He was still staring intently at his phone and was so engrossed in texting he didn't even realize Akwele's eyes were on him.

There was something about his face that made her want to study him. The more she looked, the more she recognized his expression. He was staring at his phone the same way he used to look at her. Tetteh was probably in love with whoever he was texting; he had found his new muse. How was that possible when they broke up just earlier in the day?

Akwele continued to look at him as he giggled. Without a doubt, Tetteh was in love. Her heart sank as she realized her fears were confirmed; Tetteh had another girl in his life. Was he two-timing her with another this whole time? That question shattered her confidence as a girl and a lover, and to think she had even given away her innocence to him. Akwele swung back around and ran into the main house, wanting nothing more than to be far away from him.

In her room she leaned against the door, feeling completely broken. *How can I continue living in the same house as him? I never want to see him again.* As she stuffed her clothes in her bag she told herself to forget him, but the memories were too poignant, particularly those from Mama's garden.

CHAPTER 9
Atonement

Present day

THE MUSIC FROM the reception and the sounds of the happy guests faded behind Akwele as she walked from her mother's garden toward the main house. She didn't use the shortcut, and with no energy to hurry her pace the walk seemed to take forever.

She sighed in relief as the house came into view. *Finally.* She yearned to get into her room and curl up in a ball. Just then, she spotted a familiar figure, a man in a slim-fit suit and a loose tie standing on the front steps with a small suitcase next to him. He was staring down at his phone, the light from its screen illuminating his handsome face.

She knew that face. She had picked that suit. "Kwame," she whispered.

There was no way he could have heard her. However, he lifted his eyes from his phone and called out, "Kwele!"

Akwele had never been more delighted—only her

husband called her *Kwele*. Her collected and poised bearing gave way as she sprinted toward him. Surprising she could sprint on six-inch heels, especially given how drained she'd felt only seconds earlier.

She threw herself into his arms. "Kwame," she whispered again as she hugged him. His familiar musky scent filled her as she inhaled deeply. His strong muscles hardened about her. The warmth of his embrace soothed far more effectively than the drink she'd just had and obliterated the yearn to curl up in a ball. As they embraced relief seeped into her, and for the first time that day she wasn't drowning in painful emotions. "Kwame," she murmured yet again, her arms tightening as she clung to him.

As she led him up the stairs and into her room, guilt replaced the relief she'd felt upon seeing him—guilt over being so emotional at another man's wedding. How could she have allowed herself to feel that way when she had such a wonderful husband?

He'd kept his promise and showed up despite the flight delay. Even more touching, he'd worn the suit she had picked out for him. Kwame was nothing short of magnificent and certainly didn't deserve his wife being so emotional at the wedding of a man who had not treated her right. Had she emotionally cheated on Kwame?

Her wedding ring dug into her skin, the word *cheat* being seared on her forehead for all, including Kwame, to see. Akwele worried those feelings were indicative of cracks in her marriage. Had she focused so much on her career and not been attentive enough to Kwame? Feeling disappointed in herself, Akwele vowed to atone for her undoing by loving Kwame even more passionately and prioritizing all his needs. His persistent requests that they start a family would be her top priority now—that would certainly please her mother as well.

"So, this is my room," Akwele said to Kwame as she opened the door. "Akuorkor and I used to share a room until our parents were convinced we would kill each other. We were only seven years old then, but were already clawing out each other's eyes. I have had this room since then. Akuorkor and I do share a bathroom though, right through that door, per Daddy's orders that we must share something. Would you be okay with us staying in this room while we are here? If you aren't comfortable in this room, we can have any of the guest rooms in the house."

Kwame entered the room and set down his suitcase. Silent, he looked around, walked past the neatly arranged chairs and to her bed. He then ambled to the window overlooking the front of the house, pushed aside the curtains, and peered outside.

Akwele wished Kwame would say something. He was usually very talkative and full of questions, but he had been so quiet since he arrived. She wondered if he was just tired, especially with the flight delay. "Do you want anything?" she asked him as he stared outside. "Just let me know if you want some water, tea, or dinner? Whatever you want or need, I can get it for you."

"I am sure you can," Kwame whispered.

Something was wrong, but she couldn't put a finger on it.

Kwame turned to her and stared at her flatly.

Akwele's stomach sank. Kwame had never looked at her that way. Was there something about her that was giving away the feelings she had experienced at the wedding? Was the word *cheat* really seared on her forehead like she had feared? Maybe it was the way she ran into his arms and clung to him when she saw him. She certainly couldn't tell him why she was upset. That would be the last straw.

But something about the way Kwame was peering at her made her feel very unsettled. "I will be right back, okay?" Akwele said as she escaped to the bathroom.

She shut the bathroom door and leaned against it. What was going on with Kwame? "Calm down and focus," she told herself, then laid out the facts in her head. There was something going on with both of them: something was odd about Kwame, and she felt guilty for reliving the past.

Akwele concluded she and Kwame needed a beautiful, romantic evening so he would relax and tell her what was going on with him and she would love him so passionately it would burn away all thought of Tetteh.

Feeling pleased with her plan, Akwele opened the door leading to Akuorkor's room. If there was one place in the house that had sensual attire capable of romantically firing up any mood, it would be Akuorkor's room.

Unsurprisingly, a very disarrayed room greeted Awkele as she made her way to Akuorkor's closet. She smiled as she found a drawer full of an assortment of flirty sleepwear. She decided on a sheer black one-piece, quickly changed into it, fluffed her hair, and put on some red lipstick. She barely recognized herself in the mirror, but she reminded herself that tonight didn't call for her prim and proper self.

When she returned to her room, Kwame was still looking out the window.

"You should have told me," he said, his back still turned to her.

Akwele's jaw dropped. How could Kwame have known? She felt exposed, even more naked than in the sheer sleepwear. She snatched for her red-checkered bathrobe to cover herself.

"I had a right to know." Kwame's rigid back stared at her.

"I know, and I am so s-sorry. I really did want to tell but you, but I didn't know how you would take it," Akwele stammered as she whipped the strings of the bathrobe into a messy knot.

"For the past seven years I have known you, and the three years we've been married you didn't think I had the right to know that you are an heiress to a mountain of wealth? Your father is Festus Okine!"

She and Kwame were *not* talking about the same thing. She had been so consumed with her feelings about Tetteh's wedding that she had failed to anticipate how surprised Kwame would be by the grandeur of her home.

"Look at this place." Kwame gestured around the room. "Did you think I'd get here and say, 'Nice house'? What regular person's home sits on this much land? You just casually mentioned you've had this room since you were seven. How is this a seven-year-old's room? This is bigger than our bedroom! I don't understand why you never told me about your family's wealth. Did you think I was a gold digger or something? Your dad owns a very profitable company, which you will inherit. Not just the money and properties, but the responsibilities of managing all of that, and you didn't think that I, as your husband, had a right to know. Don't you think that affects our lives?"

Although Kwame was upset, Akwele quietly sighed in relief. Kwame was hurt, and his anger was justified, but she could handle addressing his concerns better than having to explain why she had kept her history with Tetteh from him.

She crossed the room and sat on her bed in front of him. "I am so sorry I kept that from you and I am really sorry that you are hurt. Living with this secret hasn't been easy, and wondering if someone is staring at me because they've found out I am Festus Okine's daughter is difficult. However, that difficulty pales in comparison to some of my experience growing up.

"People looked at and treated me differently once they knew who my father was. I worked very hard, and it always hurt me that people thought I didn't have to do so because of what I have, or will inherit. I lost loved ones because they felt we were too different. When I got to KNUST it was refreshing because I was just like every other student. At Peprah & Anderson, I was judged on my work alone, and not by what strings could be pulled because of who my father is. When you met me you loved me for *me*, which is all I have ever wanted, and I needed it to remain that way. In the beginning it bothered me that I didn't tell you, but I loved what we had so much. The more you loved me the more I loved you, and I didn't want that to change."

He heaved a sigh and dropped heavily onto the bed next to her. "I would have still loved you if you had told me. I would have loved you even more—not because you are wealthy but because you trusted me enough to tell me. I would have loved the chance to show you that I love you for *you*, Kwele. However, I understand I haven't lived your life, and I haven't experienced the things you have and what you've lost because of your father's money." Kwame sighed. "But I think there is an important lesson here for us. A lesson that secrets don't make us stronger; they just become ticking time bombs."

Akwele's entire body stiffened, and she remained quiet.

"So, no more secrets, no more lies or omissions. Despite how much I love you, I am also human and I get hurt by these secrets. So, full transparency from now on." Kwame twisted toward her. "Why were you so upset when you saw me downstairs?"

Akwele's teeth began to chatter "I-I was just relieved to see you. I didn't know about your flight. I kept calling. I didn't know if you were okay, and I was really worried."

Kwame reached out and held her face. "I am sorry. The flight schedules and delays were all over the place. I really needed some good news before calling you because I knew how badly you wanted me to be here with you." Kwame looked straight at her. "Kwele, is there anything else I need to know?"

Akwele clenched her teeth to keep them from rattling. She broke out in a cold sweat. "Air," was all she could say when she finally spoke. "I really need some air."

"Should I open the windows? Do you need some cold water?"

"No, no, I just need to step out for a bit. You stay here." She grabbed a tablet from her desk and headed for the door. Her palms were so wet with sweat they slipped around the doorknob when she tried to open it. The memory of the last time she had run out of her room with a secret slammed her. She paused and leaned her head against the door. Running, hiding, and lying through her problems was getting old and stale. She wasn't seventeen anymore, but a self-accomplished engineer and married to a wonderful man who deserved better. He deserved the truth.

She turned around to face him. "The groom at the wedding today is called Tetteh. He was my first love, and I cared very deeply for him. I loved him more than my own life. We kept our relationship a secret, and when we broke up I ran away from home because it was too painful for me to live so close to him. His wedding was the most beautiful I have ever been to, and yet I feel like a truck hit me today."

Kwame's face was blank. No words came out of his mouth as he stood staring at her.

"Please, don't leave me," she begged before flinging the door open and running out.

"Kwele!" Kwame called out as he ran after her.

The bedroom door opened behind her, but she was

already down the stairs and Kwame probably had no idea which way she had run.

Two HOURS LATER, Akwele sat on the front steps of the main house, staring at the tablet on her lap while looking up frequently at her bedroom window. The lights were still on, which meant Kwame was probably still awake. She had been sitting on her porch since she fled her room, trying to focus on the sea of numbers on her laptop. In times of emotional turmoil, she always ran to logical tasks, her safe place. Nonetheless, she kept looking up at her window and biting on her nails. She would have to go back and face Kwame at some point, but she wanted to wait until he had fallen asleep.

Around her, a few straggling balloons and streamers bounced in the evening air along the driveway. It was hard to believe how quiet the evening was given the frenzy of activity just hours earlier.

A taxi drove down the driveway and halted before the front steps where Akwele sat. As the back door opened, Akuorkor almost tumbled out and burst out laughing as she regained her balance. Her hair looked disheveled, and she was still in her bridesmaid dress, though it now looked crumpled. Barefoot, she stumbled toward her sister, carrying her high heels in her hands, while the taxi sped away.

"You are a mess," Akwele said.

"Says the perfect twin." Akuorkor plopped down on the steps next to her. "Let me guess, you are doing math when it's almost midnight. My goodness, Akwele, you made it. You don't have to impress Ma and Daddy anymore. Look at me, sis. You got no competition. You never have."

"You are damn right," Akwele lashed out. "You've been drinking since I set eyes on you this morning. You are a disaster."

Akuorkor laughed hard and then cleared her throat. "Dearest sister, I may *look* like a mess, but you *are* the mess."

Akwele raised her eyebrows at her sister. Clearly, Akuorkor was drunk. "Have you looked at yourself in the mirror? How exactly am *I* the mess?"

Akuorkor looked squarely at her sister. "You couldn't look at Tetteh today. You stiffened like a rock when I waved him over. When he hugged you, you jumped back like he was the plague. Now, you are sitting here at almost midnight, working math. I know you, sis. Something is eating you up, and it has to do with Tetteh. I may not be the smartest, but I see and feel a lot. Maybe that's why I drink so much."

Akwele kept a neutral expression and remained silent.

"So, before you call me a mess, how about *you* look in the mirror?" With that Akuorkor stumbled to her feet as Akwele looked away, but only a moment later her shuffling steps came to a halt. "He is the reason you ran away from home," Akuorkor exclaimed as she tumbled back down. "My whole life I have had to contend with the fact I am the deviant twin while you were the success story. Akwele wins this. Akwele

116

becomes that. Princess Akwele, Saint Akwele, the hope and savior of the Okines. Meanwhile, at only seventeen you were helping yourself to Tetteh. What would Ma have thought of that? You and him right under her nose, but I guess she was too busy calling out my deviant ways to notice. You are not so perfect after all. You and Tetteh, huh." Akuorkor chuckled. "And then you had to sit through his wedding today. The wedding our parents bankrolled, and they pranced around him like the son they would be happy to switch me for."

Akwele thought Akuorkor's words were harsh, especially as she was reeling from an emotionally difficult day and a hurt husband she had to go back to face. However, Akuorkor's laughter was so infectious that Akwele, despite her misery, laughed along.

Finally, Akuorkor stopped laughing, looked at Akwele, and opened her arms. "Come here."

Akwele hugged her sister hard. Before she knew it, the tears she had been blinking away all day came running down her cheeks.

Akuorkor rubbed her back. "I'd love to comfort you all night, but I get bored easily. You need to dish on the gardener's boy. What made you two break up?"

"He said he wasn't ready for something serious. He was happy with a casual affair and I wanted more. But to this day, I don't fully understand how he went from being so romantic towards me to flat out rejecting me. I have yearned for that explanation for years. Now, I believe it just wasn't meant to be. I am very happy in my marriage. Kwame is a million times the man I could ever want, and Tetteh honestly looked so happy today too. So, it was just not meant to be for him and I, and that is okay."

Akuorkor nodded. "But?"

Akwele smiled at Akuorkor's uncanny ability to sense there was more she wasn't saying. "I wanted closure. I wanted to be free from the emotions of the past."

"Well, we all have weaknesses. Mine is the bottle, but yours is the gardener's boy." Akwele reached for her sister's hand. "I understand that you wanted to be free today, and believe me, you are. *Freedom is not in our circumstance or birthright but in our choices.* You chose your career. You chose Kwame." Akuorkor looked down at the drink in her bag. "I wish I could choose, too."

"When did this drinking start, Akuorkor? We can get you help."

"Help is mine to choose," Akuorkor said as she scowled at Akwele's chest, then pulled back the front panel of her robe. "Is that my lingerie you are wearing? Oh, my goodness. What are you thinking of doing, Akwele?"

"Oh, get your mind out of the gutter," Akwele admonished. "Yes, it's your lingerie, but I wore it for my husband. Kwame arrived a few hours ago."

"Nice! Then why are you down here. Oh dear! You told him how you felt at Tetteh's wedding. So, you are locked out of your own room." Akuorkor shook her head. "You are more messed up than I thought. Seriously, however you felt today means nothing. Dead fires leave embers, which hang around a little longer, but eventually, like the fire, they die." Akuorkor kissed her sister on the forehead and rubbed her arms.

Akwele smiled gratefully at her sister before turning to her tablet again.

"Are you going to continue sitting here and working?"

"My art is where I heal." Akwele offered up a thin smile.

Akuorkor sighed and sat back down next to her sister. "No, it's hiding not healing. I can think of more exciting ways to heal." Akuorkor gestured toward Akwele's window. "In there is a drop-dead handsome man who happens to be your husband. You should channel some of your art that way. If you don't, I will go in there and pretend I am you."

Akwele and Akuorkor laughed out loud, just like old times. Their laughter filled the night and only came to an abrupt halt when they saw the light turn on in their parents' bedroom. Their mother came to the window and opened it. "Oops," Akuorkor said under her breath.

But their mother said nothing. She just stared at them for what seemed like forever and then closed the window and turned the lights off.

"Well, that was intense," Akuorkor said. "When you left home, she didn't leave her room for days. She wouldn't eat. She wouldn't go to any of her usual events. She couldn't even get out of bed. She would call me to her room several times a day, and I had to repeat over and over that I didn't know why you had left. It was scary to see her like that, so broken."

"I am so sorry you had to through all of that. I really am. I hope someday you can understand I really couldn't stay. I loved him too much then, and I couldn't be in such proximity with him after we broke up. Then, I was convinced it would have destroyed me to stay. I am sorry my leaving home brought our family pain."

Akuorkor nodded, still looking at their mother's bedroom window.

"What finally made Ma leave her room?"

"I am not sure, but the maids whisper it had to do with Tetteh bringing her flowers. Taking into perspective what I now know about you and Tetteh, it makes for a twisted story. I also think she was relieved when you called letting us know you were safe and okay at school. But I think Ma already knew you were at KNUST before you called. I am just not sure how she knew."

Thirteen years ago

TETTEH LOOKED UP from his music notes when his father, limping heavily, entered the room with a bag filled with flowers. He sat down next to Tetteh and began sniping the stems and carefully arranging the red roses with the white daisies.

"Who are these flowers for?" Tetteh asked.

"They are for Ma Tina. She hasn't left her room since Akwele left. She barely eats anything, I hear. She's very sad, but she loves flowers, especially these roses and jasmines. I am hoping they will cheer her up."

Tetteh put aside his music sheets and went to sit beside his dad, helping him snip the stems of the roses. The final arrangement was beautiful. "These are really nice, Dad."

"Thanks, the beauty of flowers always amazes me, always brings me joy. Let's hope they do the trick for Ma Tina." His father got up, leaning heavily on his cane. "I am going to rest a bit. My leg is killing me. I will take the flowers over to the main house to Ma Tina later. Put them in a jar of water for now."

"Actually, Dad, I was going to the main house. I could take the flowers to Ma Tina."

"Oh, thank you, you just saved my poor leg," he said as he hobbled away.

When Tetteh arrived at the house, he found Aunty B dusting the tables. He noted how suspiciously she looked at him and wondered why. "My dad asked me to bring these flowers to Ma Tina."

"Ma Tina is in her room, resting," she said without looking at him. That combined with the snap in her voice said she was clearly upset at him. "Just put the flowers on the table at the foot of the stairs. I will get someone to take them up to her. When you are done, wait for me in the kitchen. I need to talk to you."

Tetteh walked over to the table and set the flowers down as Aunty B disappeared into the kitchen, dispensing a stern look that sent shivers down his spine. Was he in trouble? Did she know about he and Akwele? It was not a good thing to be in Aunty B's bad books. The woman was like the chief warden of the entire compound, and all the house helps feared her.

If he was in trouble with her, then he needed someone above her on his side.

Tetteh grabbed the flowers, climbed the stairs, and headed to Ma Tina's room. As he reached the second floor, he could hear voices coming from Ma Tina's room.

"Tell me again exactly what happened!" Ma Tina demanded.

"Ma, I already told you several times," Akuorkor sobbed. "I found her in her room. She was upset, but all she could talk about was her math problem."

"Then she asked you to steal my car keys for her, and you still didn't think there was anything wrong with her. She was probably having a nervous breakdown, and all you could do is steal a getaway car for her."

"Ma, please."

"Tell me what happened again. Maybe you missed something."

"Ma, I am tired."

"My daughter is gone."

"I am your daughter, too!"

"You helped your sister run away. This is all your fault. How could you not have called me to let me know your sister was in trouble?"

Hurried footsteps preceded Akuorkor's flight from her mother's room. She sped past Tetteh, cheeks wet, and seemed to not even notice him standing in the hallway.

As he was about to knock on Ma Tina's door, Akuorkor stopped by Mr. Okine's bar and hesitantly poured herself a drink. She tossed it back quickly and coughed loudly, and then ran to her room. Tetteh knocked on Ma Tina's door.

"Who is it?"

"It is me, Tetteh. My dad sent me to bring you some flowers."

There was a pause and then she said, "Come in."

"Good afternoon, Ma Tina." Tetteh entered the room. "I am so sorry you are sad."

"You can put the flowers there. You are kind, Tetteh, just like your mother. She was good to me, Maria. I named Akwele after her. Did you know?"

"Yes, I knew that. Please, try and get some rest."

"How can I rest now when I don't know where my daughter is? I heard she was your friend."

"She was my teacher. She was a good teacher."

Ma Tina wiped her eyes as she sobbed. "She was the best. Thank you, Tetteh. You can go now."

Tetteh turned to go and then remembered Aunty B was waiting for him downstairs. She was probably even more upset with him for bringing the flowers upstairs rather than leaving them at the foot of the stairs like she instructed. He turned to Ma Tina, who was still dabbing her eyes with her handkerchief. "Ma Tina, Akwele went to KNUST. She got accepted to their computer engineering program."

"What? I know she took the November/December exams last year, but I didn't know she had been accepted at KNUST." Ma Tina sat up suddenly. "Oh, my God, Tetteh, are you telling me that Akwele drove all the way to Kumasi? How could she do that? She took my car, and I don't think there was that much fuel in it. Please, get me my phone. I need to call my husband. We need to go and get her. She has no money and is too young to fend for herself. She is smart, but not ready for university—"

"Ma Tina, I think we should let Akwele be for a while. From what I know about her, she wants to push herself and make it on her own. She knows you can provide her with everything, but the Akwele I know wants to open her own doors and forge her own path. She will reach out to you when she is ready. But for now, please, let Akwele be."

"You know her well. What you say about her is true—Akwele has always wanted to be her own person. It still troubles me that I don't know what she's doing," Ma Tina choked out, "why she left like this, and if she's doing okay."

"She will reach out soon. You can visit or spend time with her."

Ma Tina dabbed her face with her handkerchief. "That may be a good suggestion. Hopefully, she'll reach out soon and I will go see her. Tetteh, you have brought me comfort not only with your flowers but with your wisdom. Is there anything I can do for you?"

"There is one thing. Can you walk downstairs with me?" Upon seeing the surprised look on Ma Tina's face, Tetteh continued. "This house revolves around you, and for quite some time, you haven't left your room. It will be good for people to see you again, for life to return to this household."

"Okay, please iron that shirt while I freshen up, so we can take a walk."

Tetteh smiled. "Also, I would like to be of more help to you. I won't be pursuing schooling anymore, and I will be focusing on my music. I will have more time on my hands, and I'd like to help you more. Please, let me."

"That will be my pleasure."

CHAPTER 10
The Guardian

Present day

AUNTY B HAD kept a watchful eye on Tetteh for thirteen years and often held herself back from lashing out at him as he paraded around the house like Ma Tina's anointed son.

To Aunty B's joy, the day she would carry out her revenge on him had finally arrived—the day of his wedding.

Unlike the entire household she took no part in the preparations, which was unusual given she was the main organizer of all Ma Tina's events. On the wedding day she crocheted in silence in her room, and did not go near the bustling garden.

At 11:00 p.m. her alarm shrilled loudly. It was time. She held up the place table mat she was crocheting. Almost perfect, she thought before placing her crocheting hook and yarn in her handbag.

She left the main house through the back door. Once outside, she struck a match and touched it to her lantern wick. The flame burned brightly as she walked toward the servants' quarters, humming one of her favorite gospel tunes. The skip in her stride summed up her mood; her day of retribution was finally here.

When she arrived at the servants' quarters, she peered into Tetteh's dark, empty room.

She pulled one of the chairs from the porch to the front of the house, sat down, and pulled out her crocheting hook and yarn. Only a few more stitches and she would be done.

She looked up frequently and glanced around the dimly lit servants' quarters. They still had their blue walls and low ceilings, just like fifty years ago when she first arrived.

She'd lived in the servants' quarters but dutifully cleaned the main house and cooked all the food for Mr. Okine and his parents, who were alive back then.

She'd been there when the Okines had a lavish party to celebrate Mr. Okine and Ma Tina's wedding. She also celebrated with them when the twins were born and witnessed Ma Tina's mood swings as she struggled to keep up with their care. Aunty B was happy to lend a hand to Ma Tina, offering to sleep on the floor of the nursery so she could do the night feedings. Mr. Okine noticed Aunty B's dedication and asked her to move to a nice room in the main house.

Despite the kind gestures from the Okines, Aunty B remembered who she was and where she came from no matter how close she got to them. Moreover, she was protective of them and was very upset with Tetteh for almost destroying the family.

She shook her head and continued crocheting.

Soon footsteps headed towards the servants' quarters, followed by the sound of Tetteh's voice and his wife's laughter.

Aunty B smiled and hummed her gospel tune.

When Tetteh and his wife saw Aunty B, his wife greeted, "Good evening," while he swallowed hard. He and Aunty B's eyes met and held for a few seconds, but it felt like forever.

He and his wife then went inside the quarters while Aunty B hummed and crocheted away.

When they came back out, Tetteh was holding a suitcase in one hand and his cello at his back. "You can wait for me in the car," Tetteh said to his wife, who was holding another suitcase.

Tetteh then turned to Aunty B. "Everything should be clean and in order." He dropped the keys to his quarters into her outstretched hand.

She looked him straight in the eye without blinking. "Don't think to beg. I haven't changed my mind, Tetteh. I still want you to leave this house tonight." Staring at the blank look on Tetteh's face, she added, "You turned my beautiful, smart daughter into your puppet. You broke her heart and made her run away from her own home, bringing so much pain to this household. Ma Tina fell into a depression, Mr. Okine worked till it almost killed him, and Akuorkor emptied every bottle in this house. I bet you thought no one knew you were responsible for all that.

"I know everything that happens in this house. After all the hurt you caused you moved on, at lightning speed, with another girl, insinuating my daughter is disposable. Then you chained yourself to Ma Tina's hip and dared to draw enemy lines with me. I waited and watched you prance around this house like a savior for thirteen years because I am a very patient person." Aunty B breathed heavily and then she paused to catch her breath. "But finally, today is my day. Today, I am driving you away from this house."

Tetteh gritted his teeth. "You can't lay all that blame on me. Akwele and I were two young people who fell in love. That's a normal thing that happens to boys and girls. We had fun while it lasted. It didn't work out because she wanted things I could never give her, or wasn't ready for. I don't see why you would punish me for that. I am not the one who chased her out of her own house."

"You are brazen enough to justify all the hurt you caused. Why didn't you dissuade Ma Tina with that clever tongue of yours when she told you she was inviting Akwele to the wedding? You knew it wouldn't be easy for her to be here."

"Because I wanted to see Akwele again and make amends. She left hurt, and I wanted the chance to rewrite that."

Aunty B scoffed, "At your wedding?"

"Well, I didn't know I would be driven out of my home the night of my wedding. I thought she would at least stay a few days and we would get to talk, iron things out, and maybe become friends again. I thought I would have a little time with her. Even if you don't believe me, I do care about her. She was mine once. I cared enough to know it was best to end things when they weren't going in a great direction for both of us.

Now, we are both happy with other people, except you holding on to decade-old grudges."

Aunty B shook her head. "You better leave now. You shouldn't keep your new bride waiting." Aunty B slipped the keys into her handbag while Tetteh headed for the gates with a loud scoff.

She peered at the gates until they clanged shut after Tetteh had left. Tetteh was a weed she should have nipped a long time ago, but instead she tolerated him and he had almost choked the roses she had tendered to for so long. She picked up her lantern and headed back to the main house.

She recalled how anguished she'd been when Ma Tina had told her she was going to ask Akwele to come home for Tetteh's wedding. *How could I tell Ma Tina it was a terrible idea after all the money and time she had poured into the wedding?* She hadn't believed Ma Tina could handle the truth that her anointed son caused her daughter to run away.

Aunty B decided to hold her tongue but drive Tetteh away from the house immediately after the wedding, because no matter how accomplished and happily married Akwele was she still did not trust Tetteh.

Tetteh had shaken with fury when Aunty B ordered him to leave the house. He was enjoying his role as an important person in the family and didn't want to leave. Aunty B threatened to tell Ma Tina he was the reason Akwele ran from home, which would undoubtedly make her cancel the elaborate wedding she had planned for him.

He finally agreed to leave the house after the

wedding, but true to his sly nature he told everyone he was leaving to start a new life with his wife and explore bigger opportunities.

When Akwele returned home and Aunty B saw how wide and innocent her eyes still were as she ran up the stairs to hug her, Aunty B was sure she had made the right decision by ordering Tetteh to leave. Later that night, as she'd tucked Akwele into bed, a swell of protectiveness had surged up in her, along with a sea of guilt that she hadn't done more to protect her thirteen years ago.

Thirteen years ago

AUNTY B HEAVED a sigh of relief. She had been sick with worry that Akwele was caught in the heavy rain. Everyone else was home except her. Then finally she saw her walking toward the main house, in clothes that didn't look like hers.

"Aunty B, that gardener's boy, Tetteh, was very rude to me. He refused to give me his umbrella and forced me to go to the servants' quarters. He was horrible, horrible, horrible!" Akwele stormed up the stairs and into her room, narrating the events of the afternoon to Aunty B.

"My daughter, from all you have told me, he has actually been nice to you. He helped you from the rain, fed and clothed you. Nothing about that is horrible." Aunty B entered Akwele's bedroom with her.

"Oh, you should have heard his tone, such a proud person living in those quarters." Akwele shed the clothes as if they were flea-infested and stepped into the bathroom.

"I used to live in the servants' quarters. It's not so bad there." Aunty B picked up the clothes.

"Sorry, Aunty. Anyway, you'll be glad to know that despite how horrible he was with me, I agreed to teach him and help him with his math because he is failing badly," Akwele said before turning on the shower.

"That's nice of you, daughter."

The following weeks, Aunty B would hug and listen to Akwele as she came home reeling with anger from her tutoring sessions with Tetteh. "He is too dumb to even feign interest," she would say, and "He has no brain in his head," and "He is definitely never graduating high school," and "I am never going back in there." Aunty B had encouraged Akwele to be patient and continue tutoring Tetteh despite the disinterest he showed.

Aunty B loved the twins and tried to instill good virtues in them, but she couldn't help thinking they had an altered view of reality and were used to getting everything they wanted. She thought that by Akwele working with a less-than-easy student, she could learn some important life lessons.

The next time Aunty B asked Akwele how the tutoring was going, Akwele was startled at the question. "He is, um, making some headway," she stammered.

Aunty B noted Akwele's odd reaction. However, she let out a sigh of relief that Akwele wasn't complaining about Tetteh. "I knew you would find a way. You are a good teacher."

Two months after that conversation, Aunty B was crocheting on the front porch of the house when she heard Ma Tina hurling insults at Akuorkor, who was dressed up in a stunning and very revealing red dress. But when Aunty B looked closer, she didn't think it was Akuorkor but rather Akwele.

Having brought up the twins and knowing their personalities so well, Aunty B wasn't fooled by their act. Whereas Akuorkor would have swaggered out proudly with her shoulders squared and her chin thrust in the air, the girl leaving the house hesitated in her steps and kept looking down.

What were the twins up to? She went to the library and found Akuorkor dozing off, the textbook in her hand upside down.

Back in the kitchen, she called Adamu at the main gate. "*Adamu, ani Akuorkor etsɔ agbo lɛ he lo*, has Akuorkor passed by the gate?"

"*Daabi, mɔ ko mɔ ko, ebaho ko agbo lɛ naa*. No, nobody has come by the gate."

Aunty B hung up the phone and looked through the window at the woods surrounding the main house. Akwele was on the compound somewhere, but where?

There was only one person who could know where she was. She picked up her lantern and walked straight to the servants' quarters. She knocked loudly on the gardener's door. When he opened the door, she asked, "Where is Tetteh?"

"Um, I don't know, he came home very hastily and

picked up his cello. He also changed his shirt, and then he left."

Aunty B sighed loudly as she picked up her lantern and turned to leave.

"Is there a problem, B?" Tetteh's father called after Aunty B, but she didn't respond.

Aunty B didn't go back to the main house but rather searched around for Akwele. She stopped short on her way to the garden and clutched her chest as she heard moans and Akwele's voice coming from a distance ahead. How could her daughter and the pride of the family give her innocence away to Tetteh?

Aunty B spat in fury before turning back to the main house.

Following that evening, Akwele's unusual behaviors started making sense to Aunty B. She found Akwele giggling at notes tucked between pages in her books. She once watched Akwele dip her *fufu* in water instead of soup. She also grew increasingly concerned as Akwele paid less attention to her schoolwork and spent more time with Tetteh.

She told herself it was just young love that would frizzle away without any consequence. Akwele was a sensible girl, and she would find her head soon enough.

Then came that fateful afternoon when loud and rapid footsteps pounded down the stairway, and Ma Tina's Corolla sped away from the main house.

Akwele was gone.

Aunty B wanted to dangle Tetteh upside down, but he had grown so close to Ma Tina. With Akwele gone and Akuorkor now drinking, Ma Tina really needed a child, and Tetteh had happily filled the role. Hence, she had held back on her revenge and for years waited patiently, for the Corolla to head back down the driveway and for Akwele to return home.

AKWELE WAS STILL sitting on the front steps staring down at her tablet when she saw Aunty B walking toward the main house. Where could the woman be coming from at this time of the night?

"My daughter, it's a bit late to be sitting here all alone," Aunty B said when she reached Akwele.

"I was with Akuorkor here for a while. We had a good chat," Akwele said as she looked up. "We were laughing so hard we woke Ma up. She's going to scold us tomorrow."

"I doubt that. I saw so much happiness on her face today, and it wasn't just from the wedding. It's because you are home."

"I didn't realize how much I had missed my family and home until today."

"This is a big part of you. It is important you know where you belong no matter where schooling, career, or marriage take you. You took your first breath and steps here. So, whatever this home brings you, whether happiness or sorrow, it is still yours. As you journey through life, love, and fame, remember where you belong, remember your home."

Akwele gazed up at Aunty B. The older woman's

eyes were narrowed but focused—she looked so wise. Akwele felt a tinge of worry she hadn't tapped into that wisdom as much as she should have, especially now that Aunty B was starting to age.

"Thanks for reminding me of that, Aunty." Akwele sighed. "I am concerned about Akuorkor's drinking, but she's made me aware she has help at her disposal to choose when she's ready. After our chat today, she says she's close to being ready."

"Your return home has changed many things. Akuorkor has always adored you. When she was still toddling, you were already running. When she was mouthing her first words, you were stringing sentences. She tries hard to catch up with you, which is not easy, so she finds her own ways to stand out. Those aren't always the best ways. But she loves you more than anything, and I believe she will get better." Aunty B grunted as she lowered herself next to Akwele. "Joy is finally returning to this compound."

Akwele smiled at her nanny. "Why didn't you come to the wedding today, Aunty B? Everyone was there. Tetteh is pretty much family."

"No, he is not your family," Aunty B said firmly. "Pretty clothes and a big party don't make you family."

Akwele shied from Aunty B's strong tone and changed the topic. "Why are you up so late, and where are you coming from?"

Aunty B cleared her throat. "I was just taking care of business, tying loose ends, and keeping the peace." Aunty B smiled ominously as she looked out ahead of her. "It's like everything is falling back into place, and things are returning to the way they should be. What about you? Why are you up at this time, and what is it you are working on anyway?"

"Let me show you, Aunty B." Akwele leaned over and showed her the tablet. "I designed this software platform called *Ispa,* and I have been thinking of ideas for the next version of it. While sitting here, I was inspired on how to make my work relevant to some of the projects going on here at home and with Daddy's business."

Aunty B's smile widened, and her lips trembled with emotion. "One thing I love about you is that despite all you have, you still push yourself to work hard and go the extra mile. You never rest on your laurels. This household has a future because of you." Aunty B then reached out and took the tablet from Akwele and turned it off. "But, there is a time for everything."

Akwele chuckled as she wondered where Aunty B was going with the conversation. "I know it's late, but I really need to work on this."

"I know how much you love working, but there is a man standing at the window in your room. He has been looking out and waiting for a long time. He has barely moved from the window all evening. That man is a husband looking for his wife, and he will not sleep until she comes back. I know a thing or two about waiting for loved ones to return home, and it's a difficult wait." Aunty B placed Akwele's tablet in her handbag and zipped it shut. "I was here when arrived. Once he told me who he was I wanted to him properly and give him a comfortable insisted on waiting for you at the front of the house. That's the kind of man you shouldn't keep waiting. Akwele, go to your husband."

Akwele bit her lip. "I don't think he's happy with me now. It's a long story, Aunty B."

"We all have long stories. Our hearts are bottomless pits of stories. One day we shall sit and tell these stories while we enjoy meat pies. That day is not today." Aunty B's face took on a comforting look. "Today, we let go of the old."

Akwele nodded at her nanny.

Aunty B kissed Akwele. "I raised you, and so I know you married a good man. A good man who loves you. And when I saw him today, I couldn't have been more certain. Please, don't keep a good man waiting in your own home."

Akwele smiled. "Okay, Aunty B. Will you come inside, too?"

"No, I will stay right here. I need to make sure that those who are in stay in, and those who are out stay out." Aunty B gave a knowing smile before pulling out her crocheting hook and thread. She hummed her gospel tune as she placed a stitch. Her place mat was perfect, she thought as she admired her work.

Akwele headed back inside and slowly walked up the stairs, thinking of what she would say to Kwame. She remembered Aunty B's comforting words—her past with Tetteh would always be a part of her, but it need not affect her marriage to Kwame, who she loved dearly. Sharing it with Kwame had not been easy, but it brought her a much-needed sense of relief. A great burden had been lifted off her shoulders, and she was starting a new slate with Kwame—one with no secrets.

Sharing her reasons for not telling him about her family's wealth, and learning he would have loved her nonetheless, made her feel even closer to him. Without a doubt he loved her for who she was and not what she had, which was all she had wanted.

As she finally reached the top of the stairs, she could hear Aunty B's voice bounce off the walls. *Whatever your home brings you, whether happiness or sorrow, it is still yours. As you journey through life, love, and fame, remember where you belong, remember your home.*

At the door of her room Akwele paused before reaching for the doorknob, but the door flung open anyway.

Kwame's strong form filled the space. Eyes glistening, he let out a whoosh of breath, reached for Akwele, and pulled her into his arms.

The End

eyes were narrowed but focused—she looked so wise. Akwele felt a tinge of worry she hadn't tapped into that wisdom as much as she should have, especially now that Aunty B was starting to age.

"Thanks for reminding me of that, Aunty." Akwele sighed. "I am concerned about Akuorkor's drinking, but she's made me aware she has help at her disposal to choose when she's ready. After our chat today, she says she's close to being ready."

"Your return home has changed many things. Akuorkor has always adored you. When she was still toddling, you were already running. When she was mouthing her first words, you were stringing sentences. She tries hard to catch up with you, which is not easy, so she finds her own ways to stand out. Those aren't always the best ways. But she loves you more than anything, and I believe she will get better." Aunty B grunted as she lowered herself next to Akwele. "Joy is finally returning to this compound."

Akwele smiled at her nanny. "Why didn't you come to the wedding today, Aunty B? Everyone was there. Tetteh is pretty much family."

"No, he is not your family," Aunty B said firmly. "Pretty clothes and a big party don't make you family."

Akwele shied from Aunty B's strong tone and changed the topic. "Why are you up so late, and where are you coming from?"

Aunty B cleared her throat. "I was just taking care of business, tying loose ends, and keeping the peace." Aunty B smiled ominously as she looked out ahead of her. "It's like everything is falling back into place, and things are returning to the way they should be. What about you? Why are you up at this time, and what is it you are working on anyway?"

"Let me show you, Aunty B." Akwele leaned over and showed her the tablet. "I designed this software platform called *Ispa,* and I have been thinking of ideas for the next version of it. While sitting here, I was inspired on how to make my work relevant to some of the projects going on here at home and with Daddy's business."

Aunty B's smile widened, and her lips trembled with emotion. "One thing I love about you is that despite all you have, you still push yourself to work hard and go the extra mile. You never rest on your laurels. This household has a future because of you." Aunty B then reached out and took the tablet from Akwele and turned it off. "But, there is a time for everything."

Akwele chuckled as she wondered where Aunty B was going with the conversation. "I know it's late, but I really need to work on this."

"I know how much you love working, but there is a man standing at the window in your room. He has been looking out and waiting for a long time. He has barely moved from the window all evening. That man is a husband looking for his wife, and he will not sleep until she comes back. I know a thing or two about waiting for loved ones to return home, and it's a difficult wait." Aunty B placed Akwele's tablet in her handbag and zipped it shut. "I was here when he arrived. Once he told me who he was I wanted to welcome him properly and give him a comfortable room, but he insisted on waiting for you at the front of